COLLECTION
L'IMAGINAIRE

Louis-René des Forêts

Le bavard

Gallimard

© Éditions Gallimard, 1946, renouvelé en 1973.

CHAPITRE I

Je me regarde souvent dans la glace. Mon plus grand désir a toujours été de me découvrir quelque chose de pathétique dans le regard. Je crois que je n'ai jamais cessé de préférer aux femmes qui, soit par aveuglement amoureux, soit pour me retenir près d'elles, inventaient que j'étais un vraiment bel homme ou que j'avais des traits énergiques, celles qui me disaient presque tout bas, avec une sorte de retenue craintive, que je n'étais pas tout à fait comme les autres. En effet, je me suis longtemps persuadé que ce qu'il devait y avoir en moi de plus attirant, c'était la singularité. C'est dans le sentiment de ma différence que j'ai trouvé mes principaux sujets d'exaltation. Mais aujourd'hui où j'ai perdu quelque peu de ma suffisance, comment me cacher que je ne me distingue en rien ? Je fais la grimace en écrivant ceci. Que je connaisse enfin une aussi intolérable vérité, passe encore, mais vous autres ! À vrai dire, il se glisse dans ma gêne ce léger sentiment de plaisir acide qu'on éprouve à proclamer une de ses tares, même si celle-ci n'a pas la moindre chance d'intéresser le public. On me demandera peut-être si j'ai entrepris de me confesser pour éprouver cette sorte de plaisir un peu morbide dont je parle et que je comparerais volontiers à celui que recherchent quelques personnes raffinées qui, avec une lenteur étudiée, caressent du bout de l'index une légère égratignure qu'elles se sont faite sciemment à la lèvre inférieure ou qui piquent de la pointe de la langue la pulpe d'un citron à peine mûr. À cela je suis obligé de sourire et c'est en souriant que je vous réponds que je me flatte d'avoir peu de goût pour les aveux ; mes amis disent que je suis le silence même, ils ne nieront pas qu'en dépit de leur extrême habileté, ils n'ont jamais su me tirer ce que j'avais à cœur de tenir secret. On a même convenu de voir dans cette impossibilité à me livrer une insuffisance assez grave qui excitait la pitié et je ne résiste pas au plaisir, identique à celui décrit plus haut, d'ajouter qu'une vanité sournoise me poussait à tirer profit de cette croyance en simulant ou seulement en exagérant la souffrance que me causait cette infirmité déplorable, comme si j'avais eu quelque grand secret que j'eusse été soulagé de confier si je ne l'avais tenu, à cause de son caractère à la fois exceptionnel et intime, pour absolument inavouable.

Mais si je me laisse emporter par mon zèle, je vais m'imputer des arrière-pensées que je n'ai pas eues pour me donner l'apparence d'un homme sincère qui est loin de songer à s'épargner les humiliations. Ce n'est donc pas pour le plaisir de vous entretenir de moi-même que j'ai pris la plume, ce n'est pas non plus pour mettre en vedette mes dons littéraires. Là, je suis contraint d'ouvrir une parenthèse, mais vous avez dû éprouver vous-mêmes que sitôt que vous tentez de vous expliquer avec franchise, vous vous trouvez contraints de faire suivre chacune de vos phrases affirmatives d'une dubitative, ce qui équivaut le plus souvent à nier ce que vous venez d'affirmer, bref, impossible de se débarrasser du scrupule un peu horripilant de ne rien laisser dans l'ombre. Je disais donc que je ne me soucie pas le moins du monde de l'expression que j'emprunte pour coucher ces lignes sur le papier. Pas le moins du monde est sans doute de trop. Mon goût me porte naturellement vers le style allusif, coloré, passionné, sombre et dédaigneux et j'ai pris aujourd'hui, non sans répugnance, la résolution de laisser de côté toute recherche formelle, de sorte que je me trouve écrire avec un style qui n'est pas le mien ; c'est dire que j'ai écarté tous les charmes dérisoires dont il m'arrive parfois de jouer, tout en sachant bien ce qu'ils valent : ils ne sont les fruits que d'une habileté assez ordinaire. Ajoutez à cela que mon style naturel n'est pas celui du confessionnal, rien d'étonnant s'il ressemble à une foule d'autres, mais je n'ai pas de prétention, vous êtes avertis.

Eh bien, venons aux raisons qui m'ont conduit à m'étaler sordidement. Vous remarquerez en passant le ton un peu persifleur auquel je m'abandonne, en dépit de la résolution que j'ai prise d'être aussi sérieux que sincère, aussi peu provocant que peu aimable, mais si vous faites une expérience analogue, vous découvrirez qu'il n'y a rien de plus difficile, à moins d'être échauffé par quelque conviction, que parler de soi avec gravité en laissant de côté tous les agréables jeux de l'insolence ; vous craindrez le ridicule et, pour consciencieux que soit votre épanchement intime, il y aura toujours une irrépressible ironie qui s'y donnera libre cours. Le lâche cache la vérité sous l'équivoque de l'insolence ou de la plaisanterie : tu me méprises, lecteur, mais tu vois bien que je grossis mes vices ; à toi de faire l'accommodation ; rien ne t'interdit de prendre tout ceci pour les inventions d'un exhibitionniste candide et irréprochable dans ses actes, sinon dans ses pensées. Venons-en donc à ces raisons. En vérité, il n'y en a qu'une et je dois dire qu'elle est on ne peut plus comique.

Je présume qu'il est arrivé à la plupart d'entre vous de se trouver saisi au revers de la veste par un de ces bavards qui, avides de faire entendre le son de leur voix, recherchent un compagnon dont la seule fonction consistera à prêter l'oreille sans être pour autant contraint d'ouvrir la bouche ; et encore, il n'est pas sûr que cet importun exige qu'on l'écoute, il suffit qu'on se donne un air intéressé soit en opinant de temps à autre d'un signe de tête ou d'un léger murmure que les romanciers appellent justement approbateur, soit en soutenant vaillamment le regard insistant de ce pauvre diable, malgré l'extrême fatigue que ne manquera pas de produire une telle tension musculaire. Examinons de près cet homme. Qu'il éprouve le besoin de parler et pourtant qu'il n'ait rien à dire, et plus encore, qu'il ne puisse assouvir ce besoin sans la complicité plus ou moins tacite d'un compagnon qu'il choisit, s'il en a la liberté, pour sa discrétion et son endurance, voilà qui mérite réflexion. Cet individu n'a strictement rien à dire et cependant il dit mille choses ; peu lui importe l'assentiment ou la contradiction d'un interlocuteur, et cependant il ne saurait se passer de celui-ci, auquel il a d'ailleurs la sagesse de ne demander qu'une attention toute formelle. Tout se passe comme s'il était atteint d'une affection à laquelle il serait impuissant à apporter un remède ou, pour me servir d'une comparaison familière, comme s'il se trouvait dans le même embarras que l'apprenti sorcier : la machine tourne sans nécessité, impossible d'en contrôler les mouvements désordonnés. Eh bien, j'ose dire, sans préjudice de la défection instantanée et massive de lecteurs à laquelle cet aveu m'expose, que j'appartiens précisément à cette espèce de bavards.

Mais, pour ceux qu'une aussi fâcheuse révélation n'aurait pu faire quitter des yeux ces lignes, je crois nécessaire de remonter plus haut jusqu'aux origines du mal, quoiqu'il me paraisse d'une difficulté presque insurmontable de le décrire et de le rendre sensible à des lecteurs, s'ils n'y ont jamais été sujets.

Et d'abord, le caractère très suggestif du climat et des lieux où se sont déroulées les circonstances à l'occasion desquelles je dus subir cette première crise, que je vais entreprendre de relater, justifierait sans doute une description minutieuse que seul un écrivain soucieux d'émouvoir, rompu à ce genre d'exercice et naturellement riche de dons auxquels je suis loin de prétendre, serait à même de vous donner. Pour moi, ce serait transgresser le vœu que je me suis formulé de ne pas recourir à des expédients assez bassement littéraires qui me répugnent. (Ne pas prendre trop au sérieux cette dernière phrase : si ces expédients me répugnent, c'est bien que je n'ai pas le pouvoir d'y recourir.)

Ce fut donc vers la fin d'une après-midi de dimanche où j'éprouvai une sensation d'ennui particulièrement déprimante que je me décidai brusquement à quitter ma chambre et à aller piquer une tête à la plage voisine. J'avais envie de plonger, de boire une gorgée de mer, de secouer l'eau salée de ma tête et de nager régulièrement, de me retourner pour faire la planche et de sentir la houle froide me soulever et se creuser et le soleil me brûler le visage. Mais d'abord, monter et descendre, traverser la rivière, la vallée au bois touffu, et puis arriver jusqu'au long plateau et le traverser avec de hautes herbes qui rendent la marche difficile et encore monter et descendre et traverser, m'arrêtant parfois à l'ombre d'un arbre pour souffler, et puis encore monter et descendre et traverser, toujours dans ces bois touffus de ronces dans lesquelles je devais me frayer un passage, voilà ce que je dus faire sous un soleil très chaud avant d'atteindre la falaise de craie qui surplombait la plage. J'avais tellement chaud en montant et descendant ces collines et en traversant ces bois épais que je m'étendis sur la crête de la falaise et je fus heureux d'appuyer mon dos contre le tronc d'un pin isolé qui me couvrait de son ombre fraîche et odorante. Je restai là à rêver longtemps à ma façon, c'est-à-dire tout à fait sans suite, probablement comme le font les chiens quand vous les laissez en paix et qu'ils n'ont envie ni de chasser, ni d'agiter la queue, ni même de somnoler et pour moi comme, je pense, pour les chiens, ce sont des moments d'autant plus délectables qu'ils se présentent rarement. Tout ce que je désirais maintenant, c'était ne pas bouger et attendre que la nuit tombe. Regardant le ciel absolument bleu avec très peu de nuages blancs poussés par le vent et sentant à distance la chaleur du soleil sur le roc blanc, j'étais heureux comme vous l'êtes quand vous avez laissé derrière vous tout un tas de soucis domestiques et que vous êtes enfin en possession de quelque chose que vous aimez qui vous fait vous sentir bien et entièrement seul et étranger à tout ce qui revêt une si grande importance aux yeux des hommes. Oui, c'est cela surtout que je sentais fortement, que j'étais loin des hommes et que les soucis des hommes étaient absolument dépourvus de signification. Je ne m'étendrais pas si longuement sur l'état d'euphorie où je me complaisais si je n'avais eu lieu de croire, une heure après, qu'il fut le prologue et en quelque sorte la source de la première manifestation de mon mal sous sa forme active. Couché sous le pin, je regardai longtemps le ciel, absorbé dans une contemplation animale, envahi par une paix profonde et convaincu que tout ce qui pourrait m'arriver ce soir-là m'arriverait pour le mieux. Mais quand je m'aperçus que le ciel n'était plus aussi clair, l'air aussi chaud et la rumeur de la mer déjà beaucoup moins proche, la marée devant être la plus basse à la tombée du jour, ma sérénité fit place à une exaltation étrange qui se traduisit par un besoin éperdu de prononcer sur-le-champ un discours dont je ne m'inquiétais nullement de savoir s'il présenterait quelque cohérence et encore moins quel en serait le thème ; j'étais en proie à une telle agitation que je me levai précipitamment. Cependant, je ne prononçai pas ce discours ; mes lèvres demeurèrent obstinément closes et je restai debout silencieusement à attendre que cette soif oratoire s'apaisât d'elle-même. Mais, comme l'attente se prolongeait, mon inconfort devenait plus grand. Pour me faire comprendre, je ne saurais mieux le comparer qu'à celui d'un homme qui, incommodé par un repas trop copieux, fait appel en vain au moyen le plus expéditif de s'en débarrasser. En réalité, cette crise fut de courte durée et à peine eut-elle disparu que je n'y songeai plus ; je recouvrai aussitôt mon calme, mais non pas hélas ! l'exaltation délicieuse qui l'avait précédé. Du reste, lorsque je connus, quelques jours plus tard, une nouvelle crise, je dus me résigner avec un vif déplaisir à la subir sans avoir eu le bonheur de goûter préalablement à cette exaltation que je me suis risqué plus haut à décrire tant bien que mal et que je tenais d'abord pour indissolublement liée par un rapport causal à la souffrance qui l'avait suivie, et je songeai avec amertume que, si elles n'avaient jamais été réunies que fortuitement, l'une eût compensé largement l'autre. Pour en revenir à la nature même de cette crise, il est remarquable que celle-ci se soit manifestée par un étrange besoin de discourir impossible à satisfaire, mais c'est que les mots ne me venaient pas en aide ; bref, j'avais envie de parler et je n'avais absolument rien à dire.

Sans doute, il m'est trop habituel de tenir mes faiblesses pour des maladies insolites sur lesquelles aucun traitement n'a de pouvoir, et dont je dois me contenter de suivre l'évolution avec une curiosité impuissante, pour qu'une sorte d'indifférence désabusée ne me paraisse pas, dans une certaine mesure, l'attitude la plus raisonnable à observer devant le phénomène qui m'occupe ici. En fait, c'est presque ridicule, cette obstination à me croire gravement atteint quand j'ai le cafard, quand une sombre jalousie me dévore, quand une nouvelle révélation de mon insuffisance me donne l'envie de me fourrer sous terre, ou que l'ambition me ronge, ou encore la vanité, enfin toutes défaillances auxquelles je suis fréquemment sujet et pour lesquelles je ne dispose malheureusement d'aucun remède, étant affligé d'une totale absence de volonté et ne possédant à aucun moment cette désinvolture, commune à beaucoup d'hommes heureux, qui me paraît de loin la plus enviable des qualités. Quand je suis dans le marasme, je ne prends pas sur moi d'en sortir, j'y reste jusqu'au cou. Il est vrai, comme je l'ai dit en commençant, qu'on m'a souvent plaisanté sur mon caractère taciturne, puis on m'a plaint ; c'est que là aussi j'étais enclin à déceler dans cette incapacité à m'ouvrir tous les symptômes d'une maladie incurable et, ce qui est beaucoup plus significatif, il était impossible à mes amis eux-mêmes, mis en présence de l'angoisse que leur révélaient mes traits pendant qu'ils s'épuisaient à provoquer mes confidences, de ne pas être frappés par l'analogie qui existait entre l'état où ils me voyaient et celui d'un malade qu'une souffrance interne contracte sur lui-même. Mais dans le cas présent, si mon angoisse tenait essentiellement à l'impossibilité où je me trouvais de satisfaire un désir brûlant, elle se distinguait de la précédente par la nature même de ses causes. Devant tels de mes amis, il s'agissait de m'exprimer ; sur la falaise, il ne s'agissait que de bavarder à tort et à travers sans souci de logique et de cohérence. Autre chose était de ne pouvoir communiquer et de renoncer par là même au plaisir d'une amitié pure et sincère, autre chose de souffrir d'une insuffisance apparemment organique dont le plus clair résultat était d'empêcher que ne se manifestât un vice peut-être dangereux et en tout cas stérile, puisque je n'avais pas le sentiment qu'il en pût résulter pour moi la satisfaction vitale que nous cherchons dans le fait de nous confier. Mais enfin, dans les deux cas, il y avait au moins quelque chose de commun : l'angoisse. Et cependant, à la suite de plusieurs épreuves consécutives qui ne différaient pas sensiblement de celle que j'ai décrite et sur lesquelles je ne crois pas utile de m'étendre, il m'arriva de subir une crise beaucoup plus violente, quelque peu spectaculaire et très significative pour les analogies qu'elle présentait avec celles qui nuisaient si fâcheusement aux rapports que j'aurais désiré entretenir avec mes amis.

Pour me garder contre les sourires de ceux qui, sur la foi de mon propre aveu touchant la singularité que j'affecte volontiers, seraient enclins à douter de la véracité de ce récit, je ne puis mieux faire que de recourir à une sobriété parfaite, délaissant ainsi avec une pointe de regret le pouvoir hallucinant de certaines images que j'ai dans la tête et la recherche d'effets *souhaitables*, mais qui, pour leur réputation d'instruments de fabulation, demeurent suspects aux yeux de certains lecteurs sourcilleux sur le chapitre de l'objectivité. Tant pis si c'est reculer pour mieux sauter : j'entends éviter la transposition, les complaisances, les coups de pouce et m'en tenir à une reproduction absolument rigoureuse des faits ; il ne me déplairait pas, à quelque raillerie que ma pédanterie m'expose, d'être tenu pour un esprit grave ou même, si je dois tomber dans un excès, d'une gravité un peu bouffonne. Maintenant, j'invite ceux qui ont envie de rire à le faire ouvertement ; je désire qu'ils sachent que je ne suis que trop disposé à m'associer à leur gaieté. Il me suffit de croire que quelqu'un m'honore de son attention. Qui ? N'importe ! Quelqu'un, fût-ce un lecteur que l'ennui rend un peu distrait.

Je dois dire que jusque-là, ni mes amis ni mes proches ne s'étaient inquiétés de savoir d'où me venaient ces traits tirés, ce teint pâle, ces gestes nerveux et incertains. Peut-être qu'ils ne se souciaient pas de ma santé et dans ce cas c'était parfait. Dieu sait quelle torture c'est, quand vous souffrez d'un mal que vous voulez tenir secret, d'entendre les gens vous faire une remarque sur votre mine et vous demander si vous vous sentez bien ou s'il ne vous est pas arrivé quelque ennui, et vous vous en tirez en plaisantant sur ce sale rhume que vous avez chopé ou sur quelque autre chose d'aussi inoffensif, et vous devez éviter d'avoir l'air de penser : bon, êtes-vous content, en savez-vous assez ? Mais aux vrais amis qui s'inquiètent vraiment, même si vous êtes très fort en fait de mensonge, c'est très difficile de cacher ce que vous avez en réalité, parce qu'ils ne vous croiront jamais, jusqu'à ce que la raison que vous alléguiez soit en rapport avec votre mine ou votre attitude et en définitive aussi grave que celle que vous cherchiez à dissimuler, mais alors il vous en aurait beaucoup moins coûté de dire tout de suite la vérité. Au fait, avez-vous des amis qui attachent quelque importance à ce qui vous arrive ? Si vous n'en avez pas de tels, je pense qu'après tout vous avez peut-être de la chance. Mais c'est sans motif que je me laisse aller à cette digression, puisqu'on ne m'avait jamais signifié que j'eusse l'air souffrant, jusqu'au jour où, cédant à l'attirance qu'exerce invinciblement sur moi depuis quelques années une bouteille ou seulement un verre d'alcool, je commis l'imprudence de me saouler publiquement.

La phase critique de ma crise se déroula dans une espèce de dancing où j'avais échoué avec quelques amis qui, pour avoir absorbé déjà pas mal de petits verres, s'étaient mis en tête de s'amuser quelque part, malgré la vive résistance que j'avais opposée à ce projet, ayant toujours détesté tout ce qui ressemble de près ou de loin à la débauche, mais je me rendis compte qu'ils étaient tellement en avance sur moi qu'ils n'avaient plus la force de penser que c'était déraisonnable et à la gravité avec laquelle ils parlaient d'aller faire un tour dans un endroit encore plus mal famé que je n'ose nommer ici, je compris que je devrais vider un certain nombre de verres avant d'atteindre le niveau de leur ébriété et de participer de gaieté de cœur à leurs plaisirs malsains. Ils me plaisantèrent sur ce que je ne me mêlais à la conversation que pour faire entendre des paroles de grand-mère, on préférait encore mon sempiternel silence à ces plaisants discours de morale, j'avais d'ailleurs l'esprit beaucoup trop lucide pour dire quelque chose de sensé. J'encaissai leurs sarcasmes en souriant, mais j'étais vexé. Il me suffisait de regarder un instant autour de moi pour comprendre qu'il était inutile et peut-être dangereux d'insister, je décidai donc de me retrancher dans ce mutisme auquel ils m'invitaient désobligeamment.

Le cabaret où nous pénétrâmes, le visage rougi par un vent d'hiver coupant comme des lames de couteaux, les cheveux couverts de neige et les souliers humides, était envahi par la foule la plus grouillante d'hommes et de femmes dansant ou riant, attablés devant des verres, que j'eusse encore vue. Je dois avouer que j'appréciais beaucoup les rires bruyants, le crissement des souliers sur le parquet, les interpellations de diverses natures, et le plus souvent grossières, que recouvrait avec peine un orchestre dont la musique aigre éclaboussait les murs et aussi la densité des consommateurs qui s'égayaient, dansaient, trinquaient dans une pièce relativement exiguë où l'on n'eût pas cru possible d'introduire un nouveau client : si je ne me sentis pas tout de suite à l'aise dans une atmosphère aussi trouble (c'est un fait qu'on s'attend tellement à ne voir dans un établissement de cette sorte qu'une catégorie d'individus bien définie, que l'intrusion d'individus d'une catégorie différente à laquelle mes amis et moi appartenions visiblement semble insolite et même choquante jusqu'au moment où, par la vertu de je ne sais quel extraordinaire mimétisme, vous vous apercevez que vous respirez dans ce climat étranger aussi naturellement que s'il n'y en avait pas qui vous fût plus habituel ; à la réflexion, il serait plus exact de dire que, sitôt le seuil franchi, vous percevez pendant un plus ou moins court laps de temps un courant d'hostilité à l'égard de l'intrus que vous êtes encore), du moins j'avais lieu de croire que j'y passerais inaperçu et je me réjouissais à l'idée qu'il me serait impossible de parler aux autres, faute d'espérer m'en faire entendre. C'était une bonne chose. Je resterais à l'écart, insoucieux des plaisanteries qu'on ferait sur le fait que je n'ouvrais jamais la bouche ; c'était agréable de penser que je pourrais me livrer en toute quiétude au plaisir de contempler quelque chose de vivant sans être sollicité à y prendre part ; tout ce que je désirais maintenant, c'était rester dans un coin, environné de fumée, de musique et de rires et cependant solitaire, à observer avidement et lucidement un spectacle plein de vie auquel il me plaisait d'être le seul à ne pas participer d'une manière active. Quand j'étais enfant, j'éprouvais une joie singulière et assez énigmatique à circuler avec indolence entre les manèges d'une foire, les mains dans les poches, à observer successivement et avec une avidité aussi inlassable que si j'étais moi-même participant, les ébats turbulents des enfants de mon âge qui poussaient des cris de délicieuse angoisse sur des balançoires — et je tremblais pour eux que celles-ci fassent malencontreusement le tour complet de l'axe auquel elles étaient fixées — ou bien à califourchon sur des chevaux de bois, une main serrant la baguette tendue vers un anneau qu'il s'agissait de décrocher à temps — et ma propre main tremblait dans ma poche, comme si elle-même avait été rendue malhabile par l'épuisement ou la crainte de l'échec. Au plaisir actif qui le plus souvent me paraissait astreignant, illusoire, trop limité ou encore inaccessible, je préférais celui à mon avis incomparablement plus émouvant où me jetait le spectacle d'une joie collective qu'exprimaient diversement les visages sur lesquels j'attachais un regard fasciné. Il s'agissait là proprement de sympathie. D'une sympathie qui me faisait pénétrer le plaisir des autres et me rendait capable de l'éprouver avec une intensité d'autant plus vive, d'autant plus persistante que je le partageais ensemble et tour à tour avec un grand nombre d'enfants, d'autant plus profonde qu'échappant en quelque sorte à l'étourdissement causé par des sollicitations extérieures un peu trop brutales, il m'était permis de le savourer à l'écart en toute lucidité et de le gouverner au lieu de m'y soumettre. Encore aujourd'hui, il m'est difficile d'échapper à la tentation de saisir la première occasion qui s'offre de me rendre sur le théâtre d'une manifestation populaire où j'ai des chances d'être à même d'observer sur les visages tous les signes caractéristiques de la passion dont il m'est d'ailleurs indifférent d'apprendre qu'elle est alimentée par une sotte admiration ou des rancœurs injustifiées, mais la seule crainte d'être entraîné moi-même par un flot débordant de colère ou d'enthousiasme, et précisément en vertu de ma faculté de sympathie et malgré le sang-froid que je me suis juré de conserver, me retient quelquefois d'y céder. Telle est ma curiosité que je m'enfourne volontiers dans un cinéma avec l'espoir généralement déçu de contempler en gros plan un visage pleinement expressif.

S'il ressort clairement de tout ceci que je me range dans la catégorie de ces bien tristes gens qu'on appelle voyeurs, libre au lecteur de s'en indigner, mais qui l'assure que je ne me laisse pas emporter par mon imagination ? Prouvez-moi que je dis la vérité. Comment dites-vous ? Ce mensonge ne serait pas bénéfique ? Et si je mens pour le plaisir de mentir et s'il me plaît à moi d'écrire ceci plutôt que cela, mettons : un mensonge plutôt qu'une vérité, c'est-à-dire très exactement ce qui me passe par la tête, et si je ne demande pas mieux que d'être jugé sur un faux aveu, enfin supposez qu'il me soit infiniment agréable de compromettre ma réputation ? Mais je vous vois venir : trop facile d'atténuer le fâcheux effet d'un aveu en nous donnant à entendre qu'il pourrait être mis en doute. Bon. Je vous laisse le dernier mot. Mais pour commencer, j'ai pris soin de dissiper toute équivoque en précisant que mon unique souci était de me persuader que j'avais un lecteur. Un. Et un lecteur, j'insiste, ça veut dire quelqu'un qui lit, non pas nécessairement qui juge. Au reste, je n'interdis pas qu'on me juge, mais si le lecteur brûle d'impatience, s'il se dessèche d'ennui, je le prie de n'en rien laisser paraître, je tiens à lui signifier une fois pour toutes que je n'ai que faire de ses bâillements, de ses soupirs, de ses vociférations à voix basse, de ses coups de talon sur le parquet, est-ce ma faute si j'ai un faible pour les gens polis ? Et notez que je ne vous demande pas de me lire *vraiment*, mais de m'entretenir dans cette illusion que je suis lu : vous saisissez la nuance ? — Alors, vous parlez pour mentir ? — Non, monsieur, pour parler, rien de plus, et vous-même faites-vous autre chose du matin au soir et pas seulement à votre chat ? Et un écrivain écrit-il pour une autre raison que celle qu'il a envie d'écrire ? Mais suffit. Que mon lecteur me pardonne si je n'aime pas qu'on me bourdonne aux oreilles quand je parle.

Bien qu'il me parût nécessaire pour entretenir l'état agréable où je me trouvais de conserver intacte toute ma lucidité, j'avais une connaissance assez éprouvée de ma faiblesse pour prévoir avec certitude qu'aucune considération de ce genre ne me retiendrait de céder à la tentation absurde et immédiate de vider ce verre qui brillait devant moi ; et je crois même que c'est la certitude d'une chute prochaine qui m'entraînait à en avancer l'échéance. Je bus quatre verres consécutifs, c'était bien agréable aussi. La meilleure justification à ma faiblesse me semblait résider dans le fait que ma sensibilité, au lieu de se brouiller, devenait à la fois plus nette et plus réceptive, et je me sentais plein de sympathie, une sympathie formidable, pour tous ces gens agités. Qu'ils avaient raison de rire, de danser, de boire, de se préparer par des mots et des gestes à faire l'amour ! Quel passe-temps utile ! Dans le spectacle de ces gens emplis d'espoir ou de désespoir qui s'aiment ou cherchent l'amour, dans ce bruit de rafale, dans cette odeur chaude et confinée, consiste tout le secret de la vie, me disais-je en soulevant mon verre. Vivre c'est sentir, et boire, danser et rire c'est sentir, donc boire, danser et rire c'est cela vivre et sur ce plaisant syllogisme je vidais mon verre. C'était merveilleux de voir danser des gens saouls et c'était merveilleux d'être soi-même un peu saoul. Mais c'est que j'étais complètement saoul. Assis derrière une petite table de zinc dans un coin bruyant, j'écoutais la conversation en train autour de moi et, à travers la fumée bleue des cigarettes, je regardais tour à tour les couples qui défilaient devant moi, essayant de saisir au passage un bout de conversation, mais c'était superflu : l'allure et la physionomie m'en disaient plus long que les paroles ; si une femme était l'objet de mon examen, je m'accordais tout juste le droit d'estimer d'un regard le charme de la taille avant de passer au visage que j'interrogeais passionnément et sur lequel je pouvais en général déchiffrer sans effort les déchaînements d'une ardeur causée par la danse, l'atmosphère régnante ou l'espoir d'une conquête et qui me frappait moi-même d'extase et de vertige, car de même que le reflet fulgurant du soleil sur une surface parfaitement blanche affecte bien plus cruellement le regard que la perception du soleil lui-même, le spectacle du plaisir d'autrui doit, je crois, son pouvoir contagieux et sa valeur émotive au fait que ce plaisir, par l'éclat dont il revêt la chair d'un visage, entre dans le domaine absolument convaincant pour nous de l'expérience sensible. Mais lorsque mon regard, sur ces entrefaites, rencontra celui d'une femme très belle qui dansait au bras d'un individu d'une taille ridiculement courte, au nez busqué et aux cheveux rouges qui montaient en deux vagues inégales de chaque côté d'une raie impeccable coupée en son milieu par la visière d'une casquette collée presque sur la nuque, j'eus aussitôt le sentiment réconfortant qu'il y avait encore quelqu'un dans cette salle qui, sous un masque impassible, se nourrissait secrètement du plaisir des autres avec une avidité non moins fiévreuse et non moins ordonnée que la mienne. Si d'emblée je ne parvins pas à détacher mon regard de celui de cette femme qui ne paraissait d'ailleurs pas autrement gênée de l'intérêt que, mon ivresse aidant, je lui marquais avec une insistance peut-être incorrecte, c'est que ses yeux, son visage et l'ensemble de ses manières tranchaient curieusement sur ceux des autres femmes aux rires provocants qui lançaient des œillades engageantes par-dessus l'épaule de leur danseur aux quelques hommes assis ou exhibaient négligemment des cuisses nues sans se lasser d'interpeller les uns et les autres avec une liberté de langage qu'autorisaient seuls la nature spéciale de l'endroit et les goûts vulgaires de la clientèle. Je n'éprouve aucune honte à reconnaître qu'après tant de consommations j'étais de moins en moins apte à distinguer cette femme de ses voisines et qu'en tout cas il n'y avait peut-être rien en elle qui pût me faire naïvement supposer qu'elle goûtait le même plaisir que le mien ; rien peut-être sur son beau visage qui décelât un plaisir plus raffiné que celui des autres. Mais je me plaisais à donner à sa réserve qui différait d'une manière si frappante de l'exubérance ambiante une interprétation qui pouvait très bien ne pas être la bonne. Cependant, cette impression très probablement illusoire que mon plaisir était en tous points semblable à celui auquel j'imaginais qu'elle se livrait secrètement ne provenait pas seulement de cette réserve insolite ; il y avait aussi, pendu à elle, ce petit bonhomme roux qui levait vers son visage presque inanimé des yeux ardents et, au milieu d'un débordement de soupirs, ne cessait d'exprimer des sentiments dont elle ne paraissait nullement tenir compte. Était-ce parce que lui parlait tant et plus et qu'elle ne desserrait pas les lèvres, et qu'il la dévisageait avec insistance tandis qu'elle promenait son regard partout ailleurs au-dessus de lui avec un intérêt exclusif qui eût suffi à décourager quelqu'un d'un peu moins épris, elle me semblait bien plus occupée par le plaisir des autres que par celui auquel on l'invitait avec tant de chaleur et de patience vaines.

Mais à quoi bon ces frais d'exposition, voilà bien des détours pour en venir enfin à écrire cette simple phrase : j'avais envie de danser avec elle. Et comment me retenir d'avouer que ce désir n'avait au fond pour seuls sujets que la gravité d'un visage et plus encore l'attrait tout physique qu'exerçait sur moi un corps admirablement bien balancé, et non pas du tout, comme je m'évertue sans raison à le faire croire, la stupeur émerveillée où me plongeait l'analogie vraisemblablement créée de toutes pièces par mon imagination d'ivrogne entre nos deux recettes du plaisir ? Et d'ailleurs, n'est-ce pas après coup que j'ai trompeusement substitué au désir que j'avais de tenir cette femme dans mes bras, l'enchantement que j'aurais trouvé à découvrir quelqu'un dans cette salle qui différât des autres par la façon dont elle savait comme moi tirer du plaisir tout le maximum d'effets ? Mais après tout, que vous importe ? L'ai-je désirée physiquement, a-t-elle seulement excité ma curiosité par son air sérieux ? Quelqu'un tient-il à connaître très exactement les raisons qui m'ont fait me lever et l'inviter à la prochaine danse ? Je me demande bien où les hommes ont pris ce goût surprenant pour la vérité dont le plus souvent ils n'ont que faire, pourquoi les aveux d'un homme sincère, pourquoi la lecture d'un rapport dont la clarté et la concision leur sont, disent-ils, les meilleurs garants de l'authenticité des faits exposés, les laissent tout béats d'admiration. Nous ne sommes pas ici, Dieu merci, pour courir après une vérité qui se dérobe sans cesse, ce serait un exercice aussi énervant pour notre esprit que, par exemple, pour notre main de s'appliquer à faire passer un gros fil de coton par le chas d'une aiguille. Cependant, je dois admettre et je n'ai d'ailleurs aucune envie de dissimuler, que ni l'intérêt passionné que je portais à son air énigmatique (d'où je me gardais bien de tirer des conclusions hâtives) ni la disposition un peu particulière et purement circonstancielle où je me trouvais alors ne suffiraient à expliquer le désir que j'éprouvai soudain de tenir cette femme dans mes bras au moins pendant le temps d'une danse, mais, est-il besoin de le redire, je pensais simplement que ce serait une bonne chose de presser ce corps contre ma poitrine et de voir ces yeux gris se fixer sur les miens et d'entendre tout près de mon oreille mur-

murer une voix dont le timbre devait être si saisissant. Aucune importance d'ailleurs pour la suite des événements et croyez bien que si j'analyse, si je construis des hypothèses, si je temporise, c'est moins par scrupule de ne rien laisser perdre de ce qui me vient en vrac à l'esprit que parce qu'il me plaît de me livrer à un petit jeu aussi frivole qu'inoffensif auquel je ne me targue nullement d'être passé maître : celui qui consiste en premier lieu à tenir l'interlocuteur en haleine, puis, par le simulacre d'un tic assez déplorable, à l'égarer avec ce qui aurait pu être, ce qui a peut-être été, ce qui n'a sûrement pas été, ce qu'il aurait été bon qu'il fût et ce qu'il aurait été fâcheux qu'il ne fût pas et ce qu'on a négligé de dire et ce qu'on a dit qui n'a pas été et ainsi de suite jusqu'à ce qu'enfin à bout de patience, s'écriant : « Au fait, au fait ! », on vous assure, par ce furieux rappel à l'ordre, que vous n'avez pas tout à fait perdu votre temps.

Dès que la musique cessa, je me levai et, à la grande surprise de mes amis qui m'avaient jusqu'à présent complètement négligé, j'allai droit sur la jeune femme que j'invitai à danser. Elle n'eut pas le temps d'acquiescer, le rouquin intervint en déclarant sur un ton insolent et péremptoire que la prochaine danse *aussi* était pour lui. Mais je ne tins pas compte de sa revendication et, saisissant vivement la jeune femme par la taille, je l'entraînai vers le milieu de la salle où nous commençâmes à danser. Il nous suivit, se frayant un passage entre les danseurs, il n'était nullement disposé à lâcher le morceau, et il me somma en termes désobligeants de lui rendre ce qui ne m'appartenait pas. Je lui demandai poliment si elle lui appartenait personnellement. Non ? Dans ce cas, je lui conseillai de se mêler de ses affaires et j'ajoutai que je devais l'avertir que j'étais un peu ivre, pas absolument ivre, mais juste assez pour perdre mon sang-froid. Au comble de la rage, il protesta de plus belle, les yeux avides et bouleversés fixés sur la fille dont le regard indifférent se perdait vers l'autre côté de la salle, sa voix rauque rendue furibonde par l'énormité du préjudice que je lui causais. Je lui dis de la boucler et je le priai de cesser cette mauvaise comédie : il devait prendre la chose avec plus de sérénité, chacun son tour, est-ce que ça lui serait égal de danser avec cette fille grasse et triste qui attendait là-bas dans son coin une invitation charitable ? Ces derniers mots redoublèrent sa fureur. La face blême, les mains à mi-corps, l'image même de l'amant bafoué, il se préparait visiblement à nous séparer avec ses poings et je me tenais prêt moi-même à parer aux premiers coups et à lui rendre au centuple ceux qu'il réussirait à me donner. C'est alors que la jeune femme, quittant son air distant, le dévisagea avec des yeux sombres, froids et hautains, et lui débita en espagnol une bordée de paroles apparemment très cinglantes qui parurent le sidérer et, à la façon déconfite et soumise avec laquelle il baissa les yeux, je compris que c'était un homme déjà prêt à abandonner le combat. Il resta là un moment, ne sachant que faire de ses mains, et son visage ne reflétait déjà plus qu'une colère de pure forme. Il se contenta de nous regarder tous deux à tour de rôle, la bouche ouverte ; puis il recula de quelques pas pour éviter deux couples entre lesquels il risquait de se voir cerné et il se rapprocha de nous quand nous fûmes au bord de la piste pour bégayer qu'après tout elle était libre de se donner en spectacle avec le premier gamin venu. « Très bien, merci, dis-je sur un ton sarcastique, merci beaucoup ! » Il haussa les épaules, nous tourna le dos et alla s'effondrer devant une table au bord de la piste, avec l'air avachi et légèrement penaud d'un homme éconduit. Quelque temps plus tard, je pus constater qu'il était toujours affalé sur sa chaise, devant une bouteille déjà aux trois quarts vide, les mains ceignant comme une couronne son crâne flamboyant sous l'éclat d'une lampe électrique, les yeux à demi clos entre ses paupières luisantes, le visage à la fois attentif et déformé par une colère latente. Je ne peux affirmer qu'il nous surveillait, mais certainement il avait l'œil sur nous. Il n'avait pour ainsi dire pas cessé de nous épier, rongé sans doute par une honte atroce et nourrissant, sous des dehors paisibles, des sentiments d'instant en instant plus manifestement hostiles pour ce rival qui le frustrait de son unique plaisir et le mettait dans une situation humiliante par rapport à la femme qu'il aimait.

Je déteste, cela va sans dire, cette sorte d'altercation, mais je lui trouve quelques excuses en la circonstance : l'étrange fascination qu'exerçait sur moi cette femme, la force absolument inaccoutumée de mon désir, jusqu'à l'état de demi-ivresse dans lequel je me trouvais après l'absorption de huit verres d'alcool, tout ceci accru de l'exaltation inouïe qui, pendant tout le temps où je la serrais contre moi, réussit à me délivrer de l'angoisse où me tient à peu près constamment le sentiment d'un isolement irrémédiable.

Une fois la fille tout contre moi et son

amant écarté de ma route, il ne me restait plus qu'à me plonger dans mon plaisir comme dans une marée de caresses. Plaisir tellement impétueux et bouleversant que j'en oubliais l'envie que j'avais eue d'entendre sa voix. Les yeux dans les yeux, nous dansâmes sans dire un mot. Si ses narines tremblaient, si son regard brillait d'une flamme très noire, si je sentais sous ma main son corps tressaillir longuement, comme sous l'empire d'une exquise torture, en revanche je voyais sur ses lèvres un sourire ambigu qui me faisait pourtant moins l'effet d'une trahison que d'une troublante complicité rendue encore plus évidente par le silence que nous observions au milieu du vacarme environnant. Fut-elle mise en garde par ce qu'il pouvait y avoir de louche ou de légèrement dissonant dans mon allure, de titubant dans ma démarche, de débraillé dans ma tenue, cherchait-elle à m'avertir par un léger signe d'ironie qu'elle n'était pas complètement dupe des déclarations que je pourrais être amené à lui faire et dont elle devrait mettre une bonne part sur le compte de mon ivresse, toujours est-il qu'en proie à un vertige merveilleux qui m'interdisait de penser qu'il pût y avoir disparité dans nos sentiments mutuels et qui me douait illusoirement d'une sorte d'invulnérabilité, je ne m'inquiétais pas de savoir ce qu'elle pensait de moi, et cette insouciance-là vaut d'être notée quand on saura qu'aucune préoccupation ne m'agite plus que celle de dépister, à force de discernement, de perspicacité et de ruse, l'image que se fait de moi la personne que j'aime ou du moins à l'estime de laquelle je tiens. Je ne suis pas de ceux que l'opinion d'une jolie femme laisse indifférents. Le travail qui consiste à organiser mentalement, à regrouper ou à mettre bout à bout les diverses appréciations, recueillies sur le vif ou indirectement rapportées, de telle personne sur mon compte, pour en venir ensuite à recomposer une image assez vraisemblable qui, flatteuse ou défavorable, ne correspond jamais tout à fait à la réalité permanente de ce que je suis, se reproduit à chaque nouveau contact et constitue pour moi la plus torturante des épreuves. L'esprit naturellement lucide que j'y apporte ne m'incline jamais à tricher en éludant ce qui pourrait m'être trop désagréable ; même s'il m'arrive de ne pas savoir réduire tel facteur avantageux à de plus justes proportions, je ne suis pas dupe, ayant un mépris foncier pour toute supercherie avec soi-même. Mais mon trouble et ma gaucherie n'en sont que plus vifs. Il en résulte aussi que la déception que m'inflige le plus souvent la difformité de mon image (à laquelle, il faut bien l'avouer, mon pessimisme naturel a imprimé discrètement sa marque), tout en entretenant l'équivoque, me confirme dans l'idée que la seule part de moi-même que je considère comme vraiment importante demeurant toujours cachée aux regards des êtres que je chéris le plus, tandis que tout ce que je peux montrer d'autre est sans importance, je ne serai jamais compris, *compris* se confondant pour moi avec *aimé*, et c'est là une cruelle constatation dont il m'arrive quelquefois de rire pour ce qu'elle a d'évidemment puéril. Mais ce jour-là, j'étais décidément très différent de moi-même. Entièrement absorbé par ce plaisir grisant où d'ailleurs contre toute attente je commençais à perdre pied, il ne me venait pas à l'idée d'interpréter ce sourire, d'en faire le tour, ni de tenter d'en extraire, à l'exclusion de tout le reste, ce qui pourrait servir à la fabrication ultérieure d'une image plus ou moins conforme à la réalité et c'était bien mieux ainsi. En d'autres circonstances, l'importance excessive que j'aurais attachée à l'opinion qu'on allait se faire de moi et la gêne qu'elle m'aurait causée eussent été telles qu'il ne me serait resté aucune chance de me délivrer momentanément de ce qui intérieurement me ronge, ma jouissance ayant été de ce fait très amoindrie, sinon tout à fait empoisonnée. Or, il me suffisait de sentir cette femme près de moi pour que tout devînt simple et clair ; nulle anxiété, nulle inconfiance, nul lugubre pressentiment d'un échec probable ; j'étais là au cœur d'une béatitude parfaite qui doit être celle qu'éprouvent, au sommet de leur crise, une certaine sorte de fous ; en tout cas, je la crois à peu près inexprimable. Je regardais ce visage et jamais je n'en avais vu d'aussi splendide, d'aussi ardent et d'aussi froid en même temps (je pense que quelques-unes de ces antinomies toutes extérieures, très frappantes chez cette femme, étaient pour beaucoup dans l'emprise qu'elle exerçait sur moi), d'aussi proche de moi — au point que j'identifiais ma joie avec celle qu'il me semblait exprimer — et pourtant encore assez distant pour qu'il m'imposât le respect et suscitât une curiosité à laquelle se mêlait un désir d'autant plus brûlant que son objet revêtait une apparence d'inaccessibilité.

Quand la musique cessa de nouveau, je lui demandai si elle me laissait lui offrir un verre ; elle accepta en souriant, mais, dès que nous fûmes assis, son ami s'approcha d'elle et l'invita à danser ; elle fit un geste négatif de la tête sans le regarder ; il éclata alors en imprécations, puis il fit valoir ses arguments en espagnol avec une ardeur désespérée ; elle n'y prêta aucune attention et garda le silence, avec toujours ce même sourire aigu sur les lèvres. Comprenant qu'il était inutile d'essayer de la fléchir et furieux de se sentir volé, il se tourna de mon côté et marcha vers moi en balançant ses poings avec l'air mauvais ; instinctivement je reculai en faisant glisser ma chaise sur le parquet et je me mis en garde un peu prématurément, avec une gaucherie probablement très comique. Mais, craignant sans doute qu'il me fît un mauvais parti, la jeune femme s'interposa en l'engageant d'une voix tranquille, lente et ferme, à regagner sa table où elle le rejoindrait dans un instant ; c'est là du moins ce que je crus comprendre. Cette injonction n'éveilla tout d'abord en lui qu'une étrange gesticulation muette accompagnée de sons étranglés. Sa bouche était entr'ouverte, il avait des lèvres épaisses qui semblaient enflées ; ses yeux rouges, brillant de ressentiment et de colère, essayaient de sonder jusqu'au fond les calmes yeux noirs de la jeune femme qui observait le visage amer et dérouté de sa victime avec une expression curieuse de l'effet de son pouvoir, mais sans parvenir toutefois à réprimer une sorte d'impatience que trahissait le tapotement nerveux de ses doigts sur le bord de la table. Quant à moi, je restais assis silencieusement à contempler ce spectacle atroce avec une remarquable inconscience de ce qu'une telle situation comportait d'humiliant pour moi, admettant avec une légèreté qui me semble aujourd'hui stupéfiante que mon adversaire fût évincé par un procédé féminin aussi déloyal, sans préjudice de la haine qu'il ne pourrait manquer de me vouer et dont j'aurais d'ici peu à supporter les conséquences. C'est que je ne pouvais m'empêcher de jouir intensément de la double scène que m'offraient d'une part le visage douloureux et perplexe de l'homme maté qui, secrètement furieux de l'incapacité où le reléguait sa passion dévorante, ne réussissait pas tout à fait à cacher une sorte de rage froide (et il m'importait peu qu'elle me fût destinée), d'autre part le sourire mystérieux, les yeux désarmants, le port de tête dominant et hautain de cette femme qui savait tenir à distance l'amant transi lorsqu'elle désirait se faire courtiser par d'autres. Je me prenais à tort pour un spectateur quand il était bien clair que j'étais un des acteurs, le moins intéressant des trois en raison de l'attitude lâche et passive où je me cantonnais. Cependant, si ardemment que j'aspire à la sincérité, je ne veux pas, pour la mettre en vedette, céder à une partialité dont ma réputation ferait les frais ; je crois donc pouvoir affirmer que je ne me complaisais pas dans cette inertie par insensibilité, forfanterie, scepticisme, ni même par crainte d'attirer sur moi une colère menaçante. En réalité, rien n'était plus authentique que le sentiment de calme, de détente, d'euphorie où je m'abandonnais et qu'épiçait seulement une curiosité somme toute assez légitime. De plus, pour médiocre que me semble aujourd'hui cette excuse (mais aux yeux de qui me tient-il à cœur de me justifier ? Vous avez remarqué déjà le *si ardemment que j'aspire à la sincérité*), je crois juste d'ajouter que j'étais dans un état d'hypersensibilité due à un excès de boisson qui explique en partie l'étrangeté de ma conduite. Je ne me rendais pas pleinement compte, je crois. Je faisais de mon mieux pour paraître tout à fait confortable et vraisemblablement je n'aurais jamais supporté de voir ce type souffrir devant moi et à cause de moi si, auparavant, je n'avais bu à longs traits plusieurs verres de brandy-soda. Je trouvais que ce que j'avais devant les yeux était très intéressant. Pourquoi le rouquin restait-il debout avec l'air d'un enfant qui va pleurer ? Pourquoi continuait-il à tout encaisser ? À sa place, j'aurais défoncé la figure du sale maquereau que j'étais, mais j'oubliais que j'étais précisément ce sale maquereau. Je me sentais très loin de ce que je contemplais avec une curiosité si avide, et entièrement irresponsable, aussi irresponsable qu'un honnête spectateur dans une salle de théâtre peut l'être de la sanglante tragédie qui se joue à dix pas de lui. Tout ce que je voulais pour le moment c'était savourer dans mon fauteuil, en toute tranquillité, le côté passionné, cruel et saoul de la situation. Naturellement, pas question d'intervenir.

Mais, bercé par mon agréable euphorie, je ne me doutais pas que j'allais devenir l'acteur principal, autant dire le seul, de la scène suivante que je me suis engagé plus haut à vous décrire avec la sécheresse et la rigueur qui président aux observations médicales, à supposer que je ne me laisse pas entraîner par l'émotion que pourrait bien me causer le souvenir d'une émotion ancienne. (J'ouvre ici une parenthèse pour préciser que c'est à dessein que je me suis étendu non pas tellement sur les faits, après tout épisodiques, qui l'ont précédée que sur les états successifs par lesquels j'ai dû passer à l'occasion de ces mêmes faits. En m'y consacrant avec une application si minutieuse je ne me suis proposé que d'aider à l'intelligibilité de ce qui va suivre. Je tiens à ajouter que j'ai peu de goût pour la reconstitution des souvenirs. Ni vous ni moi ne valons d'être pris si à cœur, ni tellement à la lettre. Est-ce que vous ne trouvez pas cela inconvenant : j'ai embrassé une telle, j'ai été content, elle m'a trompé, j'ai été triste, un type m'a menacé, j'ai eu peur, et ainsi de suite ? Laissez-moi vous dire que c'est tout simplement sordide et fastidieux. Je sais bien, nous avons une langue, nous avons inventé la plume à écrire, et elles ne demandent l'une et l'autre qu'à servir. Mais que diable avons-nous besoin d'une langue et d'une plume ? Et, en tout cas, d'où nous vient ce besoin pervers de faire tourner la première inconsidérément devant les auditeurs bouche bée ou paupières closes, de faire grincer la seconde en vue le plus souvent de remédier à l'insuffisance de notre vie ? Lesquels d'entre nous ont encore la pudeur de se livrer à ce fâcheux exercice seuls devant eux-mêmes ? Les maniaques, les vieux garçons, les fous. Et notez que moi-même, je ne nie pas avoir sollicité une audience, restreinte, très restreinte, il est vrai. Mais enfin une audience. Eh bien, soit : parlons, écrivons, n'hésitons pas, puisque nous ne saurions échapper au mal commun.)

Le petit homme roux, dont le visage était devenu d'une pâleur jaunâtre, hésita quelque temps sur la décision qu'il devait prendre. Il attendait debout, les mains à mi-corps, prêt à se lancer à l'assaut, avec un certain air de jouissance, comme s'il eût savouré à la fois le traitement infligé par la jeune femme aux ordres de qui il était clair qu'il se soumettrait avec délice, et sa propre colère qui témoignait publiquement de son amour. Je sentis mon sang se figer quand je vis ses genoux qui tremblaient sous le pantalon gris clair qui lui flottait amplement sur les pieds. Jusqu'alors, j'avais évité de le regarder en face, mais maintenant, pour tromper ma peur, j'essayais de le dévisager froidement avec un regard tranquille et je prenais des poses dégagées, tout en me mordant la langue très fort pour empêcher mes lèvres de trembler. Aussi fut-ce avec un soulagement indicible que je le vis soudain tourner les talons et, la tête enfoncée entre ses deux maigres épaules tombantes, regagner en trébuchant sa petite table, dans un coin de la salle, d'où il pourrait nous surveiller du coin de l'œil.

L'incident clos, je me retrouvais seul en face de cette femme et le silence tomba entre nous. Pendant que nous dansions, je m'étais déjà représenté vaguement la difficulté que j'éprouverais tôt ou tard à l'entretenir dans sa langue, mais je m'en inquiétais d'autant moins qu'un échange de paroles banales me paraissait plutôt de nature à troubler notre exaltation et je me félicitais du mutisme auquel m'obligeaient non pas tant mon incapacité habituelle de trouver à dire à un interlocuteur encore inconnu quelque chose qui puisse être le support d'une conversation que ma méconnaissance de l'espagnol probablement égale à celle qu'elle avait de ma langue. À vrai dire, dans l'état d'ébriété très avancée où je me trouvais, je n'éprouvais qu'une gêne toute passagère et je me surprenais déjà à lui confier mentalement des choses sur moi qu'il ne me serait jamais venu à l'idée, en temps normal, de révéler à mon ami le plus intime, à plus forte raison à une personne que je ne connaissais pour ainsi dire pas, même si, ressentant pour elle un très vif désir et cherchant à la courtiser, je m'étais mis, faute d'un autre sujet, à lui parler de moi-même.

À ce point de mon récit, je conçois toute la difficulté qu'il y a à retracer un événement de ma vie particulièrement obscur et confus, dont, si je veux être véridique, je devrai à la fois respecter l'incohérence et conserver les proportions, tout en m'efforçant d'éviter de lui donner dans un but tendancieux un sens qu'il n'a pas eu ou de le traiter avec un sang-froid exagéré qui le déchargerait après coup de la valeur émotive dont il était pourvu. L'angle insolite sous lequel se présentent les faits que j'entreprends de relater justifierait un mode de narration que je persiste pourtant à juger peu honnête : quelque brume, une incohérence étudiée, envoûtante par l'impression qu'elle donnerait d'un ordre inversé, une sorte de magie obtenue à l'aide de combinaisons éprouvées venant à point nommé et peu importerait lesquelles, pourvu que l'effet de vraisemblance fût atteint, le foisonnement compliqué de tous les artifices qui imposent à l'esprit du lecteur comme l'idée d'un moment à la fois essentiel et très intense et qui le frapperaient avec assez de violence pour rendre inutile toute explication dans un langage logique et discursif ; bref, beaucoup plus d'art et beaucoup moins d'honnêteté. Eh bien, non ! J'ai dit en commençant que je m'interdisais l'usage de tels procédés, sans doute efficaces par cette sorte de mirage trompeur où ils noient les faits auxquels ils restituent ce que ceux-ci pouvaient avoir à l'origine d'imprécis et de chaotique, mais auxquels en tout cas, et c'est sur ce point que j'attire l'attention du lecteur, ils font subir de telles déformations qu'on ne saurait plus songer à en donner une interprétation concluante, et ce serait naturellement sortir de mon objet qui est à la fois plus hautain et plus modeste. Plus hautain parce que je méprise ceux qui, sous couleur d'exciter la sensibilité, se vautrent dans la confusion et l'arbitraire comme des canards dans l'eau et si j'observe non sans amertume que le mensonge est toléré, bien mieux, approuvé et loué par chacun, j'entends quant à moi user de rigueur contre tout ce qui n'est pas absolument pur et lucide, du moins aujourd'hui où c'est ma fantaisie, car enfin je ne m'en fais nullement une règle d'hygiène ou un devoir. Plus modeste, parce qu'il y a un art du mensonge auquel les plus menteurs ne peuvent prétendre. L'effet théâtral n'est pas mon affaire, mieux vaut m'en tenir à décrire loyalement, comme je me propose de le faire ici, les phases successives de ma crise avec la seule préoccupation de révéler dans ses grands traits ce qui m'est apparu de son évolution. Tant pis pour qui trouvera la chose peu plaisante.

Mais, au préalable, il me paraît nécessaire de vous donner une idée sommaire du décor, des dispositions des gens à mon égard, de tous les éléments secondaires qui ont pu concourir de quelque façon à la naissance d'une crise qui ne se distingue pas seulement des précédentes par sa durée, son intensité et sa plénitude, mais aussi par la façon imprévue dont elle s'est transformée en une détresse aussi vertigineuse que l'avait été initialement le plaisir que je m'efforçais tout à l'heure de définir et à laquelle devait se substituer plus tard, sous l'effet d'un choc physique très violent, une voluptueuse hébétude qui pourrait figurer, si l'on veut, le terme de la courbe.

Le décor, c'était, à peu de chose près, celui de tous les bars maritimes où vous pouvez pénétrer à condition de n'avoir l'air ni trop sot, ni trop riche, ni trop intimidé, ni trop fendant, où il y a de belles filles qui dansent avec les clients et de moins belles qui vous font les yeux en coulisse et parfois vous versent des boissons destinées à vous égayer et à témoigner aux yeux de la patronne, par la pile de soucoupes entassées devant vous, que vous n'êtes pas venu là seulement pour vous asseoir et ne rien faire, où il y a par exemple un orchestre modestement composé de trois musiciens très dignes, mais un tantinet ivres, munis chacun d'un instrument différent, le premier d'un saxophone, le second d'un accordéon, le troisième d'un piano droit sur lequel il tapote à ses moments perdus, quand il est las de contempler par-dessus sa partition le visage et les jambes des femmes qui lui plaisent, où il survient toujours à quelque moment une bande de matelots à moitié ivres qui, tout de suite, accaparent l'attention générale par l'outrance de leurs propos et de leurs gestes, et il arrive que l'un d'entre eux, particulièrement vigoureux et exalté, s'en prenne à un petit godelureau qui ne veut pas lâcher une belle fille et proteste d'une voix rageuse ou larmoyante, selon la nature de sa saoulerie, jusqu'à ce qu'il reçoive une chaude correction et soit jeté dehors à l'approbation craintive des tenanciers, non sans avoir été préalablement délesté de son portefeuille, et, quand vous sortez de là, il peut arriver que vos poches aussi soient vides, mais généralement ce n'est que le lendemain après-midi, quand vous vous réveillez avec une couronne de fer sur la tête et une conscience redevenue claire, que vous vous rendez compte qu'après tout, votre partie nocturne, ce que vous vous refusez maintenant à appeler une partie de plaisir, n'a pas été précisément pour rien. Si je ne renonce pas tout à fait à évoquer une telle atmosphère, en dépit du romantisme un peu facile auquel elle donne lieu inévitablement et bien que je demeure constamment attentif à surmonter toute préoccupation de pittoresque, c'est que j'estime qu'elle a joué un rôle et que je ne pourrais sans arbitraire la passer sous silence.

Les dispositions des gens à mon égard s'étaient sensiblement modifiées depuis l'intervention du petit rouquin ; ce n'est pas qu'elle eût été plus remarquable que la plupart de celles qu'on voyait quotidiennement dans cet établissement ; elle n'avait pas eu de suite et n'avait revêtu à aucun moment ce caractère de violence habituel à ce genre d'altercation, mais c'est précisément ce qui l'avait rendue plus frappante aux yeux de clients qui, connaissant de longue date le tempérament agressif de l'homme, toujours prêt à faire usage de ses poings quand il se jugeait offensé par les assiduités d'un individu auprès de son amie, n'en revenaient pas de le voir lâcher prise devant un inconnu de piètre apparence, dont la combativité, à en juger par l'absence complète de ses réactions, paraissait des plus médiocres. Mais peut-être aussi pensaient-ils que mon rival, croyant que je cachais sous des dehors calmes et insouciants un monde de ruses inconnues de lui, en avait été si vivement impressionné qu'il avait jugé prudent de battre en retraite ; du moins était-ce là ce que je me plaisais à imaginer et, pour m'en convaincre, je jetai un coup d'œil circulaire dans la salle : la plupart des danseurs l'observaient avec curiosité, les hommes ouvertement, les femmes à la dérobée, et l'ensemble avec lequel les deux éléments d'un même couple reportaient leur regard sur moi, tout en conversant, me renforçait dans l'idée que j'étais l'objet de leur entretien et, naturellement, je ne doutais pas que celui-ci me fût favorable. Quoi qu'il en soit, il y avait ceci de bien clair : tandis qu'en pénétrant dans ce dancing, je n'étais qu'un personnage obscur et négligeable, je jouissais maintenant d'une certaine considération de la part de gens qui généralement ne respectent et n'admirent que plus puissant qu'eux, et je tirais de cette constatation un sentiment d'orgueil démesuré qui n'est sans doute pas étranger au fait que ma crise, à l'encontre des précédentes, revêtait un caractère d'ostentation d'autant plus surprenant que j'ai toujours jugé insoutenable l'exhibitionnisme chez autrui. Mais en société, quand je ne m'inquiète pas de passer inaperçu et de voir sans être vu, il m'arrive presque toujours de prétendre à jouer un rôle ; le plus souvent, il me plairait qu'on me crût de cette espèce d'hommes dont nul ne peut jamais prévoir ce qu'il sortira (réactions, œuvres, attitudes devant une situation donnée, etc.), de sorte que chaque nouveau rapport avec eux implique un changement total de perspective ; mon admiration allant aux êtres dont je dois sans cesse retarder le classement, il est naturel que je sois désireux de les prendre pour modèles. Au sein d'un groupe, et mieux encore s'il est composé de quelques femmes, j'éprouve une joie aiguë à jouer mon rôle, non pas dans un but concerté d'hypocrisie, mais par besoin instinctif de prendre du volume et de me couvrir d'une ombre flatteuse ; d'ailleurs, en pareil cas, ce qui me grise n'est pas tant le parfum de rouerie né de cette comédie qu'une étrange sensation de libération : il me semble qu'après une longue privation, les circonstances me permettent enfin de reprendre possession de ce qui m'est dû, d'incarner mon propre personnage. De là, qu'en dépit du souvenir horrifié que je garde de la vie de collège et de régiment, je m'y reporte quelquefois avec un sentiment de nostalgie analogue à celui d'une vieille actrice évoquant l'immense théâtre croulant sous les applaudissements où elle connut ses plus grands succès.

Quant à mes amis, ils n'en croyaient pas leurs yeux. Mon altercation avec le petit bonhomme et l'évidente beauté de ma compagne modifiaient pour quelques instants l'idée qu'ils s'étaient faite de moi. Pas tout à fait le jeune homme insignifiant qu'on traînait derrière soi comme un boulet. Tout bien considéré, je me comportais avec les femmes comme ils eussent voulu savoir le faire, je représentais en quelque sorte leur idéal de ce qu'un homme devait être, audacieux, méprisant, au besoin agressif et sarcastique, buvant un peu trop, comme devaient le faire tous les vrais hommes, flegmatique devant le danger, entreprenant avec les femmes et sachant leur plaire d'emblée, mais par-dessus tout doté d'un aplomb superbe. Je veux dire que c'était là l'idée que je pensais qu'ils se faisaient de moi. Je me plaçais orgueilleusement sur le socle de l'homme à femmes. Indiscutablement, mon attitude présente me consacrait en tant qu'homme, c'était la revanche de mes échecs passés et, par un dernier reste de puérilité, je n'étais pas loin d'y attacher un sens de révélation (à moi-même et aux autres) d'un caractère très général, ce qui me faisait passer insensiblement du plaisir intime d'en imposer au désir vaniteux de parader en public, à la manière d'un acteur qui, grisé par son succès, amplifie ses effets, faute de savoir les renouveler, et en dévoile ainsi peu à peu la grossièreté. À bien chercher, je découvrirais peut-être d'autres facteurs plus accessoires ou même douteux, mais qui, pour la plupart, ont pu contribuer secondairement à déclencher cette crise dont je ne puis, à mon grand regret, faire ici qu'amorcer le processus. Mais de telles recherches me mèneraient trop loin ; et, je l'avoue, en m'attardant sur les causes, je craindrais que mon lecteur ne me suivît pas jusqu'aux effets. Oui, je dois reconnaître que je ne suis plus trop sûr qu'on m'écoute. Je perds confiance. Il est temps, sans doute, il est grand temps que je laisse là ces tergiversations oiseuses, auxquelles je prends moi-même très peu de plaisir, que je renonce une fois pour toutes à ces grandes manœuvres autour du sujet quand c'est le sujet même qui m'intéresse. Je foncerai donc en avant. Reviens vers moi, lecteur, reviens, j'en ai fini avec les causes et je passe sans coup férir à la description du phénomène proprement dit.

Le point commun entre les deux crises, la première que j'ai décrite et celle-ci, se limite strictement à la sensation d'euphorie qui les a précédées toutes deux ; à partir du moment où elles se déclarent, toute analogie cesse. Il est important de constater que, pour qu'elles se déclenchent et trouvent à s'exercer avec une exceptionnelle efficience, il faut qu'elles découvrent en moi un terrain de réceptivité propice et par conséquent que je sois maintenu par quelque détermination de ma vie propre dans des dispositions émotionnelles toutes particulières. On a vu que dans le premier cas il s'agissait d'une étrange sensation de bien-être due sans doute à l'isolement du lieu, au bruit frais des vagues, à la pureté du ciel, aux délices de l'ombre par opposition à la perception que j'avais de rocs calcaires éclatants sous le feu inexorable du soleil et se faisant ainsi apprécier davantage comme une oasis au milieu d'un désert, sans oublier le contraste non moins vif entre le parfum d'ennui qui se dégageait d'un après-midi dans ma chambre et celui qu'un peu plus tard je respirais par tous mes pores au bord de la plage. Dans le second cas qui nous occupe maintenant, mon état, s'il avait beaucoup augmenté en intensité, conservait pourtant ses caractéristiques propres : même optimisme, même jouissance brûlante et passive, même détachement qui n'excluait pas un fort sentiment de sympathie à l'égard de ce qui m'entourait : seules, les causes avaient changé ; je ne veux pas négliger le facteur d'importance que constitue peut-être l'absorption d'une quantité appréciable d'alcools, il se peut que certains lui attribuent, non sans ironie, un rôle prédominant, mais on ne m'empêchera pas d'estimer que la vision d'une femme aussi merveilleusement belle motivait seule le plaisir fulgurant que j'éprouvais, de même qu'à son tour celui-ci était seul capable de préparer l'excellent terrain où devait éclater la plus forte crise que j'aie jamais subie. Comment me faire comprendre ? On ne pouvait rester plus longtemps muet devant un tel regard ; convaincu que ce qu'on avait d'essentiel à dire, on ne le confierait jamais à qui que ce soit d'autre et que si on persistait à demeurer silencieux, ce serait sans appel, il était logique qu'on fût désireux de sauter sur une occasion qui ne vous serait offerte qu'une fois. De même il est logique qu'à présent je sois tenté non seulement d'attribuer à l'attraction magique qu'exerçait sur moi cette femme un rôle de premier plan, mais aussi d'exprimer quelque doute sur l'importance de celui, à mon avis peu déterminant et assez aléatoire, de mon ivrognerie ou de l'atmosphère très bruyante et excitée de l'endroit ou encore de tout autre facteur de l'ordre de ceux que j'ai décrits.

Comme à l'origine des crises précédentes, mon exaltation fit place à une envie brûlante de parler, mais, chose surprenante, la substitution s'opéra si naturellement, si insidieusement que cette fois il ne me vint pas à l'esprit que je me trouvais en présence d'une nouvelle manifestation de mon mal ; et cela provenait du fait que mon désir trouvait pour la première fois, et sans délai, à se satisfaire : je parlais déjà quand je m'avisais d'en prendre conscience. La mutation se produisit en quelque sorte sans l'accord préalable de ma volonté, ce qui équivaut à dire que je n'eus même pas à passer par les tentatives angoissantes et toujours infructueuses que je faisais en vue d'aider à la libération de ce qui m'oppressait confusément et qui avaient marqué jusqu'à présent d'un sceau redoutable la seule évocation de mes dernières crises. On verra pourtant que je devais retrouver plus loin un autre enfer.

Par une singulière inconséquence qui ne fait d'ailleurs que souligner l'aspect nettement ostentatoire de ma crise, je commençai à parler au moment précis où l'orchestre cessa de jouer, où les conversations jusque-là très animées se relâchèrent tout à coup. Je parlais et c'était une sensation magnifique. Il me semblait qu'en faisant ainsi étalage de ce que j'osais tout juste m'avouer à moi-même, je me déchargeais d'un fardeau très lourd, que j'avais découvert enfin une méthode pour m'affranchir de certaines contraintes généralement reconnues nécessaires au bien public, propre à me redonner une légèreté que j'avais recherchée, mais jusqu'ici sans succès ; je me sentais délivré des tumultes malsains qu'on entretient soigneusement à l'abri des regards dans un monde clos et défendu ; les luttes, les fièvres, le désordre avaient cessé ; j'obtenais enfin un jour de sabbat ; il régnait en moi une sérénité toujours croissante qui n'était plus le fruit de l'inertie, mais celui de je ne sais combien d'efforts antérieurs dont je n'obtenais qu'aujourd'hui la récompense ; j'avais déposé mon joug d'homme condamné à la réclusion perpétuelle, je me vidais lentement, c'était un plaisir aussi bouleversant que la plus réussie des voluptés érotiques. Qu'on ne m'accuse pas de rester sciemment dans le vague quand il s'agit d'exposer la nature de mes aveux, et d'abord il n'est justement pas question de passer ceux-ci en revue ; si vous brûlez d'en prendre connaissance, je vous préviens que vous vous préparez une fameuse déception, car n'en déplaise aux gens irréfléchis, prompts à croire qu'un autobiographe est doué d'une mémoire sans défaillance et qu'il est légitime qu'on attende de lui un compte exact de ses faits et gestes, si j'ai bien promis d'étudier consciencieusement et sans détours tout le mécanisme complexe de mes crises, je n'ai pas l'ambition de tout rapporter, y compris ce que je n'ai jamais su. Il ne dépend pas de moi que le plus important m'échappe, que dis-je, m'ait échappé quand il semblerait que j'aurais pu si facilement le saisir. J'ai déjà dit que je ne dénaturerais les faits à aucun prix ; quand certains d'entre eux me feront défaut pour la compréhension de l'ensemble, je saurai renoncer au bénéfice que me vaudrait une impression plus forte produite par quelques faits inventés de toutes pièces sur l'esprit du lecteur, je ne substituerai pas aux vides de l'oubli des mensonges plus vraisemblables. Tant pis si cela doit désobliger les curieux et les méticuleux. Je préfère m'exposer à l'accusation injustifiée de passer sous silence des confidences qui me compromettraient — et j'ajoute que je veux bien être pendu s'il existe quelqu'un qui ait la naïveté de croire que j'en suis encore à éviter de me compromettre. Peu m'importe qu'une omission ou un véritable oubli jettent une ombre sur ce qui dans son ensemble ne saurait être sujet à caution. Mais j'entends qu'on me demande comment j'ai pu oublier ce qui précisément est le plus significatif ou en tout cas le plus piquant ? Je n'ai rien à répondre à cela. Et pourtant il me serait peut-être possible d'en donner une explication propre à satisfaire les personnes de bonne foi. Si fâcheuse et si invraisemblable que puisse être à certains égards cette constatation, j'ai complètement oublié quels furent mes aveux pour la bonne raison que pendant que je les prononçais, *je n'y prêtais aucune attention.* Je m'explique. L'essentiel pour moi, c'était de bavarder, peu m'importait de quelle nature était mon bavardage. Tout à l'allégresse de la délivrance, je ne me souciais pas des propos effarants que je tenais et dont je ne connaissais guère que les reflets sur les visages de mes auditeurs tour à tour illuminés d'une curiosité ardente, grimaçants de dégoût, puis blancs d'indignation, comme ceux de jurés qui doivent entendre un accusé, un peu trop communicatif pour un homme que le remords devrait accabler mais parfaitement maître de lui, leur exposer froidement les crimes immondes qui l'on conduit à se commettre devant eux. En d'autres termes, même si je devais penser que ce n'est pas ici le lieu de livrer à des inconnus certains détails intimes qui n'ont été révélés en public qu'à la faveur d'un accès maladif, même si une honte légitime m'empêchait de renouveler ici des confidences auxquelles je me suis toujours repenti après coup de m'être laissé entraîner, je serais tout à fait incapable de satisfaire la curiosité de mes lecteurs et, je l'ai dit, je suis fermement décidé à ne pas fléchir et à tenir bon devant l'incrédulité de ces mêmes lecteurs soupçonneux et déçus : ils ne me feront rien, absolument rien ajouter de mon cru.

La femme restait assise silencieusement à me regarder pérorer, les sourcils froncés, les coudes sur la table, les tempes serrées entre ses deux poings enfantins. Elle ne me quittait pas des yeux, même lorsqu'elle saisissait d'un geste vif son verre qu'elle portait gloutonnement à ses lèvres, comme si, scandalisée en même temps que fascinée par mes propos que par défi je noircissais à plaisir, elle avait cherché dans l'alcool la force d'en supporter le ton. Pas une fois je ne la vis détourner son regard ; elle observait mes lèvres, la tête penchée en avant et appuyée sur son poing droit d'où s'échappait la fumée bleue de sa cigarette qu'elle tenait précautionneusement serrée entre le pouce et l'index ; elle était immobile, raidie dans une inaction étrange, dans un repos qui ressemblait plutôt à une tension épuisante. Je crois que je ne parlai pas aussi longtemps qu'il me parut : le temps n'existait plus, ou plutôt j'étais hors du temps, car, pressé de me soulager entièrement avant qu'on me fît taire, j'accélérais mon débit tout en redoublant de cynisme avec une précipitation étourdie qui me soustrayait au temps, affrontant sans crainte et sans honte le vent de colère que je sentais se lever du sein de l'assemblée des clients qui, pour la plupart, avaient afflué en rang serré vers nous. Je veux dire que le monde des préoccupations humaines était soudain suspendu, en quelque sorte endormi et contraint à un merveilleux armistice ; le temps était annihilé, les liens avec les choses extérieures abolis.

Et cependant, à la jouissance que j'éprouvais à m'exhiber publiquement se substitua peu à peu l'effroi que me causaient l'expression devenue soudain très pathétique de cette femme et les grondements sourds accompagnés de petits sifflements de plus en plus désapprobateurs des clients qui s'agitaient derrière elle en discutant entre eux à voix basse et en tendant parfois vers moi un doigt accusateur. Je sentais qu'il y avait un parfum de désastre dans l'air ; les choses n'allaient pas aussi bien qu'il me semblait quelques instants auparavant, mais, comme je l'ai dit, ce climat lourd de drame où baignait maintenant toute la salle, au lieu de me paralyser, me poussait au contraire à défier mon auditoire en soulignant d'un trait encore plus noir des aveux déjà passablement scandaleux. J'ai déjà dit aussi que je n'échappais pas au plaisir extravagant, mais si recherché par certains hommes soucieux de l'effet qu'ils produisent, d'intriguer par tous les moyens et souvent les moins honorables, et la curiosité se lassant, de l'exciter de nouveau en allant un peu plus loin, puis beaucoup plus loin que la pudeur la plus élémentaire, d'ailleurs purement de principe, ne l'admet. Je crois pouvoir affirmer, sans qu'on puisse imputer ce jugement à un excès d'analyse, que les sentiments de curiosité, de répugnance et finalement d'hostilité qu'inspirait visiblement mon attitude, satisfaisaient d'autant plus mon désir de parade qu'ils étaient plus violents ; je pouvais en toute lucidité m'abandonner à l'idée séduisante que j'étais le personnage de la soirée (héros, tête de turc ou ennemi commun) sur lequel convergeaient tous les regards, depuis celui d'une jolie fille qui m'écoutait avec une application que j'imaginais d'autant plus soutenue et scrupuleuse que mon débit était trop rapide pour elle qui n'avait sans doute qu'une connaissance imparfaite de la langue française, jusqu'à ceux brillants de colère d'individus et de créatures qui appartenaient pourtant à un milieu où l'on est assez peu porté à s'ébahir mutuellement. Et cependant, sans oublier ce qu'une telle érection verbale pouvait avoir d'enivrant — mon corps était littéralement en transe, j'avais la foudre dans la gorge — ni la volupté positive, mais plus vulgaire, que je trouvais à détenir le privilège d'être le foyer de l'attention générale, à quoi servirait de nier que j'avais peur ? Peut-être n'est-ce pas exact. Peut-être que je n'avais pas peur. Quand je dis que j'avais peur, je veux dire que je me rendais parfaitement compte que je dévalais le long d'une pente dangereuse et, sans donner à cette image plus qu'une valeur d'évocation, que je toucherais le fond de l'abîme, quels que fussent mes efforts pour freiner et remonter. Une peur assez analogue à celles que je m'offrais quand, déjà plus tout à fait un enfant et traversant un bois la nuit, je m'appliquais à imaginer des loups, des assassins, des fantômes me guettant dans l'ombre, et que, mon cœur s'étant suffisamment contracté d'effroi, j'éprouvais une sorte de satisfaction grisante à penser que j'étais aussi maître de faire battre mon cœur et frissonner mes nerfs que de lever le petit doigt ou de disposer de mon âme. Vous auriez vu les coups d'œil provocants lancés par certains jeunes maquereaux que déconcertaient mes paroles à la fois raffinées et intolérablement indécentes par lesquelles ils se jugeaient aussi offensés que si je leur avais craché au visage (il était manifeste qu'ils n'attendaient que l'occasion de m'éconduire brutalement), vous auriez vu les ricanements de leurs amies qui, affamées de scandale et le reniflant à pleines narines, mais cette fois n'en démêlant pas clairement la nature, se retranchaient dans une attitude mi-ironique, mi-méprisante, sans éprouver le besoin naturel ni de me persifler, ni de me mépriser, vous auriez vu surtout ces yeux d'un éclat incroyable, glacés de paillettes d'argent, dans un visage sérieux et attentif et ces lèvres très rouges qu'un soupçon de sang noir épaississait, donnant à la peau très blanche une teinte livide, je crois alors, j'en demande pardon à ceux qui prétendent ne jamais se laisser égarer par des émotions incontrôlables, je crois que, placés dans une situation à peu près identique, c'est-à-dire animés par le même étrange besoin de bavarder, blessés et excités par l'animosité générale, mais passionnément désireux de conquérir une femme, fût-ce au prix de votre réputation, vous auriez éprouvé un trouble analogue à celui auquel j'étais en proie, trouble dont les éléments constitutifs que je ne parviendrai jamais à épuiser par l'analyse se trouvaient être paradoxalement l'angoisse, la fièvre, le ravissement, l'orgueil naïf, la satisfaction vaniteuse, le désir, et, y eussiez-vous seulement songé, vous n'auriez pas mieux su le dominer.

Eh bien, c'est au moment où je me représentais sans la moindre arrière-pensée tout ce qui existait, par-dessus la cécité stupide des autres, d'affinités secrètes entre cette femme et moi, où je m'enchantais de la trouver silencieuse, grave, attentive, quoique apparemment peu apte à pénétrer le sens lointain de certains de mes aveux en raison de son incapacité évidente à comprendre tous les termes d'une langue qu'elle connaissait mal, ce qui d'ailleurs m'épargnait de surveiller mes expressions et de passer sous silence certains détails un peu trop tristement révélateurs et préjudiciables à l'idée avantageuse que j'espérais bien qu'elle se ferait de moi, mais qu'en dépit de leur caractère scandaleusement intime la peur de rompre le fil de mon discours me poussait à exposer, c'est au moment où, persuadé de bonne foi qu'il venait de survenir dans mon existence, sous la forme d'une belle étrangère, un élément réel d'émotion et que notre complicité allait prendre — elle le prenait déjà avec une extraordinaire intensité — l'allure d'une expérience cruciale, tout m'invitait à croire que j'avais enfin réussi à passer d'une solitude froide et triste (le plus souvent elle n'était en réalité ni froide ni triste, elle ne me paraissait telle à cet instant que par contraste avec mon désir) à la bienfaisante chaleur d'une entente réciproque, c'est à ce moment-là, il m'en coûte de le dire, c'est exactement à ce moment-là que cette femme qui n'était somme toute qu'une putain comme les autres partit sous mon nez d'un brusque éclat de rire.

CHAPITRE II

Je courus en titubant vers la porte mais, avant de l'ouvrir, je me retournai. Elle était toujours assise, secouée par le fou rire, le visage inondé de larmes. Autour d'elle se pressaient en cercle les clients qui riaient aussi aux éclats, une main sur la hanche, leur ventre chassé en avant et de côté, ravis sans doute de sortir enfin du silence où mon long discours les avait relégués et de donner libre cours à leur exaspération qui d'ailleurs ne s'exprimait en fin de compte que par une hilarité frénétique entrecoupée de glapissements aigus et de tapes sur les cuisses. C'était un spectacle trop écœurant ! Dès que j'eus fermé la porte derrière moi, toute la salle s'emplit d'un staccato de voix semblable au tic-tac d'une mitrailleuse. Dans la rue, je me sentis d'abord heureux d'être sorti de cette salle surchauffée et bruyante. La neige avait durci et il faisait plus froid. Un froid qui pénétrait à travers les vêtements, à travers les pores dilatés par l'alcool et se glissait sournoisement jusqu'aux os. Les rues étaient désertes, les réverbères clairsemés et lointains. Les mains douillettement enfouies dans mes poches, le col de mon manteau relevé et boutonné sous le menton, je me glissai le long des murs en regardant avec prudence autour de moi et en prenant soin de me retourner de temps à autre pour m'assurer que je n'étais pas suivi. Au milieu de la chaussée vide, une ligne blanche allait s'amenuisant là-bas, en avant sur la surface blafarde et glacée de l'asphalte tigré de plaques neigeuses. Les rires et les éclats de voix parvenaient encore jusqu'à moi, lointains, assourdis par l'air ouaté, tissant une rumeur touffue que prolongeaient en sourdine les sons cuivrés de l'orchestre qui s'était remis à jouer. L'air froid me coupait le souffle, je fis halte un instant pour respirer, embrassant d'un coup d'œil satisfait la rue dans toute sa longueur bordée, à l'endroit où je m'étais arrêté, d'un côté par un long bâtiment bas dont la façade était constituée seulement par un mur blanc percé d'une immense porte aux lourds battants ouverts, tapi au fond d'un jardin grillé transformé en steppe neigeuse par la saison, de l'autre par une succession de petites maisons que rien ne distinguait sinon, si l'on veut, qu'elles étaient toutes de pierre et que leurs fenêtres étaient pourvues chacune d'un balcon de fer dont la neige qui s'étalait partout en couches minces faisait ressortir le dessin aux arabesques toutes rigoureusement identiques. Beaucoup plus loin, en face de moi, étincelait la masse volumineuse et très blanche des premiers arbres du jardin public d'où montait tout droit, pareil à un pic montagneux, le grand sapin qui en faisait depuis trente ans le principal ornement. Tout ce décor figé et abstrait, ces édifices rendus austères par la neige qui en accusait les contours et en glaçait les surfaces, l'atmosphère feutrée et comme stérilisée, le vide de ces rues propres et rectilignes qui semblaient être celles de quelque ville abandonnée, et jusqu'à ce grand portail béant sur une cour également déserte présentaient ce caractère inhumain qui m'a toujours fait battre le cœur sous quelque aspect que je l'aie rencontré, et peut-être que j'en appréciais d'autant mieux le côté à la fois velouté et sévère, géométrique et miraculeux qu'il s'opposait d'une manière très frappante à l'ambiance désordonnée du mauvais lieu dont je venais de fermer la porte derrière moi ; sans chercher à y voir autre chose qu'une coïncidence, je ne puis m'empêcher de noter avec quelle exactitude ce contraste correspondait à deux tendances de ma nature entre lesquelles j'oscillais sans cesse et qui me paraissaient parfois régir à elles seules toutes les formes de ma sensibilité : éprouvant subitement une répugnance insurmontable pour la vie en société avec son cortège d'intrigues, de méprisables agitations et de paroles creuses, toute cette chaleur d'étuve qui émanait d'une promiscuité que les sinistres obligations de la vie m'imposaient, je n'aspirais qu'à m'en dégager pour goûter aux bienfaits de l'air pur et du silence, mais je n'avais pas plutôt obéi à ce désir qu'effrayé à la perspective de me trouver désormais privé de tout contact humain et cette peur suffisant à justifier à mes yeux l'abandon d'une position que je persiste pourtant à tenir pour la meilleure, je courais me souiller avec délice au contact du monde, véritable cloaque d'où bientôt, faute de ne pouvoir raisonnablement me fixer et sûr une fois de plus que ma vie était inassociable à celle des autres, je sortais précipitamment en m'ébrouant pour me réfugier de nouveau dans le lieu inviolable auquel j'avais rêvé, et ainsi de suite. Cet état de perpétuelle alternative était des plus pénibles, mais dans le cas présent, je n'en étais pas encore au stade de l'insatisfaction : le souvenir de la salle enfumée et étouffante, l'éclairage brutal sous lequel se pressaient étroitement les danseurs, le rire vulgaire de cette femme qui prenait figure de trahison à notre pacte tacite, enfin tout cet aspect de fête populaire dont je me délectais quelques instants auparavant ne rendaient que plus vif le plaisir que j'éprouvais maintenant à contempler ce paysage immobile, glacial et silencieux où j'étais seul.

Et pourtant, tandis que je m'engageais dans une ruelle étroite où la bise venait bourdonner autour de mes oreilles, j'essayais désespérément de me rappeler comment cette femme avait souri pendant que nous dansions ensemble ; en général, je n'ai aucune peine à retenir à peu près ce que je désire d'un spectacle plaisant ou par exemple d'un visage qui m'a frappé au passage dans la rue et très souvent au cours de mes insomnies nocturnes il m'arrive d'en évoquer les traits avec une précision remarquable jusqu'à ce que las d'en épuiser les détails je passe à autre chose, mais cette fois, même en faisant de très grands efforts, je ne trouvais plus la moindre trace de ce sourire dont j'ai dit pourtant quelle attraction il avait exercée sur moi. C'était très irritant : je voulais m'en souvenir, je voulais absolument m'en souvenir, je le voulais plus encore que je n'étais disposé à me l'avouer et j'essayais d'abord de me rappeler sa chevelure, quelle sorte de pierres pendaient à ses oreilles et la façon curieuse qu'elle avait de plisser les yeux en me regardant, et son nez, comment était-il déjà ? et ainsi peu à peu et comme négligemment je m'approchais de la région brûlante, mais au moment où je croyais déjà tenir ce sourire, c'était un atroce éclat de rire qui envahissait tout le champ de ma mémoire. J'en étais quitte pour recommencer mes travaux d'approche en redoublant de prudence et de ruse, jusqu'à ce que des échecs répétés m'y fassent définitivement renoncer. En revanche, ce rire, je le voyais parfaitement, je ne le voyais que trop, et je craignais même que le souvenir pût m'en rester par-delà la mort.

En voilà assez ! Je mens ! Je viens de mentir en épiloguant gravement sur le sentiment de détente que j'aurais éprouvé à contempler ce paysage froid et silencieux ; pour dire enfin la vérité, je ne m'en souciais pas plus que d'évoquer cette femme qui avait irrémédiablement perdu à mes yeux tout le charme et le prestige qu'elle tenait pour une grande part de son sourire énigmatique. J'ai menti, je regrette de dire que mes dispositions n'étaient guère à la sérénité et quand on venait de me faire subir dans les conditions que je viens de décrire une offense qui m'avait blessé plus que ne l'eût fait un crachat reçu en pleine face, comment aurais-je pu attacher la moindre importance à la pureté glaciale de cette rue où je pressais le pas en rasant les murs comme un être honteux ? Je ne cherchais même pas à me délivrer du désespoir joint au dégoût de moi-même où m'avait jeté cet éclat de rire que je me plaisais contradictoirement à évoquer avec une bizarre insistance due sans doute à l'attrait impérieux que son souvenir exerçait sur mon esprit rongé par un double sentiment de culpabilité et de déchéance plus ou moins avoué, et je ne souhaitais rien tant que pousser à son comble une malédiction dont je tirais une sorte de jouissance analogue à celle du pénitent qui ne trouve pas seulement naturel d'encourir un juste châtiment mais encore le réclame avec une ferveur proportionnée à son désir d'expiation. C'est qu'en effet j'étais tenté de voir dans ce rire un châtiment pour m'être trop complaisamment abandonné à des confidences que, si agréable qu'eût été l'allégement éprouvé sur le moment, j'allais avoir à payer d'un rude prix. Maintenant on espère sans doute que je vais donner une explication plausible de ce mensonge, c'est là du moins où m'attendent ceux qui, désireux de me voir tomber dans le panneau d'un second mensonge, m'invitent ironiquement à me disculper. Ils seront bien surpris et qui sait ? peut-être flattés si je leur révèle que j'ai cherché à les égarer en m'attribuant des pensées de tout repos moins par crainte de la honte que j'aurais pu éprouver à me remémorer ce rire déchirant comme un coup de couteau que parce que j'avais des raisons de redouter un autre rire, je veux dire leur rire précisément, oui, votre rire, messieurs ! J'ai à faire une déclaration éminemment comique, je veux dire que je peux prévoir avec certitude qu'il ne manquera pas de gens mal intentionnés pour la juger telle. Il me paraît donc indispensable auparavant de faire remarquer que je ne m'y entends guère en matière de plaisanterie, je n'ai vraiment aucune facilité à bouffonner ; ne sauraient s'y tromper que ceux qui ont une certaine disposition à rire de ce qu'ils ne comprennent pas très bien, autrement dit qui trouvent très drôle ce qui est plutôt attristant, ce qui n'empêche nullement une autre sorte de gens de pleurer précisément quand il y aurait motif à rire. Sans bien savoir à laquelle des deux catégories je m'adresse, j'estime en tout cas que ce n'est pas trop demander aux uns et aux autres que d'afficher le plus grand sérieux une parfaite impassibilité, je n'ai pas dit une entière compréhension, ou à défaut un silence dédaigneux accompagné, je n'y vois aucun inconvénient, d'un majestueux haussement d'épaules, enfin me comprendra-t-on si je dis que j'ai moins besoin de complicité, d'approbation, de respect, d'intérêt que de silence ? Ah le silence ! Alors, voudra-t-on me croire si j'ai le front de proclamer ici même mon aversion insurmontable pour les maniaques de la confession ? Ceci va combler d'aise un certain nombre de pauvres gens qui tentent dans l'ombre de m'opposer à moi-même et confondre quelques innocents qu'une lecture consciencieuse, sinon très attentive, des pages précédentes avait inclinés à penser le contraire et je les entends déjà qui en profitent pour me demander, les premiers avec un sourire ironique, les seconds en levant les bras au ciel, à quel genre d'activité je prétends me livrer depuis un certain temps. Loin de me laisser impressionner par le caractère insolent d'une telle question, je me propose d'y répondre un peu plus tard, si j'en ai le loisir, mais, à supposer qu'on me presse d'y répondre sur-le-champ, je ferais d'abord observer à ceux qui se vantent de m'avoir pris en flagrant délit d'inconséquence qu'ils commettraient une grande erreur, pour ne pas dire une grande malhonnêteté, s'ils se refusaient à tenir compte d'une maladie qui m'est propre et dont je me propose précisément de leur soumettre ici les diverses manifestations. Pour le reste, j'y reviendrai en temps utile.

Une des raisons de ma honte résidait justement dans la répugnance que m'avaient inspirée de tout temps ceux qui succombent à la tentation de livrer leurs pensées les plus secrètes soit pour le plaisir malsain de s'affranchir d'une discipline intérieure qui est, à mon sens, l'honneur des hommes et en tout cas le fondement d'une hygiène mentale dont la nécessité n'est pas douteuse, soit pour se délivrer quelques instants d'une hantise ou encore pour l'ignoble volupté qu'ils éprouvent à s'humilier devant un de leurs pairs. Peut-être même faut-il y voir la véritable cause de cette impossibilité à me confier dont j'ai dit en commençant combien elle avait nui aux rapports intimes que j'aurais voulu entretenir avec mes amis. Pour moi, se confier si peu que ce soit ou se prêter aux confidences par pure concession à quelques êtres équivaut à vendre son âme au diable pour obtenir en échange de maigres années de faveur : dérisoire jouissance que celle qui se paie par une brûlure éternelle ! Je n'aperçois dans ce qu'on nomme noblement confession que le très coupable et très coûteux exercice d'une faiblesse et personne ne m'empêchera de tenir pour particulièrement suspecte une amitié où chacun s'applique sans cesse à provoquer chez l'autre de précieuses confidences. Je ne me souviens pas d'avoir assisté au spectacle trop fréquent de deux hommes au teint congestionné qui se penchent l'un vers l'autre avec des airs attentifs, émus et souriants par-dessus une table où refroidissent, parmi un lot de bouteilles vides, les reliefs d'un repas substantiel, voyez vous-mêmes comme ils jouent à se sentir compris et, la tête échauffée par la nourriture et le bon vin, avec quelle impudeur pleine d'ingénuité ils se livrent l'un à l'autre et ils s'en donnent à cœur joie et ils ont le cœur illuminé ainsi qu'en témoignent leurs visages radieux comme une aurore ; je ne me souviens pas non plus d'être passé par hasard auprès d'un confessionnal où, dans une obscurité propice, bourdonnaient tour à tour confesseur et pénitent, interminable chuchotement, questions et réponses, sans avoir ressenti comme une sorte de malaise quand ce n'était pas une formidable colère qui, aussi rapide qu'un tourbillon, me montait inexplicablement au cerveau ; j'ai observé qu'en moi la vue d'exercices aussi bas, légitimés pourtant par l'approbation des uns et l'indifférence des autres, ne manquait jamais de susciter un violent dégoût auquel se substituait, si par malheur j'avais été moi-même en cause, le sentiment intolérable de ma propre déchéance. À en juger par l'explosion de rire dont cette femme salua mes aveux, il faut croire que le spectacle de l'impudeur est parfois capable d'inspirer chez d'autres des sentiments moins vifs et moins hostiles mais tout aussi cruellement injurieux pour celui qui en est l'objet. Après tout, voir un homme se livrer en public à ce genre d'exercice, peut-être n'est-ce pas seulement navrant mais aussi bouffon ? Elle ne s'était pas détournée de moi avec dégoût comme il m'est permis d'affirmer que j'aurais fait à sa place : elle avait éclaté de rire. Un rire vulgaire par lequel elle proclamait ouvertement sa trahison, à supposer qu'elle ne se fût pas toujours tenue dans le camp de mes ennemis tout en s'adonnant à des manèges propres à me renforcer dans l'idée que nos deux destins s'étaient miraculeusement rejoints et que je trouverais toujours en elle une alliée sûre et loyale, mimant tous les signes de la complicité et me trompant ainsi sur ses véritables intentions avec une facilité d'autant plus grande qu'elle avait pour elle sa séduction naturelle, tout cela pour m'inspirer confiance et m'exciter à persévérer dans mon rôle comique, à moins qu'elle ait cherché simplement à obtenir de moi ce qu'en pouvait désirer une fille de son espèce. Ce qui me paraît en tout cas hors de doute, c'est que seul le souvenir de ce rire, et non pas celui des manifestations séditieuses auxquelles s'étaient livrés plus ou moins ouvertement mes autres auditeurs, avait pu en un éclair décisif me faire découvrir ce que mon attitude avait eu de dégradant et de ridicule ; seul il avait pu déclencher en moi un sentiment d'humiliation presque physique et me rendre enfin pleinement conscient de ce que je ne pouvais envisager autrement que comme une sorte de déchéance dont je ne parviendrais jamais à effacer le souvenir et par suite à me relever, quels que fussent mes efforts d'imagination pour me réhabiliter à mes propres yeux. Aussi étais-je fondé à considérer ce rire comme une juste sanction pour m'être dévoilé impudiquement par des propos qu'avec une sourde véhémence je me reprochais maintenant d'avoir tenus devant une audience si vaste et de qualité si médiocre. Viendra-t-on me dire que tout ceci frise le délire d'interprétation ? N'ai-je pas reconnu moi-même que j'avais perdu toute ma lucidité ? À quoi bon m'obstiner à décrire et à commenter des événements très communs auxquels un esprit non prévenu se refuserait à accorder toute signification ? Enfin, ce sentiment d'abjection, n'est-ce pas celui-là même qu'éprouvent maints ivrognes et en quoi se rattache-t-il à ma crise de bavardage ? Il est clair que je cherche à me distinguer et qu'au prix des plus grands efforts je m'évertue à faire remonter à des causes trop extraordinaires pour être négligeables des effets parfaitement négligeables. Ou je me refuse par orgueil à reconnaître que j'étais ivre, que cet état d'ivresse me poussait aux confidences et qu'il en résultait dans mon attitude quelque chose de grotesque dont on ne pouvait vraiment que rire, ou bien je suis une fois de plus la victime d'une simple illusion des sens. En somme on aimerait me faire admettre que mon extase, mon besoin de bavarder et la honte qui l'avait suivi sont à mettre en vrac sur le compte de ma seule ébriété, qu'ils n'en constituent en dernière analyse que les aspects variés. Jamais, sous aucun prétexte, je n'en passerai par cette manière de voir. Si j'ai été le premier à souligner le rôle joué par l'excitation où m'avait mis l'absorption d'un assez grand nombre de verres d'alcool, je prétends et je maintiendrai coûte que coûte qu'il serait absurde d'en surfaire l'importance, que mes propos n'étaient aucunement ceux d'un ivrogne et qu'ils ne comportaient rien d'incohérent qui pût prêter à rire ni même à sourire. Mon opinion inébranlable est que, si tenté que soit un homme de vider son cœur, il ne doit jamais oublier que dans la mesure où il enfreint les lois de la pudeur, il s'expose à l'ironie des uns et à la colère des autres. Pour moi, je m'étais brisé cruellement sur l'ironie.

Cependant, après avoir remonté entièrement l'étroite ruelle qui débouche sur le canal, je bifurquai et m'engageai dans une rue voisine en regardant à chaque instant derrière moi, bien qu'il me parût peu vraisemblable qu'on songeât à me filer. Aussi était-ce sans conviction aucune que je faisais mine de m'intéresser aux devantures des rares magasins de la ville dont les volets ne fussent pas rabattus, haltes qui me permettaient de surveiller furtivement les angles des rues où je m'attendais vaguement à voir une ombre se profiler sur la chaussée neigeuse ou sur les murs couverts de place en place d'affiches déchirées auxquels les becs de gaz flanquaient une volée de lumière jaune. Puis je me remis en route et je longeai la place du marché transformée par l'hiver en une sorte de terrain vague entièrement livré à l'espace, limité au fond par des bâtisses mortes où la pierre prenait un aspect de bravade à côté des derrières enfumés et ruineux de plusieurs bicoques en planches sans étage dans lesquelles quelques petits négoces avaient leur siège sans faste et souvent anonyme. Autour des fientes fraîches au relent d'ammoniaque qui, entre les traces des sabots de chevaux, s'étalaient sur la neige avec une précision obscène, tourbillonnaient et s'abattaient les volées de corbeaux dans un bruit de persiennes rouillées. Rien dans cet espace dénudé et extraordinairement perdu qui évoquât la confusion des jours de foire où toute la contrée se donne rendez-vous pour y discuter, brailler et gesticuler. Je reniflais avec plaisir l'air calme et glacé qui me piquait les narines et me cautérisait les poumons de ses vivifiantes aiguilles. Ce fut seulement quelques pas plus loin, à peu près au niveau d'une statue majestueuse où aboutit, si je ne me trompe, un grand boulevard planté d'arbres mais lui aussi désert et sans vie qui s'ouvre sur un pacage d'immeubles délabrés, que j'eus cette fois la certitude qu'on me suivait. Je me retournai vivement en scrutant d'un coup d'œil rapide et furtif la rue dans toute sa longueur. Rien d'insolite sinon une plume de neige soulevée par le vent devenu soudain assez vif et quelques vieux papiers qui roulaient en se tordant, de ces fragments de journaux que l'on voit traîner à l'aube sur les pavés des villes. Au-dessus de moi, les fils télégraphiques émettaient un son ininterrompu, aigu, étrange, comme si la froidure de l'air eût trouvé une voix. Je repris mon chemin en accélérant mon allure, mais je n'avais pas fait vingt pas qu'il me sembla de nouveau entendre derrière moi un râle léger et régulier qui scandait ma marche ; au lieu de stopper et de me retourner comme j'avais fait précédemment, je me mis à courir à toutes jambes au milieu de la chaussée du boulevard, poitrine haletante, narines ouvertes, mais bientôt un point de côté et l'essoufflement me contraignirent à ralentir sensiblement, puis je dus m'arrêter tout à fait. Au bout d'un instant, je perçus des pas précipités qui, d'après le son, ne devaient pas être éloignés de plus de cinquante mètres. Je tournai sur moi-même avec une promptitude qu'on aurait pu prendre pour un tic nerveux, mais aucun être humain, aucune ombre suspecte ne frappa mon regard, sinon, juste à la limite de l'obscurité, à une distance d'une trentaine de mètres, une charrette à bras abandonnée le long du trottoir qui dressait ses deux brancards vers le ciel voilé de brume, immobile dans la nuit vibrante de gel comme une lame de verre où les becs de gaz formaient de grandes traînées sulfureuses. Il me serait à peu près impossible d'analyser l'effet lugubre que me produisit cette charrette solitaire dont les brancards tendus vers un ciel invisible en une attitude suppliante évoquaient à mes yeux ma propre détresse, sans que j'eusse pourtant sur le moment conscience d'un tel rapport ; toujours est-il que ce spectacle me frappa de terreur et m'inspira le désir panique de courir devant moi, de me ruer à travers l'obstacle mouvant des ténèbres. Je m'étais rarement conduit d'une manière si absurde. Cependant, je pris sur moi de reprendre ma route à une allure raisonnable, me contentant seulement d'allonger le pas sans détourner la tête. Je suis tout aussi incapable de justifier la non moins mauvaise impression que me causèrent les coups rythmés des cloches qui, dans le noir au-dessus de ma tête, se mirent à sonner, tandis que je contournais l'église qui surplombait les maisons avec toute la majesté conventionnelle et figée des bâtiments publics ; les sons montaient dans l'air glacé et se fondaient en échos qui se les renvoyaient, anonymes et perdus, comme s'ils étaient devenus la voix même de ma détresse, une voix grave et déchirante, farouche et nostalgique. Mais sans doute mon malaise s'augmentait-il du fait qu'il m'était devenu désormais impossible, à cause des vibrations prolongées et soutenues des cloches, de prêter l'oreille au bruit léger des pas et au souffle de mon suiveur invisible. J'avais hâte de m'éloigner au plus vite de cette église dont la masse carrée, ingrate et même hostile ajoutait encore à l'impression franchement déplaisante que j'avais de ce quartier. Je me souviens même de l'irritation singulière que me causa une troupe de corbeaux affairés, jacassant sur un dépôt d'immondices, auxquels j'allais jusqu'à jeter des pierres, mais que mon geste fit s'ébranler d'une seule masse et retomber un peu plus loin devant moi d'un vol lourd. Je me mis à courir grand train, au prix du pire essoufflement, l'alcool ballottant dans mes entrailles comme une pierre brûlante et lourde, et au pied de la butte, au bas du boulevard, je tournai par une rue étroite bordée de maisons à galeries, aux façades mornes, construites un peu en retrait sur des terrains pelés où se dressait çà et là quelque arbre égaré et minable, tout ce décor surgissant au fur et à mesure de la pénombre avec l'apparence d'une mauvaise photo sinistre et absurde. La rue débouchait dans une autre, plus large et bordée d'une double rangée d'arbres, qui se prolongeait à droite jusqu'au jardin public. Quand je pénétrai dans celui-ci, j'eus le sentiment que c'était bien le lieu où devaient inévitablement me conduire mes pas, bien que je n'eusse aucune raison de m'aventurer là plutôt qu'ailleurs ; tout s'était passé comme si j'avais été la victime d'une machination des plus savantes de la part de mon poursuivant anonyme qui, connaissant parfaitement la topographie de la ville, ne m'avait poussé à travers tout un dédale de ruelles et de places que pour m'introduire à mon insu dans cet endroit auquel je ne pensais nullement devoir aboutir. Presqu'île triangulaire entourée d'eau et unie à la terre par un seul pont qui en permettait l'accès et qu'il fallait emprunter à nouveau pour en sortir, ce jardin constituait sans aucun doute le meilleur piège où mon ennemi pût espérer m'acculer. Je n'en continuai pas moins à m'engager dans le sentier en dos d'âne qui débouchait sur un rond-point en entonnoir à balustrade pseudo-grecque dominé par un sapin géant visible de tous les points de la ville et où tous les bancs de pierre vides étaient réunis en demi-cercle autour d'un épais tapis de neige qui à la belle saison fondait pour faire place à un gravier rouge et brillant. Je m'assis sur un banc placé au pied du sapin, non sans avoir préalablement pris soin d'en chasser la neige avec une branche morte. Il est étrange que ce fût alors seulement que j'éprouvai un véritable sentiment de détente et de sécurité. Plus question de jeter des regards inquiets autour de moi, je cessais soudain d'avoir peur ; peur de quoi ? est-ce que même je ne doutais pas de l'existence de mon ennemi ? Il se pouvait très bien qu'il eût été inventé de toutes pièces par mon imagination que l'excès de boisson avait rendue exceptionnellement inventive et qu'en proie à une panique irraisonnée, en même temps que suggestionné par l'idée d'un châtiment sans rémission auquel dans mon affolement je donnais une forme humaine, je ne m'étais sauvé à toutes jambes que pour tenter désespérément d'y échapper. Or à présent, inexplicablement délivré d'une telle hantise et toutes choses cessant de m'apparaître sous un angle tragique, rien ne m'empêchait de jouir en toute tranquillité de la beauté d'un lieu où je ne me sentais plus traqué ni menacé et que l'évocation de tout un passé dont il était le cadre douait d'un bouleversant prestige en raison de ce qu'il lui conférait de lointain et de printanier. Car ce banc, c'était celui-là même où j'aimais m'asseoir au printemps quand le jardin était aussi grouillant d'enfants turbulents et de couples enlacés, aussi criblé de pépiements d'oiseaux et de clameurs dont l'eau toute proche amplifiait étrangement la sonorité, aussi miroitant de soleil et d'ombres vertes qu'il était aujourd'hui désert, silencieux et noir. Ce jardin bâti sur pilotis m'attirait à cause du spectacle pourtant assez étourdissant des jeux enfantins, à cause aussi, j'ai honte de le dire, du sombre plaisir que je prenais à faire enrager les quelques filles assises là, solitaires, et qui d'abord ne se laissaient très complaisamment détailler par moi que parce qu'elles ne voyaient dans mon insistance qu'une indispensable entrée en matière, mais, à la longue, irritées par ce qu'elles prenaient peut-être pour de la timidité, cessaient alors toute œillade et toute exhibition de jambes quand elles ne quittaient pas subitement leur banc, les joues échauffées par la colère, pour regagner la rue, soit qu'elles eussent deviné mon manège, soit que ma passivité les eût découragées pour tout de bon. Mais ce jardin, peuplé ou non, eût été à lui seul capable de me retenir : triangle de sable et de verdure dont un des angles fendait les eaux en affectant la forme d'une proue, il me donnait l'impression d'être situé aux confins du monde et de ce banc je pouvais contempler non seulement le torrent qui au-dessous de moi se précipitait en rouleaux transparents et lumineux du sommet du barrage jusqu'à un immense bouillonnement blanc tapissé de cailloux, mais aussi toute la longue perspective du fleuve qu'enjambait une série si nombreuse de ponts que, même à la faveur d'une visibilité parfaite, il fallait renoncer à en faire le compte, enfin ce grand mur compact et impénétrable, surmonté de tilleuls, qui, par-delà le torrent, m'intriguait à cause du brouhaha mystérieux qu'on y entendait à certaines heures de la journée, fait de pieds marchant ou courant sur le gravier, de voix s'interpellant dans l'échauffement d'un jeu et auquel le tintement aigrelet d'une clochette mettait brusquement fin. Mais ce que je regrette de ne pas savoir exprimer, c'est le plaisir sensuel, à la fois très paisible et d'une acuité extrême, que j'éprouvais quand, assis sans bouger sur ce banc d'où je pouvais jouir d'un paysage composé d'eau, d'édifices, de verdures à perte de vue et de nuages auquel la lumière printanière donnait un éclat magique, le corps chauffé par un soleil doux et protégé du vent encore assez frais en cette saison par un manteau suffisamment épais, je restais longtemps à regarder tour à tour les passants qui se croisaient devant moi, l'acier étincelant du pont rigide au-dessus du barrage ou encore, renversant la tête, la voûte vert clair du sapin qui me toisait de toute sa hauteur, toutes choses assez peu remarquables en elles-mêmes, et à prêter l'oreille aux propos décousus des gens qui avaient pris place à côté de moi, aux cris joyeux des enfants, au bruissement précipité de l'eau rebondissante au-dessous du pont métallique ; la double action de regarder et d'écouter s'accompagnant depuis longtemps pour moi d'une émotion très spéciale qui pouvait surgir au moment le plus imprévu et m'être causée par quelque chose ou quelqu'un auquel je n'avais aucune raison particulière de m'intéresser. Au milieu du vaste flux des choses, ne rien faire, mais voir et écouter. Aurait-on alors cherché à m'arracher au doux vertige que me procurait une telle contemplation, peut-être aurais-je réagi violemment par instinct de défense et répondu aux questions les plus inoffensives par des paroles ou des gestes blessants, quitte à les regretter par la suite et à m'en excuser. Mais il se trouve que je n'ai jamais été amené à repousser aucune intervention fâcheuse, tant il est vrai que je passe partout inaperçu. (La plaisante contrepartie de mon aspect insignifiant dont je me lamente chaque jour, c'est pourtant une vie libre et distraite.)

On voudra bien croire que ce n'est nullement par complaisance que je m'arrête aussi longuement sur une époque de ma vie à laquelle ce banc se trouve associé dans mon esprit, c'est d'abord pour signifier que, contrairement à ce que voudraient faire croire certaines gens qui cherchent le bonheur sans jamais le trouver, celui-ci éclate sous leurs yeux et retentit dans leurs oreilles à chaque heure du jour, qu'ils le prennent donc où il est, ne fût-ce qu'un instant, et qu'ils cessent de nous fatiguer de leurs inutiles plaintes, c'est ensuite pour montrer l'importance que j'attache au rapport entre la brusque disparition de ma peur et les souvenirs de calme félicité qu'évoquait irrésistiblement pour moi la vue de ce banc sur lequel je venais de m'asseoir. Il est en effet très frappant que j'aie cessé de croire à la réalité du péril à partir du moment où je me suis introduit dans ce jardin. Ce phénomène me paraît intéressant dans la mesure où il est symptomatique de la répercussion que de tels souvenirs, pour peu qu'ils conservent leur violent parfum, peuvent avoir sur le cours d'une pensée même dominée par la peur, comme c'est le cas ici. Mais passons.

Encore une remarque. J'ai oublié de noter en son lieu un fait qui, lui aussi, revêt à mes yeux une certaine signification et je ne puis me résoudre à le passer sous silence, malgré mon souci constant de n'exposer ici que l'essentiel. On a pu observer que, dès l'instant où j'ai pris conscience du danger auquel je cherchais à échapper en courant à travers les rues de la ville, il n'a plus été question de ce douloureux sentiment de culpabilité causé, ainsi que je crois l'avoir suffisamment fait comprendre, par le souvenir de ma pitoyable conduite dans le bar et avivé ensuite par celui du rire de cette femme. C'est qu'en effet, la peur survenant, il s'était dissipé de lui-même et il me paraît non moins remarquable que, la peur me quittant à son tour dès le seuil du jardin public, il n'ait pas aussitôt repris son empire sur moi ; mais, cette fois, j'étais tout entier possédé par la musique fascinante des souvenirs, rien n'aurait pu altérer ma jouissance ; à peine avais-je encore le souci du présent. Et cependant, cette musique elle-même, combien de temps subirais-je son pouvoir ? N'allait-elle pas se dissiper à la longue et alors ne serais-je pas de nouveau exposé à expier par un cruel dégoût de moi-même la honte d'avoir parlé publiquement ? Le fait est que tout se déroula suivant le processus que je viens d'indiquer, mais cette fois, si lourd était le sentiment de ma déchéance que, tenant la peur pour le remède le plus efficace, persuadé qu'elle seule me permettrait d'éprouver un certain allégement, sinon d'échapper complètement à l'emprise du remords, j'en arrivais à la regretter ainsi qu'à souhaiter l'épreuve d'un châtiment dont je ne doutais pas de sortir régénéré.

La lune se leva, je sursautai : la grille se refermait avec un petit grincement aigrelet, quelqu'un venait d'entrer dans le jardin. Je me soulevai un peu sur les mains et je regardai au-delà du massif empâté de neige si rien n'apparaissait au tournant du sentier : le pont était désert, encombré seulement de deux tonneaux de goudron superposés et d'un tas de pavés surmonté d'un drapeau rouge que le vent agitait doucement. Je sentais l'odeur fine et glacée de l'eau, j'entendais le torrent, et le pont apparaissait à présent clairement, avec ses lignes raides et étincelantes, dans la pénombre tachée de lune. Je me secouai, je crois m'être mis à rire ; je sortis mon mouchoir pour essuyer la sueur qui perlait à mon front. Pour l'instant, j'étais encore très maître de moi, pour l'instant je voulais encore me laisser exalter lentement par cette nuit blanche, sentir encore le temps couler entre mes doigts et me refuser à tout ce qui m'engagerait à une dépense de forces excessive, et, pour cela, garder totalement vacante ma faculté d'attention. Et cependant, je ne pouvais m'empêcher de regarder fixement tour à tour le pont et le sentier qui, entre les taches rondes des réverbères, se perdait dans l'obscurité.

Une toux profonde venue de la gorge me fit tressaillir. Mes mains se crispèrent sur le banc et je jetai un regard circulaire avec une sorte d'avidité épuisante. J'allais me lever et fuir quand j'aperçus une ombre qui, près du massif, à quelques pas de moi, me coupait la retraite : de l'autre côté de l'allée, un homme se déplaçait lentement, une main dans la poche de son veston et le chapeau sur le coin de l'œil, mais, au lieu de venir vers moi, il traversa la pelouse et s'enfonça sous les tilleuls jusqu'à ce que, de mon banc, il me devînt impossible de le distinguer.

Mais, tout aussitôt, il fit volte-face, revint sur

ses pas, traversa de nouveau la pelouse à pas de loup et stoppa à la hauteur du massif en se dissimulant derrière un arbre. À ma propre stupéfaction, je m'avançai vers lui, les coudes légèrement écartés, dans la posture agressive d'un lutteur qui se dispose à engager le combat, toute la lumière dégoulinant sur mes épaules comme de l'eau blanche. Alors qu'en général je me montre incapable d'accomplir la plus légère action d'éclat ou même de me comporter avec sang-froid en face d'un ennemi de force supérieure ou seulement égale à la mienne, cette fois je me portais bravement au-devant d'un danger réel, comme si, affranchi de toute crainte ou du moins mettant mon point d'honneur à la surmonter, je m'étais jugé de taille à me mesurer à un adversaire dont j'ignorais jusqu'au nom, quand la prudence m'eût conseillé de me tenir tranquille sur ce banc, où j'étais sûr qu'il ne pouvait me voir. (Ma peur d'être dupe toujours en éveil déjoue en moi ce complot d'hypocrisie et de vanité qui mène à se croire quelqu'un d'aussi invraisemblable qu'un héros. D'ailleurs rechercher le réconfort dans l'approbation de soi-même, méritée ou non, me semble vulgaire, je ne le trouve légitime dans aucun cas. Il est inutile que je me défende d'avoir jamais pensé à mettre un acte aussi audacieux sur le compte d'une bravoure dont j'ai déjà dit que j'étais totalement dépourvu. Qu'on ne s'y trompe donc pas, j'étais mû par le désir d'en finir avec l'obsession du châtiment dont je me sentais menacé ; je rêvais d'expier, par la correction que je me ferais infliger, la honte de ma récente conduite, et ma dette acquittée, de jouir librement d'un présent où aucun remords ne viendrait s'immiscer ; la présence d'un ennemi me semblait une chance tout à fait rare qu'il s'agissait d'exploiter, au mépris de la peur, et en payant d'une souffrance physique le bénéfice de mon rachat. Ce n'était donc pas avec la fierté du combattant, avec un désir de succès, de domination ou de gloire, que j'allais l'affronter, mais avec la passive humilité d'une victime librement consentante, à laquelle il semble normal et pleinement souhaitable d'encourir le châtiment qu'elle sait avoir mérité ; je n'avais pas à vaincre un ennemi, j'avais à me livrer aux coups d'un homme qui m'apparaissait à proprement parler comme le juste exécuteur désigné pour me purifier de ma souillure et envers qui je ne devais nourrir, à ce titre, que des sentiments de gratitude.) Quand je fus à quelques mètres de lui, je ralentis, puis je stoppai devant un arbre récemment abattu qui obstruait le passage, à l'endroit où le sentier venant du pont rejoignait l'allée centrale que je venais de quitter, les yeux fixés sur l'homme qui, immobile et plaqué contre le tronc, serrait autour de ses reins un manteau trop long dont les pans battaient contre ses jambes. Pendant un instant, je pouvais me figurer que nous nous observions mutuellement, mais quand il s'écarta de l'arbre d'un bond rapide et qu'il avança la tête en me scrutant avec une sorte d'ahurissement hébété, je compris qu'il venait seulement de me découvrir. Tandis qu'il m'examinait de ses petits yeux pointus, tout mon corps crispé d'angoisse et d'indécision était animé d'un léger balancement, comme si j'avais oscillé sur place. L'ombre de l'homme qui envahissait tout le champ neigeux derrière lui, de telle sorte que celle de sa tête à présent tournée de profil par-dessus son épaule et cocassement déformée par les accidents du terrain, atteignait le pont, lui donnait un aspect gigantesque et menaçant qu'il était loin d'avoir en réalité, car il était de petite taille et apparemment peu robuste. Je le vis ouvrir son manteau et en extraire une montre ; il regarda l'heure, releva la tête et, la montre toujours en main, fit un pas vers moi en me regardant droit dans les yeux avec une expression courroucée ; un instant après, il abaissa de nouveau son regard sur la montre qu'il replaça précautionneusement dans la poche intérieure de sa veste, puis il s'efforça avec ses doigts raidis par le froid de reboutonner son manteau. Ce fut seulement lorsqu'il rejeta d'un coup sec son chapeau en arrière, découvrant un triangle de cheveux rouges et calamistrés, que je reconnus le petit rouquin du bar. Le pauvre diable, n'avait-il pas compris que j'étais désormais indifférent aux charmes de son amie, ne lui suffisait-il pas de l'avoir vue me tourner en dérision devant toute la clientèle du dancing ? J'éprouvais pour lui une vive compassion et j'étais résolu plus que jamais à le laisser me battre tout son saoul. Dans l'obscurité, je ne pouvais pas très bien voir sa figure, mais j'imaginais qu'elle était pâle et déformée par la haine, elle ne devait pas être agréable à regarder. Pauvre diable ! Il pensait sans doute qu'en me rouant de coups, il ferait triompher son amour et, en attendant, il se baignait avec délice dans sa colère. C'est en cela que consiste la vraie passion : flanquer une pile à son prochain pour l'amour de sa dame. Belle et fière conception ! Cet homme avait toute ma sympathie, j'étais heureux que le destin me l'eût envoyé en un moment tel qu'il pouvait presque sembler que, devinant mon désir d'expiation et non pas guidé par sa haine, il était venu ici pour s'offrir comme bourreau ; j'aimais à penser qu'il y avait eu entre nous, dès notre premier contact, une sorte de complicité née d'une commune insatisfaction. Il éprouvait le même besoin de me battre que j'avais celui d'être battu, ainsi chacun de nous deux mettait en pratique à sa manière un principe commun d'hygiène. Non, sa figure ne devait être ni triste ni laide, elle avait plutôt cet air béat qu'on voit aux gens devant qui brille enfin l'objet tant convoité.

La lune, un instant cachée, apparut entre les nuages qui se déchiraient et nous inonda d'une lumière glacée. Sans paraître mouvoir si peu que ce fût ses yeux injectés de sang, il m'inspectait de haut en bas, le visage figé en une double expression de ressentiment et de crainte, les deux mains enfouies dans les poches de son manteau, dont elles faisaient remuer imperceptiblement l'étoffe. Il en retira la droite avec lenteur, pour l'introduire ensuite entre les deux revers de son manteau, d'où il sortit sa montre qu'il consulta de nouveau d'un air circonspect. Il releva la tête d'un mouvement brusque et me jeta un long regard aigu et méfiant, comme s'il avait eu de bonnes raisons de croire que je profiterais d'un moment d'inattention pour prendre la fuite. Puis, d'un bond, il sauta par-dessus l'arbre abattu et, en deux enjambées, parcourut la distance qui nous séparait ; son avant-bras allait m'attraper par le milieu du corps pour me faire basculer en arrière, quand je plongeai et l'évitai d'un écart. Je ne crois pas que cette première dérobade devant la souffrance ait été causée par une incurable lâcheté, ni qu'on puisse l'interpréter comme une savante mise en garde destinée à me permettre de tirer profit de la stupeur où l'inanité de son geste avait plongé mon adversaire, et la preuve, c'est qu'il n'y eut de mon côté aucune riposte ; vraisemblablement pris de court par la rapidité de l'attaque et n'ayant donc eu ni le temps ni la présence d'esprit de dominer mon réflexe de défense, c'est tout instinctivement que j'avais esquivé le coup, m'infligeant ainsi à moi-même un cinglant démenti.

Mais, quand il sauta sur moi de nouveau je me contentai de lever le coude pour protéger mes yeux et il n'eut aucune difficulté à écraser son poing sur le coin de ma bouche qui se mit à saigner abondamment. Résolu à ne céder à la peur ou à la révolte de ce qu'il me restait de dignité qu'après avoir subi jusqu'au bout l'épreuve qui consacrerait mon rachat, je m'évertuais avec une fiévreuse application à garder les bras le long de mon corps, dans l'attitude probablement assez comique d'une victime livrée sans défense aux mains d'un cruel bourreau. Mais, irrité par l'inertie dont je faisais preuve, il se dressa de toute sa petite taille et lança un grand coup de poing qui m'atteignit au front ; je tombai assis dans la neige. Comme je tentais de me remettre sur mes pieds, il me frappa encore deux fois ; je roulai sur le dos et me tins immobile.

Bien que lié à un sentiment de chute sans fond, l'état de jubilation que je ressentis par la suite m'apparaît comme la preuve irréfutable que seule une souffrance physique avait le pouvoir d'apaiser le honteux malaise où m'entretenait le souvenir de ma faute ; cet état imprévu qui se manifestait par une sorte de gaieté, d'humeur enfantine, de disponibilité heureuse, d'entier détachement, me faisait à la fois trembler et rire et son intensité était telle qu'il n'y avait pas de torture, me semblait-il, que je n'eusse été capable d'endurer si j'avais eu des raisons de croire qu'elle entraînerait ma réhabilitation en me déchargeant cette fois entièrement du poids de mon remords ; car aucune épreuve n'était au-dessus de mes forces, je les sentais illimitées. Et c'est encore cette sorte d'extase qui vous expliquera que je n'encours en rien le reproche que vous êtes peut-être disposés à me faire de mon inertie, de mon indolence, de ma mollesse, de ma veulerie, que sais-je encore ? De là à m'accuser de lâcheté, il n'y a naturellement qu'un pas. Pourtant, afin d'aider à comprendre certaines de mes attitudes les plus ambiguës, je n'ai pu faire moins que m'étendre avec une insistance souvent lassante sur ce qui m'a toujours paru se prêter mal à l'expression, au risque de voir un grand nombre de mes lecteurs abandonner la partie, quand tout me gardait d'user de persuasion pour leur faire partager une émotion probablement intransmissible, à leurs yeux d'un intérêt douteux, et aussi dépourvue que possible des vertus particulières qui s'attachent aux émotions usuelles, mais que, pour la compréhension de l'ensemble et en dehors de toute autre considération, j'étais bien obligé de mettre en évidence.

Il se pencha sur moi en se dandinant un peu avec un air surpris ; il soufflait très fort, chaque respiration s'étouffant en une chute confuse, comme si elle devait être la dernière. Un moment s'écoula. Moi-même, j'étais essoufflé et je haletais. Mon pouls martelait douloureusement ma lèvre fendue et enflée. Peut-être que la vue de ma figure marbrée de coups lui ôterait le courage de me frapper encore, qu'il jugerait plus prudent d'en rester là et qu'il ferait demi-tour en me laissant râler dans mon sang, à plat ventre sur la neige gelée. Je craignais qu'il ne fût déjà soulagé ; pour ma part, je ne l'étais pas encore, la correction me paraissait insuffisante et c'est pourquoi je tentai de me remettre sur mes pieds espérant l'inciter, par ce regain de vitalité imprévue, à me mettre définitivement hors de combat. Il reprit une position de défense. J'essayai de me relever et je m'aperçus que je ne sentais plus mes jambes. Je savais que pour soutenir mon rôle jusqu'au bout je devrais me relever et faire mine de le frapper. Peut-être qu'il finirait par me tuer, je ne voulais pas mourir, mais, si cela devait m'arriver, je n'en avais cure. Il y eut un moment d'hésitation de part et d'autre. Malgré tout le mal que je me donnais, ma position restait extrêmement contrainte et invraisemblable. Je compris que si je n'attaquais pas le premier, il abandonnerait la partie. Je m'élançai sur lui, il eut le temps de se baisser ; son visage plongea de côté dans la clarté de la lune. Alors, il perdit patience, sauta en l'air et me tomba dessus, les pieds en avant. Il me frappa de toutes ses forces, mes jambes flageolèrent, je tombai sur les genoux. Je l'entendis s'éloigner en courant, puis je crus entendre pendant un moment le tintement des cloches. Je restai agenouillé, la tête renversée en arrière, à regarder le ciel noir avec des larmes qui coulaient sur mes joues.

Lorsque je repris connaissance, j'étais couché sur le côté, l'oreille droite enfouie dans la neige, les mains crispées sur les revers de mon manteau qu'elles serraient étroitement autour de ma poitrine. Je ressentais une douleur lancinante sur le front, entre les deux yeux. D'une torsion de reins, je réussis tant bien que mal à me mettre sur le dos et je restais ainsi étendu, immobile, regardant fixement au-dessus de moi le sapin qui se dressait, vague comme un somnambule, dans le brouillard léger et blanc, tandis que d'une main je tâtais maladroitement mon visage rendu insensible par le froid et que, de l'autre, j'explorais la couche de neige fondue sur laquelle je gisais. J'éprouvais l'impression pénible de me trouver au fond d'une crevasse d'où je ne parviendrais pas à me tirer, même au prix des efforts les plus désordonnés, soustrait à jamais aux regards humains, perdu pour le monde, dussent tous les promeneurs habituels du dimanche circuler en rangs serrés autour de moi. Les suites des coups que j'avais reçus se faisaient à présent durement sentir ; ma magnifique exaltation n'était plus qu'une immense lassitude. Rien qu'à l'évoquer, je frissonne, moins à la pensée de la souffrance qu'au sentiment de mon échec d'alors. Constatant amèrement que la punition recherchée n'avait pas amené en moi le changement que j'en attendais et rougissant d'en avoir été réduit à un aussi pitoyable expédient, je ne m'en sentais pas moins tenu de subir une nouvelle épreuve dont je craignais pourtant que l'efficacité, cette fois bien réelle, se payât par une souffrance plus atroce, probablement tout aussi humiliante et qui, d'avance, me parut si redoutable que, m'attendrissant et m'apitoyant sur moi-même, je me mis à pleurer comme un enfant. Larmes stupides d'ailleurs, peut-être causées seulement par une dépression très vive. Pourtant, mise à part cette appréhension et sachant bien que je ne pouvais demeurer impuni, j'avais hâte de me laver de mon péché et je désirais encore avec ardeur obtenir mon propre pardon, c'était même là le seul aiguillon qui pût me pousser à agir au milieu de tant de détresse. Un autre sujet de désespoir était la bise tranchante comme un rasoir qui me coupait les oreilles que protégeait à peine un misérable cache-col trop court et trop étroit. Le froid aurait été malgré tout supportable si j'avais eu la ressource de battre de la semelle pour ramener le sang à mes orteils engourdis. Mais, pour cela, il aurait fallu que je prenne la décision de me mettre sur mes pieds, or je ne me croyais pas en état de faire un tel effort. Je réussis pourtant à relever le buste et j'appuyai mon dos contre le tronc de l'arbre mort. Je restai un long moment dans cette position, sans faire un mouvement, les jambes étendues, droites devant moi et jointes hiératiquement comme une statue gisante sur un ancien tombeau, les mains posées sur mes genoux, mettant toute mon application à garder les yeux ouverts et à contempler au-dessus de moi le ciel qui était comme une voûte de fer battu. Les réverbères étaient éteints et, de fait, il faisait demi-jour. L'aube couleur de citron inondait le jardin désert, s'égouttait des branches et des corniches, émiettait les blocs d'ombre entre les arbres et déjà la fumée des chalands flottait bas sur l'eau opaque. Je me sentais frileux et fatigué. Je fis une faible tentative pour me mettre debout, mais elle n'eut aucun succès : je dus bientôt renoncer à mes efforts avec un halètement rauque et restai appuyé tout raide contre l'arbre. Mes articulations me semblaient rouillées, tous mes membres une matière morte. Pourquoi nierais-je qu'il y avait là quelque comédie ? Avec un peu plus de ténacité, je serais parvenu sans trop de peine à me mettre sur pied ; aucune de ces tentatives, à vrai dire, n'était bien pénible, mais au fort de la souffrance que me causait la morsure du froid, j'éprouvais comme la tentation de persévérer dans mon immobilité ; j'y succombais avec la même avidité qu'en été à me prélasser le corps nu au soleil, à ceci près qu'ici la cuisson ne me causait aucune volupté positive. De temps à autre, je frottais mes oreilles transies pour leur redonner un peu de vie ; mais bientôt il me devint tout à fait impossible de supporter tranquillement ce qui était au-dessus de mes forces, et je ne veux pas seulement parler de ce froid cruel dont toute ma peau était saturée et qui me transperçait jusqu'à la moelle des os, mais aussi du sentiment d'angoisse et de désolation dont je n'eus d'ailleurs véritablement conscience que lorsque je me surpris à gémir comme un animal blessé, avec un manque de retenue qu'encourageait encore le silence environnant. (Un peu plus tard, je cultivais cette tristesse, espérant ainsi apaiser la fièvre de mon organisme ; je faisais volontairement trotter dans ma tête toutes sortes d'amères réflexions relatives, par exemple, à mon noir isolement, je me traînais sciemment dans le ruisseau nauséabond de mon péché, j'en goûtais avec complaisance l'âcre et dure saveur ; la mauvaise conscience que j'entretenais ainsi en moi constituait un excellent refuge contre la souffrance physique et je me répétais mécaniquement, sans y croire, qu'il n'y aurait plus pour moi un rayon de soleil, un sourire chaleureux sur un visage, plus un son de voix humaine ; je préférais mettre ma cervelle et mon cœur à la torture, plutôt que ma chair peureuse, et si je ne pouvais m'empêcher de m'accorder une courte trêve, ce n'étaient plus seulement des larmes de feu qui venaient me brûler le visage, mais cent mille épingles qui s'enfonçaient tour à tour, avec une régularité et une précision hallucinante, dans les parties les moins vulnérables de mon corps.)

Cependant, à rester là sur le dos sans rien faire, il me sembla que, cédant à une influence pernicieuse, j'épuisais tout mon courage et que je ne pourrais plus jamais me relever ni partir. Je fis de nouveaux efforts et parvins à me tenir accroupi sur mes talons, les bras serrés autour de mes genoux, puis instantanément je fus debout, mais tout mon corps ondula, pivota sur lui-même de telle sorte que je perdis l'équilibre, étendis les deux mains devant moi et j'allais m'étaler sur le ventre quand je réussis à me remettre d'aplomb en me rattrapant d'une main à une branche. Il me sembla que toutes mes forces revenaient d'un coup et, pour savourer un avant-goût de liberté, je fis quelques pas, d'abord avec un peu d'hésitation et en prenant soin de garder ma main droite étendue vers le tronc auquel, dans le cas d'une nouvelle défaillance, je pourrais me raccrocher, puis avec de plus en plus d'assurance ; mais, craignant d'abuser de mes forces, je fis halte et m'appuyai contre un arbre ; je restai encore là un moment, sortis mon miroir de poche, me donnai un coup de peigne, ramassai mon chapeau auquel la neige amoncelée sur le sommet et sur les bords donnait l'aspect d'un gâteau à la crème ; j'essayai de le brosser soigneusement avec la main, puis avec mon mouchoir et je rajustai mon manteau froissé comme si on l'eût passé à la lessive, tordu et bouchonné. Mais, juste au moment où je me disposais à épousseter le bas de mon pantalon, une douleur aiguë dans les reins me fit pousser un cri ; je basculai en avant et je ne pus que protéger ma tête avec la main. À peine sur le sol, j'entrepris tout de suite de me relever, bien que j'eusse le sentiment que j'avais déjà perdu beaucoup de mes forces ; je m'appuyai sur le sol avec mes deux bras pour faire glisser le reste du corps, je pensais que si je pouvais atteindre l'arbre mort, il pourrait me servir d'appui et, dût une nouvelle douleur me transpercer le dos, je ne le lâcherais plus jusqu'à ce que je puisse de nouveau me redresser tout à fait. Contrairement à toute prévision, l'opération fut assez facile, j'étais beaucoup moins faible que je ne le croyais et je parvins à me relever en m'aidant d'une branche qui se terminait en fourche au-dessus de ma tête. Une fois debout, incapable de me décider à faire seulement un pas, je demeurai quelques instants sans bouger, hors d'haleine, une main crispée sur la branche, l'autre profondément enfouie dans ma poche. C'est alors que survint un fait extraordinaire.

Il se peut que je démêle un jour les raisons, qui m'échappent encore, de la curieuse sensation de réconfort que j'éprouvai bien avant d'avoir été frappé par les voix enfantines. Harassé par les coups reçus et l'insomnie, est-ce que je m'étais assoupi un très court instant, debout et les yeux ouverts, à la façon des chevaux, et au cours de mon petit somme, ce chant frais, égal et sans heurt avait-il exercé sur moi une influence apaisante dont je sentais les effets se prolonger après mon réveil, alors que pourtant j'affirme que j'en ignorais encore la cause, ce qui expliquerait peut-être ce brusque sursaut suivi d'une sorte de déchirure de mon angoisse — comme si des nuages menaçants s'étaient soudain ouverts sur un ciel serein — à laquelle s'ajoutaient en même temps la confiante certitude que j'avais de pouvoir maintenant jouir de tout sans remords et une félicité si vive que ma souffrance physique — engelures, bleus aux bras et aux jambes, migraine due en partie à ma beuverie de la veille, engourdissement — en fut presque annulée ? La seule chose certaine, c'est qu'il se passa un instant de transport complètement imprévisible avant que cette musique ne fût parvenue jusqu'à mes oreilles ou du moins avant que j'aie pu la percevoir clairement. (Quoique cela ne ressorte pas avec évidence du peu que j'ai dit, je puis bien admettre que mes nerfs étaient plus prompts que mes organes à retenir ce dont ils pouvaient avoir le besoin immédiat.) J'aurais juré d'abord que ces voix descendaient du ciel ou qu'elles venaient de l'autre bout du monde, quand en réalité elles s'élevaient toutes proches dans l'air glacé, par vagues successives, en un chœur d'une si discrète confusion qu'on aurait dit un éveil d'ailes tumultueuses. Il y avait en elles quelque chose de tellement singulier, de tellement allusif et mystérieux que je pensais qu'il n'était permis qu'à un très petit nombre d'élus de les entendre ; sans doute fallait-il être en état de les recevoir, et de plus en plus prenait corps en moi cette idée flatteuse pour ma vanité que puisque je jouissais de ce rare privilège, c'est que j'en avais été jugé digne, mieux encore, c'est que j'en étais le destinataire exclusif.

Mais cette agréable illusion ne dura que l'éclair d'un instant ; la réalité, comme j'eus tôt fait de m'en convaincre, était d'une nature beaucoup moins exaltante : ce n'était ni du ciel ni de l'autre bout du monde que cette musique me faisait signe, mais tout simplement du haut de cette grande muraille, sise en bordure du canal, derrière laquelle j'ai déjà dit que s'élevaient à certaines heures du jour les cris et les rires de ces curés-enfants aux visages malgracieux qu'on voyait sortir le jeudi par troupes, balayant la chaussée de leurs robes noires souillées de boue et guidés par un adulte au menton glabre, dont le vêtement ne se distinguait en rien du leur et qui allait et venait à leurs côtés en jetant de temps à autre une note sèche et bourrue dans le bourdonnement monotone des multiples conversations.

Ma méprise me fit pour ainsi dire toucher du doigt l'excitation folle dans laquelle je me trouvais. C'était à mourir de rire, et cependant, le plus drôle, c'est que je ne sentis même pas un sourire ironique effleurer mes lèvres. Peut-être aurais-je su, en période normale, résister à cette musique fascinante qui m'empoignait littéralement et me serais-je demandé comment des êtres de si peu d'attrait réussissaient à faire jaillir du fond d'eux-mêmes un chant si pur et si ineffable que cela tenait du miracle, et, puisque force m'était de reconnaître qu'ils en étaient les interprètes, comment ils pouvaient sans dommage vivre entre ces hauts murs qu'on avait interposés entre eux et ce paysage harmonieux que mes yeux ne se lassaient pas de parcourir tranche par tranche et sous la coupe d'hommes dans le genre de ce grand escogriffe — mais après tout, qu'est-ce qui me prouvait que sous son air gourmé il ne cachait pas un trésor de qualités ? Qui dirigeait l'exécution de ce chœur où chaque ensemble tenait inflexiblement sa partie sinon l'un des maîtres et pourquoi pas celui-là même qui jouait dans les rues le rôle dérisoire du chien de berger ? — N'importe ! tout cela aurait dû m'intriguer et me révolter au point de m'en faire presque oublier la merveilleuse suavité de ces voix, mais bien malgré moi, quelque défense que je fisse, malgré ma volonté de ne jamais me laisser égarer par quelque chose qui m'émeut à l'improviste (attitude qui, dans mon entourage, est diversement appréciée et me vaut la réputation, à mes yeux assez comique, de tête froide), j'étais tout entier la proie de cette musique qui m'inondait, m'écrasait, m'anéantissait de toute son effrayante plénitude — effrayante, parce qu'elle me laissait complètement désarmé. (Je n'ai jamais eu à me suggestionner pour m'émouvoir à l'audition de mes œuvres préférées : elles ont sur moi une vertu dominatrice à laquelle je ne cherche pas à me soustraire ; c'est ainsi que je pense volontiers qu'elles seules peuvent me porter à mon propre sommet. En revanche, me paraît éminemment suspect le bouleversement grisant que, pour peu que le cadre et les circonstances s'y prêtent, je retire de l'audition d'œuvrettes sans importance, d'une sentimentalité écœurante ou d'un pathétique de mauvais aloi débitées à la va-comme-je-te-pousse par un orchestre minable. Assis seul dans un café où trois violons et un mauvais piano exécutent un morceau en vogue ou pis encore, tel air fameux d'un opéra qui a contre lui de prétendre au sublime, si je ne me tiens pas sur mes gardes, il m'arrive d'être envahi par un délire de tristesse ou de joie auquel je ne puis honnêtement donner mon approbation : je me sens enfin ému, mais c'est vraiment à trop bon compte. Aussi me suis-je exercé à demeurer sourd à ce qui, sous couleur d'exalter ma sensibilité, ne faisait de moi qu'un absurde pleurnicheur, mais hélas ! j'ai la tête trop chaude.)

Ici, je ne songeais pas à exercer sur mon émotion un contrôle que je réservais sottement à celle que me causait l'audition d'œuvres dont je pressentais plus ou moins confusément l'inanité ; d'abord, cette musique n'était pas vulgaire, ensuite elle me remuait comme aucune autre n'aurait jamais su le faire, je me sentais plein de bien-être et comme envahi par une sérénité en tous points analogue à celle dont j'ai déjà été amené à parler à propos des symptômes de ma première crise. On m'excusera si je m'abstiens pour une fois de chercher à déceler quels sont les traits qui pourraient me permettre de caractériser et de définir une émotion dont je n'ai été que le témoin hagard, elle me paraît trop particulière, trop personnelle et par là même dénuée d'une suffisante puissance de suggestion pour que cela vaille la peine de m'y attarder. Que saurais-je en dire ? Mieux vaut à tous égards la laisser de côté, quelle que soit la place importante que j'ai la faiblesse de lui assigner dans mes souvenirs, me réservant de vous soumettre en temps utile un de ses effets gros de signification pour ce qu'il m'a ouvert de surprenantes perspectives, faisant à mes yeux figure de révélation comme le déchirement soudain d'un voile ou l'éclatement d'une vérité.

Je me bornerai cette fois à fixer ici, en quelques lignes et sommairement, ce que j'ai retenu des qualités propres à cette musique. Telle que je l'entendais dans ce jardin public où le froid paralysait tous mes membres, elle me paraissait attirante par la chaleur intense qu'elle dégageait, due à l'incandescence de certaines voix enfantines portées au rouge auxquelles s'ajoutait pourtant comme à l'arrière-plan un rideau de voix plus tendres et parfaitement sereines ; car, si, d'une manière générale, il y avait en elle quelque chose d'enveloppant et de confortable comme l'atmosphère d'une salle surchauffée où l'on pénètre après une longue station dans le froid du dehors, c'était surtout par son double caractère de liberté et d'innocence joyeuse qu'elle m'émouvait jusqu'aux larmes ; mais aussi par je ne sais quoi de large et de clair pareil au vent marin. Avec le recul du temps, il me semble que ces voix exprimaient encore une totale indifférence aux douleurs humaines, foulant aux pieds scrupules, troubles, doutes, tout ce qui constitue l'étoffe de nos soucis, se jouant de l'angoisse avec une éclatante insolence (sans lui lancer pourtant aucun de ces sombres défis, souvent ridicules par ce qu'il y a en eux d'ostentatoire et de forcé). Incantation pure, secrète, en marge du monde lourd et fade que nous portons en nous, douée de la séduction particulière qu'attire tout ce qui n'a pas cette odeur corrompue du péché, et qui enchante comme la seule évocation des mots : *allégresse, printemps, soleil* ; issue d'un univers sans sexe ni sang mais que ne dégradait pourtant aucune de ces tares propres à ce qui est exsangue et décharné ; opposant sa grâce aérienne à mon abattement d'animal blessé ; claire comme une nuit de gel, rafraîchissante comme une bolée d'eau de source ; idéale enfin comme tout ce qui suggère l'existence d'un monde harmonieux, sans commune mesure avec la réplique que nous en faisons et qui n'en est jamais qu'un détestable simulacre. Mais ce que je ne dois pas omettre de dire de ces chants, c'est la certitude que rien n'aurait pu me retirer de l'esprit qu'ils m'apportaient un parfum familier, vestige insolite d'un monde aussi radicalement distinct de celui où je me débattais que l'été l'est de l'hiver et qui, au sein même de ma jubilation, me procurait une poignante nostalgie comparable à celle qu'engendre chez un homme sur le déclin l'évocation de tout un passé glorieux ou encore à celle que vous ressentez s'il vous arrive un jour de fouler imprudemment les lieux qui ont été le théâtre d'une passion dont vous vous croyiez pourtant guéri à jamais. Restait à identifier l'épisode de ma vie auquel il se rattachait, j'étais d'autant plus anxieux d'en trouver la référence précise qu'uniquement absorbé par cette recherche qui m'importunait en m'empêchant de jouir de la musique, je me sentais gagné peu à peu par l'obsession d'une interrogation que jamais je ne m'accommoderais de laisser sans réponse ; privé de toute base d'orientation, je risquais de me tourmenter, de m'énerver et, en définitive, de voir gâché tout mon plaisir. Je voulais éclaircir ce point une fois pour toutes, et si ç'avait été nécessaire, je serais bien resté jusqu'au lendemain matin à me reporter mentalement à mon enfance, l'explorant de fond en comble, en scrutant les épisodes les plus marquants et examinant si je ne pouvais y découvrir quelque indice qui ferait fonction de clef et déclencherait brusquement la lumière, mais me laisserait-on le temps de venir à bout de ma tâche ? La musique n'allait-elle pas s'évanouir subitement et avec elle ce qui m'eût permis de trouver le mot de l'énigme ? Et s'il en était ainsi, à quoi bon me fatiguer en pure perte ? Il était sans doute préférable dans tous les cas de ne pas m'attarder à entreprendre de telles recherches qui détourneraient mon attention de ce qui les avait précisément déterminées et n'aboutiraient qu'à me soustraire au pouvoir bienfaisant de cette musique, sans que rien m'eût été donné qui puisse les justifier. En réalité, mes craintes étaient superflues. Car, tandis que je ruminais là-dessus, le jour se fit en moi peu à peu, j'avais la conviction d'être sur la bonne voie et déjà je me faisais une idée approximative du climat où s'était déroulé l'épisode dont j'attendais qu'il me donne la révélation du sens de ma nostalgie mais sans parvenir encore à le définir ni à le situer avec précision. Enfin, comme je me demandais une fois de plus ce qui avait bien pu me laisser le souvenir d'un pareil parfum, la réponse me vint comme un éclair. Et maintenant, autour de ce chœur enfantin venaient graviter des souvenirs échelonnés sur diverses périodes de ma jeunesse, mais de contenus à peu près identiques et ayant pour cadre commun la chapelle de ce collège breton où, débordant d'une ardeur violente, ressentant cruellement l'injustice de la contrainte, j'entretenais à longueur de journées mon orgueil et ma haine. Et soudain je me rappelais de quelle triomphale façon tombait le soleil de l'après-midi en faisceaux couleur de safran sur les dalles en mosaïque, sur les guipures illustrées de motifs travaillés qui ornaient l'autel, dorant les candélabres à cinq branches que brandissaient des anges en plâtre écaillé, couronnant d'un nimbe éphémère les cheveux des enfants aux joues polies et plates, aux bouches ouvertes, et la manière dont les moins pieux d'entre eux se penchaient en avant, baissaient la tête et plaquaient habilement une main sur le bas de leur visage quand, las de chanter, ils feignaient de s'abîmer en prières — genre de dissimulation où j'étais passé maître et que je pratiquais fréquemment. Et me revenait aussi à l'esprit le souvenir d'un certain dimanche de mai où j'avais aperçu un gros oiseau touffu, encadré par une des hautes fenêtres ouvertes à deux battants par laquelle s'échappaient habituellement les effluves de l'encens qui me fait vomir, se détachant en gris sur la jeune et frissonnante verdure du marronnier que je voyais resplendir chaque jour sous les couleurs du soleil comme le flanc étincelant d'un vaisseau — tandis que moi, dans mon trou sombre et froid, pareil à une larve, je dépérissais — et avec quelle application furieuse, têtue, insensée, je m'étais efforcé de prêter l'oreille au chant qui montait en boule le long de sa gorge, défiant ainsi la force torrentielle d'un *Magnificat* crié à tue-tête par deux cents voix, et de quelle poignante façon, lorsqu'un silence religieux s'établit en bas comme un majestueux point d'orgue, l'oiseau fit entendre là-haut quelques vocalises pures, presque grêles, mais dont l'ironique désinvolture me causa cette ivresse qui est le désespoir absolu voisin du bonheur. Mais ce que je me rappelais par-dessus tout, c'était l'état d'indicible ravissement auquel me portaient les *Psaumes* : tantôt je m'y abandonnais complaisamment en mêlant ma voix — peu sûre — à celles de mes camarades, tantôt, si mon orgueil hostile exigeait le défi, je m'y opposais de toute ma volonté d'autonomie, gardant alors ma bouche hermétiquement close, les lèvres seulement boursouflées d'une moue méprisante, la tête et le buste très droits, les yeux éclatants d'arrogance, avec le double espoir de signifier par la raideur de mon maintien le dégoût que m'inspiraient ces louanges serviles et d'affirmer publiquement ma liberté, et c'était dans le dernier cas surtout que j'avais le sentiment de devenir d'un coup quelqu'un de prestigieux — comme le demeurent à mes yeux celui qui, insoucieux du scandale et faisant fi d'une réprobation unanime, lutte crânement à un contre mille pour imposer ses vues, fussent-elles erronées ; le révolté qui, n'entendant pas se conformer à un état de choses qu'il réprouve et que tous admettent par veulerie ou par intérêt, n'hésite pas à braver les autorités qui le maintiennent dans l'oppression, farouchement résolu à ne céder qu'après avoir remporté la victoire, fût-elle illusoire ou trop lointaine ; l'accusé, coupable ou non, que traque dans son box une société pourrie d'honnêteté et de bon sens, bref tous les opprimés auxquels la lutte solitaire confère une auréole de pureté. Rester immobile, obstinément sourd à ce beau et solennel bavardage qui n'était qu'un leurre, dans une attitude sans geste de réfractaire, me maintenir ferme devant la supplication bêlante des autres, être considéré par mes oppresseurs, leurs serviteurs et celui qu'ils prétendaient servir, sinon comme une brebis galeuse, du moins comme un ennemi que sa pureté rend plus inquiétant, faire figure de séduisant rebelle aux yeux de mes camarades auxquels ne m'unissait pourtant aucun lien de complicité (sauf celui que nous entretenions assez habituellement contre nos maîtres), à tous inspirer une crainte respectueuse, autant de pauvres moyens — vulgaires s'ils n'avaient été si puérils — par lesquels je prétendais accéder à la puissance, me libérer de mes chaînes, en un mot me donner momentanément le change : il ne s'agissait somme toute que de supporter la contrainte en me grisant d'assurance orgueilleuse.

Mais, pour en revenir au chœur des petits séminaristes, la nostalgie qu'il éveillait en moi, ce n'était pas seulement ce plaisir mêlé de regrets que nous éprouvons toujours à ranimer des souvenirs d'enfance qui, avec le recul du temps et l'amère expérience que nous avons acquise depuis, nous reviennent parés de couleurs charmantes, mais bien plus le malaise que me causait l'antinomie, qui se révélait soudain à moi avec une horrible évidence, entre ce que je n'avais jamais douté de devenir et ce que j'étais devenu : n'avais-je pas creusé de mes propres mains le fossé infranchissable qui me séparait de ma jeunesse ? Qu'on me comprenne bien, il ne s'agissait pas de déplorer mon impuissance d'adulte à déserter le monde brutal, sec, désespérément impropre à toute aventure mythique où nous nous démenons avec une férocité d'araignée pour m'introduire ensuite, à la faveur d'une évocation précise, dans ce monde perdu auquel les hommes attachent si douloureusement leurs regards — quant à moi, je tiens celui que nous qualifions de réel pour seul digne de notre condition, préférant depuis tout temps la lumière rigide de midi aux vapeurs du soir, la rigueur d'une vérité aux replis du mensonge, la nudité aux parures. Bien au contraire, ce qui me déchirait le cœur, c'était de découvrir dans les profondeurs de mon enfance tout autre chose que des rêves dérisoires : des passions vivantes et par exemple l'impossibilité foncière de pactiser avec ce que j'exécrais, la certitude puérile d'être tout à fait maître un jour de disposer du monde qui s'étendait devant moi comme un domaine ouvert, l'incapacité de prendre mon parti du sort qui m'était fait et d'apaiser en moi une brûlante soif d'exigences. Mon passé renvoyait de moi une image étrangère dont la seule évocation jetait sur mon insuffisance actuelle une lumière implacable ; il me semblait en effet que j'y prenais une idée de moi peu compatible avec ce que des années d'auto-observation m'avaient appris. Si je souffrais alors, ce n'était pas tant de renoncer à combattre, faute d'ennemis, que de me voir talonné de près par des ennemis avec lesquels la sagesse me conseillait de ne pas entrer encore en lutte ouverte, faute d'armes suffisamment efficaces pour les confondre, tout au plus pouvais-je afficher devant eux une attitude de provocation et de rage pures ou encore les cingler d'un rire parfaitement courtois. Mais je puisais une consolation dans la pensée que lorsque viendrait le moment tant désiré de passer à l'attaque, c'est-à-dire lorsque je serais enfin en mesure de déployer toute ma force, ma souplesse et ma ruse, je connaîtrais alors l'ivresse de la victoire. Que me restait-il de cette solide confiance en moi-même, de cette volupté de détruire, de l'agressivité plus ou moins déguisée que je dirigeais contre ceux qui me faisaient subir une contrainte dont j'avais horreur, de la fascination qu'exerçaient sur moi les conquérants, les chefs de bande, les insurgés dont l'exemple éveillait au secret de moi-même une sorte de complicité intime, de l'esprit naturellement frondeur que j'apportais à toutes choses ? À mesure que j'avançais dans la vie, mon indifférence allait s'accroissant, rien ne me semblait valoir la peine d'aucun effort, et il en résultait que mon avidité n'était plus dirigée comme autrefois vers des idées de revanche ou de conquête : elle aspirait au contraire à ce qui saurait m'en délivrer. C'est qu'aujourd'hui le fracas des combats me répugne et me lasse, et j'en veux à mort à qui m'arrache de force à mon indifférence. Ne rien entreprendre, veiller, attendre, veiller...

Cela dit, je dois me garder de retenir la nostalgie dont je viens de parler comme l'élément essentiel du pouvoir de cette musique, lequel réside aussi ailleurs et serait imparfaitement défini si je me bornais à mettre l'accent sur le trouble d'importance secondaire ressenti à l'évocation de ce que j'avais tenu autrefois pour infiniment précieux et nécessaire ; je n'ai voulu insister sur ce point que parce qu'il me paraissait constituer la seule clef qui me permît d'explorer ne serait-ce qu'une part restreinte du contenu d'une émotion par ailleurs inapte à se projeter dans le cadre du monde réel. Il reste entendu que ce qui primait, c'était une joie forte à crier, celle qui déchire l'homme étreignant une femme depuis longtemps convoitée ou découvrant enfin après d'épuisantes veilles quelque vérité qui le met en contact avec ce qu'il y a au fond de lui de plus impénétrablement caché. Et que signifierait ce délicieux allégement du cœur, ce fougueux élan du sang sinon que la joie triomphale qui chantait à mes oreilles était là pour effacer la faute capitale que j'avais commise la veille et de laquelle étaient issus toute ma souffrance et mon dégoût ? Je ne puis m'expliquer autrement le désir qui m'était venu de faire quelques pas : maintenant j'avais la certitude que la honte ne me pousserait plus à trébucher comme malgré moi, à m'étaler par terre, la face cachée dans la neige, ou osant à peine ouvrir les yeux sur le ciel. Pour la première fois de la matinée, j'éprouvais une impression de bien-être physique, mes membres étaient réchauffés, je me sentais très fort, mes articulations me semblaient souples et je résolus d'en faire l'épreuve sur-le-champ. Tandis que je marchais vers le canal, je remarquai joyeusement que mes jambes m'obéissaient à merveille et brûlaient de me porter où je voudrais.

Mais avant d'aller plus loin, je voulus jeter un dernier regard sur le lieu où j'avais subi mon supplice. À cette heure-ci, entre chien et loup, tandis que de gros flocons bien séparés tombaient sur le sol un par un, dans cet air clair et glacé, il me semblait important d'en garder un souvenir précis. Je me retournai donc et je vis l'empreinte saugrenue que mon corps raidi par le froid avait gravée sur la neige boueuse et maculée de mon propre sang. Je pris sur moi de demeurer là pendant une minute à regarder cette plaie grise et rose entourée d'éclaboussures de fragments sanglants, hideuse comme un abcès sur une chair saine. Puis je m'en détournai pour me rejeter avec avidité dans le flot de la musique qui s'amplifiait peu à peu en une escalade d'une majesté infinie. Les réponses en échos que les voix se faisaient entre elles me semblaient autant d'appels à la séduction desquels, l'eussé-je voulu, je n'aurais pu me dérober. C'était bien pour moi que résonnaient ces voix impératives et pleines d'une solennité sauvage, pour moi, rien que pour moi, c'était moi qu'elles appelaient, il n'y avait pas à se tromper ni à chercher d'échappatoire : elles m'appelaient ! Pourtant je feignis par jeu d'y rester sourd et je demeurai immobile, les yeux au sol. Je me disais que j'étais encore libre, que je pouvais encore faire demi-tour et m'échapper par la grille ouverte dont je n'étais séparé que par une cinquantaine de mètres, que si je ne me dépêchais pas de quitter ce jardin, je devrais peut-être y renoncer pour toujours. Mais je m'obstinais à rester planté là, regardant à l'entour sans remuer la tête : n'était-ce pas avouer que j'avais bien compris, que j'étais bien celui qu'on appelait, que j'étais prêt à obéir ? La puissance de l'incantation devenait incroyable, j'en avais le souffle brisé. Et comme elle atteignait son apogée, je sentis un vertige s'emparer de moi par-derrière et me pousser en avant. Conscient de ma faiblesse et d'ailleurs ravi, je ne lui opposais aucune résistance. À mesure que je me rapprochais du canal, je pouvais voir devant moi l'eau briller dans la lumière pâle du petit matin et se diviser autour de la haute muraille aussi impénétrable, aussi insignifiante, aussi anonyme qu'un gros galet ou un pan de roche. Mais je ne me contentais plus de marcher à petits pas prudents, je courais littéralement sur la neige au risque de me rompre le cou. J'étreignais déjà la balustrade comme un affamé étreint un aliment. Il me sembla alors qu'un trait fulgurant me trouait le crâne derrière les yeux, l'eau qui scintillait sous moi me brûlait les paupières, remontait le sang à mes tempes.

— Assez ! m'écriai-je en sanglotant, assez ! après un tel chant, comment oserais-je encore ouvrir la bouche !

CHAPITRE III

Et maintenant, j'attends que vous me posiez la question qui vous brûle les lèvres. Allez-y. Mais, croyez-moi, abandonnez d'abord une attitude malveillante qui ne vous sied guère : espérez-vous encore me confondre ? Prenez garde **que je** ne tienne en réserve une réponse propre à saper tout l'édifice de votre ironie. Je parie que vous hochez la tête avec le sourire entendu de celui à qui on n'en fait pas accroire, vous pensez sans doute que je cherche un dernier recours dans l'intimidation, faute de ne pouvoir me tirer plus habilement d'un mauvais pas ? Alors, à vous de me prouver que vous n'êtes pas de ces gens impressionnables qui se laissent prendre à de grossières manœuvres. Mais d'abord, un instant, je vous prie. Permettez que j'invite à la patience les quelques naïfs, à supposer qu'il s'en trouve parmi vous qui, ayant pris goût au récit de mes aventures et n'entendant pas rester sur leur soif, m'interrogent, tout haletants, les yeux hors de la tête et la gorge sèche... Allons, il est vrai que je pouvais me jeter dans le canal, je n'y avais pas songé, il est vrai aussi que je pouvais m'en abstenir. Cependant, quelle que soit la sympathie que je ne puis m'empêcher d'éprouver pour ceux que tourmente une curiosité aussi légitime et sans vouloir choquer personne, la vérité m'oblige à dire qu'une telle question me paraîtrait impertinente si elle n'était d'abord si parfaitement niaise. Mais naturellement, loin de moi l'intention de la laisser si peu que ce soit en suspens : aux questions les plus variées, il se trouve que je tienne prête la même réponse. De quoi tout simplifier et contenter chacun. Quant à ceux qui ne perdent pas leur temps à se demander où j'ai voulu en venir — et par exemple, si j'ai vraiment piqué une tête dans l'eau glacée ou si je me suis détourné avec une grimace — sans doute aimeraient-ils bien savoir s'il est vrai qu'après l'audition de cette musique sublime je n'ai plus jamais osé ouvrir la bouche ? Je vois. Ce qui les excite, c'est d'apprendre *de ma bouche* ce qu'ils savent déjà. Le cruel spectacle que celui d'un homme qui s'emmêle dans les fils de ses contradictions au fur et à mesure qu'il cherche à les dévider !

Ils veulent rire, je ne leur donnerai pas ce plaisir. Croient-ils se jouer de moi, ils seront joués.

Imaginez un prestidigitateur qui, las d'abuser de la crédulité de la foule qu'il a entretenue jusqu'ici dans une illusion mensongère, se propose un beau jour de substituer à son plaisir d'enchanter celui de désenchanter, à rebours de tout ce qui fait généralement l'objet de la vanité et quitte à perdre à jamais le bénéfice qu'il tirait de sa réputation de faiseur de miracles. Qu'on ne s'y trompe pas, ce n'est pas par un tardif mais louable souci d'honnêteté qu'il lui vient la fantaisie de livrer ses recettes une à une avec la froide minutie d'un horloger qui démonte une horloge, il n'a pas de ces scrupules, c'est tout simplement par volupté de détruire ce qu'il a créé et de flétrir l'enthousiasme qu'il a soulevé, il étale donc ses pièces sur la table, donnant ainsi un air de vulgarité à ses tours les plus subtils, se délectant à décevoir ceux qu'il avait émerveillés, descendant de son propre gré du pinacle où ses dupes l'avaient porté, guettant avidement dans leurs yeux qu'agrandissait hier encore un étonnement d'enfant la première ombre de la désillusion, et pour peu que subsiste sur leur masque triste, pincé par un sourire vide, la plus légère lueur de la foi, il se hâte de l'éteindre avec autant de soin qu'il avait pris la veille à l'entretenir. Suis-je cet homme cruel et fou ?

En tout cas, je ne me pose pas en victime, je suis prêt à reconnaître le bien-fondé de la plupart des charges retenues contre moi et, s'il est une accusation à laquelle j'avoue donner facilement prise, c'est bien celle de parler inconsidérément ; il est vrai que je n'ai cessé de pérorer à tort et à travers sans craindre d'entrer à mon sujet dans des détails oiseux qui n'intéressaient que moi-même, il est vrai que j'ai cherché maintes fois par instinct de comédien à me faire passer pour ce que je ne suis pas, à me prêter des sentiments que je n'ai jamais eu l'occasion d'éprouver ou encore à m'attribuer des actions que j'étais bien incapable d'accomplir pour donner de la saveur à une vie qui n'en avait aucune ; il est vrai aussi que j'ai eu le front de renier ce qui me tenait le plus à cœur et de louer ce que j'ai de tout temps fait profession de haïr. Certes, vous avez parfaitement raison de me trouver mal venu de parler sur un ton vertueux de sincérité quand mon principal souci était de donner une entorse à la vérité pour la rendre plus excitante ou plus vraisemblable ; enfin, je ne parle pas de mes roulades, de mes contorsions, de mes subterfuges, de mes grimaces. C'est entendu, je suis un bavard, un inoffensif et fâcheux bavard, comme vous l'êtes vous-mêmes, et par surcroît un menteur comme le sont tous les bavards, je veux dire les hommes. Mais en quoi cela vous autorise-t-il à me reprocher âprement le mal dont vous êtes vous-mêmes affectés ? On ne peut me demander de rester dans mon coin, silencieux et modeste, à écouter se payer de mots des gens dont j'ai bien le droit de penser qu'ils n'ont ni plus d'expérience ni plus de réflexion que moi-même. Lequel d'entre vous me jettera la pierre ?

Ce que moins que tout autre vous paraissez disposés à me passer, c'est une certaine mauvaise conscience. Quand on a honte d'être un bavard, dites-vous, on commence par se taire. J'en conviens. Mais ce besoin fâcheux qui nous est commun constitue-t-il une tare sur laquelle ceux qui n'en rougissent pas ont le droit de me juger ? J'ai la faiblesse de croire que mieux vaut ma conscience, fût-elle mauvaise, que votre aveuglement. Est-il bien vrai qu'illuminé par la beauté de cette musique j'ai prononcé un vœu aux termes duquel j'étais tenu de garder désormais un silence décent ? Suis-je donc une sorte de vilain parjure ? Et si vous ne me rappelez opportunément la honte subie après ma grande crise que pour feindre ensuite de vous étonner qu'elle n'ait pas suffi à me corriger de mon vice, je vous répondrai... que vous répondrai-je au fait ? Rien ne m'est plus facile que de vous couper vos pauvres effets. Ce n'est pas ma faute si vos chicanes me font sourire. Reste à savoir si j'ai bien entendu cette musique, si j'ai vraiment éprouvé cette honte. Je vous répondrai donc que ce n'est pas une raison parce que je me suis donné la peine de décrire l'une et l'autre avec précision pour que leur authenticité ne puisse plus jamais être contestée par personne, et en premier lieu par moi. Est-ce que je n'aurais pas l'imagination un peu plus prompte que la mémoire ? Vous trouvez que je vais quand même un peu fort : feindre de douter de ses propres affirmations, c'est là le comble de l'impertinence ou de la mauvaise foi. Et si je ne simulais pas le doute, et si je ne doutais pas, et si je savais parfaitement à quoi m'en tenir sur la véracité de mes propos et si enfin tout mon bavardage n'était que mensonge ? Vous vous détournez avec colère : « Alors, allez au diable ! » Je ne saurais trop vous engager à considérer la situation avec sang-froid, ne craignez pas d'avoir perdu votre temps à prêter l'oreille à des mensonges, puisque vous avez eu le privilège d'assister à une crise de bavardage, ce qui était certainement plus instructif que d'en lire un rapport, fût-il pur de toute intention littéraire. Ayez le bon esprit de ne pas vous courroucer de l'abus que j'ai fait de votre crédulité, glissant à votre insu quelques vérités au milieu de tant de mensonges que je vous donnais pour des vérités, dans l'idée qui s'est vérifiée que les premières ne se distingueraient en rien des secondes. Je suis tout prêt à faire amende honorable à ceux que j'ai abusivement leurrés, je peux leur assurer qu'il m'importe très peu d'avoir le dernier mot, je demande simplement qu'il me soit permis de m'expliquer posément sur un cas qui peut être aussi bien celui de quelques-uns d'entre vous, je crois que nous allons nous entendre pour peu que vous me laissiez le temps de revenir en arrière et de tout reprendre depuis le commencement afin de dissiper définitivement ce trop long malentendu, montrant qu'il n'était fondé sur rien de si grave que nous avons pu croire.

Qui n'a pas eu, au moins une fois, envie d'élever la voix, non pas dans l'intention raisonnable de charmer un auditoire ou avec la prétention de l'instruire, mais plus simplement pour satisfaire son propre caprice ? Encore faut-il, comme je l'ai dit en commençant, qu'il croie dur comme fer qu'il existe quelque part des oreilles pour l'entendre — et, comme je le montrerai plus loin, qu'il emploie beaucoup de ruse pour s'assurer la bienveillance de l'auditeur en lui donnant le désir d'apprendre ce qu'il va dire : il y a pour celui qui parle une étrange source d'encouragement dans le visage humain qui est en face de lui. Ce n'est pas qu'il soit indispensable que vous ayez grand-chose à dire, et même vous pouvez très bien n'avoir strictement rien à dire : je ne vois pas pourquoi l'on se récrierait en m'entendant soutenir que parler et s'exprimer font deux. Se trouverait-il quelqu'un d'assez malhonnête pour prétendre qu'il n'ouvre jamais la bouche que pour communiquer une pensée, que pour faire entendre le charmant timbre de sa voix ? Le farceur ! En ouvrant la bouche, vous ne savez peut-être pas ce que vous direz, mais la conviction que vous trouverez l'abondance de mots nécessaire dans les circonstances et dans l'excitation qu'elles provoquent en vous, vous donne la hardiesse de commencer au petit bonheur : l'important est que vous assouvissiez sur-le-champ votre besoin de bavarder ; il arrive généralement que les mots répondent avec promptitude à votre appel. Mais aussi il peut arriver — et ici nous touchons à mon cas personnel — que les mots demeurent rétifs et que vous éprouviez alors une angoisse comparable à celle d'un paralytique qui veut fuir devant un danger pressant. Certains, je le sais bien, se résignent mal à l'incapacité de satisfaire leur besoin, d'autres se tiennent sur la réserve, comptant plus ou moins sincèrement sur le hasard pour les délivrer, attendant d'une manière toute passive la guérison de leur infirmité, se familiarisant peu à peu avec elle quand ils ne cherchent pas à la faire passer pour de la force d'âme, ils affectent alors de juger futile un désir que leur impuissance leur interdit de satisfaire.

Quand je brûle d'envie de parler, je ne songe pas à prendre sur moi de me taire et pourtant, le moindre de mes soucis, je le dis sans affectation, est de rendre publics mes épanchements ou même de vider mon âme dans une oreille amicale. Rien ne m'est plus étranger que le soin pris par certains hommes d'exposer leur science d'eux-mêmes aux regards de tous. Cependant, il est inutile d'espérer ouvrir la bouche si vous ne pouvez vaincre votre aversion profonde pour les feux de la rampe. Vous êtes condamné à monter sur les tréteaux, il faut vous résoudre à y faire le charlatan. Pour ma part, je ne fais pas profession de modestie : il m'est aussi indifférent de parader que de rester à l'ombre, aucun scrupule ne me retiendra de tendre des pièges à la bonne foi de mes auditeurs, si je juge que l'intérêt que mes mensonges ont éveillé chez eux m'aide à satisfaire mon vice.

Non, ce qui me préoccupe est d'un ordre moins relevé. Mon imagination pour commencer ne va-t-elle pas me faire défaut ? Où trouverai-je matière à exercer ma verve ? Car tout le monde comprendra que je ne puisse me borner à ouvrir la bouche pour produire des sons inarticulés ou pour aligner tout arbitrairement des mots sans suite : j'ai déjà dit, et je n'y reviendrai plus, qu'un bavard ne parle jamais dans le vide ; il a besoin d'être stimulé par la conviction qu'on l'écoute, fût-ce machinalement ; il n'exige pas la repartie, c'est à peine s'il cherche à établir un rapport vital entre son interlocuteur et lui ; s'il est vrai que sa loquacité grandit jusqu'à l'exaltation la plus folle devant l'assentiment ou la contradiction, elle se maintient en tout cas très honorablement devant l'indifférence et l'ennui.

J'étais donc mû par l'angoisse où me tenait l'impossibilité de faire le premier pas ; j'avais beau me recueillir et fermer les yeux — à la façon d'un prédicateur qui s'apprête à entamer un long sermon — pour puiser dans le silence l'inspiration et gagner le temps nécessaire à la fabrication d'un souvenir plausible et fertile en développements, tous ces efforts n'aboutissaient qu'à me confirmer dans l'opinion que mon imagination était sèche et froide. Cependant, mon désir se faisait plus véhément, l'ambition d'entrer en compétition avec ceux dont j'enviais l'éloquence me brûlait la gorge ; pas plus que par orgueil, je ne voulais renoncer par impuissance à une activité à laquelle j'avais une si furieuse envie de me livrer. C'est alors qu'il me vint cette illumination que ce que je cherchais si loin, je l'avais sous la main. Je parlerais de mon besoin de parler.

Mais comment me serais-je acquitté de cette tâche d'un cœur léger ? Cela n'a jamais passé pour très agréable de s'ouvrir à des gens mal intentionnés et résolument enclins à n'apercevoir autour d'eux que ce qu'il y a de plus vil et de plus corrompu, l'aveu d'un vice que personne n'ose secrètement reconnaître pour sien ne peut prêter qu'à des commentaires ironiques de la part des plus hypocrites et soulever chez les plus méchants qu'un concert d'imprécations déchaînées. N'est-ce pas fou de risquer sa réputation, de s'exposer aux sarcasmes pour la seule volupté de bavarder ?

Aussi ne tenait-il qu'à moi de brouiller par moments la piste que j'avais soigneusement tracée. Qu'est-ce qui m'empêchait de donner quelques coups de pouce à une vérité dont je redoutais les vertus explosives ? Pourquoi me serais-je fait un scrupule de ne dessiner de moi qu'une image ressemblante, donc méprisable, quand je pouvais la rendre pitoyable en invoquant habilement la maladie comme prétexte à l'irresponsabilité ? Mon plus grand souci fut donc en premier lieu de donner à la communication de faits entièrement inventés une apparence de rigueur et de logique, telle qu'il puisse sembler à mon interlocuteur qu'obéissant scrupuleusement aux données sûres fournies par ma mémoire, je n'ai jamais cédé aux tentations de l'imagination ni consenti à mettre du jeu dans les rouages de mon récit ; en second lieu de douer d'une vie acceptable certaines figures purement fictives (à commencer par celle que je donnais pour mienne) que je faisais acteurs ou figurants d'une aventure en réalité construite de toutes pièces pour les besoins de ma cause, tout en prenant soin de ne laisser autour d'elles aucune ombre suspecte qui pût faire douter en même temps de leur authenticité et de ma bonne foi. Pour mieux convaincre les plus exigeants de mes lecteurs, j'affectais de renoncer à certains effets plutôt destinés à faire valoir l'habileté de l'auteur qu'à serrer la vérité de plus près, aux beaux mouvements d'éloquence qui caractérisent en général les plaidoiries et les sermons, à mes recettes personnelles dont j'aurais su, en d'autres occasions, tirer parti avec succès. On se rappelle qu'avec une ostentation qui pouvait aussi bien passer pour une modestie excessive, je ne me suis pas fait faute de souligner la nudité volontaire de ma forme, dont j'étais le premier à regretter hypocritement qu'une certaine monotonie fût l'inévitable rançon de l'honnêteté. Mais feindre de renoncer aux artifices, c'était *aussi* un artifice, et autrement sournois. S'il m'arrivait parfois de mentir, ce n'était que pour me permettre ensuite d'en faire humblement l'aveu : bien sûr, j'avais une fâcheuse tendance à biaiser, à raconter des sornettes pour cacher ou différer ce que je n'osais dire, mais, frappé de repentir, je me reprenais aussitôt, c'est donc que je n'étais pas animé de mauvaises intentions, on pouvait faire confiance à un homme si visiblement soucieux de ne pas tomber dans le travers que nous avons tous plus ou moins de déguiser la vérité. (Permettez-moi de m'étonner en passant qu'aucun d'entre vous ne se soit jamais inquiété de soulever le voile dont j'ai la pudeur ou la lâcheté de m'envelopper. Savez-vous seulement qui vous tient ce langage ? Pourtant, vous accueillez avec plus de bienveillance et d'estime un homme qui se présente modestement en disant son nom, il y a en effet une certaine noblesse à s'offrir à la critique comme une victime résignée. Suis-je un homme, une ombre, ou rien, absolument rien ? Pour avoir longuement bavardé avec vous, ai-je pris du volume ? M'imaginez-vous pourvu d'autres organes que ma langue ? Peut-on m'identifier avec le propriétaire de la main droite qui forme les présentes lettres ? Comment le savoir ? N'attendez pas qu'il se dénonce de lui-même. Qui ne préférerait à sa place garder l'anonymat ? Je suis sûr qu'il protesterait avec une sincère indignation si j'entreprenais de le livrer en pâture à la colère des uns, au mépris des autres. Sait-il lui-même de quoi je suis fait, en admettant que je sois fait de quelque chose ? Il entend bien demeurer étranger à tout ce débat, il se lave les mains de mes écarts. Évertuez-vous à réclamer sur l'air des lampions : « L'auteur ! L'auteur ! » je parie qu'il ne montrera pas le bout de son nez ; on connaît la lâcheté de ces gens-là. Maintenant, je vous le demande : Que feriez-vous d'une étiquette qui couvre une marchandise douteuse ? À supposer que vous connaissiez enfin le nom, l'âge, les titres et qualités de celui qui n'a cessé de vous mentir sur son propre compte, en quoi seriez-vous plus avancé ? Il n'a rien dit de lui-même qui fût vrai, concluez-en qu'il n'existe pas.)

Je n'ai pas la vanité de croire que j'ai réussi à emporter votre adhésion, ni par le ton assuré que je me suis efforcé de garder jusqu'à ces derniers temps ni par l'établissement, à vrai dire assez laborieux, d'une trame logique entre les épisodes d'une aventure un peu trop manifestement invraisemblable et, par exemple, j'aurais su imposer à votre crédulité mes dissertations sur le caractère clinique de mon vice que je me déclarerais pleinement satisfait ; quelqu'un a-t-il pu sans rire m'entendre parler de ce que je qualifie pompeusement de crise ? Inutile de faire observer que je n'ai jamais subi de crises de ce genre. Elles n'ont servi qu'à masquer la honte que j'éprouve d'être affligé du vice peu exaltant auquel il me déplaît de penser que nous nous livrons tous en commun avec la même frénésie. Maintenant, n'allez pas imaginer que j'ai menti si effrontément pour le plaisir grossier de vous voir accorder créance à mes propos les plus fantaisistes ; je n'ai pas consenti sans de longs débats, et cet aveu en est la preuve, à tendre des pièges à votre bonne foi ; ma seule préoccupation, qui devrait suffire à me blanchir de toute accusation de duplicité, était d'éveiller votre intérêt et de l'entretenir en ayant recours à certains effets trompeurs qui n'avaient pour but que de vous conduire plus sûrement où je voulais vous mener, c'est-à-dire jusqu'ici. Mais j'espère que vous allez me demander pourquoi je me suis employé avec une ardeur si étrange à mettre au jour mes supercheries et, à supposer que vous n'ayez nullement l'intention de me poser une telle question, j'ai quelque raison de penser que vous me la poserez quand je ne serai plus là pour répondre. Je réponds donc séance tenante, ce qui aura du moins pour effet de me mettre à l'abri du soupçon injuste d'éluder ce qui m'embarrasse, tout en me donnant l'occasion de satisfaire le peu d'envie qu'il me reste de bavarder. Je pourrais répondre qu'un remords tardif m'a conduit à dévoiler ce que j'avais mis tant de soin à voiler, que mon horreur native du mensonge a eu enfin raison de ma honte, qu'il m'a soudain paru inacceptable d'entretenir dans l'erreur ceux de mes lecteurs qui avaient eu la courtoisie de me suivre jusqu'ici ; je pourrais répondre aussi, en me prêtant alors des sentiments moins nobles, que je trouvais une sorte de jouissance perverse à détromper moi-même mes propres dupes, que j'ai le goût d'exhiber mes tares ou qu'il me plaisait d'être honni par ceux que j'avais aguichés avec de faux appâts, ou encore je pourrais évoquer le plaisir puéril que nous prenons souvent à détruire ce qu'au prix d'un labeur sans trêve nous avons réussi à bâtir de nos propres mains. Mais naturellement, ce serait encore mentir. La vérité, c'est qu'à court d'imagination et pourtant encore peu désireux de me taire, je n'ai rien trouvé de mieux que de révéler mon escroquerie à ceux qui en étaient les victimes, et vous avez vu que je n'étais guère disposé à vous faire grâce d'aucun détail. Je ne me suis jeté si avidement sur ce nouveau sujet que parce que je n'avais alors rien d'autre qui me permît d'alimenter ma sotte et malheureuse passion. Le risible remplaçait le pathétique. Toujours est-il que je tenais bon, et c'était là l'essentiel : je parlais, je parlais, quelle jouissance ! Et je parle encore.

On me juge sévèrement. Je suis déplaisant et je sais bien qu'en cherchant les causes de votre déplaisir, je ne puis que vous déplaire davantage, mais ce ne sont pas seulement l'insolence, ni la maladresse, ni l'immodestie, ni l'affectation à la sincérité ou à la clairvoyance — encore qu'il y ait bien une certaine part de tout ceci — qui me déprécient à vos yeux. Pourquoi me suis-je exposé quand je pouvais rester dans le rang ? Pourquoi ai-je attiré l'attention sur moi ? Pourquoi suis-je à présent inscrit sur la première liste de l'ennemi ? J'ai sacrifié à mon vice les douceurs de l'obscurité et, par une fiction savante, j'ai cherché à vous donner le change, par la provocation à couvrir ma propre inanité en même temps qu'à justifier mes contradictions — c'était une façon habile de détourner l'attention et de brouiller les cartes — et, par exemple, quand pour finir je reconnais que je n'ai positivement rien à dire, vous décelez dans le ton de ma voix quelque chose comme de l'orgueil. Et maintenant encore, je ranime votre hostilité en cherchant à voir clairement en moi-même : celui qui examine ses imperfections avec un certain souci d'objectivité, vous le jugez ostentatoire : pour vous, il est manifeste que je fais état de mes dons de pénétration, et cela aussi est odieux. De sorte que si j'avais quelque imagination, j'en serais réduit à parler de tout autre sujet que de moi-même. Il me semble maintenant que j'aperçois très bien l'image méprisable qu'on peut se faire de moi, j'entends à merveille les propos malveillants que vous allez tenir sur mon compte et, à mesure que j'accumule pour ma défense des arguments spécieux, je parais à vos yeux plus haïssable, plus dépourvu de grandeur. Mais peu m'importe si vous êtes irrités par mon souci constant de me décrire, de me détailler, tout ce que je pourrais dire, qui n'exprimera jamais que ma prétention, suffira toujours à passer condamnation sur moi, soit que j'examine mon cas avec gravité, soit que j'adopte le ton de la plaisanterie. Quoi que je dise, mes propos seraient-ils absolument inoffensifs, je parlerai d'une manière telle que vous me blâmerez toujours. Vous pensez que je suis un imposteur, un outrecuidant, un provocateur, un vaurien, que sais-je ? Un paresseux qui s'abandonne à la facilité, vous ne pouvez plus écouter mes histoires, vous haïssez chaque parole qui sort de mes lèvres, c'est plus fort que vous. Et cependant, je l'ai déjà dit, faire de moi un objet de dégoût, me rouler dans la poussière à vos pieds, je n'y trouve aucun plaisir ; tant pis si cela n'est pas plus sain, mais je me suis livré à une tout autre jouissance, je veux dire à celle de parler, et vous voyez bien que je parle et que je parle encore.

Mais de même que vient un moment où la

flamme la plus vivace se tord sur elle-même, baisse le nez en fumant, vacille pour finalement s'éteindre, de même à la longue le bavard le plus invétéré éprouve une irritation grandissante au fond de la gorge, ses yeux se brouillent pour s'être trop longuement fixés sur ceux de l'interlocuteur où ils s'épuisaient à ranimer une lueur d'intérêt, il ne sait plus très bien ce qu'il avait à dire, ni comment le dire, et souhaite quelque bienfaisante relâche, de sorte qu'il se produit en lui ce qu'il ne pouvait guère prévoir et ce que l'autre avait cessé d'espérer. Le silence — ce silence pour lequel il éprouve le mélange de terreur et d'attachement que détermine la seule approche d'une chose à la fois attirante et dangereuse, prestigieuse et redoutée, ce silence aux lois arides duquel il n'a jamais consenti à se plier, qu'il n'a cessé de haïr, mais auxquelles il reste pourtant lié par une nostalgie cuisante, il se surprend à l'appeler secrètement de ses vœux, si même un reste d'orgueil ou de crainte respectueuse le retient encore de faire le premier pas (et c'est avec un soulagement joyeux que l'autre distingue chez son bourreau les signes de la fatigue qui sont aussi ceux de sa propre délivrance). Mais connaissant ses lâchetés, comment pourrait-il espérer se plaire longtemps en un pays morne et désert qu'il n'aime pas ? Il se trouve en quelque sorte dans l'état d'un homme qui, croyant avoir tout fait pour conjurer le sort contraire, doit se rendre à cette évidence que la partie est perdue, bien perdue : ne lui reste plus même, dans les conditions où elle se dénoue, l'orgueil de l'avoir jouée.

Donc, je vais me taire. Je me tais parce que je suis épuisé par tant d'excès : ces mots, ces mots, tous ces mots sans vie qui semblent perdre jusqu'au sens de leur son éteint. Je me demande si quelqu'un est encore près de moi à m'écouter ? Il y a déjà un moment que j'ai le sentiment de m'obstiner à poursuivre un ridicule et futile monologue sur une place d'où le public déçu s'est retiré en haussant les épaules, mais telle est ma puérilité que je me réjouis à l'idée que ma revanche consistera à le laisser toujours ignorer si je mentais encore quand je prétendais mentir. Que pourrais-je encore dire ? Je ne suis pas à la hauteur de mon vice, je ne me suis d'ailleurs jamais vanté de l'être. Mais, dans l'ensemble, je suis arrivé à ce que je voulais obtenir. Je me suis soulagé, et qu'on ne me dise pas que ce n'était pas la peine. Or, maintenant, je suis las. Allons, Messieurs, puisque je vous dis que je ne retiens plus personne !

DU MÊME AUTEUR

Aux Éditions Gallimard

LES MENDIANTS, roman (édition définitive en 1986)
LE BAVARD, récit (L'Imaginaire n° 32)
LA CHAMBRE DES ENFANTS, récits (L'Imaginaire n° 117)

Aux Éditions du Mercure de France

LES MÉGÈRES DE LA MER
OSTINATO

Aux Éditions Fata Morgana

UN MALADE EN FORÊT
VOIES ET DÉTOURS DE LA FICTION
LE MALHEUR AU LIDO
POÈMES DE SAMUEL WOOD
FACE À L'IMMÉMORABLE

L'IMAGINAIRE
GALLIMARD

Dernières parutions

165. René Daumal : *La Grande Beuverie.*
166. Hector Bianciotti : *L'amour n'est pas aimé.*
167. Elizabeth Bowen : *La maison à Paris.*
168. Marguerite Duras : *L'Amante anglaise.*
169. David Shahar : *Un voyage à Ur de Chaldée.*
170. Mircea Eliade : *Noces au paradis.*
171. Armand Robin : *Le temps qu'il fait.*
172. Ernst von Salomon : *La Ville.*
173. Jacques Audiberti : *Le maître de Milan.*
174. Shelby Foote : *L'enfant de la fièvre.*
175. Vladimir Nabokov : *Pnine.*
176. Georges Perros : *Papiers collés.*
177. Osamu Dazai : *Soleil couchant.*
178. William Golding : *Le Dieu scorpion.*
179. Pierre Klossowski : *Le Baphomet.*
180. A. C. Swinburne : *Lesbia Brandon.*
181. Henri Thomas : *Le promontoire.*
182. Jean Rhys : *Rive gauche.*
183. Joseph Roth : *Hôtel Savoy.*
184. Herman Melville : *Billy Budd, marin,* suivi de *Daniel Orme.*
185. Paul Morand : *Ouvert la nuit.*
186. James Hogg : *Confession du pécheur justifié.*
187. Claude Debussy : *Monsieur Croche* et autres écrits.
188. Jorge Luis Borges et Margarita Guerrero : *Le livre des êtres imaginaires.*
189. Ronald Firbank : *La Princesse artificielle,* suivi de *Mon piaffeur noir.*

190. Manuel Puig : *Le plus beau tango du monde.*
191. Philippe Beaussant : *L'archéologue.*
192. Sylvia Plath : *La cloche de détresse.*
193. Violette Leduc : *L'asphyxie.*
194. Jacques Stephen Alexis : *Romancero aux étoiles.*
195. Joseph Conrad : *Au bout du rouleau.*
196. William Goyen : *Précieuse porte.*
197. Edmond Jabès : *Le Livre des Questions,* I.
198. Joë Bousquet : *Lettres à Poisson d'Or.*
199. Eugène Dabit : *Petit-Louis.*
200. Franz Kafka : *Lettres à Milena.*
201. Pier Paolo Pasolini : *Le rêve d'une chose.*
202. Daniel Boulanger : *L'autre rive.*
203. Maurice Blanchot : *Le Très-Haut.*
204. Paul Bowles : *Après toi le déluge.*
205. Pierre Drieu la Rochelle : *Histoires déplaisantes.*
206. Vincent Van Gogh : *Lettres à son frère Théo.*
207. Thomas Bernhard : *Perturbation.*
208. Boris Pasternak : *Sauf-conduit.*
209. Giuseppe Bonaviri : *Le tailleur de la grand-rue.*
210. Jean-Loup Trassard : *Paroles de laine.*
211. Thomas Mann : *Lotte à Weimar.*
212. Pascal Quignard : *Les tablettes de buis d'Apronenia Avitia.*
213. Guillermo Cabrera Infante : *Trois tristes tigres.*
214. Edmond Jabès : *Le Livre des Questions,* II.
215. Georges Perec : *La disparition.*
216. Michel Chaillou : *Le sentiment géographique.*
217. Michel Leiris : *Le ruban au cou d'Olympia.*
218. Danilo Kiš : *Le cirque de famille.*
219. Princesse Marthe Bibesco : *Au bal avec Marcel Proust.*
220. Harry Mathews : *Conversions.*
221. Georges Perros : *Papiers collés,* II.
222. Daniel Boulanger : *Le chant du coq.*
223. David Shahar : *Le jour de la comtesse.*
224. Camilo José Cela : *La ruche.*
225. J. M. G. Le Clézio : *Le livre des fuites.*
226. Vassilis Vassilikos : *La plante.*
227. Philippe Sollers : *Drame.*

228. Guillaume Apollinaire : *Lettres à Lou.*
229. Hermann Broch : *Les somnambules.*
230. Raymond Roussel : *Locus Solus.*
231. John Dos Passos : *Milieu de siècle.*
232. Elio Vittorini : *Conversation en Sicile.*
233. Edouard Glissant : *Le quatrième siècle.*
234. Thomas De Quincey : *Les confessions d'un mangeur d'opium anglais* suivies de *Suspiria de profundis* et de *La malle-poste anglaise.*
235. Eugène Dabit : *Faubourgs de Paris.*
236. Halldor Laxness : *Le Paradis retrouvé.*
237. André Pieyre de Mandiargues : *Le Musée noir.*
238. Arthur Rimbaud : *Lettres de la vie littéraire d'Arthur Rimbaud.*
239. Henry David Thoreau : *Walden ou La vie dans les bois.*
240. Paul Morand : *L'homme pressé.*
241. Ivan Bounine : *Le calice de la vie.*
242. Henri Michaux : *Ecuador (Journal de voyage).*
243. André Breton : *Les pas perdus.*
244. Florence Delay : *L'insuccès de la fête.*
245. Pierre Klossowski : *La vocation suspendue.*
246. William Faulkner : *Descends, Moïse.*
247. Frederick Rolfe : *Don Tarquinio.*
248. Roger Vailland : *Beau Masque.*
249. Elias Canetti : *Auto-da-fé.*
250. Daniel Boulanger : *Mémoire de la ville.*
251. Julian Gloag : *Le tabernacle.*
252. Edmond Jabès : *Le Livre des Ressemblances.*
253. J. M. G. Le Clézio : *La fièvre.*
254. Peter Matthiessen : *Le léopard des neiges.*
255. Marquise Colombi : *Un mariage en province.*
256. Alexandre Vialatte : *Les fruits du Congo.*
257. Marie Susini : *Je m'appelle Anna Livia.*
258. Georges Bataille : *Le bleu du ciel.*
259. Valery Larbaud : *Jaune bleu blanc.*
260. Michel Leiris : *Biffures* (*La règle du jeu*, I).
261. Michel Leiris : *Fourbis* (*La règle du jeu*, II).
262. Marcel Jouhandeau : *Le parricide imaginaire.*

263. Marguerite Duras : *India Song*.
264. Pierre Mac Orlan : *Le tueur n° 2*.
265. Marguerite Duras : *Le théâtre de l'Amante anglaise*.
266. Pierre Drieu la Rochelle : *Beloukia*.
267. Emmanuel Bove : *Le piège*.
268. Michel Butor : *Mobile. Étude pour une représentation des États-Unis*.
269. Henri Thomas : *John Perkins* suivi de *Un scrupule*.
270. Roger Caillois : *Le fleuve Alphée*.
271. J. M. G. Le Clézio : *La guerre*.
272. Maurice Blanchot : *Thomas l'Obscur*.
273. Robert Desnos : *Le vin est tiré...*
274. Michel Leiris : *Frêle bruit* (*La règle du jeu*, IV).
275. Michel Leiris : *Fibrilles* (*La règle du jeu*, III).
276. Raymond Queneau : *Odile*.
277. Pierre Mac Orlan : *Babet de Picardie*.
278. Jacques Borel : *L'Adoration*.
279. Francis Ponge : *Le savon*.
280. D. A. F. de Sade : *Histoire secrète d'Isabelle de Bavière, Reine de France*.
281. Pierre Drieu la Rochelle : *L'homme de cheval*.
282. Paul Morand : *Milady* suivi de *Monsieur Zéro*.
283. Maurice Blanchot : *Le dernier homme*.
284. Emmanuel Bove : *Départ dans la nuit* suivi de *Non-lieu*.
285. Marcel Proust : *Pastiches et mélanges*.
286. Bernard Noël : *Le château de Cène* suivi de *Le château de Hors. L'outrage aux mots. La pornographie*.
287. Pierre Jean Jouve : *Le monde désert*.
288. Maurice Blanchot : *Au moment voulu*.
289. André Hardellet : *Le seuil du jardin*.
290. André Pieyre de Mandiargues : *L'Anglais décrit dans le château fermé*.
291. Georges Bataille : *Histoire de l'œil*.
292. Henri Thomas : *Le précepteur*.
293. Georges Perec : *W ou le souvenir d'enfance*.
294. Marguerite Yourcenar : *Feux*.
295. Jacques Audiberti : *Dimanche m'attend*.

296. Paul Morand : *Fermé la nuit.*
297. Roland Dubillard : *Olga ma vache. Les Campements. Confessions d'un fumeur de tabac français.*
298. Valery Larbaud : *Amants, heureux amants...* précédé de *Beauté, mon beau souci...* suivi de *Mon plus secret conseil.*
299. Jacques Rivière : *Aimée.*
300. Maurice Blanchot : *Celui qui ne m'accompagnait pas.*
301. Léon-Paul Fargue : *Le piéton de Paris* suivi de *D'après Paris.*
302. Joë Bousquet : *Un amour couleur de thé.*
303. Raymond Queneau : *Les enfants du limon.*
304. Marcel Schwob : *Vies imaginaires.*
305. Guillaume Apollinaire : *Le flâneur des deux rives* suivi de *Contemporains pittoresques.*
306. Arthur Adamov : *Je... Ils...*
307. Antonin Artaud : *Nouveaux écrits de Rodez.*
308. Max Jacob : *Filibuth ou La montre en or.*
309. J. M. G. Le Clézio : *Le déluge.*
310. Pierre Drieu la Rochelle : *L'homme couvert de femmes.*
311. Salvador Dali : *Journal d'un génie.*
312. D.A.F. de Sade : *Justine ou les malheurs de la vertu.*
313. Paul Nizan : *Le cheval de Troie.*
314. Pierre Klossowski : *Un si funeste désir.*
315. Paul Morand : *Les écarts amoureux.*
316. Jean Giono : *Rondeur des jours (L'eau vive I).*
317. André Hardellet : *Lourdes, lentes...*
318. Georges Perros : *Papiers collés, III.*
319. Violette Leduc : *La folie en tête.*
320. Emmanuel Berl : *Sylvia.*
321. Marc Bernard : *Pareils à des enfants...*
322. Pierre Drieu la Rochelle : *Rêveuse bourgeoisie.*
323. Eugène Delacroix : *Lettres intimes.*
324. Raymond Roussel : *Comment j'ai écrit certains de mes livres.*
325. Paul Gadenne : *L'invitation chez les Stirl.*
326. J. M. G. Le Clézio : *Voyages de l'autre côté.*
327. Gaston Chaissac : *Hippobosque au Bocage.*
328. Roger Martin du Gard : *Confidence africaine.*
329. Henri Thomas : *Le parjure.*

330. Georges Limbour : *La pie voleuse.*
331. André Gide : *Journal des faux-monnayeurs.*
332. Jean Giono : *L'oiseau bagué (L'eau vive II).*
333. Arthur Rimbaud : *Correspondance (1888-1891).*
334. Louis-René Des Forêts : *Les mendiants.*
335. Joë Bousquet : *Traduit du silence.*
336. Pierre Klossowski : *Les lois de l'hospitalité.*
337. Michel Leiris : *Langage tangage ou Ce que les mots me disent.*
338. Pablo Picasso : *Le désir attrapé par la queue.*
339. Marc Bernard : *Au-delà de l'absence.*
340. Jean Giono : *Les terrasses de l'île d'Elbe.*
341. André Breton : *Perspective cavalière.*
342. Rachilde : *La Marquise de Sade.*
343. Marcel Arland : *Terres étrangères.*
344. Paul Morand : *Tendres stocks.*
345. Paul Léautaud : *Amours.*
346. Adrienne Monnier : *Les gazettes (1923-1945).*
347. Guillaume Apollinaire : *L'Arbre à soie et autres Échos du Mercure de France (1917-1918).*
348. Léon-Paul Fargue : *Déjeuners de soleil.*
349. Henri Calet : *Monsieur Paul.*
350. Max Jacob : *Le terrain Bouchaballe.*
351. Violette Leduc : *La Bâtarde.*
352. Pierre Drieu la Rochelle : *La comédie de Charleroi.*
353. André Hardellet : *Le parc des Archers* suivi de *Lady Long Solo.*
354. Alfred Jarry : *L'amour en visites.*
355. Jules Supervielle : *L'Arche de Noé.*
356. Victor Segalen : *Peintures.*
357. Marcel Jouhandeau : *Monsieur Godeau intime.*
358. Roger Nimier : *Les épées.*
359. Paul Léautaud : *Le petit ami.*
360. Paul Valéry : *Lettres à quelques-uns.*
361. Guillaume Apollinaire : *Tendre comme le souvenir.*
362. J. M. G. Le Clézio : *Les Géants.*
363. Jacques Audiberti : *Les jardins et les fleuves.*
364. Louise de Vilmorin : *Histoire d'aimer.*

365. Léon-Paul Fargue : *Dîner de lune.*
366. Maurice Sachs : *La chasse à courre.*
367. Jean Grenier : *Voir Naples.*
368. Valery Larbaud : *Aux couleurs de Rome.*
369. Marcel Schwob : *Cœur double.*
370. Aragon : *Les aventures de Télémaque.*
371. Jacques Stephen Alexis : *Les arbres musiciens.*
372. André Pieyre de Mandiargues : *Porte dévergondée.*
373. Philippe Soupault : *Le nègre.*
374. Philippe Soupault : *Les dernières nuits de Paris.*
375. Michel Leiris : *Mots sans mémoire.*
376. Daniel-Henry Kahnweiller : *Entretiens avec Francis Crémieux.*
377. Jules Supervielle : *Premiers pas de l'univers.*
378. Louise de Vilmorin : *La lettre dans un taxi.*
379. Henri Michaux : *Passages.*
380. Georges Bataille : *Le Coupable* suivi de *L'Alleluiah.*
381. Aragon : *Théâtre/Roman.*
382. Paul Morand : *Tais-toi.*
383. Raymond Guérin : *La tête vide.*
384. Jean Grenier : *Inspirations méditerranéennes.*
385. Jean Tardieu : *On vient chercher Monsieur Jean.*
386. Jules Renard : *L'œil clair.*
387. Marcel Jouhandeau : *La jeunesse de Théophile.*
388. Eugène Dabit : *Villa Oasis ou Les faux bourgeois.*
389. André Beucler : *La ville anonyme.*
390. Léon-Paul Fargue : *Refuges.*
391. J. M. G. Le Clézio : *Terra Amata.*

Composition Nord Compo, Lille.
*Impression Bussière Camedan Imprimeries
à Saint-Amand (Cher), le 27 novembre 1998.
Dépôt légal : novembre 1998.
1er dépôt légal dans la collection : novembre 1978.
Numéro d'imprimeur : 985567/1.*
ISBN 2-07-028570-7./Imprimé en France.

83101

FU... PAPERS
PAPERS

Also by H. Beam Piper from Ace Science Fiction

EMPIRE
FEDERATION
FIRST CYCLE
FOUR DAY PLANET/LONE STAR PLANET
LORD KALVAN OF OTHERWHEN
PARATIME
SPACE VIKING

THE FUZZY PAPERS

H. Beam Piper

Illustrations by Victoria Poyser

SF
ACE BOOKS, NEW YORK

LITTLE FUZZY
Copyright © 1962 by H. Beam Piper
FUZZY SAPIENS Copyright © 1964 as THE OTHER HUMAN RACE
by H. Beam Piper
Illustrations copyright © 1980 by Victoria Poyser
All rights reserved. No part of this book may be reproduced in any form or by any means, except for the inclusion of brief quotations in a review, without permission in writing from the publisher.

All characters in this book are fictitious. Any resemblance to actual persons, living or dead, is purely coincidental.

An Ace Book

ISBN: 0-441-26194-9

First Ace Printing: September 1980
This Printing: August 1982

Manufactured in the United States of America

Ace Books, 200 Madison Avenue, New York, New York 10016

I

Jack Holloway found himself squinting, the orange sun full in his eyes. He raised a hand to push his hat forward, then lowered it to the controls to alter the pulse rate of the contragravity-field generators and lift the manipulator another hundred feet. For a moment he sat, puffing on the short pipe that had yellowed the corners of his white mustache, and looked down at the red rag tied to a bush against the rock face of the gorge five hundred yards away. He was smiling in anticipation.

"This'll be a good one," he told himself aloud, in the manner of men who have long been their own and only company. "I want to see this one go up."

He always did. He could remember at least a thousand blast-shots he had fired back along the years and on more planets than he could name at the moment, including a few thermonuclears, but they were all different and they were always something to watch, even a little one like this. Flipping the switch, his thumb found the discharger button and sent out a radio impulse; the red rag vanished in an upsurge of smoke and dust that mounted out of the gorge and turned to copper when the sunlight touched it. The big manipulator, weightless on contragravity, rocked gently; falling debris pelted the trees and splashed in the little stream.

He waited till the machine stablized, then glided it down to where he had ripped a gash in the cliff with the charge of cataclysmite. Good shot: brought down a lot of sandstone, cracked the vein of flint and hadn't thrown it around too much. A lot of big slabs were loose. Extending the forward claw-arms, he pulled and tugged, and then used the underside grapples to pick up a chunk and drop it on the flat ground between the cliff and the stream. He dropped another chunk on it, breaking both of them, and then another and another, until he had all he could work over the rest of the day. Then he set down, got the toolbox and the long-handled contragravity lifter, and climbed to the ground where he opened the box, put on gloves and an eyescreen and got out a microray scanner and a vibrohammer.

The first chunk he cracked off had nothing in it; the scanner gave the uninterrupted pattern of homogenous structure. Picking it up with the lifter, he swung it and threw it into the stream. On the fifteenth chunk, he got an interruption pattern that told him that a sunstone—or something, probably something—was inside.

Some fifty million years ago, when the planet that had been called Zarathustra (for the last twenty-five million) was young, there had existed a marine life form, something like a jellyfish. As these died, they had sunk into the sea-bottom ooze; sand had covered the ooze and pressed it tighter and tighter, until it had become glassy flint, and the entombed jellyfish little beans of dense stone. Some of them, by some ancient biochemical quirk, were intensely thermofluorescent; worn as gems, they glowed from the wearer's body heat.

On Terra or Baldur or Freya or Ishtar, a single cut of polished sunstone was worth a small fortune. Even here, they brought respectable prices from the Zarathustra Company's gem buyers. Keeping his point of expectation safely low, he got a smaller vibrohammer from the toolbox and began chipping cautiously around the foreign object, until the flint split open and revealed a smooth yellow ellipsoid, half an inch long.

"Worth a thousand sols—if it's worth anything," he commented. A deft tap here, another there, and the yellow bean came loose from the flint. Picking it up, he rubbed it between gloved palms. "I don't think it is." He rubbed harder, then held it against the hot bowl of his pipe. It still didn't respond. He dropped it. "Another jellyfish that didn't live right."

Behind him, something moved in the brush with a dry rustling. He dropped the loose glove from his right hand and turned, reaching toward his hip. Then he saw what had made the noise—a hard-shelled thing a foot in length, with twelve legs, long antennae and two pairs of clawed mandibles. He stopped and picked up a shard of flint, throwing it with an oath. Another damned infernal land-prawn.

He detested land-prawns. They were horrible things, which, of course, wasn't their fault. More to the point, they were destructive. They got into things at camp; they would try to eat anything. They crawled into machinery, possibly finding the lubrication tasty, and caused jams. They cut into electric insulation. And they got into his bedding, and bit, or rather pinched, painfully. Nobody loved a land-prawn, not even another land-prawn.

This one dodged the thrown flint, scuttled off a few feet and turned, waving its antennae in what looked like derision. Jack reached for his hip again, then checked the motion. Pistol cartridges cost like crazy; they weren't to be wasted in fits of childish pique. Then he reflected that no cartridge fired at a target is really wasted, and that he hadn't done any shooting recently. Stooping again, he picked up another stone and tossed it a foot short and to the left of the prawn. As soon as it was out of his fingers, his hand went for the butt of the long automatic. It was out and the safety off before the flint landed; as the prawn fled, he fired from the hip. The quasi-crustacean disintegrated. He nodded pleasantly.

"Ol' man Holloway's still hitting things he shoots at."

Was a time, not so long ago, when he took his abilities for granted. Now he was getting old enough to have to verify them. He thumbed on the safety and holstered the pistol, then picked up the glove and put it on again.

Never saw so blasted many land-prawns as this summer. They'd been bad last year, but nothing like this. Even the oldtimers who'd been on Zarathustra since the first colonization said so. There'd be some simple explanation, of course; something that would amaze him at his own obtuseness for not having seen it at once. Maybe the abnormally dry weather had something to do with it. Or increase of something they ate, or decrease of natural enemies.

He'd heard that land-prawns had no natural enemies; he questioned that. Something killed them. He'd seen crushed prawn shells, some of them close to his camp. Maybe stamped on by something with hoofs, and then picked clean by insects. He'd ask Ben Rainsford; Ben ought to know.

Half an hour later, the scanner gave him another interruption pattern. He laid it aside and took up the small vibrohammer. This time it was a large bean, light pink in color. He separated it from its matrix of flint and rubbed it, and instantly it began glowing.

"Ahhh! This is something like it, now!"

He rubbed harder; warmed further on his pipe bowl, it fairly blazed. Better than a thousand sols, he told himself. Good color, too. Getting his gloves off, he drew out the little leather bag from under his shirt, loosening the drawstrings by which it hung around his neck. There were a dozen and a half stones inside, all bright as live coals. He looked at them for a moment, and dropped the new sunstone in among them, chuckling happily.

Victor Grego, listening to his own recorded voice, rubbed the sunstone on his left finger with the heel of his right palm and watched it brighten. There was, he noticed, a boastful ring to his voice—not the suave, unemphatic tone considered proper on a messagetape. Well, if anybody wondered why, when they played that tape off six months from now in Johannesburg on Terra, they could look in the cargo holds of the ship that had brought it across five hundred light-years of space. Ingots of gold and platinum and gadolinium. Furs and biochemicals and brandy. Perfumes that defied synthetic imitation; hardwoods no plastic could copy. Spices. And the steel coffer full of sunstones. Almost all luxury goods, the only really dependable commodities in interstellar trade.

And he had spoken of other things. Veldbeest meat, up seven per cent from last month, twenty per cent from last year, still in demand on a dozen planets unable to produce Terran-type foodstuffs. Grain, leather, lumber. And he had added a dozen more items to the lengthening list of what Zarathustra could now produce in adequate quantities and no longer needed to import. Not fishhooks and boot buckles, either—blasting explosives and propellants, contragravity-field generator parts, power tools, pharmaceuticals, synthetic textiles. The Company didn't need to carry Zarathustra any more; Zarathustra could carry the Company, and itself.

Fifteen years ago, when the Zarathustra Company had sent him here, there had been a cluster of log and prefab huts beside an improvised landing field, almost exactly where this skyscraper now stood. Today, Mallorysport was a city of seventy thousand; in all, the planet had a population of nearly a million, and it was still growing. There were steel mills and chemical plants and reaction plants and machine works. They produced all their own fissionables, and had recently begun to export a little refined plutonium; they had even started producing collapsium shielding.

The recorded voice stopped. He ran back the spool, set for sixty-speed, and transmitted it to the radio office. In twenty minutes, a copy would be aboard the ship that would hyper out for Terra that night. While he was finishing, his communication screen buzzed.

"Dr. Kellogg's screening you, Mr. Grego," the girl in the outside office told him.

He nodded. Her hands moved, and she vanished in a polychromatic explosion; when it cleared, the chief of the Division of Scientific Study and Research was looking out of the screen instead. Looking slightly upward at the showback over his own screen, Victor was getting his warm, sympathetic, sincere and slightly too toothy smile on straight.

"Hello, Leonard. Everything going all right?"

It either was and Leonard Kellogg wanted more credit than he deserved or it wasn't and he was trying to get somebody else blamed for it before anybody could blame him.

"Good afternoon, Victor." Just the right shade of deference about using the first name—big wheel to bigger wheel. "Has Nick Emmert been talking to you about the Big Blackwater project today?"

Nick was the Federation's resident-general; on Zarathustra he was, to all intents and purposes, the Terran Federation Government. He was also a large stockholder in the chartered Zarathustra Company.

"No. Is he likely to?"

"Well, I wondered, Victor. He was on my screen just now. He says there's some adverse talk about the effect on the rainfall in the Piedmont area of Beta Continent. He was worried about it."

"Well, it would affect the rainfall. After all, we drained half a million square miles of swamp, and the prevailing winds are from the west. There'd be less atmospheric moisture to the east of it. Who's talking adversely about it, and what worries Nick?"

"Well, Nick's afraid of the effect on public opinion on Terra, You know how strong conservation sentiment is; everybody's very much opposed to any sort of destructive exploitation."

"Good Lord! The man doesn't call the creation of five hundred thousand square miles of new farmland destructive exploitation, does he?"

"Well, no, Nick doesn't call it that; of course not. But he's concerned about some garbled story getting to Terra about our upsetting the ecological balance and causing droughts. Fact is, I'm rather concerned myself."

He knew what was worrying both of them. Emmert was afraid the Federation Colonial Office would blame him for drawing fire on them from the conservationists. Kellogg was afraid he'd be blamed for not predicting the effects before his division endorsed the project. As a division chief, he had advanced as far as he would in the Company hierarchy; now he was on a Red Queen's racetrack, running like hell to stay in the same place.

"The rainfall's dropped ten per cent from last year, and fifteen per cent from the year before that," Kellogg was saying. "And some non-Company people have gotten hold of it, and so had Interworld News. Why, even some of my people are talking about ecological side-effects. You know what will happen when a story like that gets back to Terra. The conservation fanatics will get hold of it, and the Company'll be criticized."

That would hurt Leonard. He identified himself with the Company. It was something bigger and more powerful than he was, like God.

Victor Grego identified the Company with himself. It was something big and powerful, like a vehicle, and he was at the controls.

"Leonard, a little criticism won't hurt the Company," he said. "Not where it matters, on the dividends. I'm afraid you're too sensitive to criticism. Where did Emmert get this story anyhow? From your people?"

"No, absolutely not, Victor. That's what worries him. It was this man Rainsford who started it."

"Rainsford?"

Dr. Bennett Rainsford, the naturalist. Institute of Zeno-Sciences. I never trusted any of those people; they always poke their noses into things, and the Institute always reports their findings to the Colonial Office."

"I know who you mean now; little fellow with red whiskers, always looks as though he'd been sleeping in his clothes. Why, of course the Zeno-Sciences people poke their noses into things, and of course they report their findings to the government." He was beginning to lose patience. "I don't see what all this is about, Leonard. This man Rainsford just made a routine observation of meteorological effects. I suggest you have your meteorologists check it, and if it's correct pass it on to the news services along with your other scientific findings."

"Nick Emmert thinks Rainsford is a Federation undercover agent."

That made him laugh. Of course there were undercover agents on Zarathustra, hundreds of them. The Company had people here checking on him; he knew and accepted that. So did the big stockholders, like Interstellar Explorations and the Banking Cartel and Terra Baldur-Marduk Spacelines. Nick Emmert had his corps of spies and stool pigeons, and the Terran Federation had people here watching both him and Emmert. Rainsford could be a Federation agent—a roving naturalist would have a wonderful cover occupation. But this Big Blackwater business was so utterly silly. Nick Emmert had too much graft on his conscience; it was too bad that overloaded consciences couldn't blow fuses.

"Suppose he is, Leonard. What could he report on us? We are a chartered company, and we have an excellent legal department, which keeps us safely inside our charter. It is a very liberal charter, too. This is a Class-III uninhabited planet; the Company owns the whole thing outright. We can do anything we want as long as we don't violate colonial law or the Federation Constitution. As long as we don't do that, Nick Emmert hasn't anything to worry about. Now forget this whole damned business, Leonard!" He was beginning to speak sharply, and Kellogg was looking hurt. "I know you were concerned about injurious reports getting back to Terra, and that was quite commendable, but . . ."

By the time he got through, Kellogg was happy again. Victor blanked the screen, leaned back in his chair and began laughing. In a moment, the screen buzzed again. When he snapped it on, his screen-girl said:

"Mr. Henry Stenson's on, Mr. Grego."

"Well, put him on." He caught himself just before adding that it would be a welcome change to talk to somebody with sense.

The face that appeared was elderly and thin; the mouth was tight, and there were squint-wrinkles at the corners of the eyes.

"Well, Mr. Stenson. Good of you to call. How are you?"

"Very well, thank you. And you?" When he also admitted to good health, the caller continued: "How is the globe running? Still in synchronization?"

Victor looked across the office at his most prized possession, the big globe of Zarathustra that Henry Stenson had built for him, supported six feet from the floor on its own contragravity unit, spotlighted in orange to represent the KO sun, its two satellites circling about it as it revolved slowly.

"The globe itself is keeping perfect time, and Darius is all right, Xerxes is a few seconds of longitude ahead of true position."

"That's dreadful, Mr. Grego!" Stenson was deeply shocked. "I must adjust that the first thing tomorrow. I should have called to check on it long ago, but you know how it is. So many things to do, and so little time."

"I find the same trouble myself, Mr. Stenson."

They chatted for a while, and then Stenson apologized for taking up so much of Mr. Grego's valuable time. What he meant was that his own time, just as valuable to him, was wasting. After the screen blanked, Grego sat looking at it for a moment, wishing he had a hundred men like Henry Stenson in his own organization. Just men with Stenson's brains and character; wishing for a hundred instrument makers with Stenson's skills would have been unreasonable, even for wishing. There was only one Henry Stenson, just as there had been only one Antonio Stradivari. Why a man like that worked in a little shop on a frontier planet like Zarathustra . . .

Then he looked, pridefully, at the globe. Alpha Continet had moved slowly to the right, with the little speck that represented Mallorysport twinkling in the orange light. Darius, the inner moon, where the Terra-Baldur-Marduk Spacelines had their leased terminal, was almost directly over it, and the other moon, Xerxes, was edging into sight. Xerxes was the one thing about Zarathustra that the Company didn't own; the Terran Federation had retained that as a naval base. It was the one reminder that there was something bigger and more powerful than the Company.

Gerd van Riebeek saw Ruth Ortheris leave the escalator, step aside and stand looking around the cocktail lounge. He set his glass, with its inch of tepid highball, on the bar; when her eyes shifted in his direction, he waved to her, saw her brighten and wave back and then went to meet her. She gave him a quick kiss on the cheek, dodged when he reached for her and took his arm.

"Drink before we eat?" he asked.

"Oh, Lord, yes! I've just about had it for today."

He guided her toward one of the bartending machines, inserted his credit key, and put a four-portion jug under the spout, dialing the cocktail they always had when they drank together. As he did, he noticed what she was wearing: short black jacket, lavender neckerchief, light gray skirt. Not her usual vacation get-up.

"School department drag you back?" he asked as the jug filled.

"Juvenile court." She got a couple of glasses from the shelf under the machine as he picked up the jug. "A fifteen-year-old burglar."

They found a table at the rear of the room, out of the worst of the cocktail-hour uproar. As soon as he filled her glass, she drank half of it, then lit a cigarette.

"Junktown?" he asked.

She nodded. "Only twenty-five years since this planet was discovered, and we have slums already. I was over there most of the afternoon, with a pair of city police." She didn't seem to want to talk about it. "What were you doing today?"

"Ruth, you ought to ask Doc Mallin to drop in on Leonard Kellogg sometime, and give him an unobstrusive going over."

"You haven't been having trouble with him again?" she asked anxiously.

He made a face, and then tasted his drink. "It's trouble just being around that character. Ruth, to use one of those expressions your profession deplores, Len Kellogg is just plain nuts!" He drank some more of his cocktail and helped himself to one of her cigarettes. "Here," he continued, after lighting it. "A couple of days ago, he told me he'd been getting inquiries about this plague of land-prawns they're having over on Beta. He wanted me to set up a research project to find out why and what do do about it."

"Well?"

"I did. I made two screen calls, and then I wrote a report and sent it up to him. That was where I jerked my trigger; I ought to have taken a couple of weeks and made a real production out of it."

"What did you tell him?"

"The facts. The limiting factor on land-prawn increase is the weather. The eggs hatch underground and the immature prawns dig their way out in the spring. If there's been a lot of rain, most of them drown in their holes or as soon as they emerge. According to growth rings on trees, last spring was the driest in the Beta Piedmont in centuries, so most of them survived, and as they're parthenogenetic females, they all laid eggs. This spring, it was even drier, so now they have land prawns all over central Beta. And I don't know that anything can be done about them."

"Well, did he think you were just guessing?"

He shook his head in exasperation. "I don't know what he thinks. You're the psychologist, you try to figure it. I sent him that report yesterday morning. He seemed quite satisfied with it at the time. Today, just after noon, he sent for me and told me it wouldn't do at all. Tried to insist that the rainfall on Beta had been normal. That was silly; I referred him to his meteorologists and climatologists, where I'd gotten my information. He complained that the news services were after him for an explanation. I told him I'd given him the only explanation there was. He said he simply couldn't use it. There had to be some other explanation."

"If you don't like the facts, you ignore them, and if you need facts, dream up some you do like," she said. "That's typical rejection of reality. Not psychotic, not even psychoneurotic. But certainly not sane." She had finished her first drink and was sipping slowly at her second. "You know, this is interesting. Does he have some theory that would disqualify yours?"

"Not that I know of. I got the impression that he just didn't want the subject of rainfall on Beta discussed at all."

"That is odd. Has anything else peculiar been happening over on Beta lately?"

"No. Not that I know of," he repeated. "Of course, that swamp-drainage project over there was what caused the dry weather, last year and this year, but

I don't see . . ." His own glass was empty, and when he tilted the jug over it, a few drops trickled out. He looked at his watch. "Think we could have another cocktail before dinner?" he asked.

II

Jack Holloway landed the manipulator in front of the cluster of prefab huts. For a moment he sat still, realizing that he was tired, and then he climbed down from the control cabin and crossed the open grass to the door of the main living hut, opening it and reaching in to turn on the lights. Then he hesitated, looking up at Darius.

There was a wide ring around it, and he remembered noticing the wisps of cirrus clouds gathering overhead through the afternoon. Maybe it would rain tonight. This dry weather couldn't last forever. He'd been letting the manipulator stand out overnight lately. He decided to put it in the hangar. He went and opened the door of the vehicle shed, got back onto the machine and floated it inside. When he came back to the living hut, he saw that he had left the door wide open.

"Damn fool!" he rebuked himself. "Place could be crawling with prawns by now."

He looked quickly around the living room—under the big combination desk and library table, under the gunrack, under the chairs, back of the communication screen and the viewscreen, beyond the metal cabinet of the microfilm library—and saw nothing. Then he hung up his hat, took off his pistol and laid it on the table, and went back to the bathroom to wash his hands.

As soon as he put on the light, something inside the

shower stall said, "Yeeeek!" in a startled voice.

He turned quickly to see two wide eyes staring up at him out of a ball of golden fur. Whatever it was, it had a round head and big ears and a vaguely humanoid face with a little snub nose. It was sitting on its haunches, and in that position it was about a foot high. It had two tiny hands with opposing thumbs. He squatted to have a better look at it.

"Hello there, little fellow," he greeted it. "I never saw anything like you before. What are you anyhow?"

The small creature looked at him seriously and said, "Yeek," in a timid voice.

"Why, sure; you're a Little Fuzzy, that's what you are."

He moved closer, careful to make no alarmingly sudden movements, and kept on talking to it.

"Bet you slipped in while I left the door open. Well, if a Little Fuzzy finds a door open, I'd like to know why he shouldn't come in and look around."

He touched it gently. It started to draw back, then reached out a little hand and felt the material of his shirt-sleeve. He stroked it, and told it that it had the softest, silkiest fur ever. Then he took it on his lap. It yeeked in pleasure, and stretched an arm up around his neck.

"Why, sure; we're going to be good friends, aren't we? Would you like something to eat? Well, suppose you and I go see what we can find."

He put one hand under it, to support it like a baby—at least, he seemed to recall having seen babies supported in that way; babies were things he didn't fool with if he could help it—and straightened. It weighed between fifteen and twenty pounds. At first, it struggled in panic, then quieted and seemed to enjoy being carried. In the living room he sat down in his favorite armchair, under a standing lamp, and examined his new acquaintance.

It was a mammal—there was a fairly large mammalian class on Zarathustra—but beyond that he was stumped. It wasn't a primate, in the Terran sense. It wasn't like anything Terran, or anything else on Zarathustra. Being a biped put it in a class by itself for this planet. It was just a Little Fuzzy, and that was the best he could do.

That sort of nomenclature was the best anybody could do on a Class-III planet. On a Class-IV planet, say Loki, or Shesha, or Thor, naming animals was a cinch. You pointed to something and asked a native, and he'd gargle a mouthful of syllables at you, which might only mean, "Whaddaya wanna know for?" and you took it down in phonetic alphabet and the whatzit had a name. But on Zarathustra, there were no natives to ask. So this was a Little Fuzzy.

"What would you like to eat, Little Fuzzy?" he asked. "Open your mouth, and let Pappy Jack see what you have to chew with."

Little Fuzzy's dental equipment, allowing for the fact that his jaw was rounder, was very much like his own.

"You're probably omnivorous. How would you like some nice Terran Federation Space Forces Emergency Ration, Extraterrestrial, Type Three?" he asked.

Little Fuzzy made what sounded like an expression of willingness to try it. It would be safe enough; Extee Three had been fed to a number of Zarathustran mammals without ill effects. He carried Little Fuzzy out into the kitchen and put him on the floor, then got out a tin of the field ration and opened it, breaking off a small piece and handing it down. Little Fuzzy took the piece of golden-brown cake, sniffed at it, gave a delighted yeek and crammed the whole piece in his mouth.

"You never had to live on that stuff and nothing else for a month, that's for sure!"

He broke the cake in half and broke one half into manageable pieces and put it down on a saucer. Maybe Little Fuzzy would want a drink, too. He started to fill a pan with water, as he would for a dog, then looked at his visitor sitting on his haunches eating with both hands and changed his mind. He rinsed a plastic cup cap from an empty whisky bottle and put it down beside a deep bowl of water. Little Fuzzy was thirsty, and he didn't have to be shown what the cup was for.

It was too late to get himself anything elaborate; he found some leftovers in the refrigerator and combined them into a stew. While it was heating, he sat down at the kitchen table and lit his pipe. The spurt of flame from the lighter opened Little Fuzzy's eyes, but what really awed him was Pappy Jack blowing smoke. He sat watching this phenomenon, until, a few minutes later, the stew was hot and the pipe was laid aside; then Little Fuzzy went back to nibbling Extee Three.

Suddenly he gave a yeek of petulance and scampered into the living room. In a moment, he was back with something elongated and metallic which he laid on the floor beside him.

"What have you got there, Little Fuzzy? Let Pappy Jack see?"

Then he recognized it as his own one-inch wood chisel. He remembered leaving it in the outside shed after doing some work about a week ago, and not being able to find it when he had gone to look for it. That had worried him; people who got absent-minded about equipment didn't last long in the wilderness. After he finished eating and took the dishes to the sink, he went over and squatted beside his new friend.

"Let Pappy Jack look at it, Little Fuzzy," he said. "Oh, I'm not going to take it away from you. I just want to see it."

The edge was dulled and nicked; it had been used for a lot of things wood chisels oughtn't to be used for. Digging, and prying, and most likely, it had been used as a weapon. It was a handy-sized, all-purpose tool for a Little Fuzzy. He laid it on the floor where he had gotten it and started washing the dishes.

Little Fuzzy watched him with interest for a while, and then he began investigating the kitchen. Some of the things he wanted to investigate had to be taken away from him; at first that angered him, but he soon learned that there were things he wasn't supposed to have. Eventually, the dishes got washed.

There were more things to investigate in the living room. One of them was the wastebasket. He found that it could be dumped, and promptly dumped it, pulling out everything that hadn't fallen out. He bit a corner off a sheet of paper, chewed on it and spat it out in disgust. Then he found that crumpled paper could be flattened out and so he flattened a few sheets, and then discovered that it could also be folded. Then he got himself gleefully tangled in a snarl of wornout recording tape. Finally he lost interest and started away. Jack caught him and brought him back.

"No, Little Fuzzy," he said. "You do not dump wastebaskets and then walk away from them. You put things back in." He touched the container and said, slowly and distinctly, "Waste... basket." Then he righted it, doing it as Little Fuzzy would have to, and picked up a piece of paper, tossing it in from Little Fuzzy's shoulder height. Then he handed Little Fuzzy a wad of paper and repeated, "Waste... basket."

Little Fuzzy looked at him and said something that sounded as though it might be: "What's the matter with you, Pappy; you crazy or something?" After a couple more tries, however, he got it, and began throwing things in. In a few minutes, he had everything back in except a brightly colored plastic cartridge box and a wide-mouthed bottle with a screw cap. He held these up and said, "Yeek?"

"Yes, you can have them. Here; let Pappy Jack show you something."

He showed Little Fuzzy how the box could be opened and shut. Then, holding it where Little Fuzzy could watch, he unscrewed the cap and then screwed it on again.

"There, now. You try it."

Little Fuzzy looked up inquiringly, then took the

bottle, sitting down and holding it between his knees. Unfortunately, he tried twisting it the wrong way and only screwed the cap on tighter. He yeeked plaintively.

"No, go ahead. You can do it."

Little Fuzzy looked at the bottle again. Then he tried twisting the cap the other way, and it loosened. He gave a yeek that couldn't possibly be anything but "Eureka!" and promptly took it off, holding it up. After being commended, he examined both the bottle and the cap, feeling the threads, and then screwed the cap back on again.

"You know, you're a smart Little Fuzzy." It took a few seconds to realize just how smart. Little Fuzzy had wondered why you twisted the cap one way to take it off and the other way to put it on, and he had found out. For pure reasoning ability, that topped anything in the way of animal intelligence he'd ever seen. "I'm going to tell Ben Rainsford about you."

Going to the communication screen, he punched out the wave-length combination of the naturalists's camp, seventy miles down Snake River from the mouth of Cold Creek. Rainsford's screen must have been on automatic; it lit as soon as he was through punching. There was a card set up in front of it, lettered: AWAY ON TRIP, BACK THE FIFTEENTH. RECORDER ON.

"Ben, Jack Holloway," he said. "I just ran into something interesting." He explained briefly what it was. "I hope he stays around till you get back. He's totally unlike anything I've ever seen on this planet."

Little Fuzzy was disappointed when Jack turned off the screen; that had been interesting. He picked him up and carried him over to the armchair, taking him on his lap.

"Now," he said, reaching for the control panel of the viewscreen. "Watch this; we're going to see something nice."

When he put on the screen, at random, he got a view, from close up, of the great fires that were raging where the Company people were burning off the dead forests on what used to be Big Blackwater Swamp. Little Fuzzy cried out in alarm, flung his arms around Pappy Jack's neck and buried his face in the bosom of his shirt. Well, forest fires started from lightning somethimes, and they'd be bad things for a Little Fuzzy. He worked the selector and got another pickup, this time on the top of Company House in Mallorysport, three time zones west, with the city spread out below and the sunset blazing in the west. Little Fuzzy stared at it in wonder. It was pretty impressive for a little fellow who'd spent all his life in the big woods.

So was the spaceport, and a lot of other things he saw, though a view of the planet as a whole from Darius puzzled him considerably. Then, in the middle of a symphony orchestra concert from Mallorysport Opera House, he wriggled loose, dropped to the floor and caught up his wood chisel, swinging it back over his shoulder like a two-handed sword.

"What the devil? Oh-oh!"

A land-prawn, which must have gotten in while the door was open, was crossing the living room. Little Fuzzy ran after and past it, pivoted and brought the corner of the chisel edge down on the prawn's neck, neatly beheading it. He looked at his victim for a moment, then slid the chisel under it and flopped it over on its back, slapping it twice with the flat and cracking the undershell. The he began pulling the dead prawn apart, tearing out pieces of meat and eating them delicately. After disposing of the larger chunks, he used the chisel to chop off one of the prawn's mandibles to use as a pick to get at the less accessible morsels. When he had finished, he licked his fingers clean and started back to the armchair.

"No." Jack pointed at the prawn shell. "Wastebasket."

"Yeek?"

"Wastebasket."

Little Fuzzy gathered up the bits of shell, putting

them where they belonged. Then he came back and climbed up on Pappy Jack's lap, and looked at things in the screen until he fell asleep.

Jack lifted him carefully and put him down on the warm chair seat without wakening him, then went to the kitchen, poured himself a drink and brought it in to the big table, where he lit his pipe and began writing up his diary for the day. After a while, Little Fuzzy woke, found that the lap he had gone to sleep on had vanished, and yeeked disconsolately.

A folded blanket in one corner of the bedroom made a satisfactory bed, once Little Fuzzy had assured himself that there were no bugs in it. He brought in his bottle and his plastic box and put them on the floor beside it. Then he ran to the front door in the living room and yeeked to be let out. Going about twenty feet from the house, he used the chisel to dig a small hole, and after it had served its purpose he filled it in carefully and came running back.

Well, maybe Fuzzies were naturally gregarious, and were homemakers—den-holes, or nests, or something like that. Nobody wants messes made in the house, and when the young ones did it, their parents would bang them around to teach them better manners. This was Little Fuzzy's home now; he knew how he ought to behave in it.

The next morning at daylight, he was up on the bed, trying to dig Pappy Jack out from under the blankets. Besides being a most efficient land-prawn eradicator, he made a first rate alarm clock. But best of all, he was Pappy Jack's Little Fuzzy. He wanted out; this time Jack took his movie camera and got the whole operation on film. One thing, there'd have to be a little door, with a spring to hold it shut, that little Fuzzy could operate himself. That was designed during breakfast. It only took a couple of hours to make and install it; Little Fuzzy got the idea as soon as he saw it, and figured out how to work it for himself.

Jack went back to the workshop, built a fire on the hand forge and forged a pointed and rather broad blade, four inches long, on the end of a foot of quarter-inch round tool-steel. It was too point-heavy when finished, so he welded a knob on the other end to balance it. Little Fuzzy knew what that was for right away; running outside, he dug a couple of practice holes with it, and then began casting about in the grass for land-prawns.

Jack followed him with the camera and got movies of a couple of prawn killings, accomplished with smooth, by-the-numbers precision. Little Fuzzy hadn't learned that chop-clap-clap routine in the week since he had found the wood chisel.

Going into the shed, he hunted for something without more than a general idea of what it would look like, and found it where Little Fuzzy had discarded it when he found the chisel. It was a stock of hardwood a foot long, rubbed down and polished smooth, apparently with sandstone. There was a paddle at one end, with enough of an edge to behead a prawn, and the other end had been worked to a point. He took it into the living hut and sat down at the desk to examine it with a magnifying glass. Bits of soil embedded in the sharp end—that had been used as a pick. The paddle end had been used as a shovel, beheader and shell-cracker. Little Fuzzy had known exactly what he wanted when he'd started making that thing, he'd kept on until it was as perfect as possible, and had stopped short of spoiling it by overrefinement.

Finally, Jack put it away in the top drawer of the desk. He was thinking about what to get for lunch when Little Fuzzy burst into the living room, clutching his new weapon and yeeking excitedly.

"What's the matter, kid? You got troubles?" He rose and went to the gunrack, picking down a rifle and checking the chamber. "Show Pappy Jack what it is."

Little Fuzzy followed him to the big door for human-type people, ready to bolt back inside if necessary.

The trouble was a harpy—a thing about the size and general design of a Terran Jurassic pteradactyl, big enough to take a Little Fuzzy at one mouthful. It must have made one swoop at him already, and was circling back for another. It ran into a 6-mm rifle bullet, went into a backward loop and dropped like a stone.

Little Fuzzy made a very surprised remark, looked at the dead harpy for a moment and then spotted the ejected empty cartridge. He grabbed it and held it up, asking if he could have it. When told that he could, he ran back to the bedroom with it. When he returned, Pappy Jack picked him up and carried him to the hangar and up into the control cabin of the manipulator.

The throbbing of the contragravity-field generator and the sense of rising worried him at first, but after they had picked up the harpy with the grapples and risen to five hundred feet he began to enjoy the ride. They dropped the harpy a couple of miles up what the latest maps were designating as Holloway's Run, and then made a wide circle back over the mountains. Little Fuzzy thought it was fun.

After lunch, Little Fuzzy had a nap on Pappy Jack's bed. Jack took the manipulator up to the diggings, put off a couple more shots, uncovered more flint and found another sunstone. It wasn't often that he found stones on two successive days. When he returned to the camp, Little Fuzzy was picking another landprawn apart in front of the living hut.

After dinner—Little Fuzzy liked cooked food, too, if it wasn't too hot—they went into the living room. He remembered having seen a bolt and nut in the desk drawer when he had been putting the wooden prawnkiller away, and he got it out, showing it to Little Fuzzy. Little Fuzzy studied it for a moment, then ran into the bedroom and came back with his screw-top bottle. He took the top off, put it on again and then screwed the nut off the bolt, holding it up.

"See, Pappy?" Or yeeks to that effect. "Nothing to

it."

Then he unscrewed the bottle top, dropped the bolt inside after replacing the nut and screwed the cap on again.

"Yeek," he said, with considerable self-satisfaction.

He had a right to be satisfied with himself. What he'd been doing had been generalizing. Bottle tops and nuts belonged to the general class of things-that-screwed-onto-things. To take them off, you turned left; to put them on again, you turned right, after making sure that the threads engaged. And since he could conceive of right- and left-handedness, that might mean that he could think of properties apart from objects, and that was forming abstract ideas. Maybe that was going a little far, but . . .

"You know, Pappy Jack's got himself a mighty smart Little Fuzzy. Are you a grown-up Little Fuzzy, or are you just a baby Little Fuzzy? Shucks, I'll bet you're Professor Doctor Fuzzy."

He wondered what to give the professor, if that was what he was, to work on next, and he doubted the wisdom of teaching him too much about taking things apart, just at present. Sometime he might come home and find something important taken apart, or, worse, taken apart and put together incorrectly. Finally, he went to a closet, rummaging in it until he found a tin cannister. By the time he returned, Little Fuzzy had gotten up on the chair, found his pipe in the ashtray and was puffing on it and coughing.

"Hey, I don't think that's good for you!"

He recovered the pipe, wiped the stem on his shirt-sleeve and put it in his mouth, then placed the cannister on the floor, and put Little Fuzzy on the floor beside it. There were about ten pounds of stones in it. When he had first settled here, he had made a collection of the local minerals, and, after learning what he'd wanted to, he had thrown them out, all but twenty or thirty of the prettiest specimens. He was glad, now, that he had kept these.

Little Fuzzy looked the can over, decided that the lid was a member of the class of things-that-screwed-onto-things and got it off. The inside of the lid was mirror-shiny, and it took him a little thought to discover that what he saw in it was only himself. He yeeked about that, and looked into the can. This, he decided, belonged to the class of things-that-can-be-dumped, like wastebaskets, so he dumped it on the floor. Then he began examining the stones and sorting them by color.

Except for an interest in colorful views on the screen, this was the first real evidence that Fuzzies possessed color perception. He proceeded to give further and more impressive proof, laying out the stones by shade, in correct spectral order, from a lump of amethystlike quartz to a dark red stone. Well, maybe he'd seen rainbows. Maybe he'd lived near a big misty waterfall, where there was always a rainbow when the sun was shining. Or maybe that was just his natural way of seeing colors.

Then, when he saw what he had to work with, he began making arrangements with them, laying them out in odd circular and spiral patterns. Each time he finished a pattern, he would yeek happily to call attention to it, sit and look at it for a while, and then take it apart and start a new one. Little Fuzzy was capable of artistic gratification too. He made useless things, just for the pleasure of making and looking at them.

Finally, he put the stones back into the tin, put the lid on and rolled it into the bedroom, righting it beside his bed along with his other treasures. The new weapon he laid on the blanket beside him when he went to bed.

The next morning, Jack broke up a whole cake of Extee Three and put it down, filled the bowl with water, and, after making sure he had left nothing lying around that Littly Fuzzy could damage or on which he might hurt himself, took the manipulator up to the diggings. He worked all morning, cracking nearly a ton and a half of flint, and found nothing. Then he set off a string of shots, brought down an avalanche of sandstone and exposed more flint, and sat down under a pool-ball tree to eat his lunch.

Half an hour after he went back to work, he found the fossil of some jellyfish that hadn't eaten the right things in the right combinations, but a little later, he found four nodules, one after another, and two of them were sunstones; four or five chunks later, he found a third. Why, this must be the Dying Place of the Jellyfish! By late afternoon, when he had cleaned up all his loose flint, he had nine, including one deep red monster an inch in diameter. There must have been some connection current in the ancient ocean that had swirled them all into this one place. He considered setting off some more shots, decided that it was too late and returned to camp.

"Little Fuzzy!" he called, opening the living-room door. "Where are you, Little Fuzzy? Pappy Jack's rich; we're going to celebrate!"

Silence. He called again; still no reply or scamper of feet. Probably cleaned up all the prawns around the camp and went hunting farther out into the woods, thought Jack. Unbuckling his gun and dropping it onto the table, he went out to the kitchen. Most of the Extee Three was gone. In the bedroom, he found that Little Fuzzy had dumped the stones out of the biscuit tin and made an arrangement, and laid the wood chisel in a neat diagonal across the blanket.

After getting dinner assembled and in the oven, he went out and called for a while, then mixed a highball and took it into the living room, sitting down with it to go over his day's findings. Rather incredulously, he realized that he had cracked out at least seventy-five thousand sols' worth of stones today. He put them into the bag and sat sipping the highball and thinking pleasant thoughts until the bell on the stove warned him that dinner was ready.

He ate alone—after all the years he had been doing that contentedly, it had suddenly become intolerable—and in the evening he dialed through his microfilm library, finding only books he had read and reread a dozen times, or books he kept for reference. Several times he thought he heard the little door open, but each time he was mistaken. Finally he went to bed.

As soon as he woke, he looked across at the folded blanket, but the wood chisel was still lying athwart it. He put down more Extee Three and changed the water in the bowl before leaving for the diggings. That day he found three more sunstones, and put them in the bag mechanically and without pleasure. He quit work early and spent over an hour spiraling around the camp, but saw nothing. The Extee Three in the kitchen was untouched.

Maybe the little fellow ran into something too big for him, even with his fine new weapon—a hobthrush, or a bush-goblin, or another harpy. Or maybe he'd just gotten tired staying in one place, and had moved on.

No; he'd liked it here. He'd had fun, and been happy. He shook his head sadly. Once he, too, had lived in a pleasant place, where he'd had fun, and could have been happy if he hadn't thought there was something he'd had to do. So he had gone away, leaving grieved people behind him. Maybe that was how it was with Little Fuzzy. Maybe he didn't realize how much of a place he had made for himself here, or how empty he was leaving it.

He started for the kitchen to get a drink, and checked himself. Take a drink because you pity youself, and then the drink pities you and has a drink, and then two good drinks get together and that calls for drinks all around. No; he'd have one drink, maybe a little bigger than usual, before he went to bed.

III

He started awake, rubbed his eyes and looked at the clock. Past twenty-two hundred; now it really was time for a drink, and then to bed. He rose stiffly and went out to the kitchen, pouring the whisky and bringing it in to the table desk, where he sat down and got out his diary. He was almost finished with the day's entry when the little door behind him opened and a small voice said, "Yeeek." He turned quickly.

"Little Fuzzy?"

The small sound was repeated, impatiently. Little Fuzzy was holding the door open, and there was an answer from outside. Then another Fuzzy came in, and another; four of them, one carrying a tiny, squirming ball of white fur in her arms. They all had prawn-killers like the one in the drawer, and they stopped just inside the room and gaped about them in bewilderment. Then, laying down his weapon, Little Fuzzy ran to him; stooping from the chair, he caught him and then sat down on the floor with him.

"So that's why you ran off and worried Pappy Jack? You wanted your family here, too!"

The others piled the things they were carrying with Little Fuzzy's steel weapon and approached hesitantly. He talked to them, and so did Little Fuzzy—at least it sounded like that—and finally one came over and fingered his shirt, and then reached up and pulled his mustache. Soon all of them were climbing onto him, even the female with the baby. It was small enough to sit on his palm, but in a minute it had climbed to his shoulder, and then it was sitting on his head.

"You people want dinner?" he asked.

Little Fuzzzy yeeked emphatically; that was a word he recognized. He took them all into the kitchen and tried them on cold roast veldbeest and yummiyams and fried pool-ball fruit; while they were eating from a couple of big pans, he went back to the living room to examine the things they had brought with them. Two of the prawn-killers were wood, like the one Little Fuzzy had discarded in the shed. A third was of horn, beautifully polished, and the fourth looked as though it had been made from the shoulder bone of something like a zebralope. Then there was a small *coup de poing* ax, rather low paleolithic, and a chipped implement of flint the shape of a slice of orange and about five inches along the straight edge. For a hand the size of his own, he would have called it a scraper. He puzzled over it for a while, noticed that the edge was serrated, and decided that it was a saw. And there were three very good flake knives, and some shells, evidently drinking vessels.

Mamma Fuzzy came in while he was finishing the examination. She seemed suspicious, until she saw that none of the family property had been taken or damaged. Baby Fuzzy was clinging to her fur with one hand and holding a slice of pool-ball fruit, on which he was munching, with the other. He crammed what was left of the fruit into his mouth, climbed up on Jack and sat down on his head again. Have to do something to break him of that. One of these days, he'd be getting too big for it.

In a few minutes, the rest of the family came in, chasing and pummeling each other and yeeking happily. Mama jumped off his lap and joined the free-for-all, and then Baby took off from his head and landed on Mama's back. And he thought he'd lost his Little Fuzzy, and, gosh, here he had five Fuzzies and a Baby

Fuzzy. When they were tired romping, he made beds for them in the living room, and brought out Little Fuzzy's bedding and his treasures. One Little Fuzzy in the bedroom was just fine; five and a Baby Fuzzy were a little too much of a good thing.

They were swarming over the bed, Baby and all, to waken him the next morning.

The next morning he made a steel chopper-digger for each of them, and half a dozen extras for replacements in case more Fuzzies showed up. He also made a miniature ax with a hardwood handle, a handsaw out of a piece of broken power-saw blade and half a dozen little knives forged in one piece from quarter-inch coil-spring material. He had less trouble trading the Fuzzies' own things away from them than he had expected. They had a very keen property sense, but they knew a good deal when one was offered. He put the wooden and horn and bone and stone artifacts away in the desk drawer. Start of the Holloway Collection of Zarathustran Fuzzy Weapons and Implements. Maybe he'd will it to the Federation Institute of Xeno-Sciences.

Of course, the family had to try out the new chopper-diggers on land-prawns, and he followed them around with the movie camera. They killed a dozen and a half that morning, and there was very little interest in lunch, though they did sit around nibbling, just to be doing what he was doing. As soon as they finished, they all went in for a nap on his bed. He spent the afternoon pottering about camp doing odd jobs that he had been postponing for months. The Fuzzies all emerged in the late afternoon for a romp in the grass outside.

He was in the kitchen, getting dinner, when they all came pelting in through the little door into the living room, making an excited outcry. Little Fuzzy and one of the other males came into the kitchen. Little Fuzzy squatted, put one hand on his lower jaw, with thumb and little finger extended, and the other on his forehead, first finger upright. Then he thrust out his right arm stiffly and made a barking noise of a sort he had never made before. He had to do it a second time before Jack got it.

There was a large and unpleasant carnivore, called a damnthing—another example of zoological nomenclature on uninhabited planets—which had a single horn on its forehead and one on either side of the lower jaw. It was something for Fuzzies, and even for human-type people, to get excited about. He laid down the paring knife and the yummiyam he had been peeling, wiped his hands and went into the living room, taking a quick nose count and satisfying himself that none of the family were missing as he crossed to the gunrack.

This time, instead of the 6-mm he had used on the harpy, he lifted down a big 12.7 double express, making sure that it was loaded and pocketing a few spare rounds. Little Fuzzy followed him outside, pointing around the living hut to the left. The rest of the family stayed indoors.

Stepping out about twenty feet, he started around counter-clockwise. There was no damnthing on the north side, and he was about to go around to the east side when Little Fuzzy came dashing past him, pointing to the rear. He whirled, to see the damnthing charging him from behind, head down, and middle horn lowered. He should have thought of that; damnthings would double and hunt their hunters.

He lined the sights instinctively and squeezed. The big rifle roared and banged his shoulder, and the bullet caught the damnthing and hurled all half-ton of it backward. The second shot caught it just below one of the fungoid-looking ears, and the beast gave a spasmotic all-over twitch and was still. He reloaded mechanically, but there was no need for a third shot. The damnthing was as dead as he would have been except for Little Fuzzy's warning.

He mentioned that to Little Fuzzy, who was calmly retrieving the empty cartridges. Then, rubbing his shoulder where the big rifle had pounded him, he went in and returned the weapon to the rack. He used the manipulator to carry the damnthing away from the camp and drop it into a treetop, where it would furnish a welcome if puzzling treat for the harpies.

There was another alarm in the evening after dinner, The family had come in from their sunset romp and were gathered in the living room, where Little Fuzzy was demonstrating the principle of things-that-screwed-onto-things with the wide-mouthed bottle and the bolt and nut, when something huge began hooting directly overhead. They all froze, looking up at the ceiling, and then ran over and got under the gunrack. This must be something far more serious than a damnthing, and what Pappy Jack would do about it would be nothing short of catastrophic. They were startled to see Pappy Jack merely go to the door, open it and step outside. After all, none of them had ever heard a Constabulary aircar klaxon before.

The car settled onto the grass in front of the camp, gave a slight lurch and went off contragravity. Two men in uniform got out, and in the moonlight he recognized both of them: Lieutenant George Lunt and his driver, Ahmed Khadra. He called a greeting to them.

"Anything wrong?" he asked.

"No; just thought we'd drop in and see how you were making out," Lunt told him. "We don't get up this way often. Haven't had any trouble lately, have you?"

"Not since the last time." The last time had been a couple of woods tramps, out-of-work veldbeest herders from the south, who had heard about the little bag he carried around his neck. All the Constabulary had needed to do was remove the bodies and write up a report. "Come on in and hang up your guns awhile. I have something I want to show you."

Little Fuzzy had come out and was pulling at his trouser leg; he stooped and picked him up, setting him on his shoulder. The rest of the family, deciding that it must be safe, had come to the door and were looking out.

"Hey! What the devil are those things?" Lunt asked, stopping short halfway from the car.

"Fuzzies. Mean to tell me you've never seen Fuzzies before?"

"No, I haven't. What are they?"

The two Constabulary men came closer, and Jack stepped back into the house, shooing the Fuzzies out of the way. Lunt and Khadra stopped inside the door.

"I just told you. They're Fuzzies. That's all the name I know for them."

A couple of Fuzzies came over and looked up at Lietenant Lunt; one of them said, "Yeek?"

"They want to know what you are, so that makes it mutual."

Lunt hesitated for a moment, then took off his belt and holster and hung it on one of the pegs inside the door, putting his beret over it. Khadra followed his example promptly. That meant that they considered themselves temporarily off duty and would accept a drink if one were offered. A Fuzzy was pulling at Ahmed Khadra's trouser leg and asking to be noticed, and Mamma Fuzzy was holding Baby up to show to Lunt. Khadra, rather hesitantly, picked up the Fuzzy who was trying to attract his attention.

"Never saw anything like them before Jack," he said. "Where did they come from?"

"Ahmed; you don't know anything about those things," Lunt reproved.

"They won't hurt me, Lieutenant; they haven't hurt Jack, have they?" He sat down on the floor, and a couple more came to him. "Why don't you get acquainted with them? They're cute."

George Lunt wouldn't let one of his men do anything he was afraid to do; he sat down on the floor, too, and

Mamma brought her baby to him. Immediately, the baby jumped onto his shoulder and tried to get onto his head.

"Relax, George," Jack told him, "They're just Fuzzies; they want to make friends with you."

"I'm always worried about strange life forms," Lunt said. "You've been around enough to know some of the things that have happened—"

"They are not a strange life form; they are Zarathustran mammals. The same life form you've had for dinner every day since you came here. Their biochemistry's identical with ours. Think they'll give you the Polka-Dot Plague, or something?" He put Little Fuzzy down on the floor with the others. "We've been exploring this planet for twenty-five years, and nobody's found anything like that here."

"You said it yourself, Lieutenant," Khadra put in. "Jack's been around enough to know."

"Well . . . They are cute little fellows." Lunt lifted Baby down off his head and gave him back to Mamma. Little Fuzzy had gotten hold of the chain of his whistle and was trying to find out what was on the other end. "Bet they're a lot of company for you."

"You just get acquainted with them. Make yourselves at home; I'll go rustle up some refreshments."

While he was in the kitchen, filling a soda siphon and getting ice out of the refrigerator, a police whistle began shrilling in the living room. He was opening a bottle of whisky when Little Fuzzy came dashing out, blowing on it, a couple more of the family pursuing him and trying to get it away from him. He opened a tin of Extee Three for the Fuzzies, as he did, another whistle in the living room began blowing.

"We have a whole shoebox full of them at the post," Lunt yelled to him above the din. "We'll just write these two off as expended in service."

"Well, that's real nice of you, George. I want to tell you that the Fuzzies appreciate that. Ahmed, suppose you do the bartending while I give the kids their candy."

By the time Khadra had the drinks mixed and he had distributed the Extee Three to the Fuzzies, Lunt had gotten into the easy chair, and the Fuzzies were sitting on the floor in front of him, still looking him over curiously. At least the Extee Three had taken their minds off the whistles for a while.

"What I want to know, Jack, is where they came from," Lunt said, taking his drink. "I've been up here for five years, and I never saw anything like them before."

"I've been here five years longer, and I never saw them before, either. I think they came down from the north, from the country between the Cordilleras and the West Coast Range. Outside of an air survey at ten thousand feet and a few spot landings here and there, none of that country has been explored. For all anybody knows, it could be full of Fuzzies."

He began with his first encounter with Little Fuzzy, and by the time he had gotten as far as the wood chisel and the killing of the land-prawn, Lunt and Khadra were looking at each other in amazement.

"That's it!" Khadra said. "I've found prawn-shells cracked open and the meat picked out, just the way you describe it. I always wondered what did that. But they don't all have wood chisels. What do you suppose they used ordinarily?"

"Ah!" He pulled the drawer open and began getting things out. "Here's the one Little Fuzzy discarded when he found my chisel. The rest of this stuff the others brought in when they came."

Lunt and Khadra rose and came over to look at the things. Lunt tried to argue that the Fuzzies couldn't have made that stuff. He wasn't even able to convince himself. Having finished their Extee Three, the Fuzzies were looking expectantly at the viewscreen, and it occurred to him that none of them except Little Fuzzy had ever seen it on. Then Little Fuzzy jumped up on the chair Lunt had vacated, reached over to the control-panel and switched it on. What he got was an empty stretch of moonlit plain to the south, from a pickup on one of the steel towers the veldbeest herders used. That wasn't very interesting; he twiddled the selector and finally got a night soccer game at Mallorysport. That was just fine; he jumped down and joined the others in front of the screen.

"I've seen Terran monkeys and Freyan Kholphs that liked to watch screens and could turn them on and work the selector," Lunt said. It sounded like the token last salvo before the surrender.

"Kholphs are smart," Khadra agreed. "They use tools,"

"Do they make tools? Or tools to make tools with, like that saw?" There was no argument on that. "No. Nobody does that except people like us and the Fuzzies.

It was the first time he had come right out and said that; the first time he had even consciously thought it. He realized that he had been convinced of it all along, though. It startled the constabulary lieutenant and trooper.

"You mean you think—?" Lunt began.

"They don't talk, and they don't build fires," Ahmed Khadra said, as though that settled it.

"Ahmed, you know better than that. That talk-and-build-a-fire rule isn't any scientific test at all."

"It's a legal test." Lunt supported his subordinate.

"It's a rule-of-thumb that was set up so that settlers on new planets couldn't get away with murdering and enslaving the natives by claiming they thought they were only hunting and domesticating wild animals," he said. "Anything that talks and builds a fire is a sapient being, yes. That's the law. But that doesn't mean that anything that doesn't isn't. I haven't seen any of this gang building fires, and as I don't want to come home sometime and find myself burned out, I'm not going to teach them. But I'm sure they have means of communication among themselves."

"Has Ben Rainsford seen them yet?" Lunt asked.

"Ben's off on a trip somewhere. I called him as soon as Little Fuzzy, over there, showed up here. He won't be back till Friday."

"Yes, that's right; I did know that." Lunt was still looking dubiously at the Fuzzies. "I'd like to hear what he thinks about them."

If Ben said they were safe, Lunt would accept that. Ben was an expert, and Lunt respected expert testimony. Until then, he wasn't sure. He'd probably order a medical check-up for himself and Khadra the first thing tomorrow, to make sure they hadn't picked up some kind of bug.

IV

The Fuzzies took the manipulator quite calmly the next morning. That wasn't any horrible monster, that was just something Pappy Jack took rides in. He found one rather indifferent sunstone in the morning and two good ones in the afternoon. He came home early and found the family in the living room; they had dumped the wastebasket and were putting things back into it. Another land-prawn seemed to have gotten into the house; its picked shell was with the other rubbish in the basket. They had dinner early, and he loaded the lot of them into the airjeep and took them for a long ride to the south and west.

The following day, he located the flint vein on the other side of the gorge and spent most of the morning blasting away the sandstone above it. The next time he went into Mallorysport, he decided, he was going to shop around for a good power-shovel. He had to blast a channel to keep the little stream from damming up on him. He didn't get any flint cracked at all that day. There was another harpy circling around the camp when he got back; he chased it with the manipulator and shot it down with his pistol. Harpies probably found Fuzzies as tasty as Fuzzies found landprawns. The family were all sitting under the gunrack when he entered the living room.

The next day he cracked flint, and found three more stones. It really looked as though he had found the Dying Place of the Jellyfish at that. He knocked off early that afternoon, and when he came in sight of the camp, he saw an airjeep grounded on the lawn and a small man with a red beard in a faded Khaki bushjacket sitting on the bench by the kitchen door, surrounded by Fuzzies. There was a camera and some other equipment laid up where the Fuzzies couldn't get at it. Baby Fuzzy, of course, was sitting on his head. He looked up and waved, and then handed Baby to his mother and rose to his feet.

"Well, what do you think of them, Ben?" Jack called down, as he grounded the manipulator.

"My God, don't start me on that now!" Ben Rainsford replied, and then laughed. "I stopped at the constabulary post on the way home. I thought George Lunt had turned into the biggest liar in the known galaxy. Then I went home, and found your call on the recorder, so I came over here."

"Been waiting long?"

The Fuzzies had all abandoned Rainsford and come trooping over as soon as the manipulator was off contragravity. He climbed down among them, and they followed him across the grass, catching at his trouser legs and yeeking happily.

"Not so long." Rainsford looked at his watch. "Good Lord, three and half hours is all. Well, the time passed quickly. You know, your little fellows have good ears. They heard you coming a long time before I did."

"Did you see them killing any prawns?"

"I should say! I got a lot of movies of it." He shook his head slowly. "Jack, this is almost incredible."

"You're staying for dinner, of course?"

"You try and chase me away. I want to hear all about this. Want you to make a tape about them, if you're willing."

"Glad to. We'll do that after we eat." He sat down on the bench, and the Fuzzies began climbing upon and beside him. "This is the original, Little Fuzzy. He brought the rest in a couple of days later. Mamma Fuzzy, and Baby Fuzzy. And these are Mike and Mitzi.

I call this one Ko-Ko, because of the ceremonious way he beheads land-prawns."

"George says you call them all Fuzzies. Want that for the official designation?"

"Sure. That's what they are, isn't it?"

"Well, let's call the order Hollowayans," Rainsford said. "Family, Fuzzies; genus, Fuzzy. Species, Holloway's Fuzzy—*Fuzzy fuzzy holloway.* How'll that be?"

That would be all right, he supposed. At least, they didn't try to Latinize things in extraterrestrial zoology any more.

"I suppose our bumper crop of land-prawns is what brought them into this section?"

"Yes, of course. George was telling me you thought they'd come down from the north; about the only place they could have come from. This is probably just the advance guard; we'll be having Fuzzies all over the place before long. I wonder how fast they breed."

"Not very fast. Three males and two females in this crowd, and only one young one." He set Mike and Mitzi off his lap and got to his feet. "I'll go start dinner now. While I'm doing that, you can look at the stuff they brought in with them."

When he had placed the dinner in the oven and taken a couple of highballs into the living room, Rainsford was still sitting at the desk, looking at the artifacts. He accepted his drink and sipped it absently, then raised his head.

"Jack, this stuff is absolutely amazing," he said.

"It's better than that. It's unique. Only collection of native weapons and implements on Zarathustra."

Ben Rainsford looked up sharply. "You mean what I think you mean?" he asked. "Yes; you do." He drank some of his highball, set down the glass and picked up the polished-horn prawn-killer. "Anything—pardon, anybody—who does this kind of work is good enough native for me." He hesitated briefly. "Why, Jack this tape you said you'd make. Can I transmit a copy to Juan Jimenez? He's chief mammalogist with the Company science division; we exchange information. And there's another Company man I'd like to have hear it. Gerd Van Riebeek. He's a general xeno-naturalist, like me, but he's especially interested in animal evolution."

"Why not? The Fuzzies are a scientific discovery. Discoveries ought to be reported."

Little Fuzzy, Mike and Mitzi strolled in from the kitchen. Little Fuzzy jumped up on the armchair and switched on the viewscreen. Fiddling with the selector, he got the Big Blackwater woods-burning. Mike and Mitzi shrieked delightedly, like a couple of kids watching a horror show. They knew, by now, that nothing in the screen could get out and hurt them.

"Would you mind if they came out here and saw the Fuzzies?"

"Why, the Fuzzies would love that. They like company."

Mamma and Baby and Ko-Ko came in, seemed to approve what was on the screen and sat down to watch it. When the bell on the stove rang, they all got up, and Ko-Ko jumped onto the chair and snapped the screen off. Ben Rainsford looked at him for a moment.

"You know, I have married friends with children who have a hell of a time teaching eight-year-olds to turn off screens when they're through watching them," he commented.

It took an hour, after dinner, to get the whole story, from the first little yeek in the shower stall, on tape. When he had finished, Ben Rainsford made a few remarks and shut off the recorder, then looked at his watch.

"Twenty hundred; it'll be seventeen hundred in Malloyrsport," he said. "I could catch Jimenez at Science Center if I called now. He usually works a little late."

"Go ahead. Want to show him some Fuzzies?" He

moved his pistol and some other impedimenta off the table and set Little Fuzzy and Mamma Fuzzy and Baby upon it, then drew up a chair beside it, in range of the communication screen, and sat down with Mike and Mitzi and Ko-Ko. Rainsford punched out a wavelength combination. Then he picked up Baby Fuzzy and set him on his head.

In a moment, the screen flickered and cleared, and a young man looked out of it, with the momentary upward glance of one who wants to make sure his public face is on straight. It was a bland, tranquilized, life-adjusted, group-integrated sort of face—the face turned out in thousands of copies every year by the educational production lines on Terra.

"Why, Bennett, this is a pleasant surprise," he began. "I never expec—" Then he choked; at least, he emitted a sound of surprise. "What in the name of Dai-Butsu are those things on the table in front of you?" he demanded. "I never saw anything—*And what is that on year head?*"

"Family group of Fuzzies," Rainsford said. "Mature male, mature female, immature male." He lifted Baby Fuzzy down and put him in Mamma's arms. Species *Fuzzy fuzzy holloway zarathustra*. The gentleman on my left is Jack Holloway, the sunstone operator, who is the original discoverer. Jack, Juan Jimenez."

They shook their own hands at one another in the ancient Terran-Chinese gesture that was used on communication screens, and assured each other—Jimenez rather absently—that it was a pleasure. He couldn't take his eyes off the Fuzzies.

"Where did they come from?" he wanted to know. "Are you sure they're indigenous?"

"They're not quite up to spaceships, yet, Dr. Jimenez. Fairly early Paleolithic, I'd say."

Jimenez thought he was joking, and laughed. The sort of a laugh that could be turned on and off, like a light. Rainsford assured him that the Fuzzies were really indigenous.

"We have everything that's known about them on tape," he said. "About an hour of it. Can you take sixty-speed?" He was making adjustments on the recorder as he spoke. "All right, set and we'll transmit to you. And can you get hold of Gerd van Riebeek? I'd like him to hear it too; it's as much up his alley as anybody's."

When Jimenez was ready, Rainsford pressed the play-off button, and for a minute the recorder gave a high, wavering squeak. The Fuzzies all looked startled. Then it ended.

"I think, when you hear this, that you and Gerd will both want to come out and see these little people. If you can, bring somebody who's a qualified psychologist, somebody capable of evaluating the Fuzzies' mentation. Jack wasn't kidding about early Paleolithic. If they're not sapient, they only miss it by about one atomic diameter."

Jimenez looked almost as startled as the Fuzzies had. "You surely don't mean that?" He looked from Rainsford to Jack Holloway and back. "Well, I'll call you back, when we've both heard the tape. You're three time zones west of us, aren't you? Then we'll try to make it before your midnight—that'll be twenty-one hundred."

He called back half an hour short of that. This time, it was from the living room of an apartment instead of an office. There was a portable record player in the foreground and a low table with snacks and drinks, and two other people were with him. One was a man of about Jimenez's age with a good-humored, non-life-adjusted, non-group-integrated and slightly weather-beaten face. The other was a woman with glossy black hair and a Mona Lisa-ish smile. The Fuzzies had gotten sleepy, and had been bribed with Extee Three to stay up a little longer. Immediately, they registered interest. This was more fun than the viewscreen.

Jimenez introduced his companions as Gerd Van Riebeek and Ruth Ortheris. "Ruth is with Dr. Mallin's section; she's been working with the school department and the juvenile court. She can probably do as well with your Fuzzies as a regular xeno-psychologist."

"Well, I have worked with extraterrestrials," the woman said. "I've been on Loki and Thor and Shesha."

Jack nodded. "Been on the same planets myself. Are you people coming out here?"

"Oh, yes," van Riebeek said. "We'll be out by noon tomorrow. We may stay a couple of days, but that won't put you to any trouble; I have a boat that's big enough for the three of us to camp on. Now, how do we get to your place?"

Jack told him, and gave map coordinates. Van Riebeek noted them down.

"There's one thing, though, I'm going to have to get firm about. I don't want to have to speak about it again. These little people are to be treated with consideration, and not as laboratory animals. You will not hurt them, or annoy them, or force them to do anything they don't want to do."

"We understand that. We won't do anything with the Fuzzies without your approval. Is there anything you'd want us to bring out?"

"Yes. A few things for the camp that I'm short of; I'll pay you for them when you get here. And about three cases of Extee Three. And some toys. Dr. Ortheris, you heard the tape, didn't you? Well, just think what you'd like to have if you were a Fuzzy, and bring it."

V

Victor Grego crushed out his cigarette slowly and deliberately.

"Yes, Leonard," he said patiently. "It's very interesting, and doubtless an important discovery, but I can't see why you're making such a production of it. Are you afraid I'll blame you for letting non-Company people beat you to it? Or do you merely suspect that anything Bennett Rainsford's mixed up in is necessarily a diabolical plot against the Company and, by consequence, human civilization?"

Leonard Kellogg looked pained. "What I was about to say, Victor, is that both Rainsford and this man Holloway seem convinced that these things they call Fuzzies aren't animals at all. They believe them to be sapient beings."

"Well, that's—" He bit that off short as the significance of what Kellogg had just said hit him. "Good God, Leonard! I beg your pardon abjectly; I don't blame you for taking it seriously. Why, that would make Zarathustra a Class-IV inhabited planet."

"For which the Company holds a Class-III charter," Kellogg added. "For an uninhabited planet."

Automatically void if any race of sapient beings were discovered on Zarathustra.

"You know what will happen if this is true?"

"Well, I should imagine the charter would have to be renegotiated, and now that the Colonial Office knows what sort of a planet this is, they'll be anything but generous with the Company...."

"They won't renegotiate anything, Leonard. The Federation government will simply take the position that the Company has already made an adequate return on the original investments, and they'll award us what we can show as in our actual possession—I hope—and throw the rest into the public domain."

The vast plains on Beta and Delta continents, with their herds of veldbeest—all open range, and every 'beest that didn't carry a Company brand a maverick. And all the untapped mineral wealth, and the untilled arable land; it would take years of litigation even to make the Company's claim to Big Blackwater stick. And Terra-Baldur-Marduk Spacelines would lose their monopolistic franchise and get sticky about it in the courts, and in any case, the Company's import-export monopoly would go out the airlock. And the squatters rushing in and swamping everything—

"Why, we won't be any better off than the Yggdrasil Company, squatting on a guano heap on one continent!" he burst out. "Five years from now, they'll be making more money out of bat dung than we'll be making out of this whole world!"

And the Company's good friend and substantial stockholder, Nick Emmert, would be out, too, and a Colonial Governor General would move in, with regular army troops and a complicated bureaucracy. Elections, and a representative parliament, and every Tom, Dick and Harry with a grudge against the Company would be trying to get laws passed—And, of course, a Native Affairs Commission, with its nose in everything.

"But they couldn't just leave us without any kind of a charter," Kellogg insisted. Who was he trying to kid—besides himself? "It wouldn't be fair!" As though that clinched it. "It isn't our fault!"

He forced more patience into his voice. "Leonard, please try to realize that the Terran Federation government doesn't give one shrill soprano hoot on Nifflheim whether it's fair or not, or whose fault what is. The Federation government's been repenting that charter they gave the Company ever since they found out what they'd chartered away. Why, this planet is a better world than Terra ever was, even before the Atomic Wars. Now, if they have a chance to get it back, with improvements, you think they won't take it? And what will stop them? If those creatures over on Beta Continent are sapient beings, our charter isn't worth the parchment it's engrossed on, and that's an end of it." He was silent for a moment. "You heard that tape Rainsford transmitted to Jimenez. Did either he or Holloway actually claim, in so many words, that these things really are sapient beings?"

"Well, no; not in so many words. Holloway consistently alluded to them as people, but he's just an ignorant old prospector. Rainsford wouldn't come out and commit himself one way or another, but he left the door wide open for anybody else to."

"Accepting their account, could these Fuzzies be sapient?"

"Accepting the account, yes," Kellogg said, in distress. "They could be."

They probably were, if Leonard Kellogg couldn't wish the evidence out of existence.

"Then they'll look sapient to these people of yours who went over to Beta this morning, and they'll treat it purely as a scientific question and never consider the legal aspects. Leonard, you'll have to take charge of the investigation, before they make any reports everybody'll be sorry for."

Kellogg didn't seem to like that. It would mean having to exercise authority and gettng tough with people, and he hated anything like that. He nodded very reluctantly.

"Yes. I suppose I will. Let me think about it for a moment, Victor."

One thing about Leonard; you handed him something he couldn't delegate or dodge and he'd go to work on it. Maybe not cheerfully, but conscientiously.

"I'll take Ernst Mallin along," he said at length. "This man Rainsford has no grounding whatever in any of the psychosciences. He may be able to impose on Ruth Ortheris, but not on Ernst Mallin. Not after I've talked to Mallin first." He thought some more. "We'll have to get these Fuzzies away from this man Holloway. Then we'll issue a report of discovery, being careful to give full credit to both Rainsford and Holloway—we'll even accept the designation they've coined for them—but we'll make it very clear that while highly intelligent, the Fuzzies are not a race of sapient beings. If Rainsford persists in making any such claim, we will brand it as a deliberate hoax."

"Do you think he's gotten any report off to the Institute of Xeno-Sciences yet?"

Kellogg shook his head. "I think he wants to trick some of our people into supporting his sapience claims; at least, corroborating his and Holloway's alleged observations. That's why I'll have to get over to Beta as soon as possible."

By now, Kellogg had managed to convince himself that going over to Beta had been his idea all along. Probably also convincing himself that Rainsford's report was nothing but a pack of lies. Well, if he could work better that way, that was his business.

"He will, before long, if he isn't stopped. And a year from now, there'll be a small army of investigators here from Terra. By that time, you should have both Rainsford and Holloway thoroughly discredited. Leonard, you get those Fuzzies away from Holloway and I'll personally guarantee they won't be available for investigation by then. Fuzzies," he said reflectively. "Fur-bearing animals, I take it?"

"Holloway spoke, on the tape, of their soft and silky fur."

"Good. Emphasize that in your report. As soon as it's published, the Company will offer two thousand sols apiece for Fuzzy pelts. By the time Rainsford's report brings anybody here from Terra, we may have them all trapped out."

Kellogg began to look worried.

"But, Victor, that's genocide!"

"Nonsense! Genocide is defined as the extermination of a race of sapient beings. These are fur-bearing animals. It's up to you and Ernst Mallin to prove that."

The Fuzzies, playing on the lawn in front of the camp, froze into immobility, their faces turned to the west. Then they all ran to the bench by the kitchen door and scrambled up onto it.

"Now what?" Jack Holloway wondered.

"They hear the airboat," Rainsford told him. "That's the way they acted yesterday when you were coming in with your machine." He looked at the picnic table they had been spreading under the featherleaf trees. "Everything ready?"

"Everything but lunch; that won't be cooked for an hour yet. I see them now."

"You have better eyes than I do, Jack. Oh, I see it. I hope the kids put on a good show for them," he said anxiously.

He'd been jittery ever since he arrived, shortly after breakfast. It wasn't that these people from Mallorysport were so important themselves; Ben had a bigger name in scientific circles than any of this Company crowd. He was just excited about the Fuzzies.

The airboat grew from a barely visible speck, and came spiraling down to land in the clearing. When it was grounded and off contragravity, they started across the grass toward it, and the Fuzzies all jumped down from the bench and ran along with them.

The three visitors climbed down. Ruth Ortheris wore slacks and a sweater, but the slacks were bloused over a pair of ankle boots. Gerd van Riebeek had evidently done a lot of field work: his boots were stout, and he wore old, faded khakis and a serviceable-looking sidearm that showed he knew what to expect up

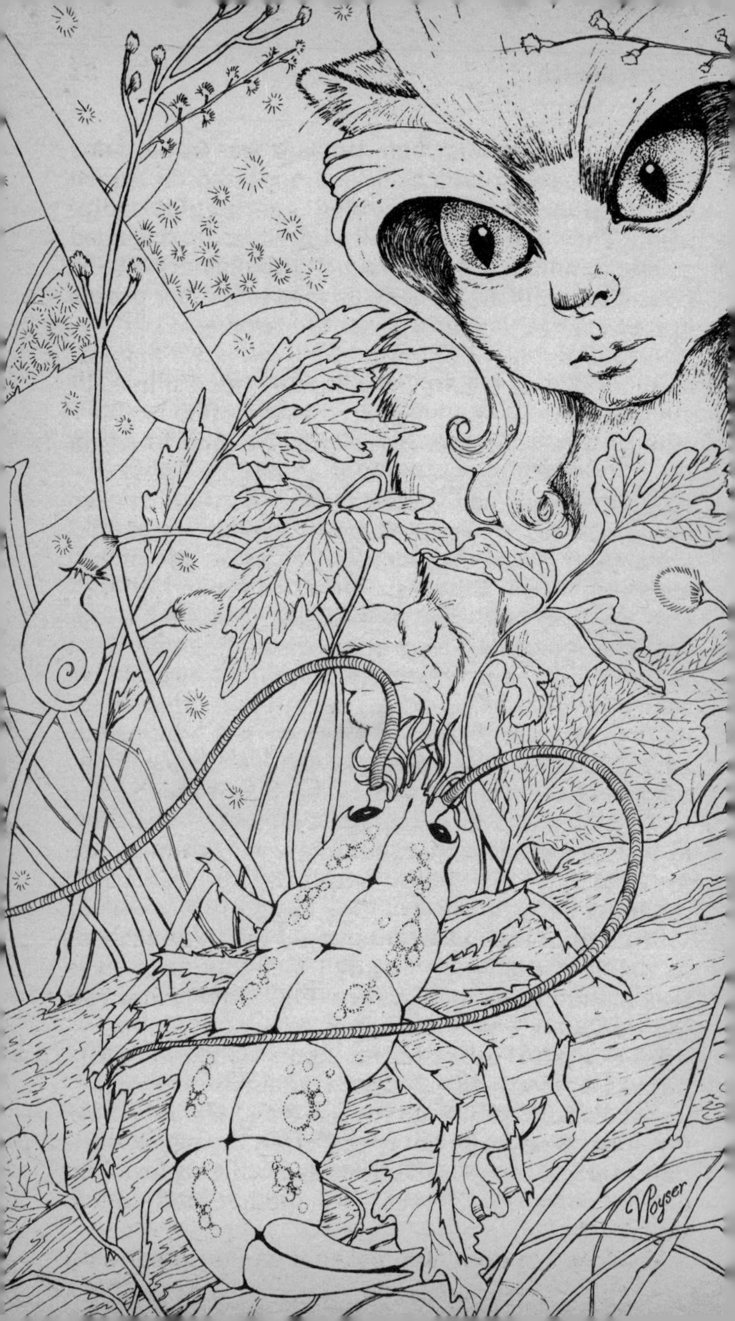
VPoyser

here in the Piedmont. Juan Jimenez was in the same sports casuals in which he had appeared on screen last evening. All of them carried photographic equipment. They shook hands all around and exchanged greetings, and then the Fuzzies began clamoring to be noticed. Finally all of them, Fuzzies and other people drifted over to the table under the trees.

Ruth Ortheris sat down on the grass with Mamma and Baby. Immediately Baby became interest in a silver charm which she wore on a chain around her neck which tinkled fascinatingly. Then he tried to sit on her head. She spent some time gently but firmly discouraging this. Juan Jimenez was squatting between Mike and Mitzi, examining them alternately and talking into a miniature recorder phone on his breast, mostly in Latin. Gerd van Riebeek dropped himself into a folding chair and took Little Fuzzy on his lap.

"You know, this is kind of surprising," he said. "Not only finding something like this, after twenty-five years, but finding something as unique as this. Look, he doesn't have the least vestige of a tail, and there isn't another tailless mammal on the planet, Fact, there isn't another mammal on this planet that has the slightest kinship to him. Take ourselves; we belong to a pretty big family, about fifty-odd genera of primates. But this little fellow hasn't any relatives at all."

"Yeek?"

"And he couldn't care less, could he?" Van Riebeek pummeled Little Fuzzy gently. "One thing, you have the smallest humanoid known; that's one record you can claim. Oh-oh, what goes on?"

Ko-Ko, who had climbed upon Rainsford's lap, jumped suddenly to the ground, grabbed the chopper-digger he had left beside the chair and started across the grass. Everybody got to their feet, the visitors getting cameras out. The Fuzzies seemed perplexed by all the excitement. It was only another land-prawn, wasn't it?

Ko-Ko got in front of it, poked it on the nose to stop

it and then struck a dramatic pose, flourishing his weapon and bringing it down on the prawn's neck. Then, after flopping it over, he looked at it almost in sorrow and hit it a couple of whacks with the flat. He began pulling it apart and eating it.

"I see why you call him Ko-Ko," Ruth said, aiming her camera. "Don't the others do it that way?"

"Well, Little Fuzzy runs along beside them and pivots and gives them a quick chop. Mike and Mitzi flop theirs over first and behead them on their backs. And Mamma takes a swipe at their legs first. But beheading and breaking the undershell, they all do that."

"Uh-huh; that's basic," she said. "Instinctive. The technique is either self-learned or copied. When Baby begins killing his own prawns, see if he doesn't do it the way Mamma does!"

"Hey, look!" Jimenez cried. "He's making a lobster pick for himself!"

Through lunch, they talked exclusively about Fuzzies. The subjects of the discussion nibbled things that were given to them, and yeeked among themselves. Gerd van Riebeek suggested that they were discussing the odd habits of human-type people. Juan Jimenez looked at him, slightly disturbed, as though wondering just how seriously he meant it.

"You know, what impressed me most in the taped account was the incident of the damnthing," said Ruth Ortheris. "Any animal associating with man will try to attract attention if something's wrong, but I never heard of one, not even a Freyan kholph or a Terran chimpanzee, that would use descriptive pantomime. Little Fuzzy was actually making a symbolic representation, by abstracting the distinguishing characteristic of the damnthing."

"Think that stiff-arm gesture and bark might have been intended to represent a rifle?" Gerd Van Riebeek asked. "He'd seen you shooting before, hadn't he?"

"I don't think it was anything else. He was telling me, 'Big nasty damnthing outside; shoot it like you did the harpy.' And if he hadn't run past me and pointed back, that damnthing would have killed me."

Jimenez, hesitantly, said, "I know I'm speaking from ignorance. You're the Fuzzy expert. But isn't it possible that you're overanthropomorphizing? Endowing them with your own characteristics and mental traits?"

"Juan, I'm not going to answer that right now. I don't think I'll answer at all. You wait till you've been around these Fuzzies a little longer, and then ask it again, only ask yourself."

"So you see, Ernst, that's the problem."

Leonard Kellogg laid the words like a paperweight on the other words he had been saying, and waited. Ernst Mallin sat motionless, his elbows on the desk and his chin in his hands. A little pair of wrinkles, like parentheses, appeared at the corners of his mouth.

"Yes. I'm not a lawyer, of course, but . . ."

"It's not a legal question. It's a question for a psychologist."

That left it back with Ernst Mallin, and he knew it.

"I'd have to see them myself before I could express an opinion. You have that tape of Holloway's with you?" When Kellogg nodded, Mallin continued: "Did either of them make any actual, overt claim of sapience?"

He answered it as he had when Victor Grego had asked the same question, adding:

"The account consists almost entirely of Holloway's uncorroborated statements concerning things to which he claims to have been the sole witness."

"Ah." Mallin permitted himself a tight little smile. "And he's not a qualified observer. Neither, for that matter, is Rainsford. Regardless of his position as a xeno-naturalist, he is complete layman in the psychosciences. He's just taken this other man's statements uncritically. As for what he claims to have observed for himself, how do we know he isn't including a lot of erroneous inferences with his descriptive statements?"

"How do we know he's not perpetrating a deliberate hoax?"

"But, Leonard, that's a pretty serious accusation."

"It's happened before. That fellow who carved a Late Upland Martian inscription in that cave in Kenya, for instance. Or Hellermann's claim to have cross-bred Terran mice with Thoran tilbras. Or the Piltdown Man, back in the first century Pre-Atomic?"

Mallin nodded. "None of us like to think of a thing like that, but, as you say, it's happened. You know, this man Rainsford is just the type to do something like that, too. Fundamentally an individualistic egoist; badly adjusted personality type. Say he wants to make some sensational discovery which will assure him the position in the scientific world to which he believes himself entitled. He finds this lonely old prospector, into whose isolated camp some little animals have strayed. The old man has made pets of them, taught them a few tricks, finally so projected his own personality onto them that he has convinced himself that they are people like himself. This is Rainsford's great opportunity; he will present himself as the discoverer of a new sapient race and bring the whole learned world to his feet." Mallin smiled again. "Yes, Leonard, it is altogether possible."

"Then it's our plain duty to stop this thing before it develops into another major scientific scandal like Hellermann's hybrids."

"First we must go over this tape recording and see what we have on our hands. Then we must make a thorough, unbiased study of these animals, and show Rainsford and his accomplice that they cannot hope to foist these ridiculous claims on the scientific world with impunity. If we can't convince them privately, there'll be nothing to do but expose them publicly."

"I've heard the tape already, but let's play if off now. We want to analyze these tricks this man Holloway has taught these animals, and see what they show."

"Yes, of course. We must do that at once," Mallin said. "Then we'll have to consider what sort of statement we must issue, and what sort of evidence we will need to support it."

After dinner was romptime for Fuzzies on the lawn, but when the dusk came creeping into the ravine, they all went inside and were given one of their new toys from Mallorysport—a big box of many-colored balls and short sticks of transparent plastic. They didn't know that it was a molecule-model kit, but they soon found that the sticks would go into holes in the balls, and that they could be built into three-dimensional designs.

This was much more fun than the colored stones. They made a few experimental shapes, then dismantled them and began on a single large design. Several times they tore it down, entirely or in part, and began over again, usually with considerable yeeking and gesticulation.

"They have artistic sense," van Riebeek said. "I've seen lots of abstract sculpture that wasn't half as good as that job they're doing."

"Good engineering, too," Jack said. "They understand balance and center-of-gravity. They're bracing it well, and not making it top-heavy."

"Jack, I've been thinking about that question I was supposed to ask myself," Jimenez said. "You know, I came out here loaded with suspicion. Not that I doubted your honesty; I just thought you'd let your obvious affection for the Fuzzies lead you into giving them credit for more intelligence than they possess. Now I think you've consistently understated it. Short of actual sapience, I've never seen anything like them."

"Why short of it?" van Riebeek asked. "Ruth, you've been pretty quiet this evening. What do you think?"

Ruth Ortheris looked uncomfortable. "Gerd, it's too early to form opinions like that. I know the way they're working together looks like cooperation on an agreed-upon purpose, but I simply can't make speech out of that yeek-yeek-yeek."

"Let's keep the talk-and-build-a-fire rule out of it," van Riebeek said. "If they're working together on a common project, they must be communicating somehow."

"It isn't communication, it's symbolization. You simply can't think sapiently except in verbal symbols. Try it. Not something like changing the spools on a recorder or field-stripping a pistol; they're just learned tricks. I mean ideas."

"How about Helen Keller?" Rainsford asked. "Mean to say she only started thinking sapiently after Anna Sullivan taught her what words were?"

"No, of course not. She thought sapiently—And she only thought in sense-imagery limited to feeling." She looked at Rainsford reproachfully; he'd knocked a breach in one of her fundamental postulates. "Of course, she had inherited the cerebroneural equipment for sapient thinking." She let that trail off, before somebody asked her how she knew that the Fuzzies hadn't.

"I'll suggest, just to keep the argument going, that speech couldn't have been invented without pre-existing sapience," Jack said.

Ruth laughed. "Now you're taking me back to college. That used to be one of the burning questions in first-year psych students' bull sessions. By the time we got to be sophomores, we'd realized that it was only an egg-and-chicken argument and dropped it."

"That's a pity," Ben Rainsford said. "It's a good question."

"It would be if it could be answered."

"Maybe it can be," Gerd said. "There's a clue to it, right there. I'll say that those fellows are on the edge of sapience, and it's an even-money bet which side."

"I'll bet every sunstone in my bag they're over."

"Well, maybe they're just slightly sapient," Jimenez

suggested.

Ruth Ortheris hooted at that. "That's like talking about being just slightly dead or just slightly pregnant," she said. "You either are or you aren't."

Gerd van Riebeek was talking at the same time. "This sapience question is just as important in my field as yours, Ruth. Sapience is the result of evolution by natural selection, just as much as a physical characteristic, and it's the most important step in the evolution of any species, our own included."

"Wait a minute, Gerd," Rainsford said. "Ruth, what do you mean by that? Aren't there degrees of sapience?"

"No. There are degrees of mentation—intelligence, if you prefer—just as there are degrees of temperature. When psychology becomes an exact science like physics, we'll be able to calibrate mentation like temperature. But sapience is qualitatively different from nonsapience. It's more than just a higher degree of mental temperature. You might call it a sort of mental boiling point."

"I think that's a damn good analogy," Rainsford said. "But what happens when the boiling point is reached?"

"That's what we have to find out," van Riebeek told him. "That's what I was talking about a moment ago. We don't know any more about how sapience appeared today than we did in the year zero, or in the year 654 Pre-Atomic for that matter."

"Wait a minite," Jack interrupted. "Before we go any deeper, let's agree on a definition of sapience."

Van Riebeek laughed. "Ever try to get a definition of life from a biologist?" he asked. "Or a definition of number from a mathematician?"

"That's about it." Ruth looked at the Fuzzies, who were looking at their colored-ball construction as though wondering if they could add anything more without spoiling the design. "I'd say: a level of mentation qualitatively different from nonsapience in that it includes ability to symbolize ideas and store and transmit them, ability to generalize and ability to form abstract ideas. There; I didn't say a word about talk-and-build-a-fire, did I?"

"Little Fuzzy symbolizes and generalizes," Jack said. "He symbolizes a damnthing by three horns, and he symbolizes a rifle by a long thing that points and makes noises. Rifles kill animals. Harpies and damnthings are both animals. If a rifle will kill a harpy, it'll kill a damnthing too."

Juan Jimenez had been frowning in thought; he looked up and asked, "What's the lowest known sapient race?"

"Yggdrasil Khooghras," Gerd van Riebeek said promptly. "Any of you ever been on Yggdrasil?"

"I saw a man shot once on Mimir, for calling another man a son of a Khooghra," Jack said. "The man who shot him had been on Yggdrasil and knew what he was being called."

"I spent a couple of years among them," Gerd said. "They do build fires; I'll give them that. They char points on sticks to make spears. And they talk. I learned their language, all eighty-two words of it. I taught a few of the intelligentsia how to use machetes without maiming themselves, and there was one mental giant I could trust to carry some of my equipment, if I kept an eye on him, but I never let him touch my rifle or my camera."

"Can they generalize?" Ruth asked.

"Honey, they can't do nothin' else but! Every word in their language is a high-order generalization. *Hroosha*, live-thing. *Noosha*, bad-thing. *Dhishta*, thing-to-eat. Want me to go on? There are only seventy-nine more of them."

Before anybody could stop him, the communication screen got itself into an uproar. The Fuzzies all ran over in front of it, and Jack switched it on. The caller was a man in gray semiformals; he had wavy gray hair and a face that looked like Juan Jimenez's twenty years from now.

"Good evening; Holloway here."

"Oh, Mr. Holloway, good evening." The caller shook hands with himself, turning on a dazzling smile. "I'm Leonard Kellogg, chief of the Company's science division. I just heard the tape you made about the—the Fuzzies?" He looked down at the floor. "Are these some of the animals?"

"These are the Fuzzies." He hoped it sounded like the correction it was intended to be. "Dr. Bennett Rainsford's here with me now, and so are Dr. Jimenez, Dr. van Riebeek and Dr. Ortheris." Out of the corner of his eye he could see Jimenez squirming as though afflicted with ants, van Riebeek getting his poker face battened down and Ben Rainsford suppressing a grin. "Some of us are out of screen range, and I'm sure you'll want to ask a lot of questions. Pardon us a moment, while we close in."

He ignored Kellogg's genial protest that that wouldn't be necessary until the chairs were placed facing the screen. As an afterthought, he handed Fuzzies around, giving Little Fuzzy to Ben, Ko-Ko to Gerd, Mitzi to Ruth, Mike to Jimenez and taking Mamma and Baby on his own lap.

Baby immediately started to climb up onto his head, as expected. It seemed to disconcert Kellogg, also as expected. He decided to teach Baby to thumb his nose when given some unobtrusive signal.

"Now, about that tape I recorded last evening," he began.

"Yes, Mr. Holloway." Kellogg's smile was getting more mechanical every minute. He was having trouble keeping his eyes off Baby. "I must say, I was simply astounded at the high order of intelligence claimed for these creatures."

"And you wanted to see how big a liar I was. I don't blame you; I had trouble believing it myself at first."

Kellogg gave a musically blithe laugh, showing even more dental equipment.

"Oh, no. Mr. Holloway; please don't misunderstand me. I never thought anything like that."

"I hope not," Ben Rainsford said, not too plesantly. "I vouched for Mr. Holloway's statements, if you'll recall."

"Of course, Bennett; that goes without saying. Permit me to congratulate you upon a most remarkable scientific discovery. An entirely new order of mammals—"

"Which may be the ninth extrasolar sapient race," Rainsford added.

"Good heavens, Bennett!" Kellogg jettisoned his smile and slid on a look of shocked surprise. "You surely can't be serious?" He looked again at the Fuzzies, pulled the smile back on and gave a light laugh.

"I thought you'd heard that tape," Rainsford said.

"Of course, and the things reported were most remarkable. But sapiences! Just because they've been taught a few tricks, and use sticks and stones for weapons—" He got rid of the smile again, and quick-changed to seriousness. "Such an extreme claim must only be made after careful study."

"Well, I won't claim they're sapient," Ruth Ortheris told him. "Not till day after tomorrow, at the earliest. But they very easily could be. They have learning and reasoning capacity equal to that of any eight-year-old Terran Human child, and well above that of the adults of some recognizedly sapient races. And they have not been taught tricks; they have learned by observation and reasoning."

"Well, Dr. Kellogg, mentation levels isn't my subject," Jimenez took it up, "but they do have all the physical characteristics shared by other sapient races— lower limbs specialized for locomotion and upper limbs for manipulation, erect posture, stereoscopic vision, color perception, erect posture, hand with opposing thumb—all the characteristics we consider as prerequisite to the development of sapience."

"I think they're sapient, myself," Gerd van Riebeek

said, "but that's not as important as the fact that they're on the very threshold of sapience. This is the first race of this mental level anybody's ever seen. I believe that study of the Fuzzies will help us solve the problem of how sapience developed in any race."

Kellogg had been laboring to pump up a head of enthusiasm; now he was ready to valve it off.

"But this is amazing! This will make scientific history! Now, of course, you all realize how pricelessly valuable these Fuzzies are. They must be brought at once to Mallorysport, where they can be studied under laboratory conditions by qualified psychologists, and —"

"No."

Jack lifted Baby Fuzzy off his head and handed him to Mamma, and set Mamma on the floor. That was reflex; the thinking part of his brain knew he didn't need to clear for action when arguing with the electronic image of a man twenty-five hundred miles away.

"Just forget that part of it and start over," he advised.

Kellogg ignored him. "Gerd, you have your airboat; fix up some nice comfortable cages—"

"Kellogg!"

The man in the screen stopped talking and stared in amazed indignation. It was the first time in years he had been addressed by his naked patronymic, and possibly the first time in his life he had been shouted at.

"Didn't you hear me the first time Kellogg? Then stop gibbering about cages. These Fuzzies aren't being taken anywhere."

"But Mr. Holloway! Don't you realize that these little beings must be carefully studied? Don't you want them given their rightful place in the hierarchy of nature?"

"If you want to study them, come out here and do it. That's so long as you don't annoy them, or me. As far as study's concerned, they're being studied now. Dr. Rainsford's studying them, and so are three of your people, and when it comes to that, I'm studying them myself."

"And I'd like you to clarify that remark about qualified psychologists," Ruth Ortheris added, in a voice approaching zero-Kelvin. "You wouldn't be challenging my professional qualifications, would you?"

"Oh, Ruth, you know I didn't mean anything like that. Please don't misunderstand me," Kellogg begged. "But this is highly specialized work—"

"Yes; how many Fuzzy specialists have you at Science Center, Leonard?" Rainsford wanted to know. "The only one I can think of is Jack Holloway, here."

"Well, I'd thought of Dr. Mallin, the Company's head psychologist."

"He can come too, just as long as he understands that he'll have to have my permission for anything he wants to do with the Fuzzies," Jack said. "When can we expect you?"

Kellogg thought some time late the next afternoon. He didn't have to ask how to get to the camp. He made a few efforts to restore the conversation to its original note of cordiality, gave that up as a bad job and blanked out. There was a brief silence in the living room. Then Jimenez said reproachfully:

"You certainly weren't very gracious to Dr. Kellogg, Jack. Maybe you don't realize it, but he is a very important man."

"He isn't important to me, and I wasn't gracious to him at all. It doesn't pay to be gracious to people like that. If you are, they always try to take advantage of it."

"Why, I didn't know you knew Len," van Riebeek said.

"I never saw the individual before. The species is very common and widely distributed." He turned to Rainsford. "You think he and this Mallin will be out tomorrow?"

"Of course they will. This is a little too big for underlings and non-Company people to be allowed to monkey with. You know, we'll have to watch out or in a year we'll be hearing from Terra about the discovery of a sapient race on Zarathustra; *Fuzzy fuzzy Kellogg.* As Juan says, Dr. Kellogg is a very important man. That's how he got important."

VI

The recorded voice ceased; for a moment the record player hummed voicelessly. Loud in the silence, a photocell acted with a double click, opening one segment of the sun shielding and closing another at the opposite side of the dome. Space Commodore Alex Napier glanced up from his desk and out at the harshly angular landscape of Xerxes and the blackness of airless space beyond the disquietingly close horizon. Then he picked up his pipe and knocked the heel out into the ashtray. Nobody said anything. He began packing tobacco into the bowl.

"Well, gentlemen?" He invited comment.

"Pancho?" Captain Conrad Greibenfeld, the Exec., turned to Lieutenant Ybarra, the chief psychologist.

"How reliable is this stuff?" Ybarra asked.

"Well, I knew Jack Holloway thirty years ago, on Fenris, when I was just an ensign. He must be past seventy now," he parenthesized. "If he says he saw anything, I'll believe it. And Bennett Rainsford's absolutely reliable, of course."

"How about the agent?" Ybarra insisted.

He and Stephen Aelborg, the Intelligence officer, exchanged glances. He nodded, and Aelborg said:

"One of the best. One of our own, lieutenant j.g., Naval Reserve. You don't need to worry about credibility, Pancho."

"They sound sapient to me," Ybarra said. "You know, this is something I've always been half hoping and half afraid would happen."

"You mean an excuse to intervene in that mess down there?" Greibenfeld asked.

Ybarra looked blankly at him for a moment. "No. No, I meant a case of borderline sapience; something our sacred talk-and-build-a-fire rule won't cover. Just how did this come to our attention, Stephen?"

"Well, it was transmitted to us from Contact Center in Mallorysport late Friday night. There seem to be a number of copies of this tape around; our agent got hold of one of them and transmitted it to Contact Center, and it was relayed on to us, with the agent's comments," Aelborg said. "Contract Center ordered a routine surveillance inside Company House and, to play safe, at the Residency. At the time, there seemed no reason to give the thing any beat-to-quarters-and-man-guns treatment, but we got a report on Saturday afternoon—Mallorysport time, that is—that Leonard Kellogg had played off the copy of the tape that Juan Jimenez had made for file, and had alerted Victor Grego immediately.

"Of course, Grego saw the implications at once. He sent Kellogg and the chief Company psychologist, Ernst Mallin, out to Beta Continent with orders to brand Rainsford's and Holloway's claims as a deliberate hoax. Then the Company intends to encourage the trapping of Fuzzies for their fur, in hopes that the whole species will be exterminated before anybody can get out from Terra to check on Rainsford's story."

"I hadn't heard that last detail before."

"Well, we can prove it," Aelborg assured him.

It sounded like a Victor Grego idea. He lit his pipe slowly. Damnit, he didn't want to have to intervene. No Space Navy C.O. did. Justifying intervention on a Colonial planet was too much bother—always a board of inquiry, often a courtmartial. And supersession of civil authority was completely against Service Doctrine. Of course, there were other and more important tenets of Service Doctrine. The sovereignty of the Terran Federation for one, and the inviolability of the Federation Constitution. And the rights of extraterrestrials, too. Conrad Greibenfeld, too, seemed to have been thinking about that.

"If those Fuzzies are sapient beings, that whole setup down there is illegal. Company, Colonial administration and all," he said. "Zarathustra's a Class-IV planet, and that's all you can make out of it."

"We won't intervene unless we're forced to. Pancho, I think the decision will be largely up to you."

Pancho Ybarra was horrified.

"Good God, Alex! You can't mean that. Who am I? A nobody. All I have is an ordinary M.D., and a Psych. D. Why, the best psychological brains in the Federation—"

"Aren't on Zarathustra, Pancho. They're on Terra, five hundred light-years, six months' ship voyage each way. Intervention, of course, is my responsibility, but the sapience question is yours. I don't envy you, but I can't relieve you of it."

Gerd van Riebeek's suggestion that all three of the visitors sleep aboard the airboat hadn't been treated seriously at all. Gerd himself was accommodated in the spare room of the living hut. Juan Jimenez went with Ben Rainsford to his camp for the night. Ruth Ortheris had the cabin of the boat to herself. Rainsford was on the screen the next morning, while Jack and Gerd and Ruth and the Fuzzies were having breakfast; he and Jimenez had decided to take his airjeep and work down from the head of Cold Creek in the belief that there must be more Fuzzies around in the woods.

Both Gerd and Ruth decided to spend the morning at the camp and get acquainted with the Fuzzies on hand. The family had had enough breakfast to leave them neutral on the subject of land-prawns, and they were given another of the new toys, a big colored ball. They rolled it around in the grass for a while, decided to save it for their evening romp and took it into the house. Then they began playing aimlessly among some junk in the shed outside the workshop. Once in a while one of them would drift away to look for a prawn, more for sport than food.

Ruth and Gerd and Jack were sitting at the breakfast table on the grass, talking idly and trying to think of excuses for not washing the dishes. Mamma Fuzzy and Baby were poking about in the tall grass. Suddenly Mamma gave a shrill cry and started back for the shed, chasing Baby ahead of her and slapping him on the bottom with the flat of her chopper-digger to hurry him along.

Jack started for the house at a run. Gerd grabbed his camera and jumped up on the table. It was Ruth who saw the cause of the disturbance.

"Jack! Look, over there!" She pointed to the edge of the clearing. "Two strange Fuzzies!"

He kept on running, but instead of the rifle he had been going for, he collected his movie camera, two of the spare chopper-diggers and some Extee Three. When he emerged again, the two Fuzzies had come into the clearing and stood side by side, looking around. Both were females, and they both carried wooden prawn-killers.

"You have plenty of film?" he asked Gerd. "Here, Ruth; take this." He handed her his own camera. "Keep far enough away from me to get what I'm doing and what they're doing. I'm going to try to trade with them."

"He went forward, the steel weapons in his hip pocket and the Extee Three in his hand, talking softly and soothingly to the newcomers. When he was as close to them as he could get without stampeding them, he stopped.

"Our gang's coming up behind you," Gerd told him. "Regular skirmish line; choppers at high port. Now they've stopped, about thirty feet behind you."

He broke off a piece of Extee Three, put it in his mouth and ate it. Then he broke off two more pieces and held them out. The two Fuzzies were tempted, but not to the point of rashness. He threw both pieces within a few feet of them. One darted forward, threw a piece to her companion and then snatched the other piece and ran back with it. They stood together, nibbling and making soft delighted noises.

His own family seemed to disapprove strenuously of this lavishing of delicacies upon outsiders. However, the two strangers decided that it would be safe to come closer, and soon he had them taking bits of field ration from his hand. Then he took the two steel chopper-diggers out of his pocket, and managed to convey the idea that he wanted to trade. The two strange Fuzzies were incredulously delighted. This was too much for his own tribe; they came up yeeking angrily.

The two strange females retreated a few steps, their new weapon ready. Everybody seemed to expect a fight, and nobody wanted one. From what he could remember of Old Terran history, this was a situation which could develop into serious trouble. Then Ko-ko advanced, dragging his chopper-digger in an obviously pacific manner, and approached the two females, yeeking softly and touching first one and then the other. Then he laid his weapon down and put his foot on it. The two females began stroking and caressing him.

Immediately the crisis evaporated. The others of the family came forward, stuck their weapons in the ground and began fondling the strangers. Then they all sat in a circle, swaying their bodies rhythmically and making soft noises. Finally Ko-Ko and the two females rose, picked up their weapons and started for the woods.

"Jack, stop them," Ruth called out. "They're going away."

"If they want to go, I have no right to stop them."

When they were almost at the edge of the woods, Ko-Ko stopped, drove the point of his weapon into the ground and came running back to Pappy Jack, throwing his arms around the human knees and yeeking. Jack stooped and stroked him, but didn't try to pick him up. One of the two females pulled his chopper-digger out, and they both came back slowly. At the same time, Little Fuzzy, Mamma Fuzzy, Mike and Mitzi came running back. For a while, all the Fuzzies embraced one another, yeeking happily. Then they all trooped across the grass and went into the house.

"Get that all, Gerd?" he asked.

"On film, yes. That's the only way I did, though. What happened?"

"You have just made the first film of intertribal social and mating customs, Zarathustran Fuzzy. This is the family's home; they don't want any strange Fuzzies hanging around. They were going to run the girls off. Then Ko-Ko decided he liked their looks, and he decided he'd team up with them. That made everything different; the family sat down with them to tell them what a fine husband they were getting and to tell Ko-Ko good-bye. Then Ko-Ko remembered that he hadn't told me good-bye, and he came back. The family decided that two more Fuzzies wouldn't be in excess of the carrying capacity of this habitat, seeing what a good provider Pappy Jack is, so now I should imagine they're showing the girls the family treasures. You know, they married into a mighty well-to-do family."

The girls were named Goldilocks and Cinderella. When lunch was ready, they were all in the living room, with the viewscreen on; after lunch, the whole gang went into the bedroom for a nap on Pappy Jack's bed. He spent the afternoon developing movie film, while Gerd and Ruth wrote up the notes they had made the day before and collaborated on an account of the adoption. By late afternoon, when they were finished, the Fuzzies came out for a frolic and prawn hunt.

They all heard the aircar before any of the human

people did, and they all ran over and climbed up on the bench beside the kitchen door. It was a constabulary cruise car; it landed, and a couple of troopers got out, saying that they'd stopped to see the Fuzzies. They wanted to know where the extras had come from, and when Jack told them, they looked at one another.

"Next gang that comes along, call us and keep them entertained till we can get here," one of them said. "We want some at the post, for prawns if nothing else."

"What's George's attitude?" he asked. "The other night, when he was here, he seemed half scared of them."

"Aah, he's got over that," one of the troopers said. "He called Ben Rainsford; Ben said they were perfectly safe. Hey, Ben says they're not animals; they're people."

He started to tell them about some of the things the Fuzzies did. He was still talking when the Fuzzies heard another aircar and called attention to it. This time, it was Ben Rainsford and Juan Jimenez. They piled out as soon as they were off contragravity, dragging cameras after them.

"Jack, there are Fuzzies all over the place up there," Rainsford began, while he was getting out. "All headed down this way; regular *Volkerwanderung*. We saw over fifty of them—four families, and individuals and pairs. I'm sure we missed ten for every one we saw."

"We better get up there with a car tomorrow," one of the troopers said. "Ben, just where were you?"

"I'll show you on the map." Then he saw Goldilocks and Cinderella. "Hey! Where'd you two girls come from? I never saw you around here before."

There was another clearing across the stream, with a log footbridge and a path to the camp. Jack guided the big airboat down onto it, and put his airjeep alongside with the canopy up. There were two men on the forward deck of the boat, Kellogg and another man who would be Ernst Mallin. A third man came out of the control cabin after the boat was off contragravity. Jack didn't like Mallin. He had a tight, secretive face, with arrogance and bigotry showing underneath. The third man was younger. His face didn't show anything much, but his coat showed a bulge under the left arm. After being introduced by Kellogg, Mallin introduced him as Kurt Borch, his assistant.

Mallin had to introduce Borch again at the camp, not only to Ben Rainsford but also to van Riebeek, to Jimenez and even to Ruth Ortheris, which seemed a little odd. Ruth seemed to think so, too, and Mallin hastened to tell her that Borch was with Personnel, giving some kind of tests. That appeared to puzzle her even more. None of the three seemed happy about the presence of the constabulary troopers, either; they were all relieved when the cruise car lifted out.

Kellogg became interested in the Fuzzies immediately, squatting to examine them. He said something to Mallin, who compressed his lips and shook his head, saying:

"We simply cannot assume sapience until we find something in their behavior which cannot be explained under any other hypothesis. We would be much safer to assume nonsapience and proceed to test that assumption."

That seemed to establish the keynote. Kellogg straightened, and he and Mallin started one of those "of course I agree, doctor, but don't you find, on the other hand, that you must agree" sort of arguments, about the difference between scientific evidence and scientific proof. Jimenez got into it to the extent of agreeing with everything Kellogg said, and differing politely with everything Mallin said that he thought Kellogg would differ with. Borch said nothing; he just stood and looked at the Fuzzies with ill-concealed hostility. Gerd and Ruth decided to help getting dinner.

They ate outside on the picnic table, with the Fuzzies watching them interestedly. Kellogg and Mallin carefully avoided discussing them. It wasn't until after dusk, when the Fuzzies brought their ball inside and everybody was in the living room, that Kellogg, adopting a presiding-officer manner, got the conversation onto the subject. For some time, without giving anyone else an opportunity to say anything, he gushed about what an important discovery the Fuzzies were. The Fuzzies themselves ignored him and began dismantling the stick-and-ball construction. For a while Goldilocks and Cinderella watched interestedly, and then they began assisting.

"Unfortunately," Kellogg continued, so much of our data is in the form of uncorroborated statements by Mr. Holloway. Now, please don't misunderstand me. I don't, myself, doubt for a moment anything Mr. Holloway said on that tape, but you must realize that professional scientists are most reluctant to accept the unsubstantiated reports of what, if you'll pardon me, they think of as nonqualified observers."

"Oh, rubbish, Leonard!" Rainsford broke in impatiently. "I'm a professional scientist, of a good many more years' standing than you, and I accept Jack Holloway's statements. A frontiersman like Jack is a very careful and exact observer. People who aren't don't live long on frontier planets."

"Now, please don't misunderstand me," Kellogg reiterated. "I don't doubt Mr. Holloway's statements. I was just thinking of how they would be received on Terra."

"I shouldn't worry about that, Leonard. The Institute accepts my reports, and I'm vouching for Jack's reliability. I can substantiate most of what he told me from personal observation."

"Yes, and there's more than just verbal statements," Gerd van Riebeek chimed in. "A camera is not a nonqualified observer. We have quite a bit of film of the Fuzzies."

"Oh, yes; there was some mention of movies," Mallin said. "You don't have any of them developed yet, do you?"

"Quite a lot. Everything except what was taken out in the woods this afternoon. We can run them off right now."

He pulled down the screen in front of the gunrack, got the film and loaded his projector. The Fuzzies, who had begun on a new stick-and-ball construction, were irritated when the lights went out, then wildly excited when Little Fuzzy, digging a toilet pit with the wood chisel, appeared. Little Fuzzy in particular was excited about that; if he didn't recognize himself, he recognized the chisel. Then there were pictures of Little Fuzzy killing and eating land-prawns, Little Fuzzy taking the nut off the bolt and putting it on again, and pictures of the others, after they had come in, hunting and at play. Finally, there was the film of the adoption of Goldilocks and Cinderella.

"What Juan and I got this afternoon, up in the woods, isn't so good, I'm afraid," Rainsford said when the show was over and the lights were on again. "Mostly it's rear views disappearing into the brush. It was very hard to get close to them in the jeep. Their hearing is remarkably acute. But I'm sure the pictures we took this afternoon will show the things they were carrying—wooden prawn-killers like the two that were traded from the new ones in that last film."

Mallin and Kellogg looked at one another in what seemed oddly like consternation.

"You didn't tell us there were more of them around," Mallin said, as though it were an accusation of duplicity. He turned to Kellogg. "This alters the situation."

"Yes, indeed, Ernst," Kellogg burbled delightedly. "This is a wonderful opportunity. Mr. Holloway, I understand that all this country up here is your property, by landgrant purchase. That's right, isn't it? Well, would you allow us to camp on that clearing across the run, where our boat is now? We'll get prefab huts—

Red Hill's the nearest town, isn't it?—and have a Company construction gang set them up for us, and we won't be any bother at all to you. We had only intended staying tonight on our boat, and returning to Mallorysport in the morning, but with all these Fuzzies swarming around in the woods, we can't think of leaving now. You don't have any objection, do you?"

He had lots of objections. The whole business was rapidly developing into an acute pain in the neck for him. But if he didn't let Kellogg camp across the run, the three of them could move seventy or eighty miles in any direction and be off his land. He knew what they'd do then. They'd live-trap or sleep-gas Fuzzies; they'd put them in cages, and torment them with maze and electric-shock experiments, and kill a few for dissection, or maybe not bother killing them first. On his own land, if they did anything like that, he could do something about it.

"Not at all. I'll have to remind you again, though, that you're to treat these little people with consideration."

"Oh, we won't do anything to your Fuzzies," Mallin said.

"You won't hurt any Fuzzies. Not more than once, anyhow."

The next morning, during breakfast, Kellogg and Kurt Borch put in an appearance, Borch wearing old clothes and field boots and carrying his pistol on his belt. They had a list of things they thought they would need for their camp. Neither of them seemed to have more than the foggiest notion of camp requirements. Jack made some suggestions which they accepted. There was a lot of scientific equipment on the list, including an X-ray machine. He promptly ran a pencil line through that.

"We don't know what these Fuzzies' level of radiation tolerance is. We're not going to find out by overdosing one of my Fuzzies."

Somewhat to his surprise, neither of them gave him any argument. Gerd and Ruth and Kellogg borrowed his airjeep and started north; he and Borch went across the run to make measurements after Rainsford and Jimenez arrived and picked up Mallin. Borch took off soon after with the boat for Red Hill. Left alone, he loafed around the camp, and developed the rest of the movie film, making three copies of everything. Toward noon, Borch brought the boat back, followed by a couple of scowlike farmboats. In a few hours, the Company construction men from Red Hill had the new camp set up. Among other things, they brought two more airjeeps.

The two jeeps returned late in the afternoon, everybody excited. Between them, the parties had seen almost a hundred Fuzzies, and had found three camps, two among rocks and one in a hollow pool-ball tree. All three had been spotted by belts of filled-in toilet pits around them; two had been abandoned and the third was still occupied. Kellogg insisted on playing host to Jack and Rainsford for dinner at the camp across the run. The meal, because everything had been brought ready-cooked and only needed warming, was excellent.

Returning to his own camp with Rainsford, Jack found the Fuzzies finished with their evening meal and in the living room, starting a new construction—he could think of no other name for it—with the molecule-model balls and sticks. Goldilocks left the others and came over to him with a couple of balls fastened together, holding them up with one hand while she pulled his trouser leg with the other.

"Yes, I see. It's very beautiful," he told her.

She tugged harder and pointed at the thing the others were making. Finally, he understood.

"She wants me to work on it, too," he said. "Ben, you know where the coffee is; fix us a pot. I'm going to be busy here."

He sat down on the floor, and was putting sticks and balls together when Ben brought in the coffee. This was more fun than he'd had in a couple of days. He said so while Ben was distributing Extee Three to the Fuzzies.

"Yes, I ought to let you kick me all around the camp for getting this started," Rainsford said, pouring the coffee. "I could make some excuses, but they'd all sound like 'I didn't know it was loaded.'"

"Hell, I didn't know it was loaded, either." He rose and took his coffee cup, blowing on it to cool it. "What do you think Kellogg's up to, anyhow? That whole act he's been putting on since he came here is phony as a nine-sol bill."

"What I told you, evening before last," Rainsford said. "He doesn't want non-Company people making discoveries on Zarathustra. You notice how hard he and Mallin are straining to talk me out of sending a report back to Terra before he can investigate the Fuzzies? He wants to get his own report in first. Well, the hell with him! You know what I'm going to do? I'm going home, and I'm going to sit up all night getting a report into shape. Tomorrow morning I'm going to give it to George Lunt and let him send it to Mallorysport in the constabulary mail pouch. It'll be on a ship for Terra before any of this gang knows it's been sent. Do you have any copies of those movies you can spare?"

"About a mile and a half. I made copies of everything, even the stuff the others took."

"Good. We'll send that, too. Let Kellogg read about it in the papers a year from now." He thought for a moment, then said: "Gerd and Ruth and Juan are bunking at the other camp now; suppose I move in here with you tomorrow. I assume you don't want to leave the Fuzzies alone while that gang's here. I can help you keep an eye on them."

"But, Ben, you don't want to drop whatever else you're doing—"

"What I'm doing, now, is learning to be a Fuzzyologist, and this is the only place I can do it. I'll see you tomorrow, after I stop at the constabulary post."

The people across the run—Kellogg, Mallin and Borch, and van Riebeek, Jimenez and Ruth Ortheris—were still up when Rainsford went out to his airjeep. After watching him lift out, Jack went back into the house, played with his family in the living room for a while and went to bed. The next morning he watched Kellogg, Ruth and Jimenez leave in one jeep and, shortly after, Mallin and van Riebeek in the other. Kellogg didn't seem to be willing to let the three who had come to the camp first wander around unchaperoned. He wondered about that.

Ben Rainsford's airjeep came over the mountains from the south in the late morning and settled onto the grass. Jack helped him inside with his luggage, and then they sat down under the big featherleaf trees to smoke their pipes and watch the Fuzzies playing in the grass. Occasionally they saw Kurt Borch pottering around outside the other camp.

"I sent the report off," Rainsford said, then looked at his watch. "It ought to be on the mail boat for Mallorysport by now; this time tomorrow it'll be in hyperspace for Terra. We won't say anything about it; just sit back and watch Len Kellogg and Ernst Mallin working up a sweat trying to talk us out of sending it." He chuckled. "I made a definite claim of sapience; by the time I got the report in shape to tape off, I couldn't see any other alternative."

"Damned if I can. You hear that, kids?" he asked Mike and Mitzi, who had come over in hope that there might be goodies for them. "Uncle Ben says you're sapient."

"Yeek?"

"They want to know if it's good to eat. What'll happen now?"

"Nothing, for about a year. Six months from now,

when the ship gets in, the Institute will release it to the press, and then they'll send an investigation team here. So will any of the other universities or scientific institutes that may be interested. I suppose the government'll send somebody, too. After all, subcivilized natives on colonized planets are wards of the Terran Federation."

He didn't know that he liked that. The less he had to do with the government the better, and his Fuzzies were wards of Pappy Jack Holloway. He said as much.

Rainsford picked up Mitzi and stroked her. "Nice fur," he said. "Fur like that would bring good prices. It will, if we don't get these people recognized as sapient beings."

He looked across the run at the new camp and wondered. Maybe Leonard Kellogg saw that, too, and saw profits for the Company in Fuzzy fur.

The airjeeps returned in the middle of the afternoon, first Mallin's, and then Kellogg's. Everybody went inside. An hour later, a constabulary car landed in front of the Kellogg camp. George Lunt and Ahmed Khadra got out. Kellogg came outside, spoke with them and then took them into the main living hut. Half an hour later, the lieutenant and the trooper emerged, lifted their car across the run and set it down on the lawn. The Fuzzies ran to meet them, possibly expecting more whistles, and followed them into the living room. Lunt and Khadra took off their berets, but made no move to unbuckle their gun belts.

"We got your package off all right Ben," Lunt said. He sat down and took Goldilocks on his lap; immediately Cinderella jumped up, also. "Jack, what the hell's that gang over there up to anyhow?"

"You got that, too?"

"You can smell it on them for a mile, against the wind. In the first place, that Borch. I wish I could get his prints; I'll bet we have them on file. And the whole gang's trying to hide something, and what they're trying to hide is something they're scared of, like a body in a closet. When we were over there, Kellogg did all the talking; anybody else who tried to say anything got shut up fast. Kellogg doesn't like you, Jack and he doesn't like Ben, and he doesn't like the Fuzzies. Most of all he doesn't like the Fuzzies."

"Well, I told you what I thought this morning," Rainsford said. "They don't want outsiders discovering things on this planet. It wouldn't make them look good to the home office on Terra. Remember, it was some non-Company people who discovered the first sunstones, back in 'Forty-eight."

George Lunt looked thoughtful. On him, it was a scowl.

"I don't think that's it, Ben. When we were talking to him, he admitted very freely that you and Jack discovered the Fuzzies. The way he talked, he didn't seem to think they were worth discovering at all. And he asked a lot of funny questions about you, Jack. The kind of questions I'd ask if I was checking up on somebody's mental competence." The scowl became one of anger now. "By God, I wish I had an excuse to question him—with a veridicator!"

Kellogg didn't want the Fuzzies to be sapient beings. If they weren't they'd be . . . fur-bearing animals. Jack thought of some overfed society dowager on Terra or Baldur, wearing the skins of Little Fuzzy and Mamma Fuzzy and Mike and Mitzi and Ko-Ko and Cinderella and Goldilocks wrapped around her adipose carcass. It made him feel sick.

VII

Tuesday dawned hot and windless, a scarlet sun coming up in a hard, brassy sky. The Fuzzies, who were in to wake Pappy Jack with their whistles, didn't like it; they were edgy and restless. Maybe it would rain today after all. They had breakfast outside on the picnic table, and then Ben decided he'd go back to his camp and pick up a few things he hadn't brought and now decided he needed.

"My hunting rifle's one," he said, "and I think I'll circle down to the edge of the brush country and see if I can pick off a zebralope. We ought to have some more fresh meat."

So, after eating, Rainsford got into his jeep and lifted away. Across the run, Kellogg and Mallin were walking back and forth in front of the camp, talking earnestly. When Ruth Ortheris and Gerd van Riebeek came out, they stopped, broke off their conversation and spoke briefly with them. Then Gerd and Ruth crossed the footbridge and came up the path together.

The Fuzzies had scattered, by this time, to hunt prawns. Little Fuzzy and Ko-Ko and Goldilocks ran to meet them; Ruth picked Goldilocks up and carried her, and Ko-Ko and Little Fuzzy ran on ahead. They greeted Jack, declining coffee; Ruth sat down in a chair with Goldilocks, Little Fuzzy jumped up on the table and began looking for goodies, and when Gerd stretched out on his back on the grass Ko-Ko sat down on his chest.

"Goldilocks is my favorite Fuzzy," Ruth was saying. "She is the sweetest thing. Of course, they're all pretty nice. I can't get over how affectionate and trusting they are; the ones we saw out in the woods were so timid."

"Well, the ones out in the woods don't have any Pappy Jack to look after them" Gerd said. "I'd imagine they're very affectionate among themselves, but they have so many things to be afraid of. You know, there's another prerequisite for sapience. It develops in some small, relatively defenseless, animal surrounded by large and dangerous enemies he can't outrun or outfight. So, to survive, he has to learn to outthink them. Like our own remote ancestors, or like Little Fuzzy; he had his choice of getting sapient or getting exterminated."

Ruth seemed troubled. "Gerd, Dr. Mallin has found absolutely nothing about them that indicates true sapience."

"Oh, Mallin be bloodied; he doesn't know what sapience is any more than I do. And a good deal less than you do, I'd say. I think he's trying to prove that the Fuzzies aren't sapient."

Ruth looked startled. "What makes you say that?"

"It's been sticking out all over him ever since he came here. You're a psychologist; don't tell me you haven't seen it. Maybe if the Fuzzies were proven sapient it would invalidate some theory he's gotten out of a book, and he'd have to do some thinking for himself. He wouldn't like that. But you have to admit he's been fighting the idea, intellectually and emotionally, right from the start. Why, they could sit down with pencils and slide rules and start working differential calculus and it wouldn't convince him."

"Dr. Mallin's trying to—" she began angrily. Then she broke it off. "Jack, excuse us. We didn't really come over here to have a fight. We came to meet some Fuzzies. Didn't we, Goldilocks?"

Goldilocks was playing with the silver charm on the

chain around her neck, holding it to her ear and shaking it to make it tinkle, making small delighted sounds. Finally she held it up and said, "Yeek?"

"Yes, sweetie-pie, you can have it." Ruth took the chain from around her neck and put it over Goldilocks' head; she had to loop it three times before it would fit. "There now; that's your very own."

"Oh, you mustn't give her things like that."

"Why not. It's just cheap trade-junk. You've been on Loki, Jack, you know what it is." He did; he'd traded stuff like that to the natives himself. "Some of the girls at the hospital there gave it to me for a joke. I only wear it because I have it. Goldilocks likes it a lot better than I do."

An airjeep rose from the other side and floated across. Juan Jimenez was piloting it; Ernst Mallin stuck his head out the window on the right, asked her if she were ready and told Gerd that Kellogg would pick him up in a few minutes. After she had gotten into the jeep and it had lifted out, Gerd put Ko-Ko off his chest and sat up, getting cigarettes from his shirt pocket.

"I don't know what the devil's gotten into her," he said, watching the jeep vanish. "Oh, yes, I do. She's gotten the Word from On High. Kellogg hath spoken. Fuzzies are just silly little animals," he said bitterly.

"You work for Kellogg, too, don't you?"

"Yes. He doesn't dictate my professional opinion, though. You know, I thought, in the evil hour when I took this job—" He rose to his feet, hitching his belt to balance the weight of the pistol on the right against the camera-binoculars on the left, and changed the subject abruptly. "Jack, has Ben Rainsford sent a report on the Fuzzies to the Institute yet?" he asked.

"Why?"

"If he hasn't, tell him to hurry up and get one in."

There wasn't time to go into that further. Kellogg's jeep was rising from the camp across the run and approaching.

He decided to let the breakfast dishes go till after lunch. Kurt Borch had stayed behind at the Kellogg camp, so he kept an eye on the Fuzzies and brought them back when they started to stray toward the footbridge. Ben Rainsford hadn't returned by lunchtime, but zebralope hunting took a little time, even from the air. While he was eating, outside, one of the rented airjeeps returned from the northeast in a hurry, disgorging Ernst Mallin, Juan Jimenez and Ruth Ortheris. Kurt Borch came hurrying out; they talked for a few minutes, and then they all went inside. A little later, the second jeep came in, even faster, and landed; Kellogg and van Riebeek hastened into the living hut. There wasn't anything more to see. He carried the dishes into the kitchen and washed them, and the Fuzzies went into the bedroom for their nap.

He was sitting at the table in the living room when Gerd van Riebeek knocked on the open door.

"Jack, can I talk to you for a minute?" he asked.

"Sure. Come in."

Van Riebeek entered, unbuckling his gun belt. He shifted a chair so that he could see the door from it, and laid the belt on the floor at his feet when he sat down. Then he began to curse Leonard Kellogg in four or five languages.

"Well, I agree, in principle; why in particular, though?"

"You know what that son of a Kooghra's doing?" Gerd asked. "He and that—" He used a couple of Sheshan words, viler than anything in Lingua Terra. "—that quack headshrinker, Mallin, are preparing a report, accusing you and Ben Rainsford of perpetrating a deliberate scientific hoax. You taught the Fuzzies some tricks; you and Rainsford, between you, made those artifacts yourselves and the two of you are conspiring to foist the Fuzzies off as sapient beings. Jack, if it weren't so goddamn stinking contemptible, it would be the biggest joke of the century!"

"I take it they wanted you to sign this report, too?"

"Yes, and I told Kellogg he could—" What Kellogg could do, it seemed, was both appalling and physiologically impossible. He cursed again, and then lit a cigarette and got hold of himself. "Here's what happened. Kellogg and I went up that stream, about twenty miles down Cold Creek, the one you've been working on, and up onto the high flat to a spring and a stream that flows down in the opposite direction. Know where I mean? Well, we found where some Fuzzies had been camping, among a lot of fallen timber. And we found a little grave, where the Fuzzies had buried one of their people."

He should have expected something like that, and yet it startled him. "You mean, they bury their dead? What was the grave like?"

"A little stone cairn, about a foot and a half by three, a foot high. Kellogg said it was just a big toilet pit, but I was sure of what it was. I opened it. Stones under the cairn, and then filled-in earth, and then a dead Fuzzy wrapped in grass. A female; she'd been mangled by something, maybe a bush-goblin. And get this Jack; they'd buried her prawn-stick with her."

"They bury their dead! What was Kellogg doing, while you were opening the grave?"

"Dithering around having ants. I'd been taking snaps of the grave, and I was burbling away like an ass about how important this was and how it was positive proof of sapience, and he was insisting that we get back to camp at once. He called the other jeep and told Mallin to get to camp immediately, and Mallin and Ruth and Juan were there when we got in. As soon as Kellogg told them what we'd found, Mallin turned fish-belly white and wanted to know how we were going to suppress it. I asked him if he was nuts, and then Kellogg came out with it. They don't dare let the Fuzzies be proven sapient."

"Because the Company wants to sell Fuzzy furs?"

Van Riebeek looked at him in surprise. "I never thought of that. I doubt if they did, either. No. Because if the Fuzzies are sapient beings, the Company's charter is automatically void."

This time Jack cursed, not Kellogg but himself.

"I am a senile old dotard! Good Lord, I know colonial law; I've been skating on the edge of it on more planets than you're years old. And I never thought of that; why, of course it would. Where are you now, with the Company, by the way?"

"Out, but I couldn't care less. I have enough in the bank for the trip back to Terra, not counting what I can raise on my boat and some other things. Xenonaturalists don't need to worry about finding jobs. There's Ben's outfit, for instance. And, brother, when I get back to Terra, what I'll spill about this deal!"

"If you get back. If you don't have an accident before you get on the ship." He thought for a moment. "Know anything about geology?"

"Why, some; I have to work with fossils. I'm as much a paleontologist as a zoologist. Why?"

"How'd you like to stay here with me and hunt fossil jellyfish for a while? We won't make twice as much, together, as I'm making now, but you can look one way while I'm looking the other, and we may both stay alive longer that way."

"You mean that, Jack?"

"I said it, didn't I?"

Van Riebeek rose and held out his hand; Jack came around the table and shook it. Then he reached back and picked up his belt, putting it on.

"Better put yours on, too, partner. Borch is probably the only one we'll need a gun for, but—"

Van Riebeek buckled on his belt, then drew his pistol and worked the slide to load the chamber. "What are we going to do?" he asked.

"Well, we're going to try to handle it legally. Fact is, I'm even going to call the cops."

He punched out a combination on the communication screen. It lighted and opened a window into the constabulary post. The sergeant who looked out of it recognized him and grinned.

"Hi, Jack. How's the family?" he asked. "I'm coming up, one of these evenings, to see them."

"You can see some now." Ko-Ko and Goldilocks and Cinderella were coming out of the hall from the bedroom; he gathered them up and put them on the table. The sergeant was fascinated. Then he must have noticed that both Jack and Gerd were wearing their guns in the house. His eyes narrowed slightly.

"You got problems, Jack?" he asked.

"Little ones; they may grow, though. I have some guests here who have outstayed their welcome. For the record, better make it that I have squatters I want evicted. If there were a couple of blue uniforms around, maybe it might save me the price of a few cartridges."

"I read you. George was mentioning that you might regret inviting that gang to camp on you." He picked up a handphone. "Calderon to Car Three," he said. "Do you read me, Three? Well, Jack Holloway's got a little squatter trouble. Yeah; that's it. He's ordering them off his grant, and he thinks they might try to give him an argument. Yeah, sure, Peace Lovin' Jack Holloway, that's him. Well, go chase his squatters for him, and if they give you anything about being Company big wheels, we don't care what kind of wheels they are, just so's they start rolling." He replaced the phone. "Look for them in about an hour, Jack."

"Why, thanks, Phil. Drop in some evening when you can hang up your gun and stay awhile."

He blanked the screen and began punching again. This time he got a girl, and then the Company construction boss at Red Hill.

"Oh, hello, Jack; is Dr. Kellog comfortable?"

"Not very. He's moving out this afternoon. I wish you'd have your gang come up with those scows and get that stuff out of my back yard."

"Well, he told us he was staying for a couple of weeks."

"He got his mind changed for him. He's to be off my land by sunset."

The Company man looked troubled. "Jack, you haven't been having trouble with Dr. Kellogg, have you?" he asked. "He's a big man with the Company."

"That's what he tells me. You'll still have to come and get that stuff, though."

He blanked the screen. "You know," he said, "I think it would be no more than fair to let Kellogg in on this. What's his screen combination?"

Gerd supplied it, and he punched it out. One of those tricky special Company combinations. Kurt Borch appeared in the screen immediately.

"I want to talk to Kellogg."

"*Doctor* Kellogg is very busy, at present."

"He's going to be a damned sight busier; this is moving day. The whole gang of you have till eighteen hundred to get off my grant."

Borch was shoved aside, and Kellogg appeared. "What's this nonsense?" he demanded angrily.

"You're ordered to move. You want to know why? I can let Gerd van Riebeek talk to you; I think there are a few things he's forgotten to call you."

"You can't order us out like this. Why, you gave us permission—"

"Permission cancelled. I've called Mike Hennen in Red Hill; he's sending his scows back for the stuff he brought here. Lieutenant Lunt will have a couple of troopers here, too. I'll expect you to have your personal things aboard your airboat when they arrive."

He blanked the screen while Kellogg was trying to tell him that it was all a misunderstanding.

"I think that's everything. It's quite a while till sundown," he added, "but I move for suspension of rules while we pour a small libation to sprinkle our new partnership. Then we can go outside and observe the enemy."

There was no observable enemy action when they went out and sat down on the bench by the kitchen door. Kellogg would be screening Mike Hennen and the constabulary post for verification, and there would be a lot of gathering up and packing to do. Finally, Kurt Borch emerged with a contragravity lifter piled with boxes and luggage, and Jimenez walking beside to steady the load. Jimenez climbed up onto the airboat and Borch floated the load up to him and then went back into the huts. This was repeated several times. In the meantime, Kellogg and Mallin seemed to be having some sort of exchange of recriminations in front. Ruth Ortheris came out, carrying a briefcase, and sat down on the edge of a table under the awning.

Neither of them had been watching the Fuzzies, until they saw one of them start down the path toward the footbridge, a glint of silver at the throat identifying Goldilocks.

"Look at that fool kid; you stay put, Gerd, and I'll bring her back."

He started down the path; by the time he had reached the bridge, Goldilocks was across and had vanished behind one of the airjeeps parked in front of the Kellogg camp. When he was across and within twenty feet of the vehicle, he heard a sound across and within twenty feet of the vehicle, he heard a sound he had never heard before—a shrill, thin shriek, like a file on saw teeth. At the same time, Ruth's voice screamed.

"Don't! Leonard, stop that!"

As he ran around the jeep, the shrieking broke off suddenly. Goldilocks was on the ground, her fur reddened. Kellogg stood over her, one foot raised. He was wearing white shoes, and they were both spotted with blood. He stamped the foot down on the little bleeding body, and then Jack was within reach of him, and something crunched under the fist he drove into Kellogg's face. Kellogg staggered and tried to raise his hands; he made a strangled noise, and for an instant the idiotic thought crossed Jack's mind that he was trying to say, "Now, please don't misunderstand me."

He caught Kellogg's shirt front in his left hand, and punched him again in the face, and again, and again. He didn't know how many times he punched Kellogg before he heard Ruth Ortheris' voice:

"Jack! Watch out! Behind you!"

He let go of Kellogg's shirt and jumped aside, turning and reaching for his gun. Kurt Borch, twenty feet away, had a pistol drawn and pointed at him.

His first shot went off as soon as the pistol was clear of the holster. He fired the second while it was still recoiling; there was a spot of red on Borch's shirt that gave him an aiming point for the third. Borch dropped the pistol he hadn't been able to fire, and started folding at the knees and then at the waist. He went down in a heap on his face.

Behind him, Gerd van Riebeek's voice was saying, "Hold it, all of you; get your hands up. You, too, Kellogg."

Kellogg, who had fallen, pushed himself erect. Blood was gushing from his nose, and he tried to stanch it on the sleeve of his jacket. As he stumbled toward his companions, he blundered into Ruth Ortheris, who pushed him angrily away from her. Then she went to the little crushed body, dropping to her knees beside it and touching it. The silver charm bell on the neck chain jingled faintly. Ruth began to cry.

Juan Jimenez had climbed down from the airboat; he was looking at the body of Kurt Borch in horror.

"You killed him!" he accused. A moment later, he changed that to "murdered." Then he started to run toward the living hut.

Gerd van Riebeek fired a bullet into the ground ahead of him, bringing him up short.

"You'll stop the next one, Juan," he said. "Go help Dr. Kellogg; he got himself hurt."

"Call the constabulary," Mallin was saying. "Ruth, you go; they won't shoot at you."

"Don't bother. I called them. Remember?"

Jimenez had gotten a wad of handkerchief tissue out

of his pocket and was trying to stop his superior's nosebleed. Through it, Kellogg was trying to tell Mallin that he hadn't been able to help it.

"The little beast attacked me; it cut me with that spear it was carrying."

Ruth Ortheris looked up. The other Fuzzies were with her by the body of Goldilocks; they must have come as soon as they had heard the screaming.

"She came up to him and pulled at his trouser leg, the way they all do when they want to attract your attention," she said. "She wanted him to look at her new jingle." Her voice broke, and it was a moment before she could recover it. "And he kicked her, and then stamped her to death."

"Ruth, keep your mouth shut!" Mallin ordered. "The thing attacked Leonard; it might have given him a serious wound."

"It did!" Still holding the wad of tissue to his nose with one hand, Kellogg pulled up his trouser leg with the other and showed a scar on his shin. It looked like a briar scratch. "You saw it yourself."

"Yes, I saw it. I saw you kick her and jump on her. And all she wanted was to show you her new jingle."

Jack was beginning to regret that he hadn't shot Kellogg as soon as he saw what was going on. The other Fuzzies had been trying to get Goldilocks onto her feet. When they realized that it was no use, they let the body down again and crouched in a circle around it, making soft, lamenting sounds.

"Well, when the constabulary get here, you keep quiet," Mallin was saying. "Let me do the talking."

"Intimidating witnesses, Mallin?" Gerd inquired. "Don't you know everybody'll have to testify at the constabulary post under veridication? And you're drawing pay for being a psychologist, too." Then he saw some of the Fuzzies raise their heads and look toward the southeastern horizon. "Here come the cops, now."

However, it was Ben Rainsford's airjeep, with a zebralope carcass lashed along one side. It circled the Kellogg camp and then let down quickly; Rainsford jumped out as soon as it was grounded, his pistol drawn.

"What happened, Jack?" he asked, then glanced around, from Goldilocks to Kellogg to Borch to the pistol beside Borch's body. "I get it. Last time anybody pulled a gun on you, they called it suicide."

"That's what this was, more or less. You have a movie camera in your jeep? Well, get some shots of Borch, and some of Goldilocks. Then stand by, and if the Fuzzies start doing anything different, get it all. I don't think you'll be disappointed."

Rainsford looked puzzled, but he holstered his pistol and went back to his jeep, returning with a camera. Mallin began insisting that, as a licensed M.D., he had a right to treat Kellogg's injuries. Gerd van Riebeek followed him into the living hut for a first-aid kit. They were just emerging, van Riebeek's automatic in the small of Mallin's back, when a constabulary car grounded beside Rainsford's airjeep. It wasn't Car Three. George Lunt jumped out, unsnapping the flap of his holster, while Ahmed Khadra was talking into the radio.

"What's happened, Jack? Why didn't you wait till we got here?"

"This maniac assaulted me and murdered that man over there!" Kellogg began vociferating.

"Is your name Jack too?" Lunt demanded.

"My name's Leonard Kellogg, and I'm a chief of division with the Company—"

"Then keep quiet till I ask you something. Ahmed, call the post; get Knabber and Yorimitsu, with investigative equipment, and find out what's tying up Car Three."

Mallin had opened the first-aid kit by now; Gerd, on seeing the constabulary, had holstered his pistol. Kellogg, still holding the sodden tissues to his nose, was wanting to know what there was to investigate.

"There's the murderer; you have him red-handed. Why don't you arrest him?"

"Jack, let's get over where we can watch these people without having to listen to them," Lunt said. He glanced toward the body of Goldilocks. "That happen first?"

"Watch out, Lieutenant! He still has his pistol!" Mallin shouted warningly.

They went over and sat down on the contragravity-field generator housing one of the rented airjeeps. Jack started with Gerd van Riebeek's visit immediately after noon.

"Yes, I thought of that angle myself," Lunt said disgustedly. "I didn't think of it till this morning, though, and I didn't think things would blow up as fast as this. Hell, I just didn't think! Well, go on."

He interrupted a little later to ask: "Kellogg was stamping on the Fuzzy when you hit him. You were trying to stop him?"

"That's right. You can veridicate me on that if you want to."

"I will; I'll veridicate this whole damn gang. And this guy Borch had his heater out when you turned around? Nothing to it, Jack. We'll have to have some kind of a hearing, but it's just plain self-defense. Think any of this gang will tell the truth here, without taking them in and putting them under veridication?"

"Ruth Ortheris will, I think."

"Send her over here, will you."

She was still with the Fuzzies, and Ben Rainsford was standing beside her, his camera ready. The Fuzzies were still swaying and yeeking plaintively. She nodded and rose without speaking, going over to where Lunt waited.

"Just what did happen, Jack?" Rainsford wanted to know. "And whose side is he on?" He nodded toward van Riebeek, standing guard over Kellogg and Mallin, his thumbs in his pistol belt.

"Ours. He's quit the Company."

Just as he was finishing, Car Three put in an appearance; he had to tell the same story over again. The area in front of the Kellogg camp was getting congested; he hoped Mike Hennen's labor gang would stay away for a while. Lunt talked to van Riebeek when he had finished with Ruth, and then with Jimenez and Mallin and Kellogg. Then he and one of the men from Car Three came over to where Jack and Rainsford were standing. Gerd van Riebeek joined them just as Lunt was saying:

"Jack, Kellogg's made a murder complaint against you. I told him it was self-defense, but he wouldn't listen. So, according to the book, I have to arrest you."

"All right." He unbuckled his gun and handed it over. "Now, George, I herewith make complaint and accusation against Leonard Kellogg, charging him with the unlawful and unjustified killing of a sapient being, to wit, an aboriginal native of the planet of Zarathustra commonly known as Goldilocks."

Lunt looked at the small battered body and the six mourners around it.

"But, Jack, they aren't legally sapient beings."

"There is no such thing. A sapient being is a being on the mental level of sapience, not a being that has been declared sapient."

"Fuzzies are sapient beings," Rainsford said. "That's the opinion of a qualified xeno-naturalist."

"Two of them," Gerd van Riebeek said. "That is the body of a sapient being. There's the man who killed her. Go ahead, Lieutenant, make your pinch."

"Hey! Wait a minute!"

The Fuzzies were rising, sliding their chopper-diggers under the body of Goldilocks and lifting it on the steel shafts. Ben Rainsford was aiming his camera as Cinderella picked up her sister's weapon and followed, carrying it; the others carried the body toward the far corner of the clearing, away from the camp. Rainsford kept just behind them, pausing to photograph and then hurrying to keep up with them.

They set the body down. Mike and Mitzi and Cinderella began digging; the others scattered to hunt for stones. Coming up behind them, George Lunt took off his beret and stood holding it in both hands; he bowed his head as the grass-wrapped body was placed in the little grave and covered.

Then, when the cairn was finished, he replaced it, drew his pistol and checked the chamber.

"That does it, Jack," he said. "I am now going to arrest Leonard Kellogg for the murder of a sapient being."

VIII

Jack Holloway had been out on bail before, but never for quite so much. It was almost worth it, though, to see Leslie Coombes's eyes widen and Mohammed Ali O'Brien's jaw drop when he dumped the bag of sunstones, blazing with the heat of the day and of his body, on George Lunt's magisterial bench and invited George to pick out twenty-five thousand sols' worth. Especially after the production Coombes had made of posting Kellogg's bail with one of those precertified Company checks.

He looked at the whisky bottle in his hand, and then reached into the cupboard for another one. One for Gus Brannhard, and one for the rest of them. There was a widespread belief that that was why Gustavus Adolphus Brannhard was practicing sporadic law out here in the boon docks of a boon-dock planet, defending gun fighters and veldbeest rustlers. It wasn't. Nobody on Zarathustra knew the reason, but it wasn't whisky. Whisky was only the weapon with which Gus Brannhard fought off the memory of the reason.

He was in the biggest chair in the living room, which was none too ample for him; a mountain of a man with tousled gray-brown hair, his broad face masked in a tangle of gray-brown beard. He wore a faded and grimy bush jacket with clips of rifle cartridges on the breast, no shirt and a torn undershirt over a shag of gray-brown chest hair. Between the bottoms of his shorts and the tops of his ragged hose and muddy boots, his legs were covered with hair. Baby Fuzzy was sitting on his head, and Mamma Fuzzy was on his lap. Mike and Mitzi sat one on either knee. The Fuzzies had taken instantly to Gus. Bet they thought he was a Big Fuzzy.

"Aaaah!" he rumbled, as the bottle and glass were placed beside him. "Been staying alive for hours hoping for this."

"Well, don't let any of the kids get at it. Little Fuzzy trying to smoke pipes is bad enough; I don't want any dipsos in the family, too."

Gus filled the glass. To be on the safe side, he promptly emptied it into himself.

"You got a nice family, Jack. Make a wonderful impression in court—as long as Baby doesn't try to sit on the judge's head. Any jury that sees them and hears that Ortheris girl's story will acquit you from the box, with a vote of censure for not shooting Kellogg, too."

"I'm not worried about that. What I want is Kellogg convicted."

"You better worry, Jack," Rainsford said. "You saw the combination against us at the hearing."

Leslie Coombes, the Company's top attorney, had come out from Mallorysport in a yacht rated at Mach 6, and he must have crowded it to the limit all the way. With him, almost on a leash, had come Mohammed Ali O'Brien, the Colonial Attorney General, who doubled as Chief Prosecutor. They had both tried to get the whole thing dismissed—self-defense for Holloway, and killing an unprotected wild animal for Kellogg. When that had failed, they had teamed in flagrant collusion to fight the inclusion of any evidence about the Fuzzies. After all it was only a complaint court; Lieutenant Lunt, as a police magistrate, had only the most limited powers.

"You saw how far they got, didn't you?"

"I hope we don't wish they'd succeeded," Rainsford said gloomily.

"What do you mean, Ben?" Brannhard asked.

"What do you think they'll do?"

"I don't know. That's what worries me. We're threatening the Zarathustra Company, and the Company's too big to be threatened safely," Rainsford replied. "They'll try to frame something on Jack."

"With veridication? That's ridiciulous, Ben."

"Don't you think we can prove sapience?" Gerd van Riebeek demanded.

"Who's going to define sapience? And how?" Rainsford asked. "Why, between them, Coombes and O'Brien can even agree to accept the talk-and-build-a-fire rule."

"Huh-uh!" Brannhard was positive. "Court ruling on that, about forty years ago, on Vishnu. Infanticide case, woman charged with murder in the death of her infant child. Her lawyer moved for dismissal on the grounds that murder is defined as the killing of a sapient being, a sapient being is defined as one that can talk and build a fire, and a newborn infant can do neither. Motion denied; the court ruled that while ability to speak and produce fire is positive proof of sapience, inability to do either or both does not constitute legal proof of nonsapience. If O'Brien doesn't know that, and I doubt if he does, Coombes will." Brannhard poured another drink and gulped it before the sapient beings around him could get at it. "You know what? I will make a small wager, and I will even give odds, that the first thing Ham O'Brien does when he gets back to Mallorysport will be to enter *nolle prosequi* on both charges. What I'd like would be for him to *nol. pros.* Kellogg and let the charge against Jack go to court. He would be dumb enough to do that himself, but Leslie Coombes wouldn't let him."

"But if he throws out the Kellogg case, that's it," Gerd van Riebeek said. "When Jack comes to trial, nobody'll say a mumblin' word about sapience."

"I will, and I will not mumble it. You all know colonial law on homicide. In the case of any person killed while in commission of a felony, no prosecution may be brought in any degree, against anybody. I'm going to contend that Leonard Kellogg was murdering a sapient being, that Jack Holloway acted lawfully in attempting to stop it and that when Kurt Borch attempted to come to Kellogg's assistance he, himself, was guilty of felony, and consequently any prosecution against Jack Holloway is illegal. And to make that contention stick, I shall have to say a great many words, and produce a great deal of testimony, about the sapience of Fuzzies."

"It'll have to be expert testimony," Rainsford said. "The testimony of psychologists. I suppose you know that the only psychologists on this planet are employed by the chartered Zarathustra Company." He drank what was left of his highball, looked at the bits of ice in the bottom of his glass and then rose to mix another one. "I'd have done the same as you did, Jack, but I still wish this hadn't happened."

"Huh!" Mamma Fuzzy looked up, startled by the exclamation. "What do you think Victor Grego's wishing, right now?"

Victor Grego replaced the hand-phone. "Leslie, on the yacht," he said. "They're coming in now. They'll stop at the hospital to drop Kellogg, and then they're coming here."

Nick Emmert nibbled a canape. He had reddish hair, pale eyes and a wide, bovine face.

"Holloway must have done him up pretty badly," he said.

"I wish Hollway'd killed him!" He blurted it angrily, and saw the Resident General's shocked expression.

"You don't really mean that, Victor?"

"The devil I don't! He gestured at the recorder-player, which had just finished the tape of the hearing, transmitted from the yacht at sixty-speed. "That's only a teaser to what'll come out at the trial. You know what the Company's epitaph will be? *Kicked to death, along with a Fuzzy, by Leonard Kellogg."*

Everything would have worked out perfectly if Kellogg had only kept his head and avoided collision with Holloway. Why, even the killing of the Fuzzy and the shooting of Borch, inexcusable as that had been, wouldn't have been so bad if it hadn't been for that asinine murder complaint. That was what had provoked Holloway's counter-complaint, which was what had done the damage.

And, now that he thought of it, it had been one of Kellogg's people, van Riebeek, who had touched off the explosion in the first place. He didn't know van Riebeek himself, but Kellogg should have, and he had handled him the wrong way. He should have known what van Riebeek would go along with and what he wouldn't.

"But, Victor, they won't convict Leonard of murder," Emmert was saying. "Not for killing one of those little things."

" 'Murder shall consist of the deliberate and unjustified killing of any sapient being, of any race,' " he quoted. "That's the law. If they can prove in court that the Fuzzies are sapient beings . . . "

Then, some morning, a couple of deputy marshals would take Leonard Kellogg out in the jail yard and put a bullet through the back of his head, which, in itself, would be no loss. The trouble was, they would also be shooting an irreparable hole in the Zarathustra Company's charter. Maybe Kellogg could be kept out of court, at that. There wasn't a ship blasted off from Darius without a couple of drunken spacemen being hustled aboard at the last moment; with the job Holloway must have done, Kellogg should look just right as a drunken spaceman. The twenty-five thousand sols' bond could be written off; that was pennies to the Company. No, that would still leave them stuck with the Holloway trial.

"You want me out of here when the others come, Victor?" Emmert asked, popping another canape into his mouth.

"No, no; sit still. This will be the last chance we'll have to get everybody together; after this, we'll have to avoid anything that'll look like collusion."

"Well, anything I can do to help; you know that, Victor," Emmert said.

Yes, he knew that. If worst came to utter worst and the Company charter were invalidated, he could still hang on here, doing what he could to salvage something out of the wreckage—if not for the Company, then for Victor Grego. But if Zarathustra were reclassified, Nick would be finished. His title, his social position, his sinecure, his grafts and perquisites, his alias-shrouded Company expense account—all out the airlock. Nick would be counted upon to do anything he could—however much that would be.

He looked across the room at the levitated globe, revolving imperceptibly in the orange spotlight. It was full dark on Beta Continent now, where Leonard Kellogg had killed a Fuzzy named Goldilocks and Jack Holloway had killed a gunman named Kurt Borch. That angered him, too; hell of a gunman! Clear shot at the broad of a man's back, and still got himself killed. Borch hadn't been any better choice than Kellogg himself. What was the matter with him; couldn't he pick men for jobs any more? And Ham O'Brien! No, he didn't have to blame himself for O'Brien. O'Brien was one of Nick Emmert's boys. And he hadn't picked Nick, either.

The squawk-box on the desk made a premonitory noise, and a feminine voice advised him that Mr. Coombes and his party had arrived.

"All right; show them in."

Coombes entered first, tall suavely elegant, with a calm, untroubled face. Leslie Coombes would wear the same serene expression in the midst of a bombardment or an earthquake. He had chosen Coombes for chief attorney, and thinking of that made him feel better. Mohammed Ali O'Brien was neither tall, elegant nor calm. His skin was almost black—he'd been born on Agni, under a hot B3 sun. His bald head glistened, and a big nose peeped over the ambuscade of a bushy white mustache. What was it they said about him? Only man on Zarathustra who could strut sitting down. And behind them, the remnant of the expedition to Beta Continent—Ernst Mallin, Juan Jimenez and Ruth Ortheris. Mallin was saying that it was a pity Dr. Kellogg wasn't with them.

"I question that, Well, please be seated. We have a great deal to discuss, I'm afraid."

Mr. Chief Justice Frederic Pendarvis moved the ashtray a few inches to the right and the slender vase with the spray of starflowers a few inches to the left. He set the framed photograph of the gentle-faced, white-haired woman directly in front of him. Then he took a thin cigar from the silver box, carefully punctured the end and lit it. Then, unable to think of further delaying tactics, he drew the two bulky loose-leaf books toward him and opened the red one, the criminal-case docket.

Something would have to be done about this; he always told himself so at this hour. Shoveling all this stuff onto Centeral Courts had been all right when Mallorysport had had a population of less than five thousand and nothing else on the planet had had more than five hundred, but that time was ten years past. The Chief Justice of a planetary colony shouldn't have to wade through all this to see who had been accused of blotting the brand on a veldbeest calf or who'd taken a shot at whom in a barroom. Well, at least he'd managed to get a few misdemeanor and small-claims courts established; that was something.

The first case, of course, was a homicide. It usually was. From Beta, Constabulary Fifteen, Lieutenant George Lunt. Jack Holloway—so old Jack had cut another notch on his gun—Cold Creek Valley, Federation citizen, race Terran human; willful killing of a sapient being, to wit Kurt Borch, Mallorysport, Federation citizen, race Terran human. Complainant, Leonard Kellogg, the same. Attorney of record for the defendant, Gustavus Adolphus Brannhard. The last time Jack Holloway had killed anybody, it had been a couple of thugs who'd tried to steal his sunstones; it hadn't even gotten into complaint court. This time he might be in trouble. Kellogg was a Company executive. He decided he'd better try the case himself. The Company might try to exert pressure.

The next charge was also homicide, from Constabulary, Beta Fifteen. He read it and blinked. Leonard Kellogg, willful killing of a sapient being, to wit, Jane Doe alias Goldilocks, aborigine, race Zarathustran Fuzzy; complainant, Jack Holloway, defendant's attorney of record, Leslie Coombes. In spite of the outrageous frivolity of the charge, he began to laugh. It was obviously an attempt to ridicule Kellogg's own complaint out of court. Every judicial jurisdiction ought to have at least one Gus Brannhard to liven things up a little. Race Zarathustra Fuzzy!

Then he stopped laughing suddenly and became deadly serious, like an engineer who finds a cataclysmite cartridge lying around primed and connected to a discharger. He reached out to the screen panel and began punching a combination. A spectacled young man appeared and greeted him deferentially.

"Good morning, Mr. Wilkins," he replied. "A couple of homicides at the head of this morning's docket—Holloway and Kellogg, both from Beta Fifteen. What is known about them?"

The young man began to laugh. "Oh, your Honor, they're both a lot of nonsense. Dr. Kellogg killed some pet belonging to old Jack Holloway, the sunstone digger, and in the ensuing unpleasantness—Holloway can be very unpleasant, if he feels he has to—this man Borch, who seems to have been Kellogg's bodyguard, made the suicidal error of trying to draw a gun on Holloway. I'm surprised at Lieutenant Lunt for letting either of those charges get past hearing court. Mr. O'Brien has entered *nolle prosequi* on both of them, so the whole thing can be disregarded."

Mohammed O'Brien knew a charge of cataclysmite when he saw one, too. His impulse had been to pull the detonator. Well, maybe this charge ought to be shot, just to see what it would bring down.

"I haven't approved the *nolle prosequi* yet, Mr. Wilkins," he mentioned gently. "Would you please transmit to me the hearing tapes on these cases, at sixty-speed? I'll take them on the recorder of this screen. Thank you."

He reached out and made the necessary adjustments. Wilkins, the Clerk of the Courts, left the screen, and returned. There was a wavering scream for a minute and a half. Going to take more time than he had expected. Well . . .

There wasn't enough ice in the glass, and Leonard Kellogg put more in. Then there was too much, and he added more brandy. He shouldn't have started drinking this early, be drunk by dinnertime if he kept it up, but what else was there to do? He couldn't go out, not with his face like this. In any case, he wasn't sure he wanted to.

They were all down on him. Ernst Mallin, and Ruth Ortheris, and even Juan Jimenez. At the constabulary post, Coombes and O'Brien had treated him like an idiot child who has to be hushed in front of company and coming back to Mallorysport they had ignored him completely. He drank quickly, and then there was too much ice in the glass again. Victor Grego had told him he'd better take a vacation till the trial was over, and put Mallin in charge of the division. Said he oughtn't to be in charge while the division was working on defense evidence. Well, maybe; it looked like the first step toward shoving him completely out of the Company.

He dropped into a chair and lit a cigarette. It tasted

badly, and after a few puffs he crushed it out. Well, what else could he have done? After they'd found that little grave, he had to make Gerd understand what it would mean to the Company. Juan and Ruth had been all right, but Gerd—The things Gerd had called him; the things he'd said about the Company. And then that call from Holloway, and the humiliation of being ordered out like a tramp.

And then that disgusting little beast had come pulling at his clothes, and he had pushed it away—well, kicked it maybe—and it had struck at him with the little spear it was carrying. Nobody but a lunatic would give a thing like that to an animal anyhow. And he had kicked it again, and it had screamed. . . .

The communication screen in the next room was buzzing. Maybe that was Victor. He gulped the brandy left in the glass and hurried to it.

It was Leslie Coombes, his face remotely expressionless.

"Oh, hello, Leslie."

"Good afternoon, Dr. Kellogg." The formality of address was studiously rebuking. "The Chief Prosecutor just called me; Judge Pendarvis has denied the *nolle prosequi* he entered in your case and in Mr. Holloway's, and ordered both cases to trial."

"You mean they're actually taking this seriously?"

"It is serious. If you're convicted, the Company's charter will be almost automatically voided. And, although this is important only to you personally, you might, very probably, be sentenced to be shot." He shrugged that off, and continued: "Now, I'll want to talk to you about your defense, for which I am responsible. Say ten-thirty tomorrow, at my office. I should, by that time, know what sort of evidence is going to be used against you. I will be expecting you, Dr. Kellogg."

He must have said more than that, but that was all that registered. Leonard wasn't really conscious of going back to the other room, until he realized that he was sitting in his relaxer chair, filling the glass with brandy. There was only a little ice in it, but he didn't care.

They were going to try him for murder for killing that little animal, and Ham O'Brien had said they wouldn't, he'd promised he'd keep the case from trial and he hadn't, they were going to try him anyhow and if they convicted him they would take him out and shoot him for just killing a silly little animal he had killed it he'd kicked it and jumped on it he could still hear it screaming and feel the horrible soft crunching under his feet. . . .

He gulped what was left in the glass and poured and gulped more. Then he staggered to his feet and stumbled over to the couch and threw himself onto it, face down, among the cushions.

Leslie Coombes found Nick Emmert with Victor Grego in the latter's office when he entered. They both rose to greet him, and Grego said "You've heard?"

"Yes. O'Brien called me immediately. I called my client—my client of record, that is— and told him. I'm afraid it was rather a shock to him."

"It wasn't any shock to me," Grego said as they sat down. "When Ham O'Brien's as positive about anything as he was about that, I always expect the worst."

"Pendarvis is going to try the case himself," Emmert said. "I always thought he was a reasonable man, but what's he trying to do now? Cut the Company's throat?"

"He isn't anti-Company. He isn't pro-Company either. He's just pro-law. The law says that a planet with native sapient inhabitants is a Class-IV planet, and has to have a Class-IV colonial government. If Zarathustra is a Class-IV planet, he wants it established, and the proper laws applied. If it's a Class-IV planet, the Zarathustra Company is illegally chartered. It's his job to put a stop to illegality. Frederic Pendarvis' religion is the law, and he is its priest. You never get anywhere by arguing religion with a priest."

They were both silent for a while after he had finished. Grego was looking at the globe, and he realized, now, that while he was proud of it, his pride was the pride in a paste jewel that stands for a real one in a bank vault. Now he was afraid that the real jewel was going to be stolen from him. Nick Emmert was just afraid.

"You were right yesterday, Victor. I wish Holloway'd killed that son of a Khooghra. Maybe it's not too late—"

"Yes, it is, Nick. It's too late to do anything like that. It's too late to do anything but win the case in court." He turned to Grego. "What are your people doing?"

Grego took his eyes from the globe. "Ernest Mallin's studying all the filmed evidence we have and all the descriptions of Fuzzy behavior, and trying to prove that none of it is the result of sapient mentation. Ruth Ortheris is doing the same, only she's working on the line of instinct and conditioned reflexes and nonsapient, single-stage reasoning. She has a lot of rats, and some dogs and monkeys, and a lot of apparatus, and some technician from Henry Stenson's instrument shop helping her. Juan Jimenez is studying mentation of Terran dogs, cats and primates, and Freyan kholphs and Mimir black slinkers."

"He hasn't turned up any simian or canine parallels to that funeral, has he?"

Grego said nothing, merely shook his head. Emmert muttered something inaudible and probably indecent.

"I didn't think he had. I only hope those Fuzzies don't get up in court, build a bonfire and start making speeches in Lingua Terra."

Nick Emmert cried out in panic. "You believe they're sapient yourself!"

"Of course. Don't you?"

Grego laughed sourly. "Nick thinks you have to believe a thing to prove it. It helps but it isn't necessary. Say we're a debating team; we've been handed the negative of the question. *Resolved: that Fuzzies are*

Sapient Beings. Personally, I think we have the short end of it, but that only means we'll have to work harder on it."

"You know, I was on a debating team at college," Emmert said brightly. When that was disregarded, he added: "If I remember, the first thing was definition of terms."

Grego looked up quickly. "Leslie, I think Nick has something. What is the legal definition of a sapient being?"

"As far as I know, there isn't any. Sapience is something that's just taken for granted."

"How about talk-and-build-a-fire?"

He shook his head. *People of the Colony of Vishnu versus Emily Morrosh,* 612 A.E." He told them about the infanticide case. "I was looking up rulings on sapience; I passed the word on to Ham O'Brien. You know, what your people will have to do will be to produce a definition of sapience, acceptable to the court, that will include all known sapient races and at the same time exclude the Fuzzies. I don't envy them."

"We need some Fuzzies of our own to study," Grego said.

"Too bad we can't get hold of Holloway's," Emmert said. "Maybe we could, if he leaves them alone at his camp."

"No. We can't risk that." He thought for a moment. "Wait a moment. I think we might be able to do it at that. Legally."

IX

Jack Holloway saw Little Fuzzy eying the pipe he had laid in the ashtray, and picked it up, putting it in his mouth. Little Fuzzy looked reproachfully at him and started to get down onto the floor. Pappy Jack was mean; didn't he think a Fuzzy might want to smoke a pipe, too? Well, maybe it wouldn't hurt him. He picked Little Fuzzy up and set him back on his lap, offering the pipestem. Little Fuzzy took a puff. He didn't cough over it; evidently he had learned how to avoid inhaling.

"They scheduled the Kellogg trial first," Gus Brannhard was saying, "and there wasn't any way I could stop that. You see what the idea is? They'll try him first, with Leslie Coombes running both the prosecution and the defense, and if they can get him acquitted, it'll prejudice the sapience evidence we introduce in your trial."

Mamma Fuzzy made another try at intercepting the drink he was hoisting, but he frustrated that. Baby had stopped trying to sit on his head, and was playing peek-a-boo from behind his whiskers.

"First," he continued, "they'll exclude every bit of evidence about the Fuzzies that they can. That won't be much, but there'll be a fight to get any of it in. What they can't exclude, they'll attack. They'll attack credibility. Of course, with veridication, they can't claim anybody's lying, but they can claim self-deception. You make a statement you believe, true or false, and the veridicator'll back you up on it. They'll attack qualifications on expert testimony. They'll quibble about statements of fact and statements of opinion. And what they can't exclude or attack, they'll accept, and then deny that it's proof of sapience.

"What the hell do they want for proof of sapience?" Gerd demanded. "Nuclear energy and contragravity and hyperdrive?"

"They will have a nice, neat, pedantic definition of sapience, tailored especially to exclude the Fuzzies, and they will present it in court and try to get it accepted, and it's up to us to guess in advance what that will be, and have a refutation of it ready, and also a definition of our own."

"Their definition will have to include Khooghras. Gerd, do the Khooghras bury their dead?"

"Hell, no; they eat them. But you have to give them this, they cook them first."

"Look, we won't get anywhere arguing about what Fuzzies do and Khooghras don't do," Rainsford said. "We'll have to get a definition of sapience. Remember what Ruth said Saturday night?"

Gerd van Riebeek looked as though he didn't want to remember what Ruth had said, or even remember Ruth herself. Jack nodded, and repeated it. "I got the impression of non-sapient intelligence shading up to a sharp line, and then sapience shading up from there, maybe a different color, or wavy lines instead of straight ones."

"That's a good graphic representation," Gerd said. "You know, that line's so sharp I'd be tempted to think of sapience as a result of mutation, except that I can't quite buy the same mutation happening in the same way on so many different planets."

Ben Rainsford started to say something, then stopped short when a constabulary siren hooted over the camp. The Fuzzies looked up interestedly. They knew what that was. Pappy Jack's friends in the blue clothes. Jack went to the door and opened it, putting the outside light on.

The car was landing; George Lunt, two of his men and two men in civilian clothes were getting out. Both the latter were armed, and one of them carried a bundle under his arm.

"Hello, George; come on in."

"We want to talk to you, Jack." Lunt's voice was strained, empty of warmth or friendliness. "At least, these men do."

"Why, yes. Sure."

He backed into the room to permit them to enter. Something was wrong; something bad had come up. Khadra came in first, placing himself beside and a little behind him. Lunt followed, glancing quickly around and placing himself between Jack and the gunrack and also the holstered pistols on the table. The third trooper let the two strangers in ahead of him, and then closed the door and put his back against it. He wondered if the court might have cancelled his bond and ordered him into custody. The two strangers—a beefy man with a scrubby black mustache and a smaller one with a thin, saturnine face—were looking expectantly at Lunt. Rainsford and van Riebeek were on their feet. Gus Brannhard leaned over to refill his glass, but did not rise.

"Let me have the papers," Lunt said to the beefy stranger.

The other took a folded document and handed it over.

"Jack, this isn't my idea," Lunt said. "I don't want to do it, but I have to. I wouldn't want to shoot you, either, but you make any resistance and I will. I'm no Kurt Borch; I know you, and I won't take any chances."

"If you're going to serve that paper, serve it," the bigger of the two strangers said. "Don't stand yakking all night."

"Jack," Lunt said uncomfortably, "this is a court order to impound your Fuzzies as evidence in the Kellogg case. These men are deputy marshals from

Central Courts; they've been ordered to bring the Fuzzies into Mallorysport."

"Let me see the order, Jack," Brannhard said, still remaining seated.

Lunt handed it to Jack, and he handed it across to Brannhard. Gus had been drinking steadily all evening; maybe he was afraid he'd show it if he stood up. He looked at it briefly and nodded.

"Court order, all right, signed by the Chief Justice." He handed it back. "They have to take the Fuzzies, and that's all there is to it. Keep that order, though, and make them give you a signed and thumbprinted receipt. Type it up for them now, Jack."

Gus wanted to busy him with something, so he wouldn't have to watch what was going on. The smaller of the two deputies had dropped the bundle from under his arm. It was a number of canvas sacks. He sat down at the typewriter, closing his ears to the noises in the room, and wrote the receipt, naming the Fuzzies and describing them, and specifying that they were in good health and uninjured. One of them tried to climb to his lap, yeeking frantically; it clutched his shirt, but it was snatched away. He was finished with his work before the invaders were with theirs. They had three Fuzzies already in sacks. Khadra was catching Cinderella. Ko-Ko and Little Fuzzy had run for the little door in the outside wall, but Lunt was standing with his heels against it, holding it shut; when they saw that, both of them began burrowing in the bedding. The third trooper and the smaller of the two deputies dragged them out and stuffed them into sacks.

He got to his feet, still stunned and only half comprehending, and took the receipt out of the typewriter. There was an argument about it; Lunt told the deputies to sign it or get the hell out without the Fuzzies. They signed, inked their thumbs and printed after their signatures. Jack gave the paper to Gus, trying not to look at the six bulging, writhing sacks, or hear the frightened little sounds.

"George, you'll let them have some of their things, won't you?" he asked.

"Sure. What kind of things?"

"Their bedding. Some of their toys."

"You mean this junk?" The smaller of the two deputies kicked the ball-and-stick construction. "All we got orders to take is the Fuzzies."

"You heard the gentleman." Lunt made the word sound worse than son of a Khooghra. He turned to the two deputies. "Well, you have them; what are you waiting for?"

Jack watched from the door as they put the sacks into the aircar, climbed in after them and lifted out. Then he came back and sat down at the table.

"They don't know anything about court orders," he said. "They don't know why I didn't stop it. They think Pappy Jack let them down."

"Have they gone, Jack?" Brannhard asked. "Sure?" Then he rose, reaching behind him, and took up a little ball of white fur. Baby Fuzzy caught his beard with both tiny hands, yeeking happily.

"Baby! They didn't get him!"

Brannhard disengaged the little hands from his beard and handed him over.

"No, and they signed for him, too." Brannhard downed what was left of his drink, got a cigar out of his pocket and lit it. "Now, we're going to go to Mallorysport and get the rest of them back."

"But . . . But the Chief Justice signed that order. He won't give them back just because we ask him to."

Brannhard made an impolite noise. "I'll bet everything I own Pendarvis never saw that order. They have stacks of those things, signed in blank, in the Chief of the Court's office. If they had to wait to get one of the judges to sign an order every time they wanted to subpoena a witness or impound physical evidence, they'd never get anything done. If Ham O'Brien didn't think this up for himself, Leslie Coombes thought it up for him."

"We'll use my airboat," Gerd said. "You coming along, Ben? Let's get started."

He couldn't understand. The Big Ones in the blue clothes had been friends; they had given the whistles, and shown sorrow when the killed one was put in the ground. And why had Pappy Jack not gotten the big gun and stopped them. It couldn't be that he was afraid; Pappy Jack was afraid of nothing.

The others were near, in bags like the one in which he had been put; he could hear them, and called to them. Then he felt the edge of the little knife Pappy Jack had made. He could cut his way out of this bag now and free the others, but that would be no use. They were in one of the things the Big Ones went up into the sky in, and if he got out now, there would be nowhere to go and they would be caught at once. Better to wait.

The one thing that really worried him was that he would not know where they were being taken. When they did get away, how would they ever find Pappy Jack again?"

Gus Brannhard was nervous, showing it by being overtalkative, and that worried Jack. He'd stopped twice at mirrors along the hallway to make sure that his gold-threaded gray neckcloth was properly knotted and that his black jacket was zipped up far enough and not too far. Now, in front of the door marked THE CHIEF JUSTICE, he paused before pushing the button to fluff his newly shampooed beard.

There were two men in the Chief Justice's private chambers. Pendarvis he had seen once or twice, but their paths had never crossed. He had a good face, thin and ascetic, the face of a man at peace with himself. With him was Mohammed Ali O'Brien, who seemed surprised to see them enter, and then apprehensive. Nobody shook hands; the Chief Justice bowed slightly and invited them to be seated.

"Now," he continued, when they found chairs, "Miss Ugatori tells me that you are making complaint against an action by Mr. O'Brien here."

"We are indeed, your Honor." Brannhard opened his briefcase and produced two papers—the writ, and the receipt for the Fuzzies, handing them across the desk. "My client and I wish to know upon what basis of legality your Honor sanctioned this act, and by what right Mr. O'Brien sent his officers to Mr. Holloway's camp to snatch these little people from their friend and protector, Mr. Holloway."

The judge looked at the two papers. "As you know, Miss Ugatori took prints of them when you called to make this appointment. I've seen them. But believe me, Mr. Brannhard, this is the first time I have seen the original of this writ. You know how these things are signed in blank. It's a practice that has saved considerable time and effort, and until now they have only been used when there was no question that I or any other judge would approve. Such a question should certainly have existed in this case, because had I seen this writ I would never have signed it." He turned to the now fidgeting Chief Prosecutor. "Mr. O'Brien," he said, "one simply does not impound sapient beings as evidence, as, say, one impounds a veldbeest calf in a brand-alteration case. The fact that the sapience of these Fuzzies is still *sub judice* includes the presumption of its possibility. Now you know perfectly well that the courts may take no action in the face of the possibility that some innocent person may suffer wrong."

"And, your Honor," Brannhard leaped into the breach, "it cannot be denied that these Fuzzies have suffered a most outrageous wrong! Picture them—no, picture innocent and artless children, for that is what these Fuzzies are, happy trusting little children, who, until then, had known only kindness and affection—

rudely kidnaped, stuffed into sacks by brutal and callous men—"

"Your Honor!" O'Brien's face turned even blacker than the hot sun of Agni had made it. "I cannot hear officers of the court so characterized without raising my voice in protest!"

"Mr. O'Brien seems to forget that he is speaking in the presence of two eye witnesses to this brutal abduction."

"If the officers of the court need defense, Mr. O'Brien, the court will defend them. I believe that you should presently consider a defense of your own actions."

"Your Honor, I insist that I only acted as I felt to be my duty," O'Brien said. "These Fuzzies are a key exhibit in the case of *People* versus *Kellogg*, since only by demonstration of their sapience can any prosecution against the defendant be maintained."

"Then why," Brannhard demanded, "did you endanger them in this criminally reckless manner?"

"Endanger them?" O'Brien was horrified. "Your Honor, I acted only to insure their safety and appearance in court."

"So you took them away from the only man on this planet who knows anything about their proper care, a man who loves them as he would his own human children, and you subjected them to abuse, which, for all you knew, might have been fatal to them."

Judge Pendarvis nodded. "I don't believe, Mr. Brannhard, that you have overstated the case. Mr. O'Brien, I take a very unfavorable view of your action in this matter. You had no right to have what are at least putatively sapient beings treated in this way, and even viewing them as mere physical evidence I must agree with Mr. Brannhard's characterization of your conduct as criminally reckless. Now, speaking judicially, I order you to produce those Fuzzies immediately and return them to the custody of Mr. Holloway."

"Well, of course, your Honor." O'Brien had been

growing progressively distraught, and his face now had the gray-over-brown hue of a walnut gunstock that has been out in the rain all day. "It'll take an hour or so to send for them and have them brought here."

"You mean they're not in this building?" Pendarvis asked.

"Oh, no, your Honor, there are no facilities here. I had them taken to Science Center—"

"*What?*"

Jack had determined to keep his mouth shut and let Gus do the talking. The exclamation was literally forced out of him. Nobody noticed; it had also been forced out of both Gus Brannhard and Judge Pendarvis. Pendarvis leaned forward and spoke with dangerous mildness:

"Do you refer, Mr. O'Brien to the establishment of the Division of Scientific Study and Research of the chartered Zarathustra Company?"

"Why, yes; they have facilities for keeping all kinds of live animals, and they do all the scientific work for—"

Pendarvis cursed blasphemously. Brannhard looked as startled as though his own briefcase had jumped at his throat and tried to bite him. He didn't look half as startled as Ham O'Brien did.

"So you think," Pendarvis said, recovering his composure with visible effort, "that the logical custodian of prosecution evidence in a murder trial is the defendant? Mr. O'Brien, you simply enlarge my view of the possible!"

"The Zarathustra Company isn't the defendant," O'Brien argued sullenly.

"Not of record, no," Brannhard agreed. "But isn't the Zarathustra Company's scientific division headed by one Leonard Kellogg?"

"Dr. Kellogg's been relieved of his duties, pending the outcome of the trial. The division is now headed by Dr. Ernst Mallin."

"Chief scientific witness for the defense; I fail to see

any practical difference."

"Well, Mr. Emmert said it would be all right," O'Brien mumbled.

"Jack, did you hear that?" Brannhard asked. "Treasure it in your memory. You may have to testify to it in court sometime." He turned to the Chief Justice. "Your Honor, may I suggest the recovery of these Fuzzies be entrusted to Colonial Marshal Fane, and may I further suggest that Mr. O'Brien be kept away from any communication equipment until they are recovered."

"That sounds like a prudent suggestion, Mr. Brannhard. Now, I'll give you an order for the surrender of the Fuzzies, and a search warrant, just to be on the safe side. And, I think, an Orphans' Court form naming Mr. Holloway as guardian of these putatively sapient beings. What are their names? Oh, I have them here on this receipt." He smiled pleasantly. "See, Mr. O'Brien, we're saving you a lot of trouble."

O'Brien had little enough wit to protest. "But these are the defendant and his attorney in another murder case I'm prosecuting," he began.

Pendarvis stopped smiling. "Mr. O'Brien, I doubt if you'll be allowed to prosecute anything or anybody around here any more, and I am specifically relieving you of any connection with either the Kellogg or the Holloway trial, and if I hear any argument out of you about it, I will issue a bench warrant for your arrest on charges of malfeasance in office."

X

Colonial Marshal Max Fane was as heavy as Gus Brannhard and considerably shorter. Wedged between them on the back seat of the marshal's car, Jack Holloway contemplated the backs of the two uniformed deputies on the front seat and felt a happy smile spread through him. Going to get his Fuzzies back. Little Fuzzy, and Ko-Ko, and Mike, and Mamma Fuzzy, and Mitzi, and Cinderella; he named them over and imagined them crowding around him, happy to be back with Pappy Jack.

The car settled onto the top landing stage of the Company's Science Center, and immediately a Company cop came running up. Gus opened the door, and Jack climbed out after him.

"Hey, you can't land here!" the cop was shouting. "This is for Company executives only!"

Max Fane emerged behind them and stepped forward; the two deputies piled out from in front.

"The hell you say, now," Fane said. "A court order lands anywhere. Bring him along, boys; we wouldn't want him to go and bump himself on a communication screen anywhere."

The Company cop started to protest, then subsided and fell in between the deputies. Maybe it was beginning to dawn on him that the Federation courts were bigger than the chartered Zarathustra Company after all. Or maybe he just thought there'd been a revolution.

Leonard Kellogg's—temporarily Ernst Mallin's—office was on the first floor of the penthouse, counting down from the top landing stage. When they stepped from the escalator, the hall was crowded with office people, gabbling excitedly in groups; they all stopped talking as soon as they saw what was coming. In the division chief's outer office three or four girls jumped to their feet; one of them jumped into the bulk of Marshal Fane, which had interposed itself between her and the communication screen. They were all shooed out into the hall, and one of the deputies was dropped there with the prisoner. The middle office was empty. Fane took his badgeholder in his left hand as he pushed through the door to the inner office.

Kellogg's—temporarily Mallin's—secretary seemed to have preceded them by a few seconds; she was standing in front of the desk sputtering incoherently. Mallin, starting to rise from his chair, froze, hunched forward over the desk. Juan Jimenez, standing in the middle of the room, seemed to have seen them first; he was looking about wildly as though for some way of escape.

Fane pushed past the secretary and went up to the desk, showing Mallin his badge and then serving the papers. Mallin looked at him in bewilderment.

"But we're keeping those Fuzzies for Mr. O'Brien, the Chief Prosecutor," he said. "We can't turn them over without his authorization."

"This," Max Fane said gently, "is an order of the court, issued by Chief Justice Pendarvis. As for Mr. O'Brien, I doubt if he's Chief Prosecutor any more. In fact, I suspect that he's in jail. *And that*," he shouted, leaning forward as far as his waistline would permit and banging on the desk with his fist, *"is where I'm going to stuff you, if you don't get those Fuzzies in here and turn them over immediately!"*

If Fane had suddenly metamorphosed himself into a damnthing, it couldn't have shaken Mallin more. Involuntarily he cringed from the marshal, and that finished him.

"But I can't," he protested. "We don't know exactly where they are at the moment."

"You don't know." Fane's voice sank almost to a whisper. "You admit you're holding them here, but you . . . don't . . . know . . . where. *Now start over again; tell the truth this time!*"

At that moment, the communication screen began making a fuss. Ruth Ortheris, in a light blue tailored costume, appeared in it.

"Dr. Mallin, what *is* going on here?" she wanted to know. "I just came in from lunch, and a gang of men are tearing my office up. Haven't you found the Fuzzies yet?"

"What's that?" Jack yelled. At the same time, Mallin was almost screaming: "Ruth! Shut up! Blank out and get out of the building!"

With surprising speed for a man of his girth, Fane whirled and was in front of the screen, holding his badge out.

"I'm Colonel Marshal Fane. Now, young woman; I want you up here right away. Don't make me send anybody after you, because I won't like that and neither will you."

"Right away, Marshal." She blanked the screen.

Fane turned to Mallin. "Now." He wasn't bothering with vocal tricks any more. "Are you going to tell me the truth, or am I going to run you in and put a veridicator on you? Where are those Fuzzies?"

"But I don't know!" Mallin wailed. "Juan, you tell him; you took charge of them. I haven't seen them since they were brought here."

Jack managed to fight down the fright that was clutching at him and got control of his voice.

"If anything's happened to those Fuzzies, you two are going to envy Kurt Borch before I'm through with you," he said.

"All right, how about it?" Fane asked Jimenez. "Start with when you and Ham O'Brien picked up the

Fuzzies at Central Courts Building last night.

"Well, we brought them here. I'd gotten some cages fixed up for them, and—"

Ruth Ortheris came in. She didn't try to avoid Jack's eyes, nor did she try to brazen it out with him. She merely nodded distantly, as though they'd met on a ship sometime, and sat down.

"What happened, Marshal?" she asked. "Why are you here with these gentlemen?"

"The court's ordered the Fuzzies returned to Mr. Holloway." Mallin was in a dither. "He has some kind a writ or something, and we don't know where they are."

"Oh, *no!*" Ruth's face, for an instant, was dismay itself. "Not when—" Then she froze shut.

"I came in about o-seven-hundred," Jimenez was saying, "to give them food and water, and they'd broken out of their cages. The netting was broken loose on one cage and the Fuzzy that had been in it had gotten out and let the others out. They got into my office—they made a perfect shambles of it—and got out the door into the hall, and now we don't know where they are. And I don't know how they did any of it."

Cages built for something with no hands and almost no brains. Ever since Kellogg and Mallin had come to the camp, Mallin had been hynotizing himself into the just-silly-little-animals doctrine. He must have succeeded; last night he'd acted accordingly.

"We want to see the cages," Jack said.

"Yeah." Fane went to the outer door. "Miguel."

The deputy came in, herding the Company cop ahead of him.

"You heard what happened?" Fane asked.

"Yeah. Big Fuzzy jailbreak. What did they do, make little wooden pistols and bluff their way out?"

"By God, I wouldn't put it past them. Come along. Bring Chummy along with you; he knows the inside of this place better than we do. Piet, call in. We want six more men. Tell Chang to borrow from the constabulary if he has to."

"Wait a minute," Jack said. He turned to Ruth. "What do you know about this?"

"Well, not much. I was with Dr. Mallin here when Mr. Grego—I mean, Mr. O'Brien—called to tell us that the Fuzzies were going to be kept here till the trial. We were going to fix up a room for them, but till that could be done, Juan got some cages to put them in. That was all I knew about it till o-nine-thirty, when I came in and found everything in an uproar and was told that the Fuzzies had gotten loose during the night. I knew they couldn't get out of the building, so I went to my office and lab to start overhauling some equipment we were going to need with the Fuzzies. About ten-hundred, I found I couldn't do anything with it, and my assistant and I loaded it on a pickup truck and took it to Henry Stenson's instrument shop. By the time I was through there, I had lunch and then came back here."

He wondered briefly how a polyencephalographic veridicator would react to some of those statements; might be a good idea if Max Fane found out.

"I'll stay here," Gus Brannhard was saying, "and see if I can get some more truth out of these people."

"Why don't you screen the hotel and tell Gerd and Ben what's happened?" he asked. "Gerd used to work here; maybe he could help us hunt."

"Good idea. Piet, tell our re-enforcements to stop at the Mallory on the way and pick him up." Fane turned to Jimenez. "Come along; show us where you had these Fuzzies and how they got away."

"You say one of them broke out of his cage and then released the others," Jack said to Jimenez as they were going down on the escalator. "Do you know which one it was?"

Jimenez shook his head. "We just took them out of the bags and put them into the cages."

That would be Little Fuzzy; he'd always been the brains of the family. With his leadership, they might have a chance. The trouble was that this place was full of dangers Fuzzies knew nothing about—radiation and poisons and electric wiring and things like that. If they really had escaped. That was a possibility that began worrying Jack.

On each floor they passed going down, he could glimpse parties of Company employees in the halls, armed with nets and blankets and other catching equipment. When they got off Jimenez led them through a big room of glass cases—mounted specimens and articulated skeletons of Zarathustran mammals. More people were there, looking around and behind and even into the cases. He began to think that the escape was genuine, and not just a cover-up for the murder of the Fuzzies.

Jimenez took them down a narrow hall beyond to an open door at the end. Inside, the permanent night light made a blue-white glow; a swivel chair stood just inside the door. Jimenez pointed to it.

"They must have gotten up on that to work the latch and open the door," he said.

It was like the doors at the camp, spring latch, with a handle instead of a knob. They'd have learned how to work it from watching him. Fane was trying the latch.

"Not too stiff," he said. "Your little fellows strong enough to work it?"

He tried it and agreed. "Sure. And they'd be smart enough to do it, too. Even Baby Fuzzy, the one your men didn't get, would be able to figure that out."

"And look what they did to my office," Jimenez said, putting on the lights.

They'd made quite a mess of it. They hadn't delayed long to do it, just thrown things around. Everything was thrown off the top of the desk. They had dumped the wastebasket, and left it dumped. He saw that and chuckled. The escape had been genuine all right.

"Probably hunting for things they could use as weapons, and doing as much damage as they could in the process." There was evidently a pretty wide streak of vindictiveness in Fuzzy character. "I don't think they like you, Juan."

"Wouldn't blame them," Fane said. Let's see what kind of a houdini they did on these cages now."

The cages were in a room—file room, storeroom, junk room—behind Jimenez's office. It had a spring lock, too, and the Fuzzies had dragged one of the cages over and stood on it to open the door. The cages themselves were about three feet wide and five feet long, with plywood bottoms, wooden frames and quarter-inch netting on the sides and tops. The tops were hinged, and fastened with hasps, and bolts slipped through the staples with nuts screwed on them. The nuts had been unscrewed from five and the bolts slipped out; the sixth cage had been broken open from the inside, the netting cut away from the frame at one corner and bent back in a triangle big enough for a Fuzzy to crawl through.

"I can't understand that," Jimenez was saying. "Why that wire looks as though it had been cut."

"It was cut. Marshal, I'd pull somebody's belt about this, if I were you. Your men aren't very careful about searching prisoners. One of the Fuzzies hid a knife out on them." He remembered how Little Fuzzy and Ko-Ko had burrowed into the bedding in apparently unreasoning panic, and explained about the little spring-steel knives he had made. "I suppose he palmed it and hugged himself into a ball, as though he was scared witless, when they put him in the bag."

"Waited till he was sure he wouldn't get caught before he used it, too," the marshal said. "That wire's soft enough to cut easily." He turned to Jimenez. "You people ought to be glad I'm ineligible for jury duty. Why don't you just throw it in and let Kellogg cop a plea?"

Gerd von Riebeek stopped for a moment in the doorway and looked into what had been Leonard Kellogg's office. The last time he'd been here, Kellogg had had him on the carpet about that land-prawn business. Now Ernst Mallin was sitting in Kellogg's chair, trying to look unconcerned and not making a very good job of it. Gus Brannhard sprawled in an armchair, smoking a cigar and looking at Mallin as he would look at a river pig when he doubted whether it was worth shooting it or not. A uniformed deputy turned quickly, then went back to studying an elaborate wall chart showing the interrelation of Zarathustran mammals—he'd made the original of that chart himself. And Ruth Ortheris sat apart from the desk and the three men, smoking. She looked up and then, when she saw that he was looking past and away from her, she lowered her eyes.

"You haven't found them?" he asked Brannhard.

The fluffy-bearded lawyer shook his head. "Jack has a gang down in the cellar, working up. Max is in the psychology lab, putting the Company cops who were on duty last night under veridication. They all claim, and the veridicator backs them up, that it was impossible for the Fuzzies to get out of the building."

"They don't know what's impossible, for a Fuzzy."

"That's what I told him. He didn't give me any argument, either. He's pretty impressed with how they got out of those cages."

Ruth spoke. "Gerd, we didn't hurt them. We weren't going to hurt them at all. Juan put them in cages because we didn't have any other place for them, but we were going to fix up a nice room, where they could play together...." Then she must have seen that he wasn't listening, and stopped, crushing out her cigarette and rising. "Dr. Mallin, if these people haven't any more questions to ask me, I have a lot of work to do."

"You want to ask her anything, Gerd?" Brannhard inquired.

Once he had had something very important he had

wanted to ask her. He was glad, now, that he hadn't gotten around to it. Hell, she was so married to the Company it'd be bigamy if she married him too.

"No, I don't want to talk to her at all."

She started for the door, then hesitated. "Gerd, I . . ." she began. Then she went out. Gus Brannhard looked after her, and dropped the ash of his cigar on Leonard Kellogg's—now Ernst Mallin's—floor.

Gerd detested her, and she wouldn't have had any respect for him if he didn't. She ought to have known that something like this would happen. It always did, in the business. A smart girl, in the business, never got involved with any one man; she always got herself four or five boyfriends, on all possible sides, and played them off one against another.

She'd have to get out of the Science Center right away. Marshal Fane was questioning people under veridication; she didn't dare let him get around to her. She didn't dare go to her office; the veridicator was in the lab across the hall, and that's where he was working. And she didn't dare—

Yes, she could do that, by screen. She went into an office down the hall; a dozen people recognized her at once and began bombarding her with questions about the Fuzzies. She brushed them off and went to a screen, punching a combination. After a slight delay, an elderly man with a thin-lipped, bloodless face appeared. When he recognized her, there was a brief look of annoyance on the thin face.

"Mr. Stenson," she began, before he could say anything. "That apparatus I brought to your shop this morning—the sensory-response detector—we've made a simply frightful mistake. There's nothing wrong with it whatever, and if anything's done with it, it may cause serious damage."

"I don't think I understand, Dr. Ortheris."

"Well, it was a perfectly natural mistake. You see, we're all at our wits' end here. Mr. Holloway and his lawyer and the Colonial Marshal are here with an order from Judge Pendarvis for the return of those Fuzzies. None of us know what we're doing at all. Why the whole trouble with the apparatus was the fault of the operator. We'll have to have it back immediately, all of it."

"I see, Dr. Ortheris." The old instrument maker looked worried. "But I'm afraid the apparatus has already gone to the workroom. Mr. Stephenson has it now, and I can't get in touch with him at present. If the mistake can be corrected, what do you want done?"

"Just hold it; I'll call or send for it."

She blanked the screen. Old Johnson, the chief data synthesist, tried to detain her with some question.

"I'm sorry, Mr. Johnson. I can't stop now. I have to go over to Company House right away."

The suite at the Hotel Mallory was crowded when Jack Holloway returned with Gerd van Riebeek; it was noisy with voices, and the ventilators were laboring to get rid of the tobacco smoke. Gus Brannhard, Ben Rainsford and Baby Fuzzy were meeting the press.

"Oh, Mr. Holloway!" somebody shouted as he entered. "Have you found them yet?"

"No; we've been all over Science Center from top to bottom. We know they went down a few floors from where they'd been caged, but that's all. I don't think they could have gotten outside; the only exit on the ground level's through a vestibule where a Company policeman was on duty, and there's no way for them to have climbed down from any of the terraces or landing stages."

"Well, Mr. Holloway, I hate to suggest this," somebody else said, "but have you eliminated the possibility that they may have hidden in a trash bin and been dumped into the mass-energy converter?"

"We thought of that. The converter's underground, in a vault that can be entered only by one door, and that was locked. No trash was disposed of between the time they were brought there and the time the search started, and everything that's been sent to the converter since has been checked piece by piece."

"Well, I'm glad to hear that, Mr. Holloway, and I know that everybody hearing this will be glad, too. I take it you've not given up looking for them?"

"Are we on the air now? No, I have not; I'm staying here in Mallorysport until I either find them or am convinced that they aren't in the city. And I am offering a reward of two thousand sols apiece for their return to me. If you'll wait a moment, I'll have descriptions ready for you...."

Victor Gregg unstoppered the refrigerated cocktail jug. "More?" he asked Leslie Coombes.

"Yes, thank you." Coombes held his glass until it was filled. "As you say, Victor, you made the decision, but you made it on my advice, and the advice was bad."

He couldn't disagree, even politely, with that. He hoped it hadn't been ruinously bad. One thing, Leslie wasn't trying to pass the buck, and considering how Ham O'Brien had mishandled his end of it, he could have done so quite plausibly.

"I used bad judgment," Coombes said dispassionately, as though discussing some mistake Hitler had made, or Napoleon. "I thought O'Brien wouldn't try to use one of those presigned writs, and I didn't think Pendarvis would admit, publicly, that he signed court orders in blank. He's been severely criticized by the press about that."

He hadn't thought Brannhard and Holloway would try to fight a court order either. That was one of the consequences of being too long in a seemingly irresistible position; you didn't expect resistance. Kellogg hadn't expected Jack Holloway to order him off his land grant. Kurt Borch had thought all he needed to do with a gun was pull it and wave it around. And Jimenez had expected the Fuzzies to just sit in their cages.

"I wonder where they got to," Coombes was saying. "I understand they couldn't be found at all in the building."

"Ruth Ortheris has an idea. She got away from Science Center before Fane could get hold of her and veridicate her. It seems she and an assistant took some apparatus out, about ten o'clock, in a truck. She thinks the Fuzzies hitched a ride with her. I know that sounds rather improbable, but hell, everything else sounds impossible. I'll have it followed up. Maybe we can find them before Holloway does. They're not inside Science Center, that's sure." His own glass was empty; he debated a refill and voted against it. "O'Brien's definitely out, I take it?"

"Completely. Pendarvis gave him his choice of resigning or facing malfeasance charges."

"They couldn't really convict him of malfeasance for that, could they? Malfeasance, maybe, but—"

"They could charge him. And then they could interrogate him under veridication about his whole conduct in office, and you know what they would bring out," Coombes said. "He almost broke an arm signing his resignation. He's still Attorney General of the Colony, of course; Nick issued a statement supporting him. That hasn't done Nick as much harm as O'Brien could do spilling what he knows about Residency affairs.

"Now Brannhard is talking about bringing suit against the Company, and he's furnishing copies of all the Fuzzy films Holloway has to the news services. Interworld News is going hog-wild with it, and even the services we control can't play it down too much. I don't know who's going to be prosecuting these cases, but whoever it is, he won't dare pull any punches. And the whole thing's made Pendarvis hostile to us. I know, the law and the evidence and nothing but the law and the evidence, but the evidence is going to filter into his conscious mind through this hostility. He's called a conference with Brannhard and myself for tomorrow afternoon; I don't know what that's going to be like."

XI

The two lawyers had risen hastily when Chief Justice Pendarvis entered; he responded to their greetings and seated himself at his desk, reaching for the silver cigar box and taking out a panatella. Gustavus Adolphus Brannhard picked up the cigar he had laid aside and began puffing on it; Leslie Coombes took a cigarette from his case. They both looked at him, waiting like two drawn weapons—a battle ax and a rapier.

"Well, gentlemen, as you know, we have a couple of homicide cases and nobody to prosecute them," he began.

"Why bother, your Honor?" Coombes asked. "Both charges are completely frivolous. One man killed a wild animal, and the other killed a man who was trying to kill him."

"Well, your Honor, I don't believe my client is guilty of anything, legally or morally," Brannhard said. "I want that established by an acquittal." He looked at Coombes. "I should think Mr. Coombes would be just as anxious to have his client cleared of any stigma of murder, too."

"I am quite agreed. People who have been charged with crimes ought to have public vindication if they are innocent. Now, in the first place, I planned to hold the Kellogg trial first, and then the Holloway trial. Are you both satisfied with that arrangement?"

"Absolutely not, your Honor," Brannhard said promptly. "The whole basis of the Holloway defense is that this man Borch was killed in commission of a felony. We're prepared to prove that, but we don't want our case prejudiced by an earlier trial."

Coombes laughed. "Mr. Brannhard wants to clear his client by preconvicting mine. We can't agree to anything like that."

"Yes, and he is making the same objection to trying your client first. Well, I'm going to remove both objections. I'm going to order the two cases combined, and both defendants tried together."

A momentary glow of unholy glee on Gus Brannhard's face; Coombes didn't like the idea at all.

"Your Honor, I trust that that suggestion was only made facetiously," he said.

"It wasn't, Mr. Coombes."

"Then if your Honor will not hold me in contempt for saying so, it is the most shockingly irregular—I won't go so far as to say improper—trial procedure I've ever heard of. This is not a case of accomplices charged with the same crime; this is a case of two men charged with different criminal acts, and the conviction of either would mean the almost automatic acquittal of the other. I don't know who's going to be named to take Mohammed O'Brien's place, but I pity him from the bottom of my heart. Why, Mr. Brannhard and I could go off somewhere and play poker while the prosecutor would smash the case to pieces."

"Well, we won't have just one prosecutor, Mr. Coombes, we will have two. I'll swear you and Mr. Brannhard in as special prosecutors, and you can prosecute Mr. Brannhard's client, and he yours. I think that would remove any further objections."

It was all he could do to keep his face judicially grave and unmirthful. Brannhard was almost purring, like a big tiger that had just gotten the better of a young goat; Leslie Coombes's suavity was beginning to crumble slightly at the edges.

"Your Honor, that is a most excellent suggestion," Brannhard declared. "I will prosecute Mr. Coombes's client with the greatest pleasure in the universe."

"Well, all I can say, your Honor, is that if the first proposal was the most irregular I had ever heard, the record didn't last long!"

"Why, Mr. Coombes, I went over the law and the rules of jurisprudence very carefully, and I couldn't find a word that could be construed as disallowing such a procedure."

"I'll bet you didn't find any precedent for it either!"

Leslie Coombes should have known better than that; in colonial law, you can find a precedent for almost anything.

"How much do you bet, Leslie?" Brannhard asked, a larcenous gleam in his eye.

"Don't let him take your money away from you. I found, inside an hour, sixteen precedents, from twelve different planetary jurisdictions."

"All right, your Honor," Coombes capitulated. "But I hope you know what you're doing. You're turning a couple of cases of the People of the Colony into a common civil lawsuit."

Gus Brannhard laughed. "What else is it?" he demanded. "*Friends of Little Fuzzy versus The chartered Zarathustra Company;* I'm bringing action as friend of incompetent aborigines for recognition of sapience, and Mr. Coombes, on behalf of the Zarathustra Company, is contesting to preserve the Company's charter, and that's all there is or ever was to this case."

That was impolite of Gus. Leslie Coombes had wanted to go on to the end pretending that the Company charter had absolutely nothing to do with it.

There was an unending stream of reports of Fuzzies seen here and there, often simultaneously in impossibly distant parts of the city. Some were from publicity seekers and pathological liars and crackpots; some were the result of honest mistakes or overimaginativeness. There was some reason to suspect that not a few had originated with the Company, to confuse the search. One thing did come to light which heartened Jack Holloway. An intensive if concealed search was being made by the Company police, and by the Mallorysport police department, which the Company controlled.

Max Fane was giving every available moment to the hunt. This wasn't because of ill will for the Company, though that was present, nor because the Chief Justice was riding him. The Colonial Marshal was pro-Fuzzy. So were the Colonial Constabulary, over whom Nick Emmert's administration seemed to have little if any authority. Colonel Ian Ferguson, the commandant, had his appointment direct from the Colonial Office on Terra. He had called by screen to offer his help, and George Lunt, over on Beta, screened daily to learn what progress was being made.

Living at the Hotel Mallory was expensive, and Jack had to sell some sunstones. The Company gem buyers were barely civil to him; he didn't try to be civil at all. There was also a noticeable coolness toward him at the bank. On the other hand, on several occasions, Space Navy officers and ratings down from Xerxes Base went out of their way to accost him, introduce themselves, shake hands with him and give him their best wishes.

Once, in one of the weather-domed business centers, an elderly man with white hair showing under his black beret greeted him.

"Mr. Holloway I want to tell you how grieved I am to learn about the disappearance of those little people of yours," he said. "I'm afraid there's nothing I can do to help you, but I hope they turn up safely."

"Why, thank you, Mr. Stenson." He shook hands with the old master instrument maker. "If you could make me a pocket veridicator, to use on some of these people who claim they saw them, it would be a big help."

"Well, I do make rather small portable veridicators

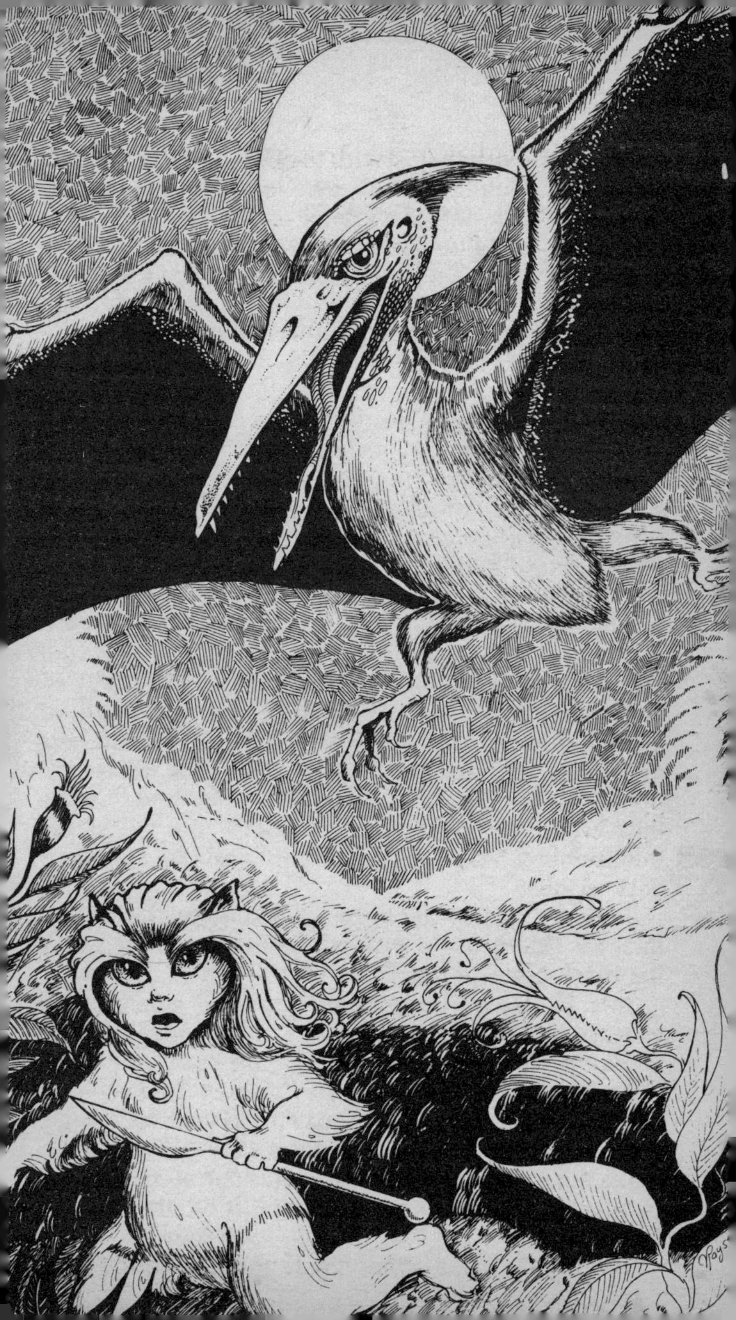

for the constabulary, but I think what you need is an instrument for detection of psychopaths, and that's slightly beyond science at present. But if you're still prospecting for sunstones, I have an improved microray scanner I just developed, and . . ."

He walked with Stenson to his shop, had a cup of tea and looked at the scanner. From Stenson's screen, he called Max Fane. Six more people had claimed to have seen the Fuzzies.

Within a week, the films taken at the camp had been shown so frequently on telecast as to wear out their interest value. Baby, however, was still available for new pictures, and in a few days a girl had to be hired to take care of his fan mail. Once, entering a bar, Jack thought he saw Baby sitting on a woman's head. A second look showed that it was only a life-sized doll, held on with an elastic band. Within a week, he was seeing Baby Fuzzy hats all over town, and shop windows were full of life-sized Fuzzy dolls.

In the late afternoon, two weeks after the Fuzzies had vanished, Marshal Fane dropped him at the hotel. They sat in the car for a moment, and Fane said:

"I think this is the end of it. We're all out of cranks and exhibitionists now."

He nodded. "That woman we were talking to. She's crazy as a bedbug."

"Yeah. In the past ten years she's confessed to every unsolved crime on the planet. It shows you how hard up we are that I waste your time and mine listening to her."

"Max, nobody's seen them. You think they just aren't, any more, don't you?"

The fat man looked troubled. "Well, Jack, it isn't so much that nobody's seen them. Nobody's seen any trace of them. There are land-prawns all around, but nobody's found a cracked shell. And six active, playful, inquisitive Fuzzies ought to be getting into things. They ought to be raiding food markets, and fruit stands, getting into places and ransacking. But there hasn't been a thing. The Company police have stopped looking for them now."

"Well, I won't. They must be around somewhere." He shook Fane's hand, and got out of the car. "You've been awfully helpful, Max. I want you to know how much I thank you."

He watched the car lift away, and then looked out over the city—a vista of treetop green, with roofs and the domes of shopping centers and business centers and amusement centers showing through, and the angular buttes of tall buildings rising above. The streetless contragravity city of a new planet that had never known ground traffic. The Fuzzies could be hiding anywhere among those trees—or they could all be dead in some man-made trap. He thought of all the deadly places into which they could have wandered. Machinery, dormant and quiet, until somebody threw a switch. Conduits, which could be flooded without warning, or filled with scalding steam or choking gas. Poor little Fuzzies, they'd think a city was as safe as the woods of home, where there was nothing worse than harpies and damnthings.

Gus Brannhard was out when he went down to the suite; Ben Rainsford was at a reading screen, studying a psychology text, and Gerd was working at a desk that had been brought in. Baby was playing on the floor with the bright new toys they had gotten for him. When Pappy Jack came in, he dropped them and ran to be picked up and held.

"George called," Gerd said. "They have a family of Fuzzies at the post now."

"Well, that's great." He tried to make it sound enthusiastic. "How many?"

"Five, three males and two females. They call them Dr. Crippen, Dillinger, Ned Kelly, Lizzie Borden and Calamity Jane."

Wouldn't it be just like a bunch of cops to hang names like that on innocent Fuzzies?

"Why don't you call the post and say hello to them?"

Ben asked.

"Baby likes them; he'd think it was fun to talk to them again."

He let himself be urged into it, and punched out the combination. They were nice Fuzzies; almost, but of course not quite, as nice as his own.

"If your family doesn't turn up in time for the trial, have Gus subpoena ours," Lunt told him. "You ought to have some to produce in court. Two weeks from now, this mob of ours will be doing all kinds of things. You ought to see them now, and we only got them yesterday afternoon."

He said he hoped he'd have his own by then; he realized that he was saying it without much conviction.

They had a drink when Gus came in. He was delighted with the offer from Lunt. Another one who didn't expect to see Pappy Jack's Fuzzies alive again.

"I'm not doing a damn thing here," Rainsford said. "I'm going back to Beta till the trial. Maybe I can pick up some ideas from George Lunt's Fuzzies. I'm damned if I'm getting away from this crap!" He gestured at the reading screen. "All I have is a vocabulary, and I don't know what half the words mean." He snapped it off. "I'm beginning to wonder if maybe Jimenez mightn't have been right and Ruth Ortheris is wrong. Maybe you can be just a little bit sapient."

"Maybe it's possible to be sapient and not know it," Gus said. "Like the character in the old French play who didn't know he was talking prose."

"What do you mean, Gus?" Gerd asked.

"I'm not sure I know. It's just an idea that occurred to me today. Kick it around and see if you can get anything out of it."

"I believe the difference lies in the area of consciousness," Ernst Mallin was saying. "You all know, of course, the axiom that only one-tenth, never more than one-eighth, of our mental activity occurs above the level of consciousness. Now let us imagine a hypothetical race whose entire mentation is conscious."

"I hope they stay hypothetical," Victor Grego, in his office across the city, said out of the screen. "They wouldn't recognize us as sapient at all."

'We wouldn't be sapient, as they'd define the term," Leslie Coombes, in the same screen with Grego, said. "They'd have some equivalent of the talk-and-build-a-fire rule, based on abilities of which we can't even conceive."

Maybe, Ruth thought, they might recognize us as one-tenth to as much as one-eighth sapient. No, then we'd have to recognize, say, a chimpanzee as being one-one-hundredth sapient, and a flatworm as being sapient to the order of one-billionth.

"Wait a minute," she said. "If I understand, you mean that nonsapient beings think, but only subconsciously?"

"That's correct, Ruth. When confronted by some entirely novel situation, a nonsapient animal will think, but never consciously. Of course, familiar situations are dealt with by pure habit and memory-response."

"You know, I've just thought of something," Grego said. "I think we can explain that funeral that's been bothering all of us in nonsapient terms." He lit a cigarette, while they all looked at him expectantly. "Fuzzies," he continued, "bury their ordure: they do this to avoid an unpleasnt sense-stimulus, a bad smell. Dead bodies quickly putrefy and smell badly; they are thus equated, subconsciously, with ordure and must be buried. All Fuzzies carry weapons. A Fuzzy's weapon is—still subconsciously—regarded as a part of the Fuzzy, hence it must also be buried."

Mallin frowned portentiously. The idea seemed to appeal to him, but of course he simply couldn't agree too promptly with a mere layman, even the boss.

"Well, so far you're on fairly safe ground, Mr. Grego," he admitted. "Association of otherwise dissimilar things because of some apparent similarity is a recognized element of nonsapient animal behavior." He frowned again. "That *could* be an explanation. I'll have to think of it."

About this time tomorrow, it would be his own idea, with grudging recognition of a suggestion by Victor Grego. In time, that would be forgotten; it would be the Mallin Theory. Grego was apparently agreeable, as long as the job got done.

"Well, if you can make anything out of it, pass it on to Mr. Coombes as soon as possible, to be worked up for use in court," he said.

XII

Ben Rainsford went back to Beta Continent, and Gerd van Riebeek remained in Mallorysport. The constabulary at Post Fifteen had made steel chopper-diggers for their Fuzzies, and reported a gratifying abatement of the land-prawn nuisance. They also made a set of scaled-down carpenter tools, and their Fuzzies were building themselves a house out of scrap crates and boxes. A pair of Fuzzies showed up at Ben Rainsford's camp, and he adopted them, naming them Flora and Fauna.

Everybody had Fuzzies now, and Pappy Jack only had Baby. He was lying on the floor of the parlor, teaching Baby to tie knots in a piece of string. Gus Brannhard, who spent most of the day in the office in the Central Courts building which had been furnished to him as special prosecutor, was lolling in an armchair in red-and-blue pajamas, smoking a cigar, drinking coffee—his whisky consumption was down to a couple of drinks a day—and studying texts on two reading screens at once, making an occasional remark into a stenomemophone. Gerd was at the desk, spoiling notepaper in an effort to work something out by symbolic logic. Suddenly he crumpled a sheet and threw it across the room, cursing. Brannhard looked away from his screens.

"Trouble, Gerd?"

Gerd cursed again. "How the devil can I tell whether Fuzzies generalize?" he demanded. "How can I tell whether they form abstract ideas? How can I prove, even, that they have ideas at all? Hell's blazes, how can I even prove, to your satisfaction, that I think consciously?"

"Working on that idea I mentioned?" Brannhard asked.

"I was. It seemed like a good idea but . . ."

"Suppose we go back to specific instances of Fuzzy behavior, and present them as evidence of sapience?" Brannhard asked. "That funeral, for instance."

"They'll still insist that we define sapience."

The communication screen began buzzing. Baby Fuzzy looked up disinterestedly, and then went back to trying to untie a figure-eight knot he had tied. Jack shoved himself to his feet and put the screen on. It was Max Fane, and for the first time that he could remember, the Colonial Marshal was excited.

"Jack, have you had any news on the screen lately?"

"No. Something turn up?"

"God, yes! The cops are all over the city hunting the Fuzzies; they have orders to shoot on sight. Nick Emmert was just on the air with a reward offer—five hundred sols apiece, dead or alive."

It took a few seconds for that to register. Then he became frightened. Gus and Gerd were both on their feet and crowding to the screen behind him.

"They have some bum from that squatters' camp over on the East Side who claims the Fuzzies beat up his ten-year-old daughter," Fane was saying. "They have both of them at police headquarters, and they've handed the story out to Zarathustra News, and Planetwide Coverage. Of course, they're Company-controlled; they're playing it for all it's worth."

"Have they been veridicated?" Brannhard demanded.

"No, and the city cops are keeping them under cover. The girl says she was playing outdoors and these Fuzzies jumped her and began beating her with sticks. Her injuries are listed as multiple bruises, fractured wrist and general shock."

"I don't believe it! They wouldn't attack a child."

"I want to talk to that girl and her father," Brannhard was saying. "And I'm going to demand that they make their statements under veridication. This thing's a frameup, Max; I'd bet my ears on it. Timing's just right; only a week till the trial."

Maybe the Fuzzies had wanted the child to play with them, and she'd gotten frightened and hurt one of them. A ten-year-old human child would look dangerously large to a Fuzzy, and if they thought they were menaced they would fight back savagely.

They were still alive and in the city. That was one thing. But they were in worse danger than they had ever been; that was another. Fane was asking Brannhard how soon he could be dressed.

"Five minutes? Good, I'll be along to pick you up," he said. "Be seeing you."

Jack hurried into the bedroom he and Brannhard shared; he kicked off his moccasins and began pulling on his boots. Brannhard, pulling his trousers up over his pajama pants, wanted to know where he thought he was going.

"With you. I've got to find them before some dumb son of a Khooghra shoots them."

"You stay here," Gus ordered. "Stay by the communication screen, and keep the viewscreen on for news. But don't stop putting your boots on; you may have to get out of here fast if I call you and tell you they've been located. I'll call you as soon as I get anything definite."

Gerd had the screen on for news, and was getting Planetwide, openly owned and operated by the Company. The newscaster was wrought up about the brutal attack on the innocent child, but he was having trouble focusing the blame. After all, who'd let the Fuzzies escape in the first place? And even a skilled semanticist had trouble in making anything called a Fuzzy sound menacing. At least he gave particulars, true or not.

The child, Lolita Lurkin, had been playing outside her home at about twenty-one hundred when she had suddenly been set upon by six Fuzzies, armed with clubs. Without provocation, they had dragged her down and beaten her severely. Her screams had brought her father, and he had driven the Fuzzies away. Police had brought both the girl and her father, Oscar Lurkin, to headquarters, where they had told their story. City police, Company police and constabulary troopers and parties of armed citizens were combing the eastern side of the city; Resident General Emmert had acted at once to offer a reward of five thousand sols apiece. . . .

"The kid's lying, and if they ever get a veridicator on her, they'll prove it", he said. "Emmert, or Grego, or the two of them together, bribed those people to tell that story."

"Oh, I take that for granted," Gerd said. "I know that place. Junktown. Ruth does a lot of work there for juvenile court." He stopped briefly, pain in his eyes, and then continued: "You can hire anybody to do anything over there for a hundred sols, especially if the cops are fixed in advance."

He shifted to the Interworld News frequency; they were covering the Fuzzy hunt from an aircar. The shanties and parked airjalopies of Junktown were floodlighted from above; lines of men were beating the brush and poking among them. Once a car passed directly below the pickup, a man staring at the ground from it over a machine gun.

"Wooo! Am I glad I'm not in that mess!" Gerd exclaimed. "Anybody sees something he thinks is a Fuzzy and half that gang'll massacre each other in ten seconds."

"I hope they do!"

Interworld News was pro-Fuzzy; the commentator in the car was being extremely sarcastic about the whole thing. Into the middle of one view of a rifle-bristling line of beaters somebody in the studio cut a view of the Fuzzies, taken at the camp, looking up appealingly while waiting for breakfast. "These," a voice said, "are the terrible monsters against whom all these brave men are protecting us."

A few moments later, a rifle flash and a bang, and then a fusillade brought Jack's heart into his throat. The pickup car jetted toward it; by the time it reached the spot, the shooting had stopped, and a crowd was gathering around something white on the ground. He had to force himself to look, then gave a shuddering breath of relief. It was a zaragoat, a three-horned domesticated ungulate.

"Oh-Oh! Some squatter's milk supply finished." The commentator laughed. "Not the first one tonight either. Attorney General—former Chief Prosecutor— O'Brien's going to have quite a few suits against the administration to defend as a result of this business."

"He's going to have a goddamn thundering big one from Jack Holloway!"

The communication screen buzzed; Gerd snapped it on.

"I just talked to Judge Pendarvis," Gus Brannhard reported out of it. "He's issuing an order restraining Emmert from paying any reward except for Fuzzies turned over alive and uninjured to Marshal Fane. And he's issuing a warning that until the status of the Fuzzies is determined, anybody killing one will face charges of murder."

"That's fine, Gus! Have you seen the girl or her father yet?"

Brannhard snarled angrily. "The girl's in the Company hospital, in a private room. The doctors won't let anybody see her. I think Emmert's hiding the father in the Residency. And I haven't seen the two cops who brought them in, or the desk sergeant who booked the complaint, or the detective lieutenant who was on duty here. They've all lammed out. Max has a couple of men over in Junktown, trying to find out who called the cops in the first place. We may get something out of that."

The Chief Justice's action was announced a few minutes later; it got to the hunters a few minutes after that and the Fuzzy hunt began falling apart. The City and Company police dropped out immediately. Most of the civilians, hoping to grab five thousand sols' worth of live Fuzzy, stayed on for twenty minutes, and so, apparently to control them, did the constabulary. Then the reward was cancelled, the airborne floodlights went off and the whole thing broke up.

Gus Brannhard came in shortly afterward, starting to undress as soon as he heeled the door shut after him. When he had his jacket and neckcloth off, he dropped into a chair, filled a water tumbler with whisky, gulped half of it and then began pulling off his boots.

"If that drink has a kid sister, I'll take it," Gerd muttered. "What happened, Gus?"

Brannhard began to curse. "The whole thing's a fake; it stinks from here to Nifflheim. It would stink on Nifflheim." He picked up a cigar butt he had laid aside when Fane's call had come in and relighted it. "We found the woman who called the police. Neighbor; she says she saw Lurkin come home drunk, and a little later she heard the girl screaming. She says he beats her up every time he gets drunk, which is about five times a week, and she'd made up her mind to stop it the next chance she got. She denied having seen anything that even looked like a Fuzzy anywhere around."

The excitement of the night before had incubated a new brood of Fuzzy reports; Jack went to the marshal's office to interview the people making them. The first dozen were of a piece with the ones that had come in originally. Then he talked to a young man who had something of different quality.

"I saw them as plain as I'm seeing you, not more than fifty feet away," he said. "I had an autocarbine, and I pulled up on them, but gosh, I couldn't shoot them. They were just like little people, Mr. Holloway, and they looked so scared and helpless. So I held over their heads and let off a two-second burst to scare them away before anybody else saw them and shot them."

"Well, son, I'd like to shake your hand for that. You know, you thought you were throwing away a lot of money there. How many did you see?"

"Well, only four. I'd heard that there were six, but the other two could have been back in the brush where I didn't see them."

He pointed out on the map where it had happened. There were three other people who had actually seen Fuzzies; none were sure how many, but they were all positive about locations and times. Plotting the reports on the map, it was apparent that the Fuzzies were moving north and west across the outskirts of the city.

Brannhard showed up for lunch at the hotel, still swearing, but half amusedly.

"They've exhumed Ham O'Brien, and they've put him to work harassing us," he said. "Whole flock of civil suits and dangerous-nuisance complaints and that sort of thing; idea's to keep me amused with them while Leslie Coombes is working up his case for the trial. Even tried to get the manager here to evict Baby; I threatened him with a racial-discrimination suit, and that stopped that. And I just filed suit against the Company for seven million sols on behalf of the Fuzzies—million apiece for them and a million for their lawyer."

"This evening," Jack said, "I'm going out in a car with a couple of Max's deputies. We're going to take Baby, and we'll have a loud-speaker on the car." He unfolded the city map. "They seem to be traveling this way; they ought to be about here, and with Baby at the speaker, we ought to attract their attention."

They didn't see anything, though they kept at it till dusk. Baby had a wonderful time with the loudspeaker; when he yeeked into it, he produced an ear-splitting noise, until the three humans in the car flinched every time he opened his mouth. It affected dogs too; as the car moved back and forth, it was followed by a chorus of howling and baying on the ground.

The next day, there were some scattered reports, mostly of small thefts. A blanket spread on the grass behind a house had vanished. A couple of cushions had been taken from a porch couch. A frenzied mother reported having found her six-year-old son playing with some Fuzzies; when she had rushed to rescue him, the Fuzzies had scampered away and the child had begun weeping. Jack and Gerd rushed to the scene. The child's story, jumbled and imagination-colored, was definite on one point—the Fuzzies had been nice to him and hadn't hurt him. They got a recording of that on the air at once.

When they got back to the hotel, Gus Brannhard was there, bubbling with glee.

"The Chief Justice gave me another job of special prosecuting," he said. "I'm to conduct an investigation into the possibility that this thing, the other night, was a frame-up, and I'm to prepare complaints against anybody who's done anything prosecutable. I have authority to hold hearings, and subpoena witnesses, and interrogate them under veridication. Max Fane has specific orders to cooperate. We're going to start, tomorrow, with Chief of Police Dumont and work down. And maybe we can work up, too, as far as Nick Emmert and Victor Grego." He gave a rumbling laugh. "Maybe that'll give Leslie Coombes something to worry about."

Gerd brought the car down beside the rectangular excavation. It was fifty feet square and twenty feet deep, and still going deeper, with a power shovel in it and a couple of dump scows beside. Five or six men in coveralls and ankle boots advanced to meet them as they got out.

"Good morning, Mr. Holloway," one of them said. "It's right down over the edge of the hill. We haven't disturbed anything."

"Mind running over what you saw again? My partner here wasn't in when you called."

The foreman turned to Gerd. "We put off a couple of shots about an hour ago. Some of the men, who'd gone down over the edge of the hill, saw these Fuzzies run out from under that rock ledge down there, and up the hollow, that way." He pointed. "They called me, and I went down for a look, and saw where they'd been camping. The rock's pretty hard here, and we used pretty heavy charges. Shock waves in the ground was what scared them."

They started down a path through the flower-dappled tall grass toward the edge of the hill, and down past the gray outcropping of limestone that formed a miniature bluff twenty feet high and a hundred in length. Under an overhanging ledge, they found two cushions, a red-and-gray blanket, and some odds and ends of old garments that looked as though they had once been used for polishing rags. There was a broken kitchen spoon, and a cold chisel, and some other metal articles.

"That's it, all right. I talked to the people who lost the blanket and the cushions. They must have made camp last night, after your gang stopped work; the blasting chased them out. You say you saw them go up that way?" he asked, pointing up the little stream that came down from the mountains to the north.

The stream was deep and rapid, too much so for easy fording by Fuzzies; they'd follow it back into the foothills. He took everybody's names and thanked them. If he found the Fuzzies himself and had to pay off on an information-received basis, it would take a mathematical genius to decide how much reward to pay whom.

"Gerd, if you were a Fuzzy, where would you go up

there?" he asked.

Gerd looked up the stream that came rushing down from among the wooded foothills.

"There are a couple more houses farther up," he said. "I'd get above them. Then I'd go up one of those side ravines, and get up among the rocks, where the damnthings couldn't get me. Of course, there are no damnthings this close to town, but they wouldn't know that."

"We'll need a few more cars. I'll call Colonel Ferguson and see what he can do for me. Max is going to have his hands full with this investigation Gus started."

Piet Dumont, the Mallorysport chief of police, might have been a good cop once, but for as long as Gus Brannhard had known him, he had been what he was now—an empty shell of unsupported arrogance, with a sagging waistline and a puffy face that tried to look tough and only succeeded in looking unpleasant. He was sitting in a seat that looked like an old fashioned electric chair, or like one of those instruments of torture to which beauty-shop customers submit themselves. There was a bright conical helmet on his head, and electrodes had been clamped to various portions of his anatomy. On the wall behind him was a circular screen which ought to have been a calm turquoise blue, but which was flickering from dark blue through violet to mauve. That was simple nervous tension and guilt and anger at the humiliation of being subjected to veridicated interrogation. Now and then there would be a stabbing flicker of bright red as he toyed mentally with some deliberate misstatement of fact.

"You know, yourself, that the Fuzzies didn't hurt that girl," Brannhard told him.

"I don't know anything of the kind," the police chief retorted. "All I know's what was reported to me."

That had started out a bright red; gradually it faded into purple. Evidently Piet Dumont was adopting a rules-of-evidence definition of truth.

"Who told you about it?"

"Luther Woller. Detective lieutenant on duty at the time."

The veridicator agreed that that was the truth and not much of anything but the truth.

"But you know that what really happened was that Lurkin beat the girl himself, and Woller persuaded them both to say the Fuzzies did it," Max Fane said.

"I don't know anything of the kind!" Dumont almost yelled. The screen blazed red. "All I know's what they told me; nobody said anything else. Red and blue, juggling in a typical quibbling pattern. "As far as I know, it was the Fuzzies done it."

"Now, Piet," Fane told him patiently. "You've used this same veridicator here often enough to know you can't get away with lying on it. Woller's making you the patsy for this, and you know that, too. Isn't it true, now, that to the best of your knowledge and belief those Fuzzies never touched that girl, and it wasn't till Woller talked to Lurkin and his daughter at headquarters that anybody even mentioned Fuzzies?"

The screen darkened to midnight blue, and then, slowly, it lightened.

"Yeah, that's true," Dumont admitted. He avoided their eyes, and his voice was surly. "I thought that was how it was, and I asked Woller. He just laughed at me and told me to forget it." The screen seethed momentarily with anger. "That son of a Khooghra thinks he's chief, not me. One word from me and he does just what he damn pleases!"

"Now you're being smart, Piet," Fane said. "Let's start all over. . . .

A constabulary corporal was at the controls of the car Jack had rented from the hotel: Gerd had taken his place in one of the two constabulary cars. The third car shuttled between them, and all three talked back and forth by radio.

"Mr. Holloway." It was the trooper in the car Gerd had been piloting. "Your partner's down on the ground; he just called me with his portable. He's found a cracked prawn-shell."

"Keep talking; give me direction," the corporal at the controls said, lifting up.

In a moment, they sighted the other car, hovering over a narrow ravine on the left bank of the stream. The third car was coming in from the north. Gerd was still squatting on the ground when they let down beside him. He looked up as they jumped out.

"This is it, Jack" he said. "Regular Fuzzy job."

So it was. Whatever they had used, it hadn't been anything sharp; the head was smashed instead of being cleanly severed. The shell, however, had been broken from underneath in the standard manner, and all four mandibles had been broken off for picks. They must have all eaten at the prawn, share alike. It had been done quite recently.

They sent the car up, and while all three of them circled about, they went up the ravine on foot, calling: "Little Fuzzy! Little Fuzzy!" They found a footprint, and then another, where seepage water had moistened the ground. Gerd was talking excitedly into the portable radio he carried slung on his chest.

"One of you, go ahead a quarter of a mile, and then circle back. They're in here somewhere."

"I see them! I see them!" a voice whooped out of the radio. "They're going up the slope on your right, among the rocks!"

"Keep them in sight; somebody come and pick us up, and we'll get above them and head them off."

The rental car dropped quickly, the corporal getting the door open. He didn't bother going off contragravity; as soon as they were in and had pulled the door shut behind them, he was lifting again. For a moment, the hill sung giddily as the car turned, and then Jack saw them, climbing the steep slope among the rocks. Only four of them, and one was helping another. He wondered which ones they were, what had happened to the other two and if the one that needed help had been badly hurt.

The car landed on the top, among the rocks, settling at an awkward angle. He, Gerd and the pilot piled out and started climbing and sliding down the declivity. Then he found himself within reach of a Fuzzy and grabbed. Two more dashed past him, up the steep hill. The one he snatched at had something in his hand, and aimed a vicious blow at his face with it; he had barely time to block it with his forearm. Then he was clutching the Fuzzy and disarming him; the weapon was a quarter-pound ballpeen hammer. He put it in his hip pocket and then picked up the struggling Fuzzy with both hands.

"You hit Pappy Jack!" he said reproachfully. "Don't you know Pappy any more? Poor scared little thing!"

The Fuzzy in his arms yeeked angrily. Then he looked, and it was no Fuzzy he had ever seen before—not Little Fuzzy, nor funny, pompous Ko-Ko, nor mischievous Mike. It was a stranger Fuzzy.

"Well, no wonder; of course you didn't know Pappy Jack. You aren't one of Pappy Jack's Fuzzies at all!"

At the top, the constabulary corporal was sitting on a rock, clutching two Fuzzies, one under each arm. They stopped struggling and yeeked piteously when they saw their companion also a captive.

"Your partner's down below, chasing the other one," the corporal said. "You better take these too; you know them and I don't."

"Hang onto them; they don't know me any better than they do you."

With one hand, he got a bit of Extee Three out of his coat and offered it; the Fuzzy gave a cry of surprised pleasure, snatched it and gobbled it. He must have eaten it before. When he gave some to the corporal, the other two, a male and a female, also seemed familiar with it. From below, Gerd was calling:

"I got one. It's a girl Fuzzy; I don't know if it's Mitzi

or Cinderella. And, my God, wait till you see what she was carrying."

Gerd came into sight, the fourth Fuzzy struggling under one arm and a little kitten, black with a white face, peeping over the crook of his other elbow. He was too stunned with disappointment to look at it with more than vague curiosity.

"They aren't our Fuzzies, Gerd. I never saw any of them before."

"Jack, are you sure."

"Of course I'm sure!" He was indignant. "Don't you think I know my own Fuzzies? Don't you think they'd know me?"

"Where'd the pussy come from?" the corporal wanted to know.

"God knows. They must have picked it up somewhere. She was carrying it in her arms, like a baby."

"They're somebody's Fuzzies. They've been fed Extee Three. We'll take them to the hotel. Whoever it is, I'll bet he misses them as much as I do mine."

His own Fuzzies, whom he would never see again. The full realization didn't hit him until he and Gerd were in the car again. There had been no trace of his Fuzzies from the time they had broken out of their cages at Science Center. This quartet had appeared the night the city police had manufactured the story of the attack on the Lurkin girl, and from the moment they had been seen by the youth who couldn't bring himself to fire on them, they had left a trail that he had been able to pick up at once and follow. Why hadn't his own Fuzzies attracted as much notice in the three weeks since they had vanished?

Because his own Fuzzies didn't exist any more. They had never gotten out of Science Center alive. Somebody Max Fane hadn't been able to question under veridication had murdered them. There was no use, any more, trying to convince himself differently.

"We'll stop at their camp and pick up the blanket and the cushions and the rest of the things. I'll send the people who lost them checks," he said. "The Fuzzies ought to have those things."

XIII

The management of the Hotel Mallory appeared to have undergone a change of heart, or of policy, toward Fuzzies. It might have been Gus Brannhard's threats of action for racial discrimination and the possibility that the Fuzzies might turn out to be a race instead of an animal species after all. The manager might have been shamed by the way the Lurkin story had crumbled into discredit, and influenced by the revived public sympathy for the Fuzzies. Or maybe he just decided that the chartered Zarathustra Company wasn't as omnipotent as he'd believed. At any rate, a large room, usually used for banquets, was made available for the Fuzzies George Lunt and Ben Rainsford were bringing in for the trial, and the four strangers and their black-and-white kitten were installed there. There were a lot of toys of different sorts, courtesy of the management, and a big view screen. The four strange Fuzzies dashed for this immediately and turned it on, yeeking in delight as they watched landing craft coming down and lifting out at the municipal spaceport. They found it very interesting. It only bored the kitten.

With some misgivings, Jack brought Baby down and introduced him. They were delighted with Baby, and Baby thought the kitten was the most wonderful thing he had ever seen. When it was time to feed them, Jack had his own dinner brought in, and ate with them. Gus and Gerd came down and joined him later.

"We got the Lurkin kid and her father," Gus said,

and then falsettoed: " 'Naw, Pop gimme a beatin', and the cops told me to say it was the Fuzzies.' "

"She say that?"

"Under veridication, with the screen blue as a sapphire, in front of half a dozen witnesses and with audiovisuals on. Interworld's putting it on the air this evening. Her father admitted it, too; named Woller and the desk sergeant. We're still looking for them; till we get them, we aren't any closer to Emmert or Grego. We did pick up the two car cops, but they don't know anything on anybody but Woller."

That was good enough, as far as it went, Brannhard thought, but it didn't go far enough. There were those four strange Fuzzies showing up out of nowhere, right in the middle of Nick Emmert's drive-hunt. They'd been kept somewhere by somebody—that was how they'd learned to eat Extee Three and found out about viewscreens. Their appearance was too well synchronized to be accidental. The whole thing smelled to him of a booby trap.

One good thing had happened. Judge Pendarvis had decided that it would be next to impossible, in view of the widespread public interest in the case and the influence of the Zarathustra Company, to get an impartial jury, and had proposed a judicial trial by a panel of three judges, himself one of them. Even Leslie Coombes had felt forced to agree to that.

He told Jack about the decision. Jack listened with apparent attentiveness, and then said:

"You know, Gus, I'll always be glad I let Little Fuzzy smoke my pipe when he wanted to, that night out at camp."

The way he was feeling, he wouldn't have cared less if the case was going to be tried by a panel of three zaragoats.

Ben Rainsford, his two Fuzzies, and George Lunt, Ahmed Khadra and the other constabulary witnesses and their family, arrived shortly before noon on Saturday. The Fuzzies were quartered in the stripped-out banquet room, and quickly made friends with the four already there, and with Baby. Each family bedded down apart, but they ate together and played with each others' toys and sat in a clump to watch the viewscreen. At first, the Ferny Creek family showed jealousy when too much attention was paid to their kitten, until they decided that nobody was trying to steal it.

It would have been a lot of fun, eleven Fuzzies and a Baby Fuzzy and a black-and-white kitten, if Jack hadn't kept seeing his own family, six quiet little ghosts watching but unable to join the frolicking.

Max Fane brightened when he saw who was on his screen.

"Well, Colonel Ferguson, glad to see you."

"Marshal," Ferguson was smiling broadly. "You'll be even gladder in a minute. A couple of my men, from Post Eight, picked up Woller and that desk sergeant, Fuentes."

"Ha!" He started feeling warm inside, as though he had just downed a slug of Baldur honey-rum. "How?"

"Well, you know Nick Emmert has a hunting lodge down there. Post Eight keeps an eye on it for him. This afternoon, one of Lieutenant Obefemi's cars was passing over it, and they picked up some radiation and infrared on their detectors, as though the power was on inside. When they went down to investigate, they found Woller and Fuentes making themselves at home. They brought them in, and both of them admitted under veridication that Emmert had given them the keys and sent them down there to hide out till after the trial.

"They denied that Emmert had originated the frameup. That had been one of Woller's own flashes of genius, but Emmert knew what the score was and went right along with it. They're being brought up here the first thing tomorrow morning."

"Well, that's swell, Colonel! Has it gotten out to the

news services yet?"

"No. We would like to have them both questioned here in Mallorysport, and their confessions recorded, before we let the story out. Otherwise, somebody might try to take steps to shut them up for good."

That had been what he had been thinking of. He said so, and Ferguson nodded. Then he hesitated for a moment, and said:

"Max, do you like the situation here in Mallorysport? Be damned if I do."

"What do you mean?"

"There are too many strangers in town," Ian Ferguson said. "All the same kind of strangers—husky-looking young men, twenty to thirty, going around in pairs and small groups. I've been noticing it since day before last, and there seem to be more of them every time I look around."

"Well, Ian, it's a young man's planet, and we can expect a big crowd in town for the trial. . . ."

He didn't really believe that. He just wanted Ian Ferguson to put a name on it first. Ferguson shook his head.

"No, Max. This isn't a trial-day crowd. We both know what they're like; remember when they tried the Gawn brothers? No whooping it up in bars, no excitement, no big crap games; this crowd's just walking around, keeping quiet, as though they expected a word from somebody."

"Infiltration." Goddamit, he'd said it first, himself after all! "Victor Grego's worried about this."

"I know it, Max. And Victor Grego's like a veldbeest bull; he isn't dangerous till he's scared, and then watch out. And against the gang that's moving in here, the men you and I have together would last about as long as a pint of trade-gin at a Sheshan funeral."

"You thinking of pushing the panic-button?"

The constabulary commander frowned. "I don't want to. A dim view would be taken back on Terra if I did it without needing to. Dimmer view would be taken of needing to without doing it, though. I'll make another check, first."

Gerd van Riebeek sorted the papers on the desk into piles, lit a cigarette and then started to mix himself a highball.

"Fuzzies are members of a sapient race," he declared. "They reason logically, both deductively and inductively. They learn by experiment, analysis and association. They formulate general principles, and apply them to specific instances. They plan their activities in advance. They make designed artifacts, and artifacts to make artifacts. They are able to symbolize, and convey ideas in symbolic form, and form symbols by abstracting from objects.

"They have aesthetic sense and creativity," he continued. "They become bored in idleness, and they enjoy solving problems for the pleasure of solving them. They bury their dead ceremoniously, and bury artifacts with them."

He blew a smoke ring, and then tasted his drink. "They do all these things, and they also do carpenter work, blow police whistles, make eating tools to eat land-prawns with and put molecule-model balls together. Obviously they are sapient beings. But don't *please* don't ask me to define sapience, because God damn it to Nifflheim, I still can't!"

"I think you just did," Jack said.

"No, that won't do. I need a definition."

"Don't worry, Gerd," Gus Brannhard told him. "Leslie Coombes will bring a nice shiny new definition into court. We'll just use that."

XIV

They walked together, Frederic and Claudette Pendarvis, down through the roof garden toward the landing stage, and, as she always did, Claudette stopped and cut a flower and fastened it in his lapel.

"Will the Fuzzies be in court?" she asked.

"Oh, they'll have to be. I don't know about this morning; it'll be mostly formalities." He made a grimace that was half a frown and half a smile. "I really don't know whether to consider them as witnesses or as exhibits, and I hope I'm not called on to rule on that, at least at the start. Either way, Coombes or Brannhard would accuse me of showing prejudice."

"I want to see them. I've seen them on screen, but I want to see them for real."

"You haven't been in one of my courts for a long time, Claudette. If I find that they'll be brought in today, I'll call you. I'll even abuse my position to the extent of arranging for you to see them outside the courtroom. Would you like that?"

She'd love it. Claudette had a limitless capacity for delight in things like that. They kissed good-bye, and he went to where his driver was holding open the door of the aircar and got in. At a thousand feet he looked back; she was still standing at the edge of the roof garden, looking up.

He'd have to find out whether it would be safe for her to come in. Max Fane was worried about the possibility of trouble, and so was Ian Ferguson, and neither was given to timorous imaginings. As the car began to descend toward the Central Courts buildings, he saw that there were guards on the roof, and they weren't just carrying pistols—he caught the glint of rifle barrels, and the twinkle of steel helmets. Then, as he came in, he saw that their uniforms were a lighter shade of blue than the constabulary wore. Ankle boots and red-striped trousers; Space Marines in dress blues. So Ian Ferguson had pushed the button. It occurred to him that Claudette might be safer here than at home.

A sergeant and a couple of men came up as he got out; the sergeant touched the beak of his helmet in the nearest thing to a salute a Marine ever gave anybody in civilian clothes.

"Judge Pendarvis? Good morning, sir."

"Good morning, sergeant. Just why are Federation Marines guarding the court building?"

"Standing by, sir. Orders of Commodore Napier. You'll find that Marshal Fane's people are in charge below-decks, but Marine Captain Casagra and Navy Captain Greibenfeld are waiting to see you in your office."

As he started toward the elevators, a big Zarathustra Company car was coming in. The sergeant turned quickly, beckoned a couple of his men and went toward it on the double. He wondered what Leslie Coombes would think about those Marines.

The two officers in his private chambers were both wearing sidearms. So, also, was Marshal Fane, who was with them. They all rose to greet him, sitting down when he was at his desk. He asked the same question he had of the sergeant above.

"Well, Constabulary Colonel Ferguson called Commodore Napier last evening and requested armed assistance, your Honor," the officer in Space Navy black said. "He suspected, he said, that the city had been infiltrated. In that, your Honor, he was perfectly correct; beginning Wednesday afternoon, Marine Captain

Casagra, here, on Commodore Napier's orders, began landing a Marine infiltration force, preparatory to taking over the Residency. That's been accomplished now; Commodore Napier is there, and both Resident General Emmert and Attorney General O'Brien are under arrest, on a variety of malfeasance and corrupt-practice charges, but that won't come into your Honor's court. They'll be sent back to Terra for trial."

"Then Commodore Napier's taken over the civil government?"

"Well, say he's assumed control of it, pending the outcome of this trial. We want to know whether the present administration's legal or not."

"Then you won't interfere with the trial itself?"

"That depends, your Honor. We are certainly going to participate." He looked at his watch. "You won't convene court for another hour? Then perhaps I'll have time to explain."

Max Fane met them at the courtroom door with a pleasant greeting. Then he saw Baby Fuzzy on Jack's shoulder and looked dubious.

"I don't know about him, Jack. I don't think he'll be allowed in the courtroom."

"Nonsense!" Gus Brannhard told him. "I admit, he is both a minor child and an incompetent aborigine, but he is the only surviving member of the family of the decedent Jane Doe alias Goldilocks, and as such has an indisputable right to be present."

"Well, just as long as you keep him from sitting on people's heads. Gus, you and Jack sit over there; Ben, you and Gerd find seats in the witness section."

It would be half an hour till court would convene, but already the spectators' seats were full, and so was the balcony. The jury box, on the left of the bench, was occupied by a number of officers in Navy black and Marine blue. Since there would be no jury, they had apparently appropriated it for themselves. The press box was jammed and bristling with equipment.

Baby was looking up interestedly at the big screen behind the judges' seats; while transmitting the court scene to the public, it also showed, like a nonreversing mirror, the same view to the spectators. Baby wasn't long in identifying himself in it, and waved his arms excitedly. At that moment, there was a bustle at the door by which they had entered, and Leslie Coombes came in, followed by Ernst Mallin and a couple of his assistants, Ruth Ortheris, Juan Jimenez—and Leonard Kellogg. The last time he had seen Kellogg had been at George Lunt's complaint court, his face bandaged and his feet in a pair of borrowed moccasins because his shoes, stained with the blood of Goldilocks, had been impounded as evidence.

Coombes glanced toward the table where he and Brannhard were sitting, caught sight of Baby waving to himself in the big screen and turned to Fane with an indignant protest. Fane shook his head. Coombes protested again, and drew another headshake. Finally he shrugged and led Kellogg to the table reserved for them, where they sat down.

Once Pendarvis and his two associates—a short, roundfaced man on his right, a tall, slender man with white hair and a black mustache on his left—were seated, the trial got underway briskly. The charges were read, and then Brannhard, as the Kellogg prosecutor, addressed the court—"being known as Goldilocks...sapient member of a sapient race...willful and deliberate act of the said Leonard Kellogg...brutal and unprovoked murder." He backed away, sat on the edge of the table and picked up Baby Fuzzy, fondling him while Leslie Coombes accused Jack Holloway of brutally assaulting the said Leonard Kellogg and ruthlessly shooting down Kurt Borch.

"Well, gentlemen, I believe we can now begin hearing the witnesses," the Chief Justice said. "Who will start prosecuting whom?"

Gus handed Baby to Jack and went forward: Coombes stepped up beside him.

"Your Honor, this entire trial hinges upon the question of whether a member of the species *Fuzzy fuzzy holloway zarathustra* is or is not a sapient being," Gus said. "However, before any attempt is made to determine this question, we should first establish, by testimony, just what happened at Holloway's Camp, in Cold Creek Valley, on the afternoon of June 19, Atomic Era Six Fifty-Four, and once this is established, we can then proceed to the question of whether or not the said Goldilocks was truly a sapient being."

"I agree," Coombes said equably. "Most of these witnesses will have to be recalled to the stand later, but in general I think Mr. Brannhard's suggestion will be economical of the court's time."

"Will Mr. Coombes agree to stipulate that any evidence tending to prove or disprove the sapience of Fuzzies in general be accepted as proving or disproving the sapience of the being referred to as Goldilocks?"

Coombes looked that over carefully, decided that it wasn't booby-trapped and agreed. A deputy marshal went over to the witness stand, made some adjustments and snapped on a switch at the back of the chair. Immediately the two-foot globe in a standard behind it lit, a clear blue. George Lunt's name was called; the lieutenant took his seat and the bright helmet was let down over his head and the electrodes attached.

The globe stayed a calm, untroubled blue while he stated his name and rank. Then he waited while Coombes and Brannhard conferred. Finally Brannhard took a silver half-sol piece from his pocket, shook it between cupped palms and slapped it onto his wrist. Coombes said, "Heads," and Brannhard uncovered it, bowed slightly and stepped back.

"Now, Lieutenant Lunt," Coombes began, "when you arrived at the temporary camp across the run from Holloway's camp, what did you find there?"

"Two dead people," Lunt said. "A Terran human,

who had been shot three times through the chest, and a Fuzzy, who had been kicked or trampled to death."

"Your Honors!" Coombes expostulated, "I must ask that the witness be requested to rephrase his answer, and that the answer he has just made be stricken from the record. The witness, under the circumstances, has no right to refer to the Fuzzies as 'people.' "

"Your Honors," Brannhard caught it up, "Mr. Coombes's objection is no less prejudicial. He has no right, under the circumstances, to deny that the Fuzzies be referred to as 'people.' This is tantamount to insisting that the witness speak of them as nonsapient animals."

It went on like that for five minutes. Jack began doodling on a notepad. Baby picked up a pencil with both hands and began making doodles too. They looked rather like the knots he had been learning to tie. Finally, the court intervened and told Lunt to tell, in his own words, why he went to Holloway's camp, what he found there, what he was told and what he did. There was some argument between Coombes and Brannhard, at one point, about the difference between hearsay and *res gestae*. When he was through, Coombes said, "No questions."

"Lieutenant, you placed Leonard Kellogg under arrest on a complaint of homicide by Jack Holloway. I take it that you considered this complaint a valid one?"

"Yes, sir. I believed that Leonard Kellogg had killed a sapient being. Only sapient beings bury their dead."

Ahmed Khadra testified. The two troopers who had come in the other car, and the men who had brought the investigative equipment and done the photographing at the scene testified. Brannhard called Ruth Ortheris to the stand, and, after some futile objections by Coombes, she was allowed to tell her own story of the killing of Goldilocks, the beating of Kellogg and the shooting of Borch. When she had finished, the Chief Justice rapped with his gavel.

"I believe that this testimony is sufficient to establish the fact that the being referred to as Jane Doe alias Goldilocks was in fact kicked and trampled to death by the defendant Leonard Kellogg, and that the Terran human known as Kurt Borch was in fact shot to death by Jack Holloway. This being the case, we may now consider whether or not either or both of these killings constitute murder within the meaning of the law. It is now eleven forty. We will adjourn for lunch, and court will reconvene at fourteen hundred. There are a number of things, including some alterations to the courtroom, which must be done before the afternoon session . . . Yes, Mr. Brannhard?"

"Your Honors, there is only one member of the species *Fuzzy fuzzy holloway zarathustra* at present in court, an immature and hence nonrepresentative individual." He picked up Baby and exhibited him. "If we are to take up the question of the sapience of this species, or race, would it not be well to send for the Fuzzies now staying at the Hotel Mallory and have them on hand?"

"Well, Mr. Brannhard," Pendarvis said, "we will certainly want Fuzzies in court, but let me suggest that we wait until after court reconvenes before sending for them. It may be that they will not be needed this afternoon. Anything else?" He tapped with his gavel. "Then court is adjourned until fourteen hundred."

Some alterations in the courtroom had been a conservative way of putting it. Four rows of spectators' seats had been abolished, and the dividing rail moved back. The witness chair, originally at the side of the bench, had been moved to the dividing rail and now faced the bench, and a large number of tables had been brought in and ranged in an arc with the witness chair in the middle of it. Everybody at the tables could face the judges, and also see everybody else by looking into the big screen. A witness on the chair could also see the veridicator in the same way.

Gus Brannhard looked around, when he entered with Jack, and swore softly.

"No wonder they gave us two hours for lunch. I wonder what the idea is." Then he gave a short laugh. "Look at Coombes; he doesn't like it a bit."

A deputy with a seating diagram came up to them.

"Mr. Brannhard, you and Mr. Holloway over here, at this table." He pointed to one a little apart from the others, at the extreme right facing the bench. "And Dr. van Riebeek, and Dr. Rainsford over here, please."

The court crier's loud-speaker, overhead, gave two sharp whistles and began:

"Now hear this! Now hear this! Court will convene in five minutes—"

Brannhard's head jerked around instantly, and Jack's eyes followed his. The court crier was a Space Navy petty officer.

"What the devil is this?" Brannhard demanded. "A Navy court-martial?"

"That's what I've been wondering, Mr. Brannhard," the deputy said. "They've taken over the whole planet, you know."

"Maybe we're in luck, Gus. I've always heard that if you're innocent you're better off before a court-martial and if you're guilty you're better off in a civil court."

He saw Leslie Coombes and Leonard Kellogg being seated at a similar table at the opposite side of the bench. Apparently Coombes had also heard that. The seating arrangements at the other tables seemed a little odd too. Gerd van Riebeek was next to Ruth Ortheris, and Ernst Mallin was next to Ben Rainsford, with Juan Jiminez on his other side. Gus was looking up at the balcony.

"I'll bet every lawyer on the planet's taking this in," he said. "Oh-oh! See the white-haired lady in the blue dress, Jack? That's the Chief Justice's wife. This is the first time she's been in court for years."

"Hear ye! Hear ye! Hear ye! Rise for the Honorable Court!"

Somebody must have given the petty officer a quick briefing on courtroom phraseology. He stood up, holding Baby Fuzzy, while the three judges filed in and took their seats. As soon as they sat down, the Chief Justice rapped briskly with his gavel.

"In order to forestall a spate of objections, I want to say that these present arrangements are temporary, and so will be the procedures which will be followed. We are not, at the moment, trying Jack Holloway or Leonard Kellogg. For the rest of this day, and, I fear, for a good many days to come, we will be concerned exclusively with determining the level of mentation of *Fuzzy fuzzy holloway zarathustra*.

"For this purpose, we are temporarily abandoning some of the traditional trial procedures. We will call witnesses; statements of purported fact will be made under veridication as usual. We will also have a general discussion, in which all of you at these tables will be free to participate. I and my associates will preside; as we can't have everybody shouting disputations at once, anyone wishing to speak will have to be recognized. At least, I hope we will be able to conduct the discussion in this manner.

"You will all have noticed the presence of a number of officers from Xerxes Naval Base, and I suppose you have all heard that Commodore Napier has assumed control of the civil government. Captain Greibenfeld, will you please rise and be seen? He is here participating as *amicus curiae*, and I have given him the right to question witnesses and to delegate that right to any of his officers he may deem proper. Mr. Coombes and Mr. Brannhard may also delegate that right as they see fit."

Coombes was on his feet at once. "Your Honors, if we are now to discuss the sapience question, I would suggest that the first item on our order of business be the presentation of some acceptable definition of sapience. I should, for my part, very much like to know what it is that the Kellogg prosecution and the Holloway defense mean when they use that term."

That's it. They want us to define it. Gerd van Riebeek was looking chagrined; Ernst Mallin was smirking. Gus Brannhard, however, was pleased.

"Jack, they haven't any more damn definition than we do," he whispered.

Captain Greibenfeld, who had seated himself after rising at the request of the court, was on his feet again.

"Your Honors, during the past month we at Xerxes Naval Base have been working on exactly that problem. We have a very considerable interest in having the classification of this planet established, and we also feel that this may not be the last time a question of disputable sapience may arise. I believe, your Honors, that we have approached such a definition. However, before we begin discussing it, I would like the court's permission to present a demonstration which may be of help in understanding the problems involved."

"Captain Greibenfeld has already discussed this demonstration with me, and it has my approval. Will you please proceed, Captain," the Chief Justice said.

Greibenfeld nodded, and a deputy marshal opened the door on the right of the bench. Two spacemen came in, carrying cartons. One went up to the bench; the other started around in front of the tables, distributing small battery-powered hearing aids.

"Please put them in your ears and turn them on," he said. "Thank you."

Baby Fuzzy tried to get Jack's. He put the plug in his ear and switched on the power. Instantly he began hearing a number of small sounds he had never heard before, and Baby was saying to him: *"He-inta sa-wa'aka; igga sa geeda?"*

"Muhgawd, Gus, he's talking!"

"Yes, I hear him; what do you suppose—?"

"Ultrasonic; God, why didn't we think of that long

ago?"

He snapped off the hearing aid. Baby Fuzzy was saying, "Yeeek." When he turned it on again, Baby was saying, "*Kukk-ina za zeeva.*"

"No, Baby, Pappy Jack doesn't understand. We'll have to be awfully patient, and learn each other's language."

"*Pa-pee Jaaak!*" Baby cried. "*Ba-bee za-hinga; Pa-pee Jaak za zag ga he-izza!*"

"That yeeking is just the audible edge of their speech; bet we have a lot of transsonic tones in our voices, too."

"Well, he can hear what we say; he's picked up his name and yours."

"Mr. Brannhard, Mr. Holloway," Judge Pendarvis was saying, "may we please have your attention? Now, have you all your earplugs in and turned on? Very well; carry on, Captain."

This time, an ensign went out and came back with a crowd of enlisted men, who had six Fuzzies with them. They set them down in the open space between the bench and the arc of tables and backed away. The Fuzzies drew together into a clump and stared around them, and he stared, unbelievingly, at them. They couldn't be; they didn't exist any more. But they were—Little Fuzzy and Mamma Fuzzy and Mike and Mitzi and Ko-Ko and Cinderella. Baby whooped something and leaped from the table, and Mamma came stumbling to meet him, clasping him in her arms. Then they all saw him and began clamoring: "*Pa-pee Jaaak! Pa-pee Jaaak!*"

He wasn't aware of rising and leaving the table; the next thing he realized, he was sitting on the floor, his family mobbing him and hugging him, gabbling with joy. Dimly he heard the gavel hammering, and the voice of Chief Justice Pendarvis: "Court is recessed for ten minutes!" By that time, Gus was with him; gathering the family up, they carried them over to their table.

They stumbled and staggered when they moved, and that frightened him for a moment. Then he realized that they weren't sick or drugged. They'd just been in low-G for a while and hadn't become reaccustomed to normal weight. Now he knew why he hadn't been able to find any trace of them. He noticed that each of them was wearing a little shoulder bag—a Marine Corps first-aid pouch—slung from a webbing strap. Why the devil hadn't he thought of making them something like that? He touched one and commented, trying to pitch his voice as nearly like theirs as he could. They all babbled in reply and began opening the little bags and showing him what they had in them—little knives and minature tools and bits of bright or colored junk they had picked up. Little Fuzzy produced a tiny pipe with a hardwood bowl, and a little pouch of tobacco from which he filled it. Finally, he got out a small lighter.

"Your Honors!" Gus shouted, "I know court is recessed, but please observe what Little Fuzzy is doing."

While they watched, Little Fuzzy snapped the lighter and held the flame to the pipe bowl, puffing.

Across on the other side, Leslie Coombes swallowed once or twice and closed his eyes.

When Pendarvis rapped for attention and declared court reconvened, he said:

"Ladies and gentlemen, you have all seen and heard this demonstration of Captain Greibenfeld's. You have heard these Fuzzies uttering what certainly sounds like meaningful speech, and you have seen one of them light a pipe and smoke. Incidentally, while smoking in court is discountenanced, we are going to make an exception, during this trial, in favor of Fuzzies. Other people will please not feel themselves discriminated against."

That brought Coombes to his feet with a rush. He started around the table and then remembered that under the new rules he didn't have to.

"Your Honors, I objected strongly to the use of that

term by a witness this morning; I must object even more emphatically to its employment from the bench. I have indeed heard these Fuzzies make sounds which might be mistaken for words, but I must deny that this is true speech. As to this trick of using a lighter, I will undertake, in not more than thirty days, to teach it to any Terran primate or Freyan kholph."

Greibenfeld rose immediately. "Your Honors, in the past thirty days, while these Fuzzies were at Xerxes Navel Base, we have compiled a vocabulary of a hundred-odd Fuzzy words, for all of which definite meanings have been established, and a great many more for which we have not as yet learned the meanings. We even have the beginning of a Fuzzy grammar. As for this so-called trick of using a lighter, Little Fuzzy—we didn't know his name then and referred to him as M2—learned that for himself, by observation. We didn't teach him to smoke a pipe either; he knew that before we had anything to do with him."

Jack rose while Greibenfeld was still speaking. As soon as the Space Navy captain had finished, he said:

"Captain Greibenfeld, I want to thank you and your people for taking care of the Fuzzies, and I'm very glad you learned how to hear what they're saying, and thank you for all the nice things you gave them, but why couldn't you have let me know they were safe? I haven't been very happy the last month, you know."

"I know that, Mr. Holloway, and if it's any comfort to you, we were all very sorry for you, but we could not take the risk of compromising our secret intelligence agent in the Company's Science Center, the one who smuggled the Fuzzies out the morning after their escape." He looked quickly across in front of the bench to the table at the other end of the arc. Kellogg was sitting with his face in his hands, oblivious to everything that was going on, but Leslie Coombes's well-disciplined face had broken, briefly, into a look of consternation. "By the time you and Mr. Brannhard and Marshal Fane arrived with an order of the court for the Fuzzies' recovery, they had already been taken from Science Center and were on a Navy landing craft for Xerxes. We couldn't do anything without exposing our agent. That, I am glad to say, is no longer a consideration."

"Well, Captain Greibenfeld," the Chief Justice said, "I assume you mean to introduce further testimony about the observations and studies made by your people on Xerxes. For the record, we'd like to have it established that they were actually taken there, and when, and how."

"Yes, your Honor. If you will call the fourth name on the list I gave you, and allow me to do the questioning, we can establish that."

The Chief Justice picked up a paper. "Lieutenant j.g. Ruth Ortheris, TFN Reserve," he called out.

This time, Jack Holloway looked up into the big screen, in which he could see everybody. Gerd van Riebeek, who had been trying to ignore the existence of the woman beside him, had turned to stare at her in amazement. Coombes's face was ghastly for an instant, then froze into corpselike immobility; Ernst Mallin was dithering in incredulous anger; beside him Ben Rainsford was grinning in just as incredulous delight. As Ruth came around in front of the bench, the Fuzzies gave her an ovation; they remembered and liked her. Gus Brannhard was gripping his arm and saying: "Oh, brother! This is it, Jack; it's all over but shooting the cripples!"

Lieutenant j.g. Ortheris, under a calmly blue globe, testified to coming to Zarathustra as a Federation Naval Reserve officer recalled to duty with Intelligence, and taking a position with the Company.

"As a regularly qualified doctor of psychology, I worked under Dr. Mallin in the scientific division, and also with the school department and the juvenile court. At the same time I was regularly transmitting reports to Commander Aelborg, the chief of Intelligence on Xerxes. The object of this surveillance was to make sure that the Zarathustra Company was not violating the provisions of their charter or Federation law. Until the middle of last month, I had nothing to report beyond some rather irregular financial transactions involving Resident General Emmert. Then, on the evening of June fifteen—"

That was when Ben had transmitted the tape to Juan Jimenez; she described how it had come to her attention.

"As soon as possible, I transmitted a copy of this tape to Commander Aelborg. The next night, I called Xerxes from the screen on Dr. van Riebeek's boat and reported what I'd learned about the Fuzzies. I was then informed that Leonard Kellogg had gotten hold of a copy of the Holloway-Rainsford tape and had alerted Victor Grego; that Kellogg and Ernst Mallin were being sent to Beta Continent with instructions to prevent publication of any report claiming sapience for the Fuzzies and to fabricate evidence to support an accusation that Dr. Rainsford and Mr. Holloway were perpetrating a deliberate scientific hoax."

"Here, I'll have to object to this, your Honor," Coombes said, rising. "This is nothing but hearsay."

"This is part of a Navy Intelligence situation estimate given to Lieutenant Ortheris, based on reports we had received from other agents," Captain Greibenfeld said. "She isn't the only one we have on Zarathustra, you know. Mr. Coombes, if I hear another word of objection to this officer's testimony from you, I am going to ask Mr. Brannhard to subpoena Victor Grego and question him under veridication about it."

"Mr. Brannhard will be more than happy to oblige, Commander," Gus said loudly and distinctly.

Coombes sat down hastily.

"Well, Lieutenant Ortheris, this is most interesting, but at the moment, what we're trying to establish is how these Fuzzies got to Xerxes Naval Base," the chubby associate justice, Ruiz, put in.

"I'll try to get them there as quickly as possible,

your Honor," she said. "On the night of Friday the twenty-second, the Fuzzies were taken from Mr. Holloway and brought into Mallorysport; they were turned over by Mohammed O'Brien to Juan Jimenez, who took them to Science Center and put them in cages in a room back of his office. They immediately escaped. I found them, the next morning, and was able to get them out of the building, and to turn them over to Commander Aelborg, who had come down from Xerxes to take personal charge of the Fuzzy operation. I will not testify as to how I was able to do this. I am at present and was then an officer of the Terran Federation Armed Forces; the courts have no power to compel a Federation officer to give testimony involving breach of military security. I was informed, through my contact in Mallorysport, from time to time, of the progress of the work of measuring the Fuzzies' mental level there; I was able to pass on suggestions occasionally. Any time any of these suggestions was based on ideas originating with Dr. Mallin, I was careful to give him full credit.'"

Mallin looked singularly unappreciative.

Brannhard got up. "Before this witness is excused, I'd like to ask if she knows anything about four other Fuzzies, the ones found by Jack Holloway up Ferny Creek on Friday."

"Why, yes; they're my Fuzzies, and I was worried about them. Their names are Complex, Syndrome, Id and Superego."

"Your Fuzzies, Lieutenant?"

"Well, I took care of them and worked with them; Juan Jimenez and some Company hunters caught them over on Beta Continent. They were kept at a farm center about five hundred miles north of here, which had been vacated for the purpose. I spent all my time with them, and Dr. Mallin was with them most of the time. Then, on Monday night, Mr. Coombes came and got them."

"Mr. Coombes, did you say?" Gus Brannhard asked.

"Mr. Leslie Coombes, the Company attorney. He said they were needed in Mallorysport. It wasn't till the next day that I found out what they were needed for. They'd been turned loose in front of that Fuzzy hunt, in the hope that they would be killed."

She looked across at Coombes; if looks were bullets, he'd have been deader than Kurt Borch.

"Why would they sacrifice four Fuzzies merely to support a story that was bound to come apart anyhow?" Brannhard asked.

"That was no sacrifice. They had to get rid of those Fuzzies, and they were afraid to kill them themselves for fear they'd be charged with murder along with Leonard Kellogg. Everybody, from Ernst Mallin down, who had anything to do with them was convinced of their sapience. For one thing, we'd been using those hearing aids ourselves; I suggested it, after getting the idea from Xerxes. Ask Dr. Mallin about it, under veridication. Ask him about the multiordinal polyencephalograph experiments, too."

"Well, we have the Holloway Fuzzies placed on Xerxes," the Chief Justice said. "We can hear the testimony of the people who worked with them there at any time. Now, I want to hear from Dr. Ernst Mallin."

Coombes was on his feet again. "Your Honors, before any further testimony is heard, I would like to confer with my client privately."

"I fail to see any reason why we should interrupt proceedings for that purpose, Mr. Coombes. You can confer as much as you wish with your client after this session, and I can assure you that you will be called upon to do nothing on his behalf until then." He gave a light tap with his gavel and then said: "Dr. Ernst Mallin will please take the stand."

XV

Ernst Mallin shrank, as though trying to pull himself into himself, when he heard his name. He didn't want to testify. He had been dreading this moment for days. Now he would have to sit in that chair, and they would ask him questions, and he couldn't answer them truthfully and the globe over his head—

When the deputy marshal touched his shoulder and spoke to him, he didn't think, at first, that his legs would support him. It seemed miles, with all the staring faces on either side of him. Somehow, he reached the chair and sat down, and they fitted the helmet over his head and attached the electrodes. They used to make a witness take some kind of an oath to tell the truth. They didn't any more. They didn't need to.

As soon as the veridicator was on, he looked up at the big screen behind the three judges; the glove above his head was a glaring red. There was a titter of laughter. Nobody in the courtroom knew better than he what was happening. He had screens in his laboratory that broke it all down into individual patterns—the steady pulsing waves from the cortex, the alpha and beta waves; beta-aleph and beta-beth and beta-gimel and beta-daleth. The thalamic waves. He thought of all of them, and of the electromagnetic events which accompanied brain activity. As he did, the red faded and the globe became blue. He was no longer suppressing statements and substituting other statements he knew to be false. If he could keep it that way. But, sooner or later, he knew, he wouldn't be able to.

The globe stayed blue while he named himself and stated his professional background. There was a brief flicker of red while he was listing his publication—that paper, entirely the work of one of his students, which he had published under his own name. He had forgotten about that, but his conscience hadn't.

"Dr. Mallin," the oldest of the three judges, who sat in the middle, began, "what, in your professional opinion, is the difference between sapient and non-sapient mentation?"

"The ability to think consciously," he stated. The globe stayed blue.

"Do you mean that nonsapient animals aren't conscious, or do you mean they don't think?"

"Well, neither. Any life form with a central nervous system has some consciousness—awareness of existence and of its surroundings. And anything having a brain thinks, to use the term at its loosest. What I meant was that only the sapient mind thinks and knows that it is thinking."

He was perfectly safe so far. He talked about sensory stimuli and responses, and about conditioned reflexes. He went back to the first century Pre-Atomic, and Pavlov and Korzybski and Freud. The globe never flickered.

"The nonsapient animal is conscious only of what is immediately present to the senses and responds automatically. It will perceive something and make a single statement about it—this is good to eat, this sensation is unpleasant, this is a sex-gratification object, this is dangerous. The sapient mind, on the other hand, is conscious of thinking about these sense stimuli, and makes descriptive statements about them, and then makes statements about those statements, in a connected chain. I have a structural differential at my seat; if somebody will bring it to me—"

"Well, never mind now, Dr. Mallin. When you're off the stand and the discussion begins you can show what you mean. We just want your opinion in general terms, now."

"Well, the sapient mind can generalize. To the nonsapient animal, every experience is either totally novel or identical with some remembered experience. A rabbit will flee from one dog because to the rabbit mind it is identical with another dog that has chased it. A bird will be attracted to an apple, and each apple will be a unique red thing to peck at. The sapient being will say, 'These red objects are apples; as a class, they are edible and flavorsome.' He sets up a class under the general label of apples. This, in turn, leads to the formation of abstract ideas—redness, flavor, et cetera—conceived of apart from any specific physical object, and to the ordering of abstractions—'fruit' as distinguished from apples, 'food' as distinguished from fruit."

The globe was still placidly blue. The three judges waited, and he continued:

"Having formed these abstract ideas, it becomes necessary to symbolize them, in order to deal with them apart from the actual object. The sapient being is a symbolizer, and a symbol communicator; he is able to convey to other sapient beings his ideas in symbolic form."

"Like *'Pa-pee Jaak'*?" the judge on his right, with the black mustache, asked.

The globe flashed red at once.

"Your Honors, I cannot consider words picked up at random and learned by rote speech. The Fuzzies have merely learned to associate that sound with a specific human, and use it as a signal, not as a symbol."

The globe was still red. The Chief Justice, in the middle, rapped with his gavel.

"Dr. Mallin! Of all the people on this planet, you at least should know the impossibility of lying under veridication. Other people just know it can't be done; you know why. Now I'm going to rephrase Judge Janiver's question, and I'll expect you to answer truthfully. If you don't I'm going to hold you in contempt. When those Fuzzies cried out, 'Pappy Jack!' do you or do you not believe that they were using a verbal expression which stood, in their minds, for Mr. Holloway?"

He couldn't say it. This sapience was all a big fake; he had to believe that. The Fuzzies were only little mindless animals.

But he didn't believe it. He knew better. He gulped for a moment.

"Yes, your Honor. The term 'Pappy Jack' is, in their minds, a symbol standing for Mr. Jack Holloway."

He looked at the globe. The red had turned to mauve, the mauve was becoming violet, and then clear blue. He felt better than he had felt since the afternoon Leonard Kellogg had told him about the Fuzzies.

"Then Fuzzies do think consciously, Dr. Mallin?" That was Pendarvis.

"Oh, yes. The fact that they use verbal symbols indicates that, even without other evidence. And the instrumental evidence was most impressive. The mentation pictures we got by encephalography compare very favorably with those of any human child of ten or twelve years old, and so does their learning and puzzle-solving ability. On puzzles, they always think the problem out first, and then do the mechanical work with about the same mental effort, say, as a man washing his hands or tying his neckcloth."

The globe was perfectly blue. Mallin had given up trying to lie; he was simply gushing out everything he thought.

Leonard Kellogg slumped forward, his head buried in his elbows on the table, and misery washed over him in tides.

I am a murderer; I killed a person. Only a funny little person with fur, but she was a person, and I knew it when I killed her, I knew it when I saw that little grave out in the woods, and they'll put me in that chair and make me admit it to everybody, and then they'll take me out in the jail yard and somebody will shoot me through the head with a pistol, and—

And all the poor little thing wanted was to show me her new jingle!

"Does anybody want to ask the witness any questions?" the Chief Justice was asking.

"I don't," Captain Greibenfeld said. "Do you, Lieutenant?"

"No, I don't think so," Lieutenant Ybarra said. "Dr. Mallin's given us a very lucid statement of his opinions."

He had, at that, after he'd decided he couldn't beat the veridicator. Jack found himself sympathizing with Mallin. He'd disliked the man from the first, but he looked different now—sort of cleaned and washed out inside. Maybe everybody ought to be veridicated, now and then, to teach them that honesty begins with honesty to self.

"Mr. Coombes?" Mr. Coombes looked as though he never wanted to ask another witness another question as long as he lived. "Mr. Brannhard?"

Gus got up, holding a sapient member of a sapient race who was hanging onto his beard, and thanked Ernst Mallin fulsomely.

"In that case, we'll adjourn until o-nine-hundred tomorrow. Mr. Coombes, I have here a check on the chartered Zarathustra Company for twenty-five thousand sols. I am returning it to you and I am canceling Dr. Kellogg's bail," Judge Pendarvis said, as a couple of attendants began getting Mallin loose from the veridicator.

"Are you also canceling Jack Holloway's?"

"No, and I would advise you not to make an issue of it, Mr. Coombes. The only reason I haven't dismissed the charge against Mr. Holloway is that I don't want to handicap you by cutting off your foothold in the prosecution. I do not consider Mr. Holloway a bail risk. I do so consider your client, Dr. Kellogg."

"Frankly, your Honor, so do I," Coombes admitted. "My protest was merely an example of what Dr. Mallin would call conditioned reflex."

Then a crowd began pushing up around the table; Ben Rainsford, George Lunt and his troopers, Gerd and Ruth, shoving in among them, their arms around each other.

"We'll be at the hotel after a while, Jack," Gerd was saying. "Ruth and I are going out for a drink and something to eat; we'll be around later to pick up her Fuzzies."

Now his partner had his girl back, and his partner's girl had a Fuzzy family of her own. This was going to be real fun. What were their names now? Syndrome, Complex, Id and Superego. The things some people named Fuzzies!

XVI

They stopped whispering at the door, turned right, and ascended to the bench, bearing themselves like images in a procession, Ruiz first, then himself and then Janiver. They turned to the screen so that the public whom they served might see the faces of the judges, and then sat down. The court crier began his chant. They could almost feel the tension in the courtroom. Yves Janiver whispered to them:

"They all know about it."

As soon as the crier had stopped, Max Fane approached the bench, his face blankly expressionless.

"Your Honors, I am ashamed to have to report that the defendant, Leonard Kellogg, cannot be produced in court. He is dead; he committed suicide in his cell last night. While in my custody," he added bitterly.

The stir that went through the courtroom was not shocked surprise, it was a sigh of fulfilled expectation. They all knew about it.

"How did this happen, Marshal?" he asked, almost conversationally.

"The prisoner was put in a cell by himself; there was a pickup eye, and one of my deputies was keeping him under observation by screen." Fane spoke in a toneless, almost robotlike voice. "At twenty-two thirty, the prisoner went to bed, still wearing his shirt. He pulled the blankets up over his head. The deputy observing him thought nothing of that; many prisoners do that, on account of the light. He tossed about for a while, and then appeared to fall asleep.

"When a guard went in to rouse him this morning, the cot, under the blanket, was found saturated with blood. Kellogg had cut his throat, by sawing the zipper track of his shirt back and forth till he severed his jugular vein. He was dead."

"Good heavens, Marshal!" He was shocked. The way he'd heard it, Kellogg had hidden a penknife, and he was prepared to be severe with Fane about it. But a thing like this! He found himself fingering the toothed track of his own jacket zipper. "I don't believe you can be at all censured for not anticipating a thing like that. It isn't a thing anybody would expect."

Janiver and Ruiz spoke briefly in agreement. Marshal Fane bowed slightly and went off to one side.

Leslie Coombes, who seemed to be making a very considerable effort to look grieved and shocked, rose.

"Your Honors, I find myself here without a client," he said. "In fact, I find myself here without any business at all; the case against Mr. Holloway is absolutely insupportable. He shot a man who was trying to kill him, and that's all there is to it. I therefore pray your Honors to dismiss the case against him and discharge him from custody."

Captain Greibenfeld bounded to his feet.

"Your Honors, I fully realize that the defendant is now beyond the jurisdiction of this court, but let me point out that I and my associates are here participating in this case in the hope that the classification of this planet may be determined, and some adequate definition of sapience established. These are most serious questions, your Honors."

"But, your Honors," Coombes protested, "we can't go through the farce of trying a dead man."

"*People of the Colony of Baphomet versus Jamshar Singh, Deceased*, charge of arson and sabotage, A.E. 604," the Honorable Gustavus Adolphus Brannhard interrupted.

Yes, you could find a precedent in colonial law for

almost anything.

Jack Holloway was on his feet, a Fuzzy cradled in the crook of his left arm, his white mustache bristling truculently.

"I am not a dead man, your Honors, and I am on trial here. The reason I'm not dead is why I am on trial. My defense is that I shot Kurt Borch while he was aiding and abetting in the killing of a Fuzzy. I want it established in this court that it is murder to kill a Fuzzy."

The judge nodded slowly. "I will not dismiss the charges against Mr. Holloway," he said. "Mr. Holloway had been arraigned on a charge of murder; if he is not guilty, he is entitled to the vindication of an acquittal. I am afraid, Mr. Coombes, that you will have to go on prosecuting him."

Another brief stir, like a breath of wind over a grain field, ran through the courtroom. The show was going on after all.

All the Fuzzies were in court this morning; Jack's six, and the five from the constabulary post, and Ben's Flora and Fauna, and the four Ruth Ortheris claimed. There was too much discussion going on for anybody to keep an eye on them. Finally one of the constabulary Fuzzies, either Dillinger or Dr. Crippen, and Ben Rainsford's Flora and Fauna, came sauntering out into the open space between the tables and the bench dragging the hose of a vacuum-duster. Ahmed Khadra ducked under a table and tried to get it away from them. This was wonderful; screaming in delight, they all laid hold of the other end, and Mike and Mitzi and Superego and Complex ran to help them. The seven of them dragged Khadra about ten feet before he gave up and let go. At the same time, an incipient fight broke out on the other side of the arc of tables between the head of the language department at Mallorysport Academy and a spinsterish amateur phoneticist. At this point, Judge Pendarvis, deciding that if you can't prevent it, relax and enjoy it, rapped a few times with his gavel, and announced that court was recessed.

"You will all please remain here; this is not an adjournment, and if any of the various groups who seem to be discussing different aspects of the problem reach any conclusion they feel should be presented in evidence, will they please notify the bench so that court can be reconvened. In any case, we will reconvene at eleven thirty."

Somebody wanted to know if smoking would be permitted during the recess. The Chief Justice said that it would. He got out a cigar and lit it. Mamma Fuzzy wanted a puff: she didn't like it. Out of the corner of his eye, he saw Mike and Mitzi, Fora and Fauna scampering around and up the steps behind the bench. When he looked again, they were all up on it, and Mitzi was showing the court what she had in her shoulder bag.

He got up, with Mamma and Baby, and crossed to where Leslie Coombes was sitting. By this time, somebody was bringing in a coffee urn from the cafeteria. Fuzzies ought to happen oftener in court.

The gavel tapped slowly. Little Fuzzy scrambled up onto Jack Holloway's lap. After five days in court, they had all learned that the gavel meant for Fuzzies and other people to be quiet. It might be a good idea, Jack thought, to make a little gavel, when he got home, and keep it on the table in the living room for when the family got too boisterous. Baby, who wasn't gavel-trained yet, started out onto the floor; Mamma dashed after him and brought him back under the table.

The place looked like a courtroom again. The tables were ranged in a neat row facing the bench, and the witness chair and the jury box were back where they belonged. The ashtrays and the coffee urn and the ice tubs for beer and soft drinks had vanished. It looked like the party was over. He was almost regretful; it had been fun. Especially for seventeen Fuzzies and a Baby

Fuzzy and a little black-and-white kitten.

There was one unusual feature; there was now a fourth man on the bench, in gold-braided Navy black; sitting a little apart from the judges, trying to look as though he weren't there at all—Space Commodore Alex Napier.

Judge Pendarvis laid down his gavel. "Ladies and gentlemen, are you ready to present the opinions you have reached?" he asked.

Lieutenant Ybarra, the Navy psychologist, rose. There was a reading screen in front of him; he snapped it on.

"Your Honors," he began, "there still exists considerable difference of opinion on matters of detail but we are in agreement on all major points. This is quite a lengthy report, and it has already been incorporated into the permanent record. Have I the court's permission to summarize it?"

The court told him he had. Ybarra glanced down at the screen in front of him and continued:

"It is our opinion," he said, "that sapients may be defined as differing from nonsapience in that it is characterized by conscious thought, by ability to think in logical sequence and by ability to think in terms other than mere sense data. We—meaning every member of every sapient race—think consciously, and we know what we are thinking. This is not to say that all our mental activity is conscious. The science of psychology is based, to a large extent, upon our realization that only a small portion of our mental activity occurs above the level of consciousness, and for centuries we have been diagraming the mind as an iceberg, one-tenth exposed and nine-tenths submerged. The art of psychiatry consists largely in bringing into consciousness some of the content of this submerged nine-tenths, and as a practitioner I can testify to its difficulty and uncertainty.

"We are so habituated to conscious thought that when we reach some conclusion by any nonconscious process, we speak of it as a 'hunch," or an 'intuition,' and question its validity. We are so habituated to acting upon consciously formed decisions that we must laboriously acquire, by systematic drill, those automatic responses upon which we depend for survival in combat or other emergencies. And we are by nature so unaware of this vast submerged mental area that it was not until the first century Pre-Atomic that its existence was more than vaguely suspected, and its nature is still the subject of acrimonious professional disputes."

There had been a few of those, off and on, during the past four days, too.

"If we depict sapient mentation as an iceberg, we might depict nonsapient mentation as the sunlight reflected from its surface. This is a considerably less exact analogy; while the nonsapient mind deals, consciously, with nothing but present sense data, there is a considerable absorption and re-emission of subconscious memories. Also, there are occasional flashes of what must be conscious mental activity, in dealing with some novel situation. Dr. van Riebeek, who is especially interested in the evolutionary aspect of the question, suggests that the introduction of novelty because of drastic environmental changes may have forced nonsapient beings into more or less sustained conscious thinking and so initiated mental habits which, in time, gave rise to true sapience.

"The sapient mind not only thinks consciously by habit, but it thinks in connected sequence. It associates one thing with another. It reasons logically, and forms conclusions, and uses those conclusions as premises from which to arrive at further conclusions. It groups associations together, and generalizes. Here we pass completely beyond any comparison with nonsapience. This is not merely more consciousness, or more thinking; it is thinking of a radically different kind. The nonsapient mind deals exclusively with crude sensory material. The sapient mind translates sense impressions into ideas, and then forms ideas *of* ideas, in ascending orders of abstraction, almost without limit.

"This, finally, brings us to one of the recognized overt manifestations of sapience. The sapient being is a symbol user. The nonsapient being cannot symbolize, because the nonsapient mind is incapable of concepts beyond mere sense images."

Ybarra drank some water, and twisted the dial of his reading screen with the other hand.

"The sapient being," he continued, "can do one other thing. It is a combination of the three abilities already enumerated, but combining them creates something much greater than the mere sum of the parts. The sapient being can imagine. He can conceive of something which has no existence whatever in the sense-available world of reality, and then he can work and plan toward making it a part of reality. He can not only imagine, but he can also create."

He paused for a moment. "This is our definition of sapience. When we encounter any being whose mentation includes these characteristics, we may know him for a sapient brother. It is the considered opinion of all of us that the beings called Fuzzies are such beings."

Jack hugged the small sapient one on his lap, and Little Fuzzy looked up and murmured, *"He-inta?"*

"You're in, kid," he whispered. "You just joined the people."

Ybarra was saying, "They think consciously and continuously. We know that by instrumental analysis of their electroencephalographic patterns, which compare closely to those of an intelligent human child of ten. They think in connected sequence; I invite consideration of all the different logical steps involved in the invention, designing and making of their prawn-killing weapons, and in the development of tools with which to make them. We have abundant evidence of their ability to think beyond present sense data, to associate, to generalize, to abstract and to symbolize.

"And above all, they can imagine, not only a new implement, but a new way of life. We see this in the first human contact with the race which, I submit, should be designated as *Fuzzy sapiens*. Little Fuzzy found a strange and wonderful place in the forest, a place unlike anything he had ever seen, in which lived a powerful being. He imagined himself living in this place, enjoying the friendship and protection of this mysterious being. So he slipped inside, made friends with Jack Holloway and lived with him. And then he imagined his family sharing this precious comfort and companionship with him, and he went and found them and brought them back with him. Like so many other sapient beings, Little Fuzzy had a beautiful dream; like a fortunate few, he made it real."

The Chief Justice allowed the applause to run on for a few minutes before using his gavel to silence it. There was a brief colloquy among the three judges, and then the Chief Justice rapped again. Little Fuzzy looked perplexed. Everybody had been quiet after he did it the first time, hadn't they?

"It is the unanimous decision of the court to accept the report already entered into the record and just summarized by Lieutenant Ybarra, TFN, and to thank him and all who have been associated with him.

"It is now the ruling of this court that the species known as *Fuzzy fuzzy holloway zarathustra* is in fact a race of sapient beings, entitled to the respect of all other sapient beings and to the full protection of the law of the Terran Federation." He rapped again, slowly, pounding the decision into the legal framework.

Space Commodore Napier leaned over and whispered; all three of the judges nodded emphatically. The naval officer rose.

"Lieutenant Ybarra, on behalf of the Service and of the Federation, I thank you and those associated with you for a lucid and excellent report, the culmination of work which reflects credit upon all who participated in it. I also wish to state that a suggestion made to me by Lieutenant Ybarra regarding possible instrumental detection of sapient mentation is being credited to him in my own report, with the recommendation that it be given important priority by the Bureau of Research and Development. Perhaps the next time we find people who speak beyond the range of human audition, who have fur and live in a mild climate, and who like their food raw, we'll know what they are from the beginning."

Bet Ybarra gets another stripe, and a good job out of this. Jack hoped so. Then Pendarvis was pounding again.

"I had almost forgotten; this is a criminal trial," he confessed. "It is the verdict of this court that the defendant, Jack Holloway, is not guilty as here charged. He is herewith discharged from custody. If he or his attorney will step up here, the bail bond will be refunded." He puzzled Little Fuzzy by hammering again with his gavel to adjourn court.

This time, instead of keeping quiet, everybody made all the noise they could, and Uncle Gus was holding him high over his head and shouting:

"The *winnah!* By unanimous decision!"

XVII

Ruth Ortheris sipped at the tart, cold cocktail. It was good; oh, it was good, all good! The music was soft, the lights were dim, the tables were far apart; just she and Gerd, and nobody was paying any attention to them. And she was clear out of the business, too. An agent who testified in court always was expended in service like a fired round. They'd want her back, a year from now, to testify when the board of inquiry came out from Terra, but she wouldn't be Lieutenant j.g. Ortheris then, she'd be Mrs. Gerd van Riebeek. She set down the glass and rubbed the sunstone on her finger. It was a lovely sunstone, and it meant such a lovely thing.

And we're getting married with a ready-made family, too. Four Fuzzies and a black-and-white kitten.

"You're sure you really want to go to Beta?" Gerd asked. "When Napier gets this new government organized, it'll be taking over Science Center. We could both get our old jobs back. Maybe something better."

"You don't want to go back?" He shook his head. "Neither do I. I want to go to Beta and be a sunstone digger's wife."

"And a Fuzzyologist."

"And a Fuzzyologist. I couldn't drop that now. Gerd, we're only beginning with them. We know next to nothing about their psychology."

He nodded seriously. "You know, they may turn out to be even wiser than we are."

She laughed. "Oh, Gerd! Let's don't get too excited about them. Why, they're like little children. All they think about is having fun."

"That's right. I said they were wiser than we are. They stick to important things." He smoked silently for a moment. "It's not just their psychology; we don't know anything much about their physiology, or biology either." He picked up his glass and drank. "Here; we had eighteen of them in all. Seventeen adults and one little one. Now what kind of ratio is that? And the ones we saw in the woods ran about the same. In all, we sighted about a hundred and fifty adults and only ten children."

"Maybe last year's crop have grown up," she began.

"You know any other sapient races with a one-year maturation period?" he asked. "I'll bet they take ten or fifteen years to mature. Jack's Baby Fuzzy hasn't gained a pound in the last month. And another puzzle; this craving for Extee Three. That's not a natural food; except for the cereal bulk matter, it's purely synthetic. I was talking to Ybarra; he was wondering if there mightn't be something in it that caused an addiction."

"Maybe it satisfies some kind of dietary deficiency."

"Well, we'll find out." He inverted the jug over his glass. "Think we could stand another cocktail before dinner?"

Space Commodore Napier sat at the desk that had been Nick Emmert's and looked at the little man with the red whiskers and the rumpled suit, who was looking back at him in consternation.

"Good Lord, Commodore; you can't be serious?"

"But I am. Quite serious, Dr. Rainsford."

"Then you're nuts!" Rainsford exploded. "I'm no more qualified to be Governor General than I'd be to command Xerxes Base. Why, I never held an administrative position in my life."

"That might be a recommendation. You're replacing a veteran administrator."

"And I have a job. The Institute of Zeno-Sciences—"

"I think they'll be glad to give you leave, under the circumstances. Doctor, you're the logical man for this job. You're an ecologist; you know how disastrous the effects of upsetting the balance of nature can be. The Zarathustra Company took care of this planet, when it was their property, but now nine-tenths of it is public domain, and people will be coming in from all over the Federation, scrambling to get rich overnight. You'll know how to control things."

"Yes, as Commissioner of Conservation, or something I'm qualified for."

"As Governor General. Your job will be to make policy. You can appoint the administrators."

"Well, who, for instance?"

"Well, you're going to need an Attorney General right away. Who will you appoint for that position?"

"Gus Brannhard," Rainsford said instantly.

"Good. And who—this question is purely rhetorical—will you appoint as Commissioner of Native Affairs?"

Jack Holloway was going back to Beta Continent on the constabulary airboat. Official passenger: Mr. Commissioner Jack Holloway. And his staff: Little Fuzzy, Mamma Fuzzy, Baby Fuzzy, Mike, Mitzi, Ko-Ko and Cinderella. Bet they didn't know they had official positions!

Somehow he wished he didn't have one himself.

"Want a good job, George?" he asked Lunt.

"I have a good job."

"This'll be a better one. Rank of major, eighteen thousand a year. Commandant, Native Protection Force. And you won't lose seniority in the constabulary; Colonel Ferguson'll give you indefinite leave."

"Well, cripes, Jack, I'd like to, but I don't want to leave the kids. And I can't take them away from the rest of the gang."

"Bring the rest of the gang along. I'm authorized to borrow twenty men from the constabulary as a training cadre, and you only have sixteen. Your sergeants'll get commissions, and all your men will be sergeants. I'm going to have a force of a hundred and fifty for a start."

"You must think the Fuzzies are going to need a lot of protection."

"They will. The whole country between the Cordilleras and the West Coast Range will be Fuzzy Reservation and that'll have to be policed. Then the Fuzzies outside that will have to be protected. You know what's going to happen. Everybody wants Fuzzies; why, even Judge Pendarvis approached me about getting a pair for his wife. There'll be gangs hunting them to sell, using stun-bombs and sleepgas and everything. I'm going to have to set up an adoption bureau; Ruth will be in charge of that. And that'll mean a lot of investigators—"

Oh, it was going to be one hell of a job! Fifty thousand a year would be chicken feed to what he'd lose by not working his diggings. But somebody would have to do it, and the Fuzzies were his responsibility.

Hadn't he gone to law to prove their sapience?

They were going home, home to the Wonderful Place. They had seen many wonderful places, since the night they had been put in the bags: the place where everything had been light and they had been able to jump so high and land so gently, and the place where they had met all the others of their people and had so much fun. But now they were going back to the old Wonderful Place in the woods, where it had all started.

And they had met so many Big Ones, too. Some Big Ones were bad, but only a few; most Big Ones were good. Even the one who had done the killing had felt sorry for what he had done; they were all sure of that. And the other Big Ones had taken him away, and they had never seen him again.

He had talked about that with the others—with Flora and Fauna, and Dr. Crippen, and Complex, and Superego, and Dillinger and Lizzie Borden. Now that they were all going to live with the Big Ones, they would have to use those funny names. Someday they would find out what they meant, and that would be fun, too. And they could; now the Big Ones could put things in their ears and hear what they were saying, and Pappy Jack was learning some of their words, and teaching them some of his.

And soon all the people would find Big Ones to live with, who would take care of them and have fun with them and love them, and give them the Wonderful Food. And with the Big Ones taking care of them, maybe more of their babies would live and not die so soon. And they would pay the Big Ones back. First they would give their love and make them happy. Later, when they learned how, they would give their help, too.

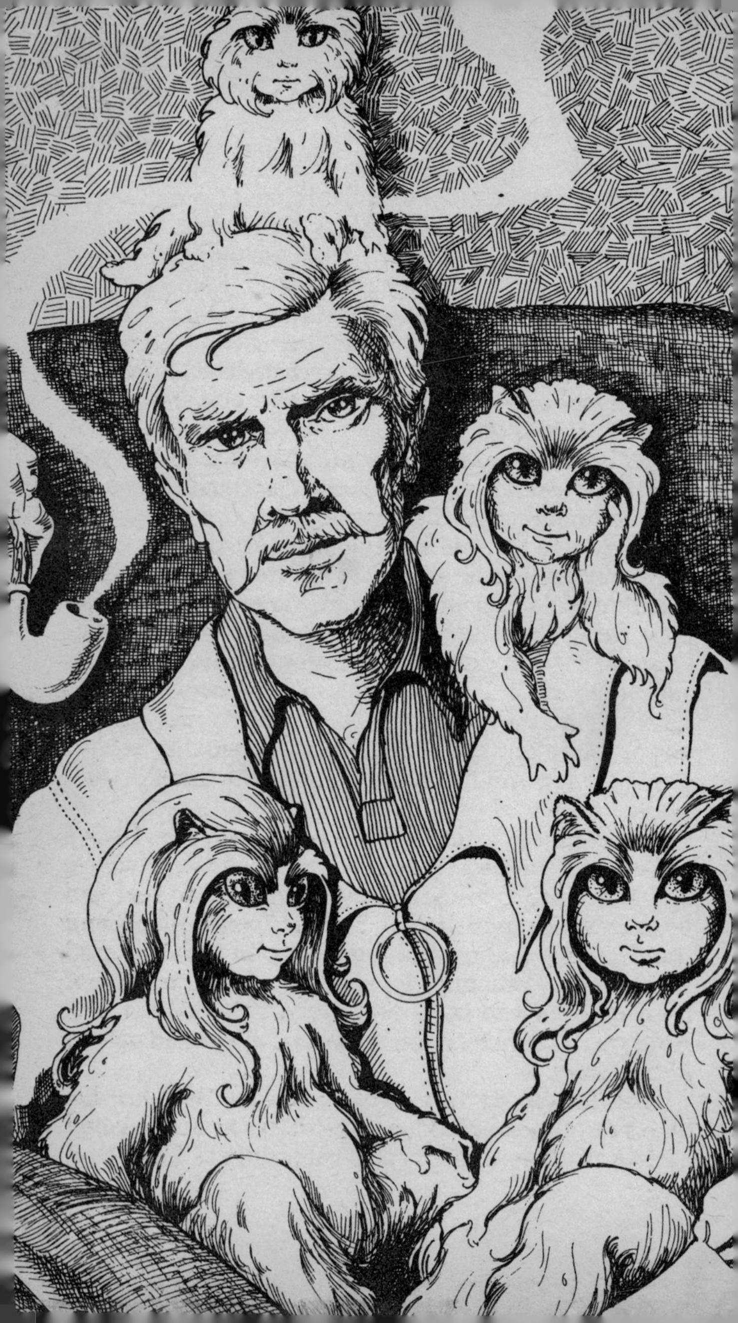

I

VICTOR GREGO finished the chilled fruit juice and pushed the glass aside, then lit a cigarette and poured hot coffee into the half-filled cup that had been cooling. This was going to be another Nifflheim of a day, and the night's sleep had barely rested him from the last one and the ones before that. He sipped the coffee, and began to feel himself rejoining the human race.

Staff conferences, all day, of course, with everybody bickering and recriminating. He hoped, not too optimistically, that this would be the end of it. By this evening all the division chiefs ought to know what had to be done. If only they wouldn't come running back to him for decisions they ought to make themselves, or bother him with a lot of nit-picking details. Great God, wasn't a staff supposed to handle staff work?

The trouble was that for the last fifteen years, twelve at least, all the decisions had been made in advance, and the staff work had all been routine, but that had been when Zarathustra had been a Class-III planet and the company had owned it outright. In the Chartered Zarathustra Company, emergencies had simply not been permitted to arise. Not, that was, until old Jack Holloway had met a small person whom he had named Little Fuzzy.

Then everybody had lost their heads. He'd lost his own a few times, and done some things he now wished he hadn't done. Most of his subordinates hadn't recovered theirs, yet, and the Charterless Zarathustra Company was operating, if that were the word for it, in a state of total and permanent emergency.

The cup was half empty, again; he filled it to the top and lit a fresh cigarette from the old one before crushing it out. Might as well get it started. He reached to the switch and flicked on the communication screen across the breakfast table.

In a moment, Myra Fallada appeared in it. She had elaborately curled white hair, faintly yellowish, a round face, protuberant blue eyes, and a lower lip of the sort associated with the ancient Hapsburg family. She had been his secretary ever since he had come to Zarathustra, and she thought that what had happened a week ago in Judge Pendarvis' court had been the end of the world.

"Good morning, Mr. Grego." She was eyeing his dressing gown and counting the cigarette butts in the ashtray, trying to estimate how soon he'd be down at his desk. "An awful lot of business has come in this morning."

"Good morning, Myra. What kind of business?"

"Well, things are getting much worse in the cattle country. The veldbeest herders are all quitting their jobs; just flying off and leaving the herds . . ."

"Are they flying off in company aircars? If they are, have Harry Steefer put out wants for them on stolen-vehicle charges."

"And the *City of Malverton*; she's spacing out from Darius today." She went on to tell him about that.

"I know. That was all decided yesterday. Just tell them to carry on with it. Now, is there anything I really have to attend to personally? If there is, bundle it up and send it to the staff conference room; I'll handle it there with the people concerned. Rubber-stamp the rest and send it back where it belongs, which is not on my desk. I won't be in; I'm going straight to the conference room. That will be in half an hour. Tell the houseboy he can come in to clean up then, and tell the chef I won't be eating here at all. I'll have lunch off a tray somewhere, and dinner with Mr. Coombes in the Executive Room."

Then he waited, mentally counting to a hundred. As he had expected, before he reached fifty Myra was getting into a flutter.

"Mr. Grego, I almost forgot!" She usually did. "Mr. Evins went inside the gem-reserve vault; he's down there now."

"Yes, I told him to make inventory and appraisal today. I'd forgotten about that myself. Well, we can't keep him waiting. I'll go down directly."

He blanked the screen, gulped what was left of the coffee and rose, leaving the kitchenette-breakfast room and crossing the short hall to his bedroom, taking off his dressing gown as he went. That he should not have forgotten: the problem represented by the contents of the gem-reserve vault was of greater importance, though of less immediacy, than what was going on in the cattle country.

Up to a week ago, when Chief Justice Pendarvis had smashed the company's charter with a few taps of his gavel, sunstones had been a company monopoly. It had been illegal for anybody but the company to buy sunstones, or for anybody to sell one except to a company gem buyer, but that had been company law, and the Pendarvis decisions had wiped out the company's lawmaking powers. Sunstone deposits were always too scattered for profitable large-scale mining. They were found by free-lance prospectors, who sold them to the company at the company's prices. Jack Holloway, who had started the whole trouble, had been one of the most successful of prospectors.

Now sunstones were in the open competitive market on Zarathustra, and something would have to be done about establishing a new gem-buying policy. Before he could do that, he wanted to know just how many of them the company had in reserve.

So he had to go down and open the vault, before

Conrad Evins, the chief gem buyer, could get in to find out. He knew the combination. So—in case anything happened to him—did Leslie Coombes, the head of the legal division, and, against the possibility that both he and Coombes were killed or incapacitated, there was a copy of it neatly typed on a slip of paper in a special-security box at the Bank of Mallorysport, which could only be gotten out by the Colonial Marshal with a court order. It was a bother, but too many people couldn't be trusted with that combination.

The gem rooms were on the fifteenth level down; they were surrounded by the company police headquarters, and there was only one way in, through a door barred by a heavy steel portcullis. The guard who controlled this sat in a small cubicle fronted by two inches of armor glass; several other guards, with submachine guns, sat or stood behind a low counter in front of it. Harry Steefer, the chief of company police, was there, and so was Conrad Evins, the gem buyer, a small man with graying hair and a bulging brow and narrow chin. With them were two gray-smocked assistants.

"Sorry to keep you gentlemen waiting," he greeted them. "Ready, Mr. Evins?"

Evins was. Steefer nodded to the men inside the armor-glass cubicle; the portcullis rose silently. They entered a bare hallway, covered by viewscreen pickups at either end and with sleep-gas release nozzles on the ceiling. The door at the other end opened, and in the small anteroom beyond they all showed their identity cards to a guard: Evins and his two assistants, the sergeant and the two guards accompanying them, Grego, even Chief Steefer. The guard spoke into a phone; somebody completely out of sight and reach pressed a button or flipped a switch and the door beyond opened. Grego went through alone, and down a short flight of steps to another door, brightly iridescent with a plating of collapsium, like a spaceship's hull or a nuclear reactor.

There was a keyboard, like the keyboard of a linotype machine. He went to it, punching out the letters of a short sentence, then waited ten seconds. The huge door receded slowly, then slid aside.

"All right, gentlemen," he called out. "The vault's open."

Then he walked through, into a circular room beyond. In the middle of it was a round table, its top covered with black velvet, with a wide circular light-shade above it. The wall was lined by a steel cabinet with many shallow drawers. The Chief, a sergeant with a submachine gun, Evins, and his two assistants followed him in. He lit a cigarette, watching the smoke draw up around the light-shade and vanish out the ventilator above. Evins' two assistants began getting out paraphernalia and putting things on the table; the gem buyer felt the black velvet and nodded. Grego put his hand on it, too. It was warm, almost hot.

One of the assistants brought a drawer from the cabinet and emptied it on the table—several hundred smooth, translucent pebbles. For a moment they looked like so much gravel. Then, slowly, they began to glow, until they were blazing like burning coals.

Some fifty million years ago, when Zarathustra had been almost completely covered by seas, there had been a marine life-form, not unlike a big jellyfish, and for a million or so years the seas had abounded with them, and as they died they had sunk into the ooze and been covered by sand. Ages of pressure had reduced them to hard little beans of stone, and the ooze to gray flint. Most of them were just pebbles, but by some ancient biochemical quirk, a few were intensely thermofluorescent. Worn as gems, they would glow from the body heat of the wearer, as they were glowing now on the electrically heated table top. They were found nowhere in the galaxy but on Zarathustra, and even a modest one was worth a small fortune.

"Just for a quick estimate, in round figures, how much money have we in this room?" he asked Evins.

Evins looked pained. He had the sort of mind which detested expressions like "quick estimate," and "round figures."

"Well, of course, the Terra market quotation, as of six months ago, was eleven hundred and twenty-five sols a carat, but that's just the average price. There are premium-value stones . . ."

He saw one of those, and picked it up; an almost perfect sphere, an inch in diameter, deep blood-red. It lay burning in his palm, it was beautiful. He wished he owned it himself, but none of this belonged to him. It belonged to an abstraction called the Chartered— no, Charterless—Zarathustra Company, which represented thousands of stockholders, including a number of other abstractions called Terra-Baldur-Marduk Spacelines, and Interstellar Explorations, Ltd., and the Banking Cartel. He wondered how Conrad Evins felt, working with these beautiful things, knowing how much each of them was worth, and not owning any of them.

"But I can tell you how little they are worth," Evins was saying, at the end of a lecture on the Terra gem market. "The stones in this vault are worth not one millisol less than one hundred million sols."

That sounded like a lot of money, if you said it quickly and didn't think. The Chartered, even the Charterless, Zarathustra Company was a lot of company, too, and all its operations were fantastically expensive. That wouldn't be six months' gross business for the company. They couldn't let the sunstone business live on its reserve.

"This is new, isn't it?" he asked, laying the red globe of light back on the heated table top.

"Yes, Mr. Grego. We bought that less than two months ago. Shortly before the Trial." He capitalized the word; the day Pendarvis beat the company down with his gavel would be First Day, Year Zero, On Zarathustra from now on. "It was bought," he added, "from Jack Holloway."

II

Snapping off the shiny new stenomemophone, Jack Holloway relit his pipe and pushed back his chair, looking around what had been the living room of his camp before it had become the office of the Commissioner of Native Affairs for the Class-IV Colonial Planet of Zarathustra. It had been a pleasant room, a place where a man could spread out by himself, or entertain the infrequent visitors who came this far into the wilderness. The hardwood floor was scattered with rugs made from the skins of animals he had shot; the deep armchairs and the couch were covered with smaller pelts. Like the big table at which he worked, he had built them himself. There was a reading screen, a metal-cased library of microbooks; the gunrack reflected soft gleams from polished stocks and barrels. And now look at the damn place!

Two extra viewscreens, another communication screen, a vocowriter, a teleprint machine, all jammed together. An improvised table on trestles at right angles to the one at which he sat, its top littered with plans and blueprints and things; mostly things. And this red-upholstered swivel chair; he hated that worst of all. Forty years ago, he'd left Terra to get the seat of his pants off the seat of a chair like that, and here he was in the evening of life—well, late afternoon, call it around second cocktail time—trapped in one.

It wasn't just this room, either. Through the open door he could hear what was happening outside. The thud of axes, and the howl of chain-saws; he was going to miss all those big featherleaf trees from around the house. The machine-gun banging of power-hammers, the clanking and grunting of bulldozers. A sudden warning cry, followed by a falling crash and a multivoiced burst of blasphemy. He hoped none of the Fuzzies had been close enough to whatever had happened to get hurt.

Something tugged gently at his trouser-leg, and a small voice said, "Yeek?" His hands went to his throat, snapping on the ultrasonic hearing-aid and inserting the earplug. Immediately, he began to hear a number of small sounds that had been previously inaudible, and the voice was saying, "Pappy Jack?"

He looked down at the Zarathustran native whose affairs he had been commissioned to administer. He was an erect biped, two feet tall, with a wide-eyed humanoid face, his body covered with soft golden fur. He wore a green canvas pouch lettered TFMC, and a two-inch silver disc on a chain about his neck, and nothing else. The disc was lettered LITTLE FUZZY, and *Jack Holloway, Cold Creek Valley, Beta Continent*, and the numeral I. He was the first Zarathustran aborigine he or any other Terran human had ever seen.

He reached down and stroked his small friend's head.

"Hello, Little Fuzzy. You want to visit with Pappy Jack for a while?"

Little Fuzzy pointed to the open door. Five other Fuzzies were peeping bashfully into the room, making comments among themselves.

"Fuzzee no shu do-bizzo do-mitto zat-hakko," Little Fuzzy informed him. *"Heeva so si do-mitto."*

Some Fuzzies who hadn't been here before had just come; they wanted to stay. At least, that was what he thought Little Fuzzy was saying; it had only been ten days since he had known that Fuzzies could talk at all. He pressed a button to start the audiovisual recorder; it was adjusted to transform their ultrasonic voices to audible frequencies.

"Make talk." He picked his way through his hundred-word Fuzzy vocabulary. "Pappy Jack friend. Not hurt, be good to them. Give good things."

"*Josso shoddabag?*" Little Fuzzy asked. "*Josso shoppo-diggo? Josso t'heet? Esteefee?*"

"Yes. Give shoulder-bags and chopper-diggers and treats," he said. "Give Extee-Three."

Friendly natives; distribution of presents to. Function of the Commissioner of Native Affairs. Little Fuzzy began a speech. This was Pappy Jack, the greatest and wisest of all the Big Ones, the Hagga, the friend of all the People, the Gashta, only the Big Ones called the Gashta Fuzzies. He would give wonderful things. *Shoddabag*, in which things could be carried, leaving the hands free. He displayed his own. And weapons so hard that they never wore out. He ran to the jumbled pile of bedding under the gunrack and came back with a six-inch leaf-shaped blade on a twelve-inch shaft. And Pappy Jack would give the *Hoksu-Fusso*, the Wonderful Food, *esteefee*.

Rising, he went out to what had been his kitchen before it had been crammed with supplies. There were plenty of chopper-diggers; he'd had a couple of hundred made up before he left Mallorysport. Shoulder-bags were in shorter supply. They were all either Navy black or Marine Corps green, first-aid pouches and tool-kit pouches and belt pouches for submachine gun and autorifle magazines, all fitted with shoulder straps. He hung five of them over his arm, then unlocked a cupboard and got out two rectangular tins with blue labels marked EMERGENCY FIELD RATION, EXTRATERRESTRIAL SERVICE TYPE THREE. All Fuzzies were crazy about Extee-Three, which demonstrated that, while sapient beings, they were definitely not human. Only a completely starving human would eat the damn stuff.

When he returned, the five newcomers were squatting in a circle inside the door with Little Fuzzy, examining his steel weapon and comparing it with the paddle-shaped hardwood sticks they had made for themselves. The word *zatku* was being frequently used.

It was an important word to Fuzzies, their name for a big pseudocrustacean Terrans called a land-prawn. Fuzzies hunted *zatku* avidly, and, until they had tasted Extee-Three, preferred them to any other food. If it hadn't been for the *zatku*, the Fuzzies would have stayed in the unexplored country of northern Beta Continent, and it would have been years before any Terran would have seen one.

Quite a few Terrans, especially Victor Grego, the Zarathustra Company manager-in-chief, were wishing the Fuzzies had stayed permanently undiscovered. Zarathustra had been listed as a Class-III planet, inhabitable by Terran humans but uninhabited by any native race of sapient beings, and on that misunderstanding the Zarathustra Company had been chartered to colonize and exploit it and had been granted outright ownership of the planet and one of the two moons, Darius. The other moon, Xerxes, had been retained as a Federation Navy base, which had been fortunate, because suddenly Zarathustra had turned into a Class-IV planet, with a native population.

The members of the native population here present looked up expectantly as he opened one of the tins and cut the gingerbread-colored cake into six equal portions. The five newcomers sniffed at theirs and waited until Little Fuzzy began to eat. Then, after a tentative nibble, they gobbled avidly, with full-mouthed sounds of delight.

From the first, he had suspected that they weren't just cute little animals, but people—sapient beings, like himself and like the eight other sapient races discovered since Terrans had gone out to the stars. When Bennett Rainsford, then a field naturalist for the Institute of Xeno-Sciences, had seen them, he had agreed, and had named the species *Fuzzy fuzzy hol-*

loway. They had both been excited, and very proud of the discovery, and neither of them had thought, until it was brought forcibly to their attention, of the effect on the Zarathustra Company's charter.

Victor Grego had thought of that at once; he had fought desperately, viciously, and with all the resources of the company, to prevent the recognition of the Fuzzies as sapient beings and the invalidation of the company's charter. The battle had ended in court, with Jack Holloway charged with murder for shooting a company gunman and a company executive named Leonard Kellogg similarly charged for kicking to death a Fuzzy named Goldilocks. The two cases, tried as one, had hinged on the question of the sapience of the Fuzzies. On the docket, it had been *People of the Colony of Zarathustra versus Holloway and Kellogg*. His lawyer, Gus Brannhard, had insisted on referring to it as *Friends of Little Fuzzy versus The Chartered Zarathustra Company*.

Little Fuzzy and his friends had won, and with their sapience recognized, the company's charter was out the airlock, and so was the old Class-III Colonial Government, and Space Commodore Napier, the commandant of Xerxes Base, had been compelled, since Zarathustra was without legal government, to proclaim martial rule and supervise the establishment of a new Class-IV Government. He had appointed Bennett Rainsford Governor.

And just who do you suppose Ben Rainsford appointed as Commissioner of Native Affairs?

Well, somebody had to take it, and who'd started all this Fuzzy business, anyhow?

The five newcomers had finished their Extee-Three, and been given their shoulder-bags and their steel chopper-diggers, and were trying the balance of the latter and beheading imaginary land-prawns with them. He opened the other tin of Extee-Three and divided it. This time, they nibbled slowly, with appreciative comments. Little Fuzzy gathered up the two empty tins and put them in the wastebasket.

"How you come this place?" he asked, when Little Fuzzy had rejoined the circle.

They all began talking at once; with Little Fuzzy's help, he got the general sense of it. They had heard strange noises and had come to the edge of the woods, and seen frightening things. But Fuzzies were people; they investigated, even if they were frightened. Then they had seen other people. *Hagga-gashta*, big people, and *shi-mosh-gashta*, people like us.

Little Fuzzy instantly corrected the speaker. *Hagga-gashta* were just Hagga, Big Ones, and *shi-mosh-gashta* were Fuzzies. Why were the Gashta called Fuzzies? Because Pappy Jack said so, that was why. That seemed to settle it.

"But why come this place? You come from other place, far away. Why come here?"

More argument. Little Fuzzy was explaining what he meant, and the newcomers were answering.

"Tell them here are many-many *zatku*. They come, many lights and darks. Many-many."

Fuzzies could count up to five, the fingers of one hand. The other hand had to be used to count with. They could count in multiples of five to a hand of hands, and after that it was many, and then many-many. Somewhere in the mass of Fuzzy study notes that were piling up was a suggestion to see what Fuzzies could do with an abacus.

So, maybe three months ago and six or eight hundred miles north of here, this gang had heard that the country to the south was teeming with *zatku*, and they had joined the *volkerwanderung*. Little Fuzzy and his family had been in the advance-guard; the big rush was still coming. He tried to find out how they had learned of it. Other Fuzzies had told them: that was as far as he could get.

Anyhow, they had gotten into the pass to the north and come down into Cold Creek Valley, and here they were. They had come to the edge of the woods, seen the activity at the camp, and decided, from the presence of other Fuzzies, that there was nothing to hurt them, and had come in.

"Many things to hurt!" Little Fuzzy contradicted, instantly and vehemently. "Must watch all-time. Not go in front of things that move. Not go under things that go up off ground. Not touch strange things. Ask Big Ones what will hurt. Big Ones try not to hurt Fuzzies, Fuzzies must help."

He continued at length; the newcomers exchanged apprehensive glances and low-voiced comments. Finally, he picked up his chopper-digger and rose.

Bizzo," he said. "*Aki-pokko-so.*"

Come; I show you. He got that easily enough. "First, show police place," he advised. "Make marks with fingers; get bright things for necks."

"Hokay," Little Fuzzy agreed. "Go *polis*, make *fingap'int*, get *idee-disko.*"

About the time Terrans had mastered classical native Fuzzy, the Fuzzies would all be talking pigin-Fuzzy. The newcomers made way for Little Fuzzy, and trooped outside after him, like tourists following a guide. He watched them cross the open space in front of the house and turn left toward the bridge over the little stream. Then he went back to his desk and made a screen-call to prod up the tentmaker in Red Hill on the order of shoulder-bags—"Maybe tomorrow, Mr. Holloway; we're doing all we can."—and then made a stenomemo about finding more Extee-Three. Then he went back to doodling and scribbling notes on the table of organization and operation-scheme for the Commission of Native Affairs, on which he seemed to be getting nowhere at a terrific speed.

"Hello, Jack. Another gang joined up?"

He raised his head. The speaker was coming in the door, a stocky, square-faced man in blue. There was a lighter oval on the side of his beret, where something had been removed, and the collar of his tunic showed that his major's single star had quite recently replaced a first lieutenant's double bars. He wore a band on his left arm hand-lettered ZNPF, otherwise his uniform was Colonial Constabulary.

"Hello, George. Come in and rest your feet. You look as though they need it."

Major George Lunt, Commandant, Zarathustra Native Protection Force, agreed wearily and profanely, taking off his beret and his pistol-belt and dropping them on the makeshift table. Then, looking around, he went to a chair and lifted from it four loose-leaf books and a fiberboard carton full of papers, marked OLD ATOMBOMB BOURBON, and set them on the floor. Then he unzipped his tunic, sat down, and got out his cigarettes.

"Office hut's all up, now," he reported. "They're waiting on a scow-load of flooring for it."

"I was talking on screen about that an hour ago. It'll be here by this evening." By this time tomorrow, all this junk could be moved out, and the place would be home again. "Any men coming out on the afternoon boat?"

"Three. They only got the recruiting office opened yesterday, and there isn't any big rush of recruits. Captain Casagra says he'll lend us fifty Marines and some vehicles, temporarily. How many Fuzzies have we, now, with this new bunch?"

He counted mentally. His own family: Little Fuzzy and Mamma Fuzzy and Baby Fuzzy and Mike and Mitzi and Ko-Ko and Cinderella. George Lunt's Fuzzies. Dr. Crippen and Dillinger and Ned Kelly and Lizzie Borden and Calamity Jane. The nine whom they had found at the camp when they returned from Mallorysport after the trial, and the six who came in day before yesterday, and four yesterday morning, and the two last evening, and now this gang.

"Thirty-eight, counting Baby. That's a lot of Fuzzies," he observed.

"You just think it is," Lunt told him. "The patrols

we've had out north of here say they're still coming. This time next week, we'll have a couple of hundred."

And before then, the ones who were here would begin to feel overcrowded, and a lot of nice new *shoppo-diggo* would get bloodied. He said so, adding:

"You have a tactical plan for dealing with a native uprising, Major?"

"I've been worrying about it. You know, we could get rid of a lot of them," Lunt said. "Just mention on telecast that we have more Fuzzies than we know what to do with, and we'd have to start rationing them."

They'd have to do that, anyhow. With all the publicity since the trial, everybody was Fuzzy-crazy. Everybody wanted Fuzzies of their own, and where there's a demand, there are suppliers, legitimate or otherwise. It was a wonder the woods weren't full of people catching Fuzzies to sell now. For all he knew, maybe they were.

And a lot of people shouldn't be allowed to have Fuzzies. Not just sadists and perverts, either. People who'd want Fuzzies because the Joneses had them, and then neglect them. People who would get tired of them after a while and dump them outside town. People who couldn't get it through their moronic heads that Fuzzies were people too. So they'd have to set up some regular system of Fuzzy adoption.

He'd thought, at first, of Ruth Ortheris, Ruth van Riebeek she was, now, for that, but she and her husband were needed too urgently here at the camp on the Fuzzy-study program. There were just too many things about Fuzzies neither he nor anybody else knew yet, and he'd have to find out what was good for them and what wasn't.

He looked at the clock; 0935; that would be 0635 in Mallorysport. After lunch, which would be midmorning there, he'd call her and find out how soon she'd be coming out.

III

Ruth van Riebeek—she had resigned both her Navy commission and her maiden name simultaneously five days ago—ought, she told herself, to be happy and excited. She was clear out of Navy Intelligence and its dark corridors of deceit and suspicion, and she and Gerd were married, and any scientific worker in the Federation would give anything to be in her place. A whole new science, the study of a new race of sapient beings; why, it was only the ninth time that had happened in the five centuries since the first Terran starship left the Sol System. A tiny spot of light—what they really knew about the Fuzzies—surrounded by a twilight zone of what they thought they knew, mostly erroneous. And beyond that, the dark of ignorance, full of strange surprises, waiting to be conquered. And she was in on the very beginning of it. It was a wonderful opportunity.

But wasn't it just one Nifflheim of a way to spend a honeymoon?

When she and Gerd were married, everything was going to be so wonderful. They would spend a lazy week here in the city, just being happy together and making plans and gathering things for their new home. Then they would go back to Beta Continent, and Gerd would work the sunstone diggings in partnership with Jack Holloway while she kept house, and they would spend the rest of their lives being happy together in the woods, with their four Fuzzies, Id and Superego and Complex and Syndrome.

The honeymoon, as such, had lasted one night, here at the Hotel Mallory. The next morning, before they were through breakfast, Jack Holloway was screening them. Space Commodore Napier had appointed Ben Rainsford Governor, and Ben had immediately appointed Jack Commissioner of Native Affairs, and now Jack was appointing Gerd to head his study and research bureau, taking it for granted that Gerd would accept. Gerd had, taking it for granted that she would agree, as, after a rebellious moment, she had.

After all, weren't they all responsible for what had happened? The Fuzzies certainly weren't; they hadn't gone to law to be declared sapient. All a Fuzzy wanted was to have fun. And they were responsible to the Fuzzies for what would happen to them hereafter, all of them together, Ben Rainsford and Jack Holloway and she and Gerd, and Pancho Ybarra. And now, Lynne Andrews.

Through the open front of the room, on the balcony, she could hear Lynne's voice, half amused and half exasperated:

"You little devils! Bring that back here! *Do-bizzo. So-josso-aki!*"

A Fuzzy—one of the two males, Superego—dashed inside with a lighted cigarette, the other male, Id, and one of the girls, Syndrome, pursuing. She put in her earplug and turned on her hearing-aid, wishing for the millionth time that Fuzzies had humanly audible voices. Id was clamoring that it was his turn and trying to take the cigarette away from Superego, who pushed him off with his free hand, took a quick puff, and handed it to Syndrome, who began puffing hastily on it. Id started to grab it, then saw the cigarette she was smoking and ran to climb on her lap, pleading:

"Mummy Woof; *josso-aki smokko.*"

Lynne Andrews, slender and blonde, followed them into the room, the earplug wire of her hearing-aid leading down from under the green bandezu around her head. She carried Complex, squirming in her arms. Complex was complaining that Auntie Lynne wouldn't give her *smokko*.

"That's one Terran word they picked up soon enough," Lynne was commenting.

"Let her have one; it won't hurt her." With scientific caution, she added, "It doesn't seem to hurt them."

She knew what Lynne was thinking. She had been recruited—shanghaied would probably be a better word—from Mallorysport General Hospital because they had wanted somebody whose M.D. was a little less a matter of form than hers or Pancho Ybarra's. Lynne was a pediatrician, which had seemed appropriate because Fuzzies were about the size of year-old human children and because a pediatrician, like a veterinarian, has to be able to get along with a minimum of cooperation from the patient. Unfortunately, she was carrying it beyond analogy and equating Fuzzies with human children. A year-old human oughtn't to be allowed to smoke, so neither should a Fuzzy, who might be fifty for all anybody knew to the contrary.

She gave Id her cigarette. Lynne, apparently much against her better judgment, sat down on a couch and lit one for Complex, and one for herself, and then lit a third for Superego. Now all the Fuzzies had *smokko*. Syndrome ran to one of the low cocktail tables and came back with an ashtray, which she put on the floor. The others sat down with her around it, all but Id, who stayed on Mummy Woof's lap.

"Lynne, they won't take anything that hurts them," she argued. "Alcohol, for instance."

Lynne had to agree. Any Fuzzy would take a drink, just to do what the Big Ones were doing—once. The smallest quantity affected a Fuzzy instantly, and a tipsy Fuzzy was really something to see, and then the Fuzzy would have a sick hangover, and never took a second drink. That was one of the things she'd found out while working with Ernst Mallin, the Company psychologist, and doublecrossing him and the company for Navy Intelligence.

"Well, some of them don't like *smokko*."

"Some human-type people don't, either. Some human-type people have allergies. What kind of allergies do Fuzzies have? That's something else for you to find out."

She set Id on the table and pulled one of the looseleaf books toward her, picking up a pen and writing the word at the top of the blank page. Id picked up another pen and began making a series of little circles on a notepad.

The door from the hallway opened into the next room; she heard Pancho Ybarra's voice and her husband laughing. The three on the floor put their cigarettes in the ashtray and jumped to their feet, shrieking, "Pappy Ge'hd! Unka Panko!" and dashed through the door into the next room. Id, dropping the pen, jumped down and ran after them. In a moment, they were all back. Syndrome had a Navy officer's cap on her head, holding it up with both hands to see from under it. Id followed, with Gerd's floppy gray sombrero, and Complex and Superego came in carrying a bulky briefcase between them. Gerd and Pancho followed. Gerd's suit, freshly pressed that morning, already rumpled, but the Navy psychologist was still miraculously handbox-neat. She rose and greeted them, kissing Gerd; Pancho crossed to the couch and sat down with Lynne.

"Well, what's new?" Gerd asked.

"Jack called me, about an hour ago. They have the lab hut up, and all the equipment they have for it moved in. They have some bungalows up, a double one for us. Jack showed me a view of it; it's nice. And I was bullying people about the computer and the rest of the stuff. We can all go out as soon as we have everything here together."

"This evening, if we want to run ourselves ragged and get in in the middle of the night," Gerd said.

"After lunch tomorrow, if we want to take our time. Ben Rainsford wants us for dinner this evening."

Lynne thought that sounded a trifle cannibalistic, and voted for tomorrow. "How did you make out at the hospital?" she asked.

"They gave us everything we asked for, no argument at all," Gerd said. "And the same at Science Center. I was surprised."

"I wasn't," Pancho said. "There's a lot of scuttlebutt about the Government taking both over. In a couple of weeks, we may be their bosses. What are we going to do about lunch; go out or have it sent in?"

"Let's have it sent in," she said. "We can check over these equipment lists, and you two can chase up anything that's left out this afternoon."

Pancho got out his cigarette case, and discovered that it was empty.

"Hey, Lynne; *so-josso-aki smokko*," he said.

Well, it would be a honeymoon. Sort of crowded, but fun. And Pancho and Lynne were beginning to take an interest in each other. She was glad of that.

Chief Justice Frederic Pendarvis leaned his elbows on the bench and considered the three black-coated lawyers before him in the action of *John Doe, Richard Roe,* et alii, *An Unincorporated Voluntary Association,* versus *The Colonial Government of Zarathustra.*

One, at the defendants' lectern, was a giant; well over six feet and two hundred pounds, his big-nosed face masked by a fluffy gray-brown beard, an unruly mop of gray-brown hair suggesting, incongruously, a halo. His name was Gustavus Adolphus Brannhard, and until he had been rocketed to prominence in what everybody was calling the Fuzzy Trial, he had been chiefly noted for his ability to secure the acquittal of obviously guilty clients, his prowess as a big-game hunter, and his capacity, without visible effect, for whisky. For the past five days, he had been Attorney-General of the Colony of Zarathustra.

The man standing beside and slightly behind him would have seemed tall, too, in the proximity of anybody but Gus Brannhard. He was slender and suavely elegant, and his thin, aristocratic features wore an habitually half-bored, half-amused expression, as though life were a joke he heard too many times before. His name was Leslie Coombes, he was the Zarathustra Company's chief attorney, and from the position he had taken it looked as though he were here to support his erstwhile antagonist in *People* versus *Holloway and Kellogg*.

The third, at the plaintiff's lectern, was Hugo Ingermann; Judge Pendarvis was making a determined effort not to let that prejudice him against his clients. To his positive knowledge, Ingermann had been in court at least seven times in the last six years representing completely honest and respectable people, and it was possible, though scarcely probable, that this might be the eighth occasion. He was, of course, a member of the Bar, due to lack of evidence to support disbarment proceedings, so he had a right to stand here and be heard.

"This is an action, is it not, to require the Colonial Government to make available for settlement and exploitation lands now in the public domain, and to set up offices where claims to such lands may be filed?" he asked.

"It is, your Honor. I represent the plaintiffs," Ingermann said. He was shorter than either of the others; plump, with a smooth, pink-cheeked face, and beginning to lose his hair in front. There was an expression of complete and utter sincerity in his round blue eyes which might have deceived anybody who had not been on Zarathustra long enough to have heard of him. He would have continued had Pendarvis not turned to Brannhard.

"I represent the Colonial Government, your Honor; we are contesting the plaintiff's action."

"And you, Mr. Coombes?"

"I represent the Charterless Zarathustra Company," Coombes said. "We are not a party to this action. I am here merely as observer and *amicus curiae.*"

"The . . . Charterless, did you say, Mr. Coombes? . . . Zarathustra Company has a right to be so represented here; they have a substantial interest." He wondered whose idea "Charterless" was; it sounded like a typical piece of Grego gallows-humor. "Mr. Ingermann?"

"Your Honor, it is the contention of the plaintiffs whom I represent that since approximately eighty percent of the land surface of this planet is now public domain, by virtue of a recent ruling of the Honorable Supreme Court, it is now obligatory upon the Colonial Government to make this land available to the public. This, your Honor, is plainly stated in Federation Law . . ."

He began citing acts, sections, paragraphs; precedents; relevant decisions of Federation Courts on other planets. He was talking entirely for the record; all this had been included in the brief he had submitted. It should be heard, but enough was enough.

"Yes, Mr. Ingermann; the Court is aware of the law, and takes notice that it has been upheld in other cases," he said. "The Government doesn't dispute this, Mr. Brannhard?"

"Not at all, your Honor. Far from it. Governor Rainsford is, himself, most anxious to transfer unseated land to private ownership . . ."

"Yes, but when?" Ingermann demanded. "How long is Governor Rainsford going to drag his feet . . ."

"I question the justice of Mr. Ingermann's so characterizing the situation," Brannhard interrupted. "It must be remembered that it is less than a week since there was any public land at all on this planet."

"Or since the Government Mr. Ingermann's clients are suing has existed," Coombes added. "And I could endure knowing who these Messieurs Doe and Roe are. The names sound faintly familiar, but . . ."

"Your Honor, my clients are an association of individuals interested in acquiring land," Ingermann said. "Prospectors, woodsmen, tenant farmers, small veldbeest ranchers..."

"Loan-sharks, shylocks, percentage grubstakers, speculators, would-be claim brokers," Brannhard continued.

"They are the common people of this planet!" Ingermann declared. "The workers, the sturdy and honest farmers, the frontiersmen, all of whom the Zarathustra Company has held in peonage until liberated by the great and historic decisions which bear your Honor's name."

"Just a moment," Coombes almost drawled. "Your Honor, the word 'peonage' has a specific meaning at law. I must deny most vehemently that it has ever described the relationship between the Zarathustra Company and anybody on this planet."

"The word was ill-chosen, Mr. Ingermann. It will be deleted from the record."

"We still haven't found out who Mr. Ingermann's clients are, your Honor," Brannhard said. "May I suggest that Mr. Ingermann be placed on the stand and asked to name them?"

Ingermann shot a quick, involuntary glance at the witness stand: a heavy chair, with electrode attachments and a bright metal helmet over it, and a translucent globe on a standard. Then he began clamoring protests. So far, Hugo Ingermann had always managed to avoid having to testify to anything under veridication. That was probably why he was still a member of the Bar, instead of a convict.

"No, Mr. Brannhard," he said, with real sadness. "Mr. Ingermann is not compelled to divulge the names of his clients. Mr. Ingermann would be within his rights in bringing this action on his own responsibility, out of his deep love of justice and well-known zeal for the public welfare."

Brannhard shrugged massively. Nobody could blame

him for not trying. Coombes spoke:

"Your Honor, we are all agreed about the Government's obligation, but has it occurred, either to Mr. Ingermann or to the Court, that the present Government is merely a fiat-government set up by military authority? Commodore Napier acted, as he was obliged to, as the ranking officer of the Terran Federation Armed Forces present, to constitute civil government to replace the former one, declared illegal by your Honor. Until elections can be held and a popularly elected Colonial Legislature can be convened, there may be grave doubts as to the validity of some of Governor Rainsford's acts, especially in granting titles to land. Your Honor, do we want to see the courts of this planet vexed, for years to come, with litigation over such titles?"

"That's the Government's attitude precisely," Brannhard agreed. "We're required by law to hold such elections within a year; to do that we'll have to hold an election for delegates to a constitutional convention and get a planetary constitution adopted. That will take six to eight months. Until this can be done, we petition the Court to withhold action on this matter."

"That's quite reasonable, Mr. Brannhard. The Court recognizes the Government's legal obligation, but the Court does not recognize any immediacy in fulfilling it. If, within a year, the Government can open the public lands and establish land-claim offices, the Court will be quite satisfied." He tapped lightly with his gavel. "Next case, if you please," he told the crier.

"Now I see it!" Ingermann almost shouted. "The Zarathustra Company's taken over this new Class-IV Government, and the courts along with it!"

He hit the bench again with his gavel; this time it cracked like a rifle shot.

"Mr. Ingermann! You are not deliberately placing yourself in contempt, are you?" he asked. "No? I'd hoped not. Next case, please."

Leslie Coombes accepted the cocktail with a word of absent minded thanks, tasted it, and set it down on the low table. It was cool and quiet up here on the garden-terrace around Victor Grego's penthouse at the top of Company House; the western sky was a conflagration of sunset reds and oranges and yellows.

"No, Victor; Gus Brannhard is not our friend. He's not our enemy, but as Attorney-General he is Ben Rainsford's lawyer, and the Government's—at the moment, it's hard to distinguish between the two—and Ben Rainsford hates all of us vindicatively."

Victor Grego looked up from the drink he was pouring for himself. He had a broad-cheeked, wide-mouthed face. A few threads of gray were visible in the sunset glow among the black at his temples; they hadn't been there before the Fuzzy Trial.

"I don't see why," he said, "It's all over now. They made their point about the Fuzzies; that was all they were interested in, wasn't it?"

He was being quite honest about it, too, Coombes thought. Grego was simply incapable of animosity about something that was over and done with.

"It was all Jack Holloway and Gerd van Riebeek were interested in. Brannhard was their lawyer; he'd have fought just as hard to prove that bush-goblins were sapient beings. But Rainsford is taking this personally. The Fuzzies were his great scientific discovery, and we tried to discredit it, and that makes us Bad Guys. And in the last chapter, the Bad Guys should all be killed or sent to jail."

Grego stoppered the cocktail jug and picked up his glass.

"We haven't come to the last chapter yet," he said. "I don't want any more battles; we haven't patched up the combat damage from the last one. But if Ben Rainsford wants one, I'm not bugging out on it. You know, we could make things damned nasty for him." He sipped slowly and set the glass down. "This so-called Government of his is broke; you know that, don't you? And it'll take from six to eight months to get a Colonial Legislature organized and in session, and he can't levy taxes by executive decree; that's purely a legislative function. In the meantime, he'll have to borrow, and the only place he can borrow is from the bank we control."

That was the trouble with Victor. If anybody or anything challenged him, his first instinct was to hit back. Following that instinct when he had first heard of the Fuzzies that had gotten the Company back of the eightball in the first place.

"Well, don't do any fighting with planet busters at twenty paces," he advised. "Gus Brannhard and Alex Napier, between them, talked him out of prosecuting us for what we did before the trial, and convinced him he'd wreck the whole planetary economy if he damaged the company too badly. We're in the same spot; we can't afford to have a bankrupt Government on top of everything else. Let him borrow all the money he wants."

"And then tax it away from us to pay it back?"

"Not if we get control of the Legislature and write the tax laws ourselves. This is a political battle; let's use political weapons."

"You mean organize a Zarathustra Company Party?" Grego laughed. "You have any idea how unpopular the company is, right now?"

"No, no. Let the citizens and voters organize the parties. We'll just pick out the best one and take it over. All we'll need to organize will be a political organization."

Grego smiled slowly over the rim of his glass and swallowed.

"Yes, Leslie. I don't think I need to tell you what to do. You know it better than I do. Have you anybody in mind to head it? They shouldn't be associated with the Company at all; at least, not out where the public can see it."

He named a few names—independent business

men, freeholding planters, professional people, a clergyman or so. Grego nodded approvingly at each.

"Hugo Ingermann," he said.

"Good God!" Coombes doubted his ears for a moment. Then he was shocked. "We want nothing whatever to do with that fellow. Why, there isn't a crooked operation in Mallorysport, criminal or just plain dishonest, that he isn't mixed up in. And I told you how he was talking in court today."

Grego nodded again. "Precisely. Well, we won't have anything to do with him. We'll just let Hugo go his malodorous way, and cash in on any scandals he creates. You say Rainsford thinks in terms of Good Guys and Bad Guys? Well, Hugo Ingermann is the baddest Bad Guy on the planet, and if Rainsford doesn't know that, and he probably doesn't, Gus Brannhard'll tell him. I just hope Hugo Ingermann goes on attacking the company every time he opens his mouth." He finished what was in his glass and unstoppered the jug. "Still with me, Leslie? It's a half hour yet to dinner."

As Gus Brannhard started across the lawn on the south side of Government House, two Fuzzies came dashing to meet him. Their names were Flora and Fauna, and as usual he had to pause and remember that fauns were male and that Flora was a regular feminine name. The names some people gave Fuzzies. Of course, Ben was a naturalist. If he had a pair of Fuzzies of his own, he'd probably have called them Felony and Misdemeanor, or Misfeasance and Malfeasance. He put in his earphone and squatted to get down to their level.

"Hello, sapient beings. Now keep your hands out of Uncle Gus's whiskers." He glanced up and saw the small man with the red beard approaching. "Hello, Ben. They pull yours much?"

"Sometimes. I haven't so much to pull. Yours is more fun. Jack Holloway says they think you're a Big Fuzzy." The Fuzzies were pointing across the lawn, clamoring for him to come and see something. "Oh, sure; their new home. I'll bet there isn't a Fuzzy anywhere who has a nicer home. *Hokay*, kids; *bizzo*."

The new home was a Marine Corps pup-tent, pitched in an open glade beside a fountain; it would be a lot roomier for two Fuzzies than for two Marines. There were Fuzzy treasures scattered around it, things from toy shops, and odds and ends of bright or colored or oddly-shaped junk they had scavanged for themselves. He noticed, and commented on, a stout toy wheelbarrow.

"Oh, yes; we have discovered the wheel," Ben said. "They were explaining it to me yesterday; very intelligently, as far as I could follow. They give each other rides, and they are very good about taking turns. And they use it to collect loot. Very good about that, too; always ask if they can have anything they find."

"Well, this is just wonderful," he told them, and then repeated it in Fuzzy. Ben complimented him on his progress in the language.

"I damn well better learn it. Pendarvis is going to set up a Native Cases Court, like the ones on Loki and Gimli and Thor. Be anybody's guess how soon I'll have to listen to a flock of Fuzzy witnesses."

He looked inside the tent. The blankets and cushions were all piled at one end; bedmaking, it seemed, wasn't a Fuzzy accomplishment. A bed was to sleep in, and no Fuzzy could see the sense in making a bed and then having to un-make it before he could use it. He looked at some of their things, and picked up a little knife, trying the edge on his thumb. Immediately, Flora cried out:

"*Keffu, Unka Gus! Sha'ap; kuttsu!*"

"Muhgawd, Ben; you hear what she said? She speaks Lingua Terra!"

"That's right. That was one of the first things I taught them. And you don't have to teach them anything more than once, either." He looked at his watch, and spoke to the Fuzzies. They seemed disappointed, but

Fauna said, "*Hokay*," and ran into the tent, bringing out his shoulder-bag and chopper-digger, and Flora's. "Told them we have to make Big One talk, to go hunt land-prawns. I had a bunch brought in, this morning, and turned loose for them."

Fauna piled into the wheelbarrow; Flora got between the shafts and picked it up, starting off at a run, the passenger whooping loudly. Ben watched them vanish among the shrubbery, and got out his pipe and tobacco.

"Gus, why in Nifflheim did Leslie Coombes show up in court today and back you against this fellow Ingermann?" he demanded. "I thought Grego put Ingermann up to that himself."

That's right; any time anything happens, blame Grego.

"No, Ben. The company doesn't want a big landrush starting, any more than we do. They don't want their whole labor force bugging out on them, and that's what it would come to. I don't know why I can't pound it into your head that Victor Grego has as big a stake in keeping things together on this planet as you have."

"Yes, if he can control it the way he used to. Well, I'm not going to let him . . ."

He made an impatient noise. "And Ingermann; Grego wouldn't touch him with a ten-light-year pole. You call Grego a criminal? Well, maybe you were too busy, over on Beta, counting tree rings and checking on the love life of bush-goblins, to know about the Mallorysport underworld, but as a criminal lawyer I had to. Beside Hugo Ingermann, Victor Grego is a saint, and they have images of him in all the churches and work miracles with them. You name any kind of a racket—dope, prostitution, gambling, protection-shakedowns, illicit-gem buying, shylocking, stolen goods—and Ingermann's at the back of it. This action of his, today; he has a ring of crooks who want to make a killing in land speculation. That's why I wanted to stop him, and that's why Grego sent Coombes to help me. Ben, you're going to find that this is only the first of many occasions when you and Grego are going to be on the same side."

Rainsford started an angry reply; before he could speak, Gerd van Riebeek's voice floated down from the escalator-head on the terrace above.

"Anybody home down there?"

"No, nobody but us Fuzzies," Rainsford called back. "Come on down."

IV

With a sigh of relief, Victor Grego entered the living room of his penthouse apartment. His hand rose to the switch beside the door, then dropped; the faint indirect glow from around the edge of the ceiling was enough. He'd just pour himself a drink and sit here in the crepuscular silence, resting. His body was tired, more so than it should be, at his age, but his brain was still racing at top speed. No use trying to go to sleep now.

He took off his jacket and neckcloth and dropped them on a chair, opening his shirt collar as he went to the cellaret; he poured a big inhaler-glass half full of brandy and started for his favorite chair, then returned to get the bottle. It would take more than one glass to brake the speeding wheels inside his head. He placed the bottle on a low table, beside the fluted glass bowl, and sat down, wondering what he had noticed that had disturbed him. Nothing important; he sipped from the glass and leaned back, closing his eyes.

They had the trouble in the veldbeest country on Beta and Delta Continents worked out, at least to where they knew what to do about it. Close down all the engineering jobs, the Big Blackwater drainage project on Beta, and the various construction jobs, and shift men to the cattle ranges; issue them combat equipment and put them on fighting pay, to deal with these gangs of rustlers that were springing up. Maybe if they started a couple of range-wars, Ian Ferguson and his Colonial Constabulary would have to take a hand. But the main thing was to keep the herds together. And the wild veldbeest; Ben Rainsford was a conservationist, he ought to be interested in protecting them.

And he still hadn't decided on a sunstone buying policy. Not enough information on the present situation. He'd have to do something about that.

Oh, Nifflheim with it; think about it tomorrow.

He drank more brandy, and reached to the glass bowl on the low table, and found that it was empty. That was what had bothered him. It had been half full of the sort of tidbits he privately called nibblements—salted nuts, wafers, things like that—when he and Leslie Coombes had gone through the room on their way down for dinner.

Or had it? Maybe he just thought it had been. He began worrying about that, too. And the way he'd forgotten, this morning, about the sunstone inventory. Better call in Ernst Mallin to give him a checkup.

Then he laughed mirthlessly. If anybody needed a checkup, it was the company psychologist himself. Poor Ernst; he'd had a pretty shattering time of it, and now he probably thought he was being blamed for everything.

He wasn't, of course. Mallin had done the best anybody could have done, in an impossible situation. The Fuzzies had been sapient beings, and that was all there'd been to it, and that wasn't Mallin's fault. That Mallin had been forced so to testify in court had been the fault of his immediate subordinate, Dr. Ruth Ortheris, who had also, it developed, been Lieutenant j.g. Ortheris, TFN Intelligence. She'd been the one who tipped Navy Intelligence about the Fuzzies in the first place. She'd been the one who'd smuggled Jack Holloway's Fuzzy family out of Science Center after Leslie Coombes had gotten hold of them on a bogus court order. And she'd been the one who'd insisted on live-trapping that other Fuzzy family and exposing

Mallin to them.

That had been a beautiful piece of work. He'd watched the trial by screen; he could still see poor Mallin on the stand, trying to insist that Fuzzies were just silly little animals, with the red-blazing globe of the veridicator calling him a liar every time he opened his mouth. Why, she'd made the company defeat itself with its own witness.

He ought to hate her for that. He didn't; he admired her for it, as he admired anybody who had a job to do and did it competently. He had too damned few people like that in his own organization.

Have to do something nice for Ernst, though. He couldn't stay in charge at Science Center, but he'd have to be promoted out of it. Probably have to invent a job for him.

Finally, he decided that he could go to sleep, now. He took the brandy bottle back to the cellaret, gathered up the garments he had thrown down, and went into the bedroom, putting on the lights.

Then he looked at the bed and saw the golden-furred shape snuggled against the pillows. He swore. One of those life-size Fuzzy dolls that had been on sale ever since the Fuzzies had gotten into the news. If this was somebody's idea of a joke . . .

Then the thing he had taken for a doll sat up, blinked, and said, "Yeek?"

"Why, the damn thing's alive!" he yelled. "It's a *real* Fuzzy!" The Fuzzy was afraid; watching him and at the same time seeking an avenue of escape. "Don't be scared, kid," he soothed. "I won't hurt you. How'd you get in here, anyhow?"

One thing, the puzzle of the empty bowl was solved; the contents were now inside the Fuzzy. This, however, posed the question of how the Fuzzy got there. When he had thought this was a joke, he had been angry. Now he doubted that it was a joke, and he was on the edge of being worried.

The Fuzzy, who had been regarding him warily, had

evidently decided that he was not hostile and might even be friendly. He got to his feet, tried to walk on the yielding pneumatic mattress, and tumbled heels-over-head. Instantly he was on his feet again, leaping twice his height into the air, bouncing, and yeeking happily. He caught him on the second bounce and sat down on the bed with him.

"Are you hungry, kid?" That bowl of nibblements wasn't much of a meal, even for a Fuzzy. The stuff was all heavily salted, too. "Bet you're thirsty." What was it Jack Holloway's Fuzzies called him? Pappy Jack. "Well, Pappy Vic'll get you something."

In the kitchenette-breakfast room, the uninvited guest drank two small aperitif-glasses of water and part of a third, while his host wondered about what he'd like to eat. Jack Holloway gave his Fuzzies Extee-Three, but he didn't have . . . Oh, yes; maybe he did.

He went into the bedroom and opened one of the closets, where his field equipment was kept—rifles, sleeping-bag, cameras and binoculars, and a couple of rectangular steel cases to be carried in an aircar, full of camping paraphernalia. He opened one, which contained mess-gear he'd brought with him from Terra and used on field trips ever since, and sure enough, there were a couple of tins of Extee-Three.

The Fuzzy, who had been watching beside him, yeeked excitedly when he saw the blue labels, and ran ahead of him to the kitchenette. He could hardly wait till the tin was open. Somebody had given him Extee-Three before.

He made a sandwich for himself and sat down at the table while the Fuzzy ate, and he was still worried. There were only four doors into Company House from the ground, and all of them were constantly guarded. There were no windows less than sixty feet from the ground. While no bet on what Fuzzies couldn't do was really safe, he doubted that they had learned to pilot aircars just yet. So somebody had brought this Fuzzy here, and beside *How*, which would be by aircar, the question branched out into When and Who and Why.

Why was what worried him most. Fuzzies, as he didn't need to remind himself, were people, and wards of the Terran Federation, and all sort of crimes could be committed against them. Leonard Kellogg would have been executed for killing one of them, if he hadn't done the job for himself in his cell at the jail. And beside murder, there was abduction, and illegal restraint. Maybe somebody was trying to frame him.

He put on the communication screen and punched the call combination of the Chief's office at company police headquarters. He got Captain Morgan Lansky, who held down Chief Steefer's desk from midnight to six. As soon as Lansky saw who was calling, he got rid of his cigar, zipped up his tunic, and tried to look alert, wide awake and busy.

"Why, Mr. Grego! Is anything wrong?"

"That's what I want to know, Captain. I have a Fuzzy up here in my apartment. I want to know how he got here."

"A Fuzzy? Are you sure, Mr. Grego?"

He stooped and picked up his visitor, setting him on the table. The Fuzzy was clutching half a cake of Extee-Three. He saw Lansky looking out of the wall at him and yeeked in astonishment.

"What is your opinion, Captain?"

Captain Lansky's opinion was that he'd be damned. "How did he get in, Mr. Grego?"

Grego prayed silently for patience. "That is precisely what I want to know. To begin with, have you any idea how he got in the building?"

"Somebody," the captain decided, after deliberation, "must have brought him in. In an aircar," he added, after more cogitation.

"I had gotten that far, myself. Would you have any idea when?"

Lansky began to shake his head. Then he was smitten with an idea.

"Hey, Mr. Grego! The pilfering!"

"What pilfering?"

"Why, the pilfering. Pilfering, and ransacking; in offices and like that. And somebody's getting into supply rooms at some of the cafeterias, and where they keep the candy and stuff for the vending robots. The first musta been the night of the sixteenth." That would be three days ago. "The first report came in day before yesterday morning, after the 0600-1200 shift came on. It's been like that ever since; every morning, places being ransacked and candy and stuff like that taken. You think that Fuzzy's been doing all of it?"

He could see no reason why not. Fuzzies were small people, able to make themselves very inconspicuous when they wanted to. Hadn't they survived for oomphty-thousand years in the woods, dodging harpies and bush-goblins. And Company House was full of hiding places. It had been built twelve years ago, three years after he came to Zarathustra, and it had been built big. It wasn't going to be like the buildings they ran up on Terra, to be torn down in a couple of decades; it was meant to be the headquarters of the Chartered Zarathustra Company for a couple of centuries. Eighteen levels, six to eight floors to a level; more than half of them were empty and many unfinished, waiting for the CZC to grow into them.

"The ones Dr. Jimenez trapped for Dr. Mallin," Lansky said. "Maybe this is one of them."

He winced, mentally, at the thought of those Fuzzies. Catching them and letting Mallin study them had been the worst error of the whole business, and the way they had gotten rid of them had been a close runner-up.

It had been a Mallorysport police lieutenant, on his own lame-brained responsibility, who had started the story about a ten-year-old girl, Lolita Lurkin, being attacked by Fuzzies, and it had been Resident-General Nick Emmert, now bound for Terra aboard a destroyer from Xerxes to face malfeasance charges, who had posted a reward of five thousand sols apiece on Jack Holloway's Fuzzies, supposed to be at large in the city. Dead or alive; that had touched off a hysterical Fuzzy-hunt.

That had been when he and Leslie Coombes had perpetrated their own masterpiece of imbecility, by turning loose the Fuzzies Mallin had been studying, whom everybody was now passionately eager to see the last of, in the hope that they would be shot for Emmert's reward money. Instead, Jack Holloway, hunting for his own Fuzzies in ignorance of the fact that they were safe on Xerxes Naval Base, had found them, and now he was very glad of it. Gerd and Ruth van Riebeek had them now.

"No, Captain. Those Fuzzies are all accounted for. And Dr. Jimenez didn't bring any others to Mallorysport."

That put Lansky back where he had started. He went off on another tangent:

"Well, I'll send somebody up right away to get him, Mr. Grego."

"You will do nothing of the sort, Captain. The Fuzzy's quite all right here; I'm taking care of him. All I want to know is how he got into Company House. And I want the investigation made discreetly. Tell the Chief when he comes in." He thought of something else. "Get hold of a case of Extee-Three; do it before you go off duty. And have it put on my delivery lift, where I'll find it the first thing tomorrow."

The Fuzzy was disappointed when he blanked the screen; he wondered where the funny man in the wall had gone. He finished his Extee-Three, and didn't seem to want anything else. Well, no wonder; one of those cakes would keep a man going for twenty-four hours.

He'd have to fix up some place for the Fuzzy to sleep. And some way for him to get water; the sink in the kitchenette was too high to be convenient. There was a low sink outside, which the gardener used; he turned the faucet on slightly, set a bowl under it, and put a little metal cup beside it. The Fuzzy understood about that, and yeeked appreciatively. He'd have to get one of those earphones the Navy people had developed, and learn the Fuzzy language.

Then he remembered that Fuzzies were most meticulous about their sanitary habits. Going back inside, he entered the big room behind the kitchenette which served the chef as a pantry, the houseboy for equipment storage, the gardener as a seedhouse and tool shed, and all of them as a general junkroom. He hadn't been inside the place, himself, for some time. He swore disgustedly when he saw it, then began rummaging for something the Fuzzy could use as a digging tool.

Selecting a stout-handled basting spoon, he took it out into the garden and dug a hole in a flower bed, sticking the spoon in the ground beside it. The Fuzzy knew what the hole was for, and used it, and then filled it in and stuck the spoon back where he found it. He made some ultrasonic remarks, audible as yeeks, in gratification at finding that human-type people had civilized notions about sanitation too.

Find him something better tomorrow, a miniature spade. And fix up a real place for him to sleep, and put in a little fountain, and . . .

It suddenly occurred to him that he was assuming that the Fuzzy would want to stay with him permanently, and also to wonder whether he wanted a Fuzzy living with him. Of course he did. A Fuzzy was fun, and fun was something he ought to have more of. And a Fuzzy would be a friend. A Fuzzy wouldn't care whether he was manager-in-chief of the Charterless Zarathustra Company or not, and friends like that were hard to come by, once you'd gotten to the top.

Except for Leslie Coombes, he didn't have any friends like that.

Some time during the night, he was awakened by

something soft and warm squirming against his shoulder.

"Hey; I thought I fixed you a bed of your own."

"Yeek?"

"Oh, you want to bunk with Pappy Vic. All right."

They both went back to sleep.

V

It was fun having company for breakfast, especially company small enough to sit on the table. The Fuzzy tasted Grego's coffee; he didn't care for it. He liked fruit juice and sipped some. Then he nibbled Extee-Three, and watched quite calmly while Grego lit a cigarette, but manifested no desire to try one. He'd probably seen humans smoking, and may have picked up a lighted cigarette and either burned himself or hadn't liked it.

Grego poured more coffee, and then put on the screen. The Fuzzy turned to look at it. Screens were fun: interesting things happened in them. He was fascinated by the kaleidoscopic jumble of color. Then it cleared, and Myra Fallada appeared in it.

"Good morning, Mr. Grego," she started. Then she choked. Her mouth stayed open, and her eyes bulged as though she had just swallowed a glass of hundred-and-fifty-proof rum thinking it iced tea. Her hand rose falteringly to point.

"Mr. Grego! That . . . Is that a *Fuzzy?*"

The Fuzzy was delighted; this was a lot more fun than the man in the blue clothes, last night.

"That's right. I found him making himself at home, here, last evening." He wondered how many more times he'd have to go over that. "All I can get out of him is yeeks. For all I know, he may be a big stockholder."

After consideration, Myra decided this was a joke.

A sacrilegious joke; Mr. Grego oughtn't to make jokes like that about the company.

"Well, what are you going to do with it?"

"Him? Why, if he wants to stay, fix up a place for him here."

"But . . . But it's a Fuzzy!"

The company lost its charter because of Fuzzies. Fuzzies were the enemy, and loyal company people oughtn't to fraternize with them, least of all Mr. Grego.

"Miss Fallada, the Fuzzies were on this planet for a hundred thousand years before the company was ever thought of." Pity he hadn't taken that attitude from the start. "This Fuzzy is a very nice little fellow, who wants to be friends with me. If he wants to stay with me, I'll be very happy to have him." He closed the subject by asking what had come in so far this morning.

"Well, the girls have most of the morning reports from last night processed; they'll be on your desk when you come down. And then . . ."

And then, the usual budget of gripes and queries. He thought most of them had been settled the day before.

"All right; pile it up on me. Has Mr. Coombes called yet?"

Yes. He was going to be busy all day. He would call again before noon, and would be around at cocktail time. That was all right. Leslie knew what he had to do and how to do it. When he got Myra off the screen, he called Chief Steefer.

Harry Steefer didn't have to zip up his tunic or try to look wide awake; he looked that way already. He was a retired Federation Army officer and had a triple row of ribbon on his left breast to prove it.

"Good morning, Mr. Grego." Then he smiled and nodded at the other person in view in his screen. "I see you still have the trespasser."

"Guest, Chief. What's been learned about him?"

"Well, not too much, yet. I have what you gave

Captain Lansky last night; he's tabulated all the reports and complaints on this wave of ransackings and petty thefts. A rather imposing list, by the way. Shall I give it to you in full?"

"No; just summarize it."

"Well, it started, apparently, with ransacking in a couple of offices and a ladies' lounge on the eighth level down. No valuables taken, but things tossed around and left in disorder, and candy and other edibles taken. It's been going on like that ever since, on progressively higher levels. There were reports that somebody was in a couple of cafeteria supply rooms, without evidence of entrance."

"Human entrance, that is."

"Yes. Lansky had a couple of detectives look those places over last night; he says that a Fuzzy could have squirmed into all of them. I had reports on all of it as it happened. Incidentally, there was nothing reported for last night, which confirms the supposition that your Fuzzy was responsible for all of it."

"Regular little vest-pocket crime wave, aren't you." He pummeled the Fuzzy gently. "And there was nothing before the night of the sixteenth or below the eighth level down?"

"That's right, Mr. Grego. I wanted to talk to you before I did anything, but there may be a chance that either Dr. Mallin or Dr. Jimenez may know something about it."

"I'll talk to both of them, myself. Dr. Jimenez was over on Beta until a day or so before the trial; after he'd trapped the four Dr. Mallin was studying, he stayed on to study the Fuzzies in habitat. He had a couple of men helping him, paid hunters or rangers or something of the sort."

"I'll find out who they were," Steefer said. "And, of course, almost anybody who works out of Company House on Beta Continent may have picked the Fuzzy up and brought him back and let him get away. We'll do all we can to find out about this, Mr. Grego."

He thanked Steefer and blanked the screen, and punched out the call-combination of Leslie Coombes' apartment. Coombes, in a dressing gown, answered at once; he was in his library, with a coffee service and a stack of papers in front of him. He smiled and greeted Grego; then his eyes shifted, and the smile broadened.

"Well! Touching scene; Victor Grego and his Fuzzy. If you can't lick them, join them" he commented. "When and where did you pick him up?"

"I didn't; he joined me." He told Coombes about it. "What I want to find out now is who brought him here."

"My advice is, have him flown back to Beta and turned loose in the woods where he came from. Rainsford agreed not to prosecute us for what we did before the trial, but if he finds you're keeping a Fuzzy at Company House now, he'll throw the book at you."

"But he likes it here. He wants to stay with Pappy Vic. Don't you, kid?" he asked. The Fuzzy said something that sounded like agreement. "Suppose you go to Pendarvis and make application for papers of guardianship for me, like the ones he gave Holloway and George Lunt and Rainsford."

A gleam began to creep into Leslie Coombes' eyes. He'd like nothing better than a chance at a return bout with Gus Brannhard, with a not-completely-hopeless case.

"I believe I could . . ." Then he banished temptation. "No; we have too much on our hands now, without another Fuzzy trial. Get rid of him, Victor." He held up a hand to forestall a protest. "I'll be around for cocktails, about 1730-ish," he said, "You think it over till then."

Well, maybe Leslie was right. He agreed, and for a while they talked about the political situation. The Fuzzy became bored and jumped down from the table. After they blanked their screens he looked around and couldn't see him. The door to the pantry-storeroomtoolroom-junkroom was open; maybe he was in there investigating things. That was all right; he couldn't make the existing mess any worse. Grego poured more coffee and lit another cigarette.

There was a loud crash from beyond the open door, and an alarmed yeek, followed by more crashing and thumping and Fuzzy cries of distress. Jumping to his feet, he ran to the door and looked inside.

The Fuzzy was in the middle of a puddle of brownish gunk that had spilled from an open five-gallon can which seemed to have fallen from a shelf. Sniffing, he recognized it—a glaze for baked meats, mostly molasses, that the chef had mixed from a recipe of his own. It took about a pint to glaze a whole ham, so the damned fool had mixed five gallons of it. Most of it had gone on the Fuzzy, and in attempting to get away from the deluge he had upset a lot of jars of spices and herbs, samples of which were sticking to his fur. Then he had put his foot on a sheet of paper, and it had stuck; trying to pull it loose, it had stuck to his hands, too. As soon as he saw Pappy Vic, he gave a desperate yeek of appeal.

"Yes, yeek yourself." He caught the Fuzzy, who flung both adhesive arms around his neck. "Come on, here; let's get you cleaned up."

Carrying the Fuzzy into the bathroom, he dumped him into the tub, then tore off the hopelessly ruined shirt. Trousers all spotted with the stuff, too; change them when he finished the job. He brought a jar of shampoo soap from the closet and turned on the hot water, tempering it to what he estimated the Fuzzy could stand.

Now, wasn't this a Nifflheim of a business? As if he hadn't anything to do but wash Fuzzies.

He rubbed the soap into the Fuzzy's fur; the Fuzzy first resented and then decided he liked it, shrieked in pleasure, and grabbed a handful of the soap and tried to shampoo Grego. Finally, they got finished with it. The Fuzzy liked the hot-air dryer, too. He'd never had a shampoo before.

His fur clean and dry and fluffy, he sat on the bed and watched Pappy Vic change clothes. It was amazing the way the Big Ones could change their outer skins; must be very convenient. He made remarks, from time to time, and Grego carried on a conversation with him.

After he had dressed, Grego recorded a message for the houseboy, to be passed on to the chef and the gardener, to get everything to Nifflheim out of that back room that didn't belong there, and to keep what little did in some kind of decent order. If that place could be kept in order, now, the Fuzzy had one positive accomplishment to his credit.

They took the lift down to the top executive level—lifts appeared to be a new experience for the Fuzzy, too—and into his private office. The Fuzzy looked around in wonder, especially at the big globe of Zarathustra, floating six feet off the floor on its own built-in contragravity unit, spotlighted from above to simulate Zarathustra's KO-class sun, its two satellites circling around it. Finally, for a better view, he jumped up on a chair.

"If I had any idea you'd stay there . . ." He flipped the screen switch and got Myra on it. "I had a few things to clean up before I could come down," he told her, with literal truthfulness. "How many girls have we in the front office, this morning?"

There were eight, and they were all busy. Myra started to tell him what with; maybe four could handle it at a pinch, and six without undue strain. That was another thing the Charterless Zarathustra Company would have to economize on.

"Well, they can look after the Fuzzy, too," he said. "Take turns with him. He's in here, trying to make up his mind what kind of deviltry to get into next. Come get him, and take him out and tell the girls to keep him innocently amused."

"But, Mr. Grego; they have work . . ."

"This is more work. We'll find out which one gets along best with him, and promote her to chief Fuzzy-sitter. Are we going to let one Fuzzy disrupt our whole organization?"

Myra started to remind him of what the Fuzzies had done to the company already, then said, "Yes, Mr. Grego," and blanked the screen. A moment later she entered.

She and the Fuzzy looked at one another in mutual hostility and suspicion. She took a hesitant step forward; the Fuzzy yeeked angrily, dodged when she reached for him, and ran to Grego, jumping onto his lap.

"She won't hurt you," he soothed. "This is Myra; she likes Fuzzies. Don't you, Myra?" He stroked the Fuzzy. "I'm afraid he doesn't like you."

"Well, that makes it mutual," Myra said. "Mr. Grego, I am your secretary. I am not an animal keeper."

"Fuzzies are not animals. They are sapient beings. The Chief Justice himself said so. Have you never heard of the Pendarvis Decisions?"

"Have I heard of anything else, lately? Mr. Grego, how you can make a pet of that little demon, after all that's happened . . ."

"All right, Myra. I'll take him."

He went through Myra's office and into the big room they called executive operations center, through which reports from all over the company's shrunken but still extensive empire reached him and his decisions and directives and orders and instructions were handed down to his subjects. There were eight girls there, none particularly busy. One was reading alternately from several sets of clipboarded papers and talking into a vocowriter. Another was making a subdued clatter with a teleprint machine. A third was at a drawing board, constructing one of those multicolored zigzag graphs so dear to the organizational heart. The rest sat smoking and chatting; they all made hasty pretense of busying themselves as he entered. Then one of them saw the Fuzzy in his arms.

"Look! Mr. Grego has a Fuzzy!"

"Why, it's a real live Fuzzy!"

Then they were all on their feet and crowding forward in a swirl of colored dresses and perfumes and eager, laughing voices and pretty, smiling faces.

"Where did you get him, Mr. Grego?"

"Oh, can we see him?"

"Yes, girls." He set the Fuzzy down on the floor. "I don't know where he came from, but I think he wants to stay with us. I'm going to leave him here for a while. Don't let him interfere too much with your work, but keep an eye on him and don't let him get into any trouble. It'll be at least an hour before I have anything ready to go out. You can give him anything you'd eat yourselves; if he doesn't want, he won't take it. I don't think he's very hungry right now. And don't kill him with affection."

When he went out, they were all sitting on the floor in a circle around the Fuzzy, who was having a wonderful time. He told Myra to leave the doors of her office open so he could go through when he wanted to. Then he went through another door, into the computer room.

It was quarter-circular; two straight walls twenty feet long at right angles and the curved wall between, the latter occupied by the input board for the situation-analysis and operation-guidance computers. This was a band of pale green plastic, three feet wide, divided into foot squares by horizontal and vertical red lines, each square perforated with thousands of tiny holes, in some of them, little plug-in lights twinkled in every color of the spectrum. Three levels down, a whole floor was occupied with the computers this board serviced. From it, new information was added in the quasi-mathematical symbology computers understood.

He stood for a moment, looking at the Christmas-tree lights. Nothing in the world would have tempted him to touch it; he knew far too little about it. He wondered if they had started the computers working on the sunstone-buying policy problem, then went out into his own office, closing the door behind him, and sat down at his desk.

In the old, pre-Fuzzy days, he would have spent a leisurely couple of hours here, drinking more coffee and going over reports. Once in a while he would have made some comment, or asked a question, or made a suggestion, to show that he was keeping up with what was going on. Only rarely would any situation arise requiring his personal action.

Now everybody was having situations; things he had thought settled at the marathon staff conference of the past four days were coming unstuck; conflicts were developing. He had to make screen-calls to people he would never have bothered talking to under ordinary circumstances—the superintendent of the meat-packing plant on Delta Continent, the chief engineer on the now-idle Big Blackwater drainage project, the master mechanic at the nuclear-electric power-unit plant. He welcomed one such necessity, the master mechanic at the electronics-equipment factory; they were starting production of ultrasonic hearing-aids for the Government, and he ordered half a dozen sent around to his office. When he got one of them, he could hear what his new friend was saying.

Myra Fallada came in, dithering in the doorway till he had finished talking to the chief of chemical industries about a bottleneck in blasting-explosive production. As soon as he blanked the screen, she began.

"Mr. Grego, you will simply have to get that horrid creature out of operations center. The girls aren't doing a bit of work, and the noise is driving me simply *mad!*"

He could hear shrieks of laughter, and the running scamper of Fuzzy feet. Now that he thought of it, he had been hearing that for some time.

"And I positively can't work . . . *Aaaaaa!*"

Something bright red hit her on the back of the head and bounced into the room. A red plastic bag, a sponge bag or swimsuit bag or something like that, stuffed with tissue paper. The Fuzzy ran into the room, dodging past Myra, and hurled it back, within inches of her face, then ran after it.

"Well, yes, Myra. I'm afraid this is being carried a bit far." He rose and went past her into her office, in time to see the improvised softball come whizzing at him from the big office beyond. He caught it and went on through; the Fuzzy ran ahead of him to a tall girl with red hair who stopped and caught him up.

"Look, girls," he said, "I said keep the Fuzzy amused; I didn't say turn this into a kindergarten with the teacher gone AWOL. It's bad enough to have the Fuzzies tear up our charter, without letting them stop work on what we have left."

"Well, it did get a little out of hand," the tall redhead understated.

"Yes. Slightly." Nobody was going to under-understate him. What was her name? Sandra Glenn. "Sandra, he seems to like you. You take care of him. Just keep him quiet and keep him from bothering everybody else."

He hoped she wouldn't ask him how. She didn't; she just said, "I'll try, Mr. Grego." He decided to settle for that; that was all anybody could do.

By the time he got back to his desk, there was a call from the head of Public Services, wanting to know what he was going to tell the school teachers about their job futures. When he got rid of that, he called Dr. Ernst Mallin at Science Center.

The acting head of Science Center was fussily neat in an uncompromisingly black and white costume which matched his uncompromisingly black and white mind. He had a narrow face and a small, tight mouth; it had been an arrogantly positive face once. Now it was the face of a man who expects the chair he is sitting on to collapse under him at any moment.

"Good morning, Mr. Grego." Apprehensive, and trying not to show it.

"Good morning, Doctor. Those Fuzzies you were working with before the trial; the ones Dr. and Mrs. van Riebeek have now. Were they the only ones you had?"

The question took Mallin by surprise. They were, he stated positively. And to the best of his knowledge Juan Jimenez, who had secured them for him, had caught no others.

"Have you talked to Dr. Jimenez yet?" he asked, after hearing about the Fuzzy in Company House. "I don't believe he brought any when he came in from Beta Continent."

"No, not yet. I wanted to talk to you, first, about the Fuzzy and about something else. Dr. Mallin, I gather you're not exactly happy in charge of Science Center."

"No, Mr. Grego. I took it over because it was the only thing to do at the time, but now that the trial is over, I'd much rather go back to my own work."

"Well, so you shall, and your salary definitely won't suffer because of it. And I want to assure you again of my complete confidence in you, Doctor. During the Fuzzy trouble you did the best any man could have, in a thoroughly impossible situation . . ."

He watched the anxiety ebb out of Mallin's face; before he was finished, the psychologist was smiling one of his tight little smiles.

"Now, there's the matter of your successor. What would you think of Juan Jimenez?"

Mallin frowned. Have to make a show of thinking it over, and he was one of those people who thought with his face.

"He's rather young, but I believe it would be a good choice, Mr. Grego. I won't presume to speak of his ability as a scientist, his field is rather far from mine. But he has executive ability, capacity for decisions and for supervision, and gets along well with people. Yes; I should recommend him." He paused, then asked, "Do you think he'll accept it?"

"What do you think, Doctor?"

Mallin chuckled. "That was a foolish question," he admitted. "Mr. Grego; this Fuzzy. You still have him at Company House? What are you going to do with him?"

"Well, I had hoped to keep him, but I'm afraid I can't. He is a little too enterprising. He made my apartment look like a slightly used battlefield this morning, and now he's turning the office into a three-ring circus. And Leslie Coombes advises me to get rid of him; he thinks it may start Rainsford after us again. I think I'll have him taken back to Beta and liberated there."

"I'd like to have him, myself, Mr. Grego. Just keep him at my home and play with him and talk to him and try to find how he thinks about things. Mr. Grego, those Fuzzies are the sanest people I have ever seen. I know; I tried to drive the ones I had psychotic with frustration-situation experiments, and I simply couldn't. If we could learn their basic psychological patterns, it would be the greatest advance in psychology and psychiatry since Freud."

He meant it. He was a different Ernst Mallin now; ready to learn, to conquer his own ignorance instead of denying it. But what he wanted was out of the question.

"I'm sorry, believe me I am. But if I gave you the Fuzzy, Leslie Coombes would have a fit, and that's nothing to what Ben Rainsford would have; he'd bring prosecutions against the lot of us. If I do keep him, you'll have opportunity to study him, but I'm afraid I can't."

He brought the conversation to a close, and blanked the screen. The noise had stopped in operation center; the work probably had, too. He didn't want to get rid of the Fuzzy. He was a nice little fellow. But . . .

VI

He wasn't able to get Juan Jimenez immediately. Juan was doing something at the zoo, and the zoo was spread over too much area to track him down. He left word to call him as soon as possible, and went back to his own work, and finally had his lunch brought in and ate it at the desk. The outside office got noisy again, for a while. The girls seemed to be feeding the Fuzzy, and he wondered apprehensively on what. Some of the things those girls ate would give a billygoat indigestion. About an hour afterward, Jimenez was on the screen.

The chief mammalogist was a young man, with one of those cheerful, alert, agreeable, sincere and accommodating faces you saw everywhere on the upper echelons of big corporations or institutions. He might or might not be a good scientist, but he was a real two-hundred-proof company man.

"Hello, Juan; calling from Science Center?"

"Yes, Mr. Grego. I was at the zoo; they have some new panzer pigs from Gamma. When I got back, they told me you wanted to talk to me."

"Yes. When you came back, just before the trial, from Beta, did you bring any Fuzzies along with you?"

"Good Lord, no!" Jimenez was startled. "I got the impression that we needed Fuzzies like we needed a hole in the head. I got the impression that the one was about equal to the other."

"Just like Ernst Mallin: the more you saw of them,

the more sapient they looked. Well, dammit, what else were they? What were you doing on Beta?"

"Well, as I told you, Mr. Grego, we had a camp and we'd attracted about a dozen of them around it with Extee-Three, and we were photographing them and studying behavior, but we never made any attempt to capture any, after the first four."

"Beside yourself, who were 'we'?"

"The two men helping me, a couple of rangers from Survey Division; their names were Herckerd and Novaes. They helped me live-trap the four I gave to Dr. Mallin, and they helped with the camp work, and with photographing and so on."

"Well, here's the situation." He went into it again, realizing why witnesses in court who have been taken a dozen times over their stories by the police and the prosecuting attorney's people always sounded so glib. "So, you see, I want to find out what this is. It may be something quite innocent, but I want to be sure."

"Well, I didn't bring him in, and Herckerd and Novaes came in along with me; they didn't."

"I wish you, or they, had brought him; then I'd know what this is all about. Oh, another thing, Juan. As you know, Dr. Mallin was only in temporary charge at Science Center after Kellogg was arrested. He's going back to what's left of his original job, most happily, I might add. Do you think you could handle it? If you do, you can have it."

One thing you had to give Jimenez, he wasn't a hypocrite. He didn't pretend to be overcome with the honor, and he didn't question his own fitness. "Why, thank you, Mr. Grego!" Then he went into a little speech of acceptance which sounded suspiciously premeditated. Yes; he would definitely accept. So Grego made a little speech of his own, ending:

"I suggest you contact Dr. Mallin at once. He knows of my decision to appoint you, and you'll find him quite pleased to turn over to you. Oh, suppose we have lunch together tomorrow; by that time you should know what you have, and we can talk over future plans."

As soon as he had Jimenez off the screen he got Harry Steefer onto it.

"Mallin says he knows nothing about it, and so does Juan Jimenez. I have the names of two men who were helping Jimenez on Beta . . ."

Steefer grinned. "Phil Novaes and Moses Herckerd; they both worked for the Survey Division. Herckerd's a geologist, and Novaes is a hunter and wildlife man. They came in along with Jimenez the day before the trial, and then they vanished. A company aircar vanished along with them. My guess is they either went prospecting or down into the veldbeest country to do a little rustling. Want me to put out a wanted for them?"

"Yes, do that, Chief, about the car. Too many company vehicles have been vanishing along with employees since this turned into a Class-IV planet. And I still want to know who brought that Fuzzy here—and why."

"We're working on it," Steefer said. "There are close to a hundred people in half a dozen divisions who might have been over on Beta, in Fuzzy country, and picked up a Fuzzy for a pet. Then, say the Fuzzy got away here in Company House. Whoever was responsible would keep quiet about it afterward. I'm trying to find out, but you said you wanted it done discreetly."

"As discreetly as possible; I want it done, though. And you might start a search on some of the unoccupied floors on the eighth and ninth levels down, for evidence of where the Fuzzy was kept before he got away."

Steefer nooded. "We haven't any more men than we need," he mentioned. "Well, I'll do the best I can."

On past performance, Harry Steefer's best was likely to be pretty good. He nodded, satisfied, and went back to work, trying to figure what sort of a cargo could be scraped up for the Terra-Baldur-Marduk liner *City of Kapstaad*, which would be getting in in a week. He was still at it, calculating values on the Terra market against cubic feet of hold-space, when the door from the computer room opened behind him.

He turned, to see Sandra Glenn in the doorway. Her red hair and lipstick and her green eyes were vivid against a face that was white as paper.

"Mr. Grego." It was a barely audible whisper, shocked and frightened. "Were you doing anything with the board?"

"Good God, no!" He shoved his chair back and came to his feet. "I keep my ignorant fingers off that. What's been done to it?"

She stepped forward and aside and pointed. When he looked he saw the middle of the board a blaze of many-colored lights; not the random-looking pattern that would make sense only to a computer or a computerman, but a studied design, symmetrical and harmonious. A beautiful design. But God—Allah to Zeus, take your pick—only knew what gibbering nonsense it was putting into the trusting innards of that computer. Sandra was close to the screaming meemies; she had some idea of what kind of a computation would emerge.

"That," he said, "was our little friend *Fuzzy fuzzy holloway*. He came in here and saw the lights and found out they could be pulled out and shifted around, and he decided to make a real pretty thing. Weren't you, or any of the other girls, watching him?"

"Well, I had some work, and Gertrude was watching him, and then he lay down for a nap after lunch, and somebody called Gertrude to the screen . . ."

"All right. You're not the first one to be fooled by a Fuzzy, and neither's Gertrude. They fooled a guy named Grego pretty badly a few times. Has anything been done about this?"

"No; I just saw it a moment ago . . ."

"All right. Call Joe Verganno. No; I'll do it, his

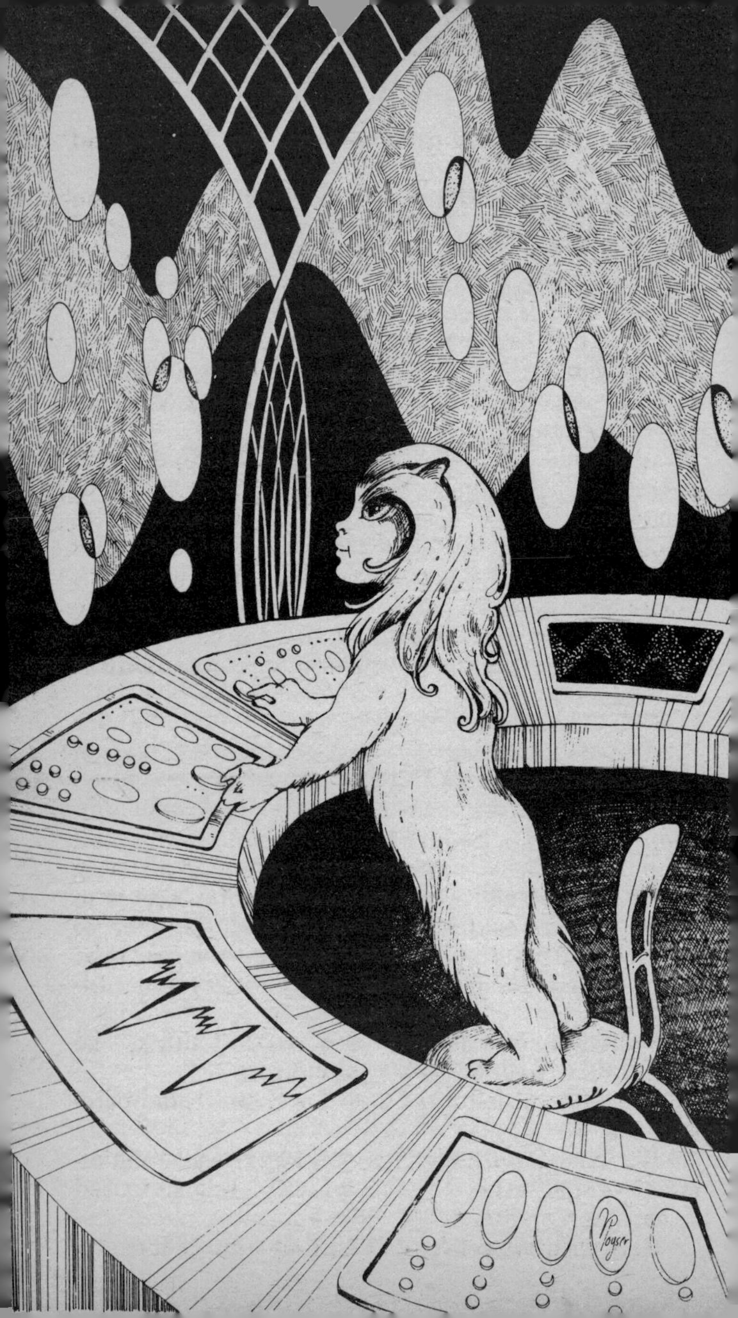

screen girl won't try to argue with me. You go find that Fuzzy."

He crossed in two long steps to the communication screen and punched a combination from the card taped up beside it. The girl who answered started to say, "Master computerman's office," and then saw who she had on screen. "Why, Mr. Grego!"

"Give me Verganno, quick."

Her hand moved; the screen exploded into a shatter of light and cleared with the computerman looking out of it.

"Joe, hell's to pay," he said, before Verganno could speak. "Somebody shoved a lot of plugs into the input board here and bitched everything up. Here." He reached under the screen and grabbed something that looked vaguely like a pistol, with a wide-angle lens where the muzzle should be, connected with the screen by a length of minicable. Aiming at the colored pattern on the board, he squeezed the trigger switch. Behind him, Joe Verganno's voice howled:

"Good God! Who did that?"

"A Fuzzy. No, I'm not kidding; that's right. You got it?"

"Just a sec. Yeah, turn it off." In the screen, Verganno grabbed a handphone. "General warning, all computer outlets. False data has been added affecting Executive One and Executive Two; no reliance is to be placed on computations from Executive One or Two until further notice. All right, Mr. Grego, I'll be right up. You mean there's a Fuzzy loose in your office?"

"Yes, he's been here all day. I don't think," he added, "that he'll be here much longer."

One of the girls looked into the room from operation-center.

"We can't find him anywhere, Mr. Grego!" she almost wailed. "And it's all my fault; I was supposed to be watching him!"

"Hell with whose fault it is; find him. If it's anybody's fault it's mine for bringing him here."

That was a fault that would be rectified directly. He saw Myra dithering at the door of her office.

"Get Ernst Mallin. Tell him to come here and get that damned Fuzzy to Nifflheim out of here."

Argue about the legal aspects later; if Mallin wanted a Fuzzy to study, he could have one. Myra said something about better late than never, and retracted into her office. The door from the outside hall opened cautiously, and a couple of police and three mechanics from one of the aircar hangars entered; somebody's had sense enough to call for reinforcements. One of the mechanics had a blanket over his arm; that was smart, too. The girls were searching the big room, and keeping watch on the doors. The hall door opened again, and Joe Verganno and one of his technicians came in with a hand lifter loaded with tools.

"Anything been done to the board yet?" he asked.

"Nifflheim, no! We're not making a bad matter worse than it is. See if you can figure out what's happening in the computer."

"A couple of my men are going to find that out down below. Lemme see this screen, now." He went into the room, followed by the technician with the lifter. The technician said something obscenely blasphemous a moment later.

He went back to the big room; through the open door of her office, he could hear Myra talking to somebody. "Come and get him, right away. No, we don't know where he is . . . *Eeeeeeh!* Get away from me, you little monster! Mr. Grego, here he is!"

"Grab him and hold him," he ordered. "Go help her," he told one of the cops. "Don't hurt the Fuzzy; just get hold of him."

Then he turned and ran through the computer room almost colliding with Verganno's helper, and ran into his own office. As he skidded around his desk, the Fuzzy dashed through the door of Myra's office. The blanket the aircar mechanic had been carrying sailed after him, missing him. Myra, the cop, and the mechanic came running after it; the mechanic caught his feet in it and went down. The cop tripped over him, and Myra tripped over the cop. The cop was cursing. Myra was screaming. The mechanic, knocked breathless under both of them, was merely gasping. The Fuzzy landed on top of the desk, saw Grego, and took off from there, landing against his chest and throwing his arms around Grego's neck. One of the girls, coming through from Myra's office and avoiding the struggling heap in front of the door, whooped, "Come on, everybody! Mr. Grego's caught him!"

The cop, who had gotten to his feet, said, "I'll take him, Mr. Grego," and reached for the Fuzzy. The Fuzzy yeeked loudly, and clung tighter to Grego.

"No, I'll hold him. He isn't afraid of me." He sat down in his desk chair, holding the Fuzzy and stroking him. "It's all right, kid. Nobody's going to hurt you. And we're going to take you out of here, to a nice place where you can have fun, and people'll be good to you . . ."

The words meant nothing to the Fuzzy; the voice, and the stroking hands, were comforting and reassuring. He snuggled closer, making happy little sounds. He was safe, now.

"What are you gonna do with him, Mr. Grego?" the cop asked.

Grego hugged the Fuzzy to him. "I'm not going to do anything with him. Look at him; he trusts me; he thinks I won't let anybody do anything to him. Well, I won't. I never let anybody who trusted me down yet, and be damned if I'll start now, with a Fuzzy."

"You mean, you're going to keep him?" Myra demanded. "After what he did?"

"He didn't mean to do anything bad, Myra. He just wanted to make a pretty thing with the lights. I'll bet he's as proud as anything of it. It's just going to be up to me to see that he doesn't get at anything else he can make trouble with."

"Dr. Mallin said he was coming right away. He'll be disappointed."

"He'll have to be disappointed, then. He can study the Fuzzy here. And get the building superintendent and the chief decorator; tell them I want them to start putting in a Fuzzy garden up on my terrace. Tell both of them to come up to my suite personally; tell them I want work started immediately, and I'll authorize double time for overtime till it's finished."

The Fuzzy wasn't scared, any more. Pappy Vic was taking care of him. And all these other Big Ones were listening to Pappy Vic; they wouldn't hurt him or chase him any more.

"And call Tregaskis at Electronics Equipment; ask him what's holding up those hearing-aids he was going to send me. And I'll need somebody to help look after the kid. Sandra, do you do anything we can't replace you at? Then you've just been appointed Fuzzy Sitter in Chief. You start immediately; ten percent raise as of this morning.

Sandra was happy. "I'll love that, Mr. Grego. What's, his name?"

"Name? I don't have a name for him, yet. Anybody have any ideas?"

"I have a few!" Myra said savagely.

"Call him Diamond," Joe Verganno, in the doorway of the computer room, suggested.

"Because he's so small and precious? I like that. But don't be a piker. Call him Sunstone."

"No; that was probably why the original Diamond was named, but I was thinking of calling him after a little dog that belonged to Sir Isaac Newton," Verganno said. "It seems Diamond got hold of a manuscript Sir Isaac had just finished and was going to send to his publisher. Mostly math, all done with a quill pen, no carbons of course. So Diamond got this manuscript down on the floor and he tore hell out of it, which meant about three months' work to do over. When Newton saw it, he just looked at it, and then sat down with the dog on his lap, and said, 'Oh, Diamond, poor Diamond; how little you know what mischief you have done!''

"That's a nice little story, Joe. It's something I'll want to remind myself of, now and then. Bet you'll give a lot of reasons to, won't you, Diamond?"

VII

Jack Holloway leaned back in his chair, resting one ankle across the corner of the desk and propping the other foot on a partly open bottom drawer. If he had to work in an office, it was nice working in a real one, and it was a big improvement to be able to use his living quarters exclusively for living in again. The wide doors at either end of the arched prefab hut were open and a little breeze was drawing through, just enough to keep the place cool and carry off his pipe smoke. There wasn't so much noise outside any more; most of the new buildings were up now. He could hear a distant popping of small arms as the dozen and a half ZNPF recruits fired for qualification.

A hundred yards away, at the other end, Sergeant Yorimitsu was monitoring screen-views transmitted in from a couple of cars up on patrol, and Lieutenant Ahmed Khadra and Sergeant Knabber were taking the fingerprints of a couple of Fuzzies that had come in an hour ago. Little Fuzzy, resting the point of his chopper-digger on the floor with his hands on the knob pommel, watched boredly. Fingerprinting was old stuff, now. The space between was mostly vacant; a few unoccupied desks and idle business machines scattered about. Some of these days they'd have a real office force, and then he'd be able to get out and move around among the natives, the way a Commissioner ought to.

One thing, they had the Fuzzy Reservation question

settled, at least for now. Ben Rainsford was closing everything north of the Little Blackwater and the East Fork of the Snake to settlement; that country all belonged to the Fuzzies and nobody else. Now if the Fuzzies could only be persuaded to stay there. And Gerd and Ruth and Pancho Ybarra and the Andrews girl were here, now, and set up. Maybe they'd begin to find out a few of the things they had to know.

The stamp machine banged twice, putting numbers on the ID discs for the two newcomers. Khadra brought the discs back and squatted to put them on the two Fuzzies.

"How many is that, now, Ahmed?" he called down the hut.

"These are Fifty-eight and Fifty-nine," Khadra called back. "Deduct three, two for Rainsford's, and one for Goldilocks."

Poor little Goldilocks; she'd have loved having an ID disc. She'd been so proud of the little jingle-charm Ruth had given her, just before she'd been killed. Fifty-six Fuzzies; getting quite a population here.

The communication screen buzzed. He flipped a switch on the edge of his desk and dropped his feet to the floor, turning. It was Ben Rainsford, and he was furiously angry about something. His red whiskers bristled as though electrically charged, and his blue eyes were almost shooting sparks.

"Jack," he began indignantly, "I've just found out that Victor Grego has a Fuzzy cooped up at Company House. What's more, he's had the effrontery to have Leslie Coombes apply to Judge Pendarvis to have him appointed guardian."

That surprised him slightly. To date, Grego hadn't exactly established himself as one of the Friends of Little Fuzzy.

"How did he get him, do you know?"

Rainsford gobbled in rage for a moment, then said:

"He claims he found this Fuzzy in his apartment, night before last, up at the top of Company House.

Now isn't that one Nifflheim of a story; does he think anybody's silly enough to believe that?"

"Well, it is a funny place for a Fuzzy to be," he admitted. "You suppose it might be one that was live-trapped for Mallin to study, before the trial? Ruth says there were only four, and they were all turned loose the night of the Lurkin business."

"I don't know. All I know is what Gus Brannhard told me that Pendarvis' secretary told him, that Pendarvis told her, that Coombes told Pendarvis." That sounded pretty roundabout, but he supposed that was the way Colonial Governors had to get things. "Gus says Coombes claims Grego says he doesn't know where the Fuzzy came from or how he got into Company House. That is probably a thumping big lie."

"It's probably the truth. Victor Grego's too smart to lie to his lawyer, and Coombes is too smart to lie to the Chief Justice. Judges are funny about that; they want statements veridicated, and after what you saw happen to Mallin in court, you don't suppose any of that crowd would try to lie under veridication."

Rainsford snorted scornfully. Grego was lying; if the veridicator backed him up, the veridicator was as big a liar as he was.

"Well, I don't care how he got the Fuzzy; what I'm concerned with is what he's doing to him," Rainsford replied. "And Ernst Mallin; Coombes admitted to Pendarvis that Mallin was helping Grego look after the Fuzzy. *Look after* him! They're probably torturing the poor thing, Grego and that sadistic quack head-shrinker. Jack, you've got to get that Fuzzy away from Grego!"

"Oh, I doubt that. Grego wouldn't mistreat the Fuzzy, and if he was, he wouldn't apply for papers of guardianship and make himself legally responsible. What do you want me to do?"

"Well, I told Gus to get a court order; Gus told me you were the Native Commissioner, that it was your job to act to protect the Fuzzy . . ."

Gus didn't think the Fuzzy needed any protecting;

he thought Grego was treating him well, and ought to be allowed to keep him. Se he'd passed the buck. He nodded.

"All right. I'm coming in to Mallorysport now. You're three hours behind us here, and if I use Gerd's boat I can make it in three hours. I'll be at Government House at 1530, your time. I'll bring either Pancho or Ruth along. You have Gus meet us when we get in. And I'll want to borrow your Flora and Fauna."

"What for?"

"Interpreters, and to interrogate Grego's Fuzzy. And I want them instead of any of our crowd here because they may have to testify in court and they won't have to travel back and forth. And tell Gus to get all the papers we'll need to crash Company House with. This is the first time anything like this has come up. We're going to give it the full treatment."

He blanked the screen, scribbled on a notepad and tore off the sheet, then looked around. Ko-Ko and Cinderella and Mamma Fuzzy and a couple of the Constabulary Fuzzies were working on a jigsaw puzzle on the floor near his desk.

"Ko-Ko," he called. *"Do-bizzo."* When Ko-Ko got to his feet and came over, he handed him the note. "Give to Unka Panko," he said. "Make run fast."

Victor Grego had Leslie Coombes on screen; the lawyer was saying:

"The Chief Justice is not hostile. Hospitable, I'd say. I think he's trying to be careful not to establish any precedent that might embarrass the Native Affairs Commission later. He was rather curious about how the Fuzzy got into Company House, though."

"Tell him that makes two of us. So am I."

"Have Steefer's men found out anything yet?"

"Not that he's reported. I'm going to talk to him shortly. The way things are, he's spread out pretty thin."

"It would help a lot if we could explain that. Would

you be willing to make a veridicated statement of what you know?"

"With adequate safeguards. Not for anybody to pump me about business matters."

"Naturally. How about Mallin and Jimenez?"

"They will if they want to keep on working for the company." It surprised him that Coombes would even ask such a question. "You think it's necessary?"

"I think it very advisable. Rainsford will certainly oppose your application; possibly Holloway. How about getting a statement from the Fuzzy?"

"Mallin and I tried, last evening. I don't know any of the language, and he only has a few tapes he got from Lieutenant Ybarra at the time of the trial. We have hearing-aids, now. It's a hell of a language; sounds like Old Terran Japanese more than anything else. The Fuzzy was trying to tell us something, but we couldn't make out what. We have it all on tape.

"And we showed him audio-visual portraits of those two Survey rangers who were helping Jimenez. He made both of them; I doubt if he likes them very much. We're looking for them. We are also looking for a Company scout car that vanished along with them."

"Vehicle theft's a felony; that will do to hold and interrogate them on," Coombes mentioned. "Well, shall I see you for cocktails?"

"Yes. You'd better call me, say every half-hour. If Rainsford gets nasty about this, I may need you before then."

After that, he called Chief Steefer. Steefer greeted him with:

"Mr. Grego, how red is my face?"

"Not noticeably so. Should it be?"

Steefer swore. "Mr. Grego, I want your authorization to make an inch-by-inch search of this whole building."

"Good God, Harry!" He was thinking of how many millions on millions of inches that was. "Have you found something?"

"Not about the Fuzzy, but—you have no idea what's been going on here, on these unoccupied levels. We found places where people had been camping for weeks. We found one place where there must have been a non-stop party going on for a month; there was almost a lifter scow full of empty bottles. And we found a tea pad."

"Yes? What was that like?"

"Nothing much; lot of mattresses thrown around, and the floor covered with butts—mostly chuckle-weed or opiate-impregnated tobacco. I don't think that was any of our people; everybody and his girl friend in Mallorysport seems to have been sneaking in here. We have men at all the landing stages, of course, but there aren't enough to..." His face hardened. "I've just gone slack on the job. That's the only explanation I can make."

"We've all gone slack, Harry." He thought of the mess in his pantry; that was symptomatic. "You know, we may owe the Fuzzies a debt of gratitude, if what's happened to us will make us start acting like a business concern instead of a bunch of kids in fairyland. All right; go ahead. Finding out how the Fuzzy got in here is still of top importance, but clean house generally while you're at it and see that it stays cleaned up."

Then he called Juan Jimenez at Science Center. Jimenez had gotten a new suit since yesterday, less casual, more executive. His public face had been done over too, to emphasize efficiency rather than agreeableness.

"Good morning, Victor." He stumbled a little over the first name, which was a prerogative of a division chief but to which he was not yet accustomed.

"Good morning, Juan. I know you haven't forgotten we're lunching together, but I wondered if you could make it a little early. There are a couple of things we want to go over first. In twenty minutes?"

"Easily; sooner than that if you wish."

"As soon as you can make it. Just come in the back way."

Then he made another screen call. This was an outside call, for which he had to look up the combination. When the screen cleared, a thin-faced, elderly man with white hair looked out of it. He wore a gray work smock, the breast pockets full of small tools and calibrating instruments. His name was Henry Stenson, and he might have been called an instrument maker, just as Benvenuto Cellini might have been called a jeweler.

"Why, Mr. Grego," he greeted, in pleased surprise, or reasonable facsimile. "I haven't heard from you for some time."

"No. Not since that gadget you planted in my globe stopped broadcasting. Incidentally, the globe's about thirty seconds slow, and both moons are impossibly out of synchronization. We had to stop it to take out that thing you built into it, and none of my people have your fine touch."

Stenson grimaced slightly. "I suppose you know for whom I did that?"

"Well, I'm not certain whether you're Navy Intelligence, like our former employee, Ruth Ortheris, or Colonial Office Investigative Bureau; but that's minor. Whoever, they're to be congratulated on an excellent operative. You know, I could get quite nasty about that; planting radio-transmitted microphones in people's offices is a felony. I don't intend doing anything, but I definitely want no more of it. You can understand my attitude."

"Well, naturally, Mr. Grego. You know," he added, "I thought that thing was detection-proof."

"Instrumentally, yes. My people were awed when they saw the detection-baffles on that thing. Have you patented them? If you have, we owe you some money, because we're copying them. But nothing is proof against physical search, and we practically tore my office apart as soon as it became evident that anything said in it was known almost immediately on Xerxes Base."

Stenson nodded gravely. "You didn't call me just to tell me you'd caught me out? I knew that as soon as the radio went dead."

"No. I want you to put the globe back in synchronization, as soon as possible. And there's another thing. You helped the people on Xerxes design those ultrasonic hearing-aids, didn't you? Well, could you attack the problem from the other side, Mr. Stenson? I mean, design a little self-powered hand-phone, small enough for a Fuzzy to carry, that would transform the Fuzzy's voice to audible frequencies?"

Stenson was silent for all of five seconds. "Yes, of course, Mr. Grego. If anything, it should be simpler. Of course, teaching the Fuzzy to carry and use it would be a problem, but not in my line of work."

"Well, try and get an experimental model done as soon as possible. I have a Fuzzy available to try it. And if there's anything patentable about it, get it protected. Talk to Leslie Coombes. This may be of commercial value to both of us."

"You think there'll be a demand?" Stenson asked. "How much do you think a Fuzzy would pay for one?"

"I think the Native Affairs Commission would pay ten to fifteen sols apiece for them, and I'm sure our electronics plant could turn them out to sell profitably for that."

Somebody had entered the office; in one of the strategically-placed mirrors, he saw that it was Juan Jimenez keeping out of the field of the screen-pickup. He nodded to him and went on talking to Stenson, who would be around the next morning to look at the globe. When they finished the conversation and blanked screens, he motioned Jimenez to his deskside chair.

"How much of that did you hear?" he asked.

"Well, I heard that white-haired old Iscariot say he'd be around tomorrow to fix the globe . . ."

"Henry Stenson is no Iscariot, Juan. He is a Terran Federation secret agent, and the Federation is to be congratulated on his loyalty and ability. Now that I know just what he is, and now that he knows I know it, we can do business on a friendly basis of mutual respect and distrust. He's going to work up a gadget by which the Fuzzies can speak audibly to us.

"Now, about Fuzzies," he continued. "We're sure that your two helpers, Herckerd and Novaes, brought this Fuzzy of mine here to Mallorysport. You say they didn't have him when they came back with you?"

"Absolutely not, Mr. Grego."

"Would you veridicate that?"

Jimenez didn't want to, that was plain. But he did want to work for the Company, especially now that he had just been promoted to chief of Scientific Study and Research. He was as close to the top of the Company House hierarchy as he could get, and he wanted to stay there.

"Yes, of course. I'd hoped, though, that my word would be good enough..."

"Nobody's word's going to be good enough. I'm going to veridicate what I know about it, myself; so's Ernst Mallin. There will be quite a few veridicated statements taken in the next few days. Now, I want you to meet this Fuzzy. See if you know him, or if he knows you."

They went out to the private lift and up to the penthouse. In the living room, Sandra Glenn was lounging in his favorite chair, listening to something from a record player with an earphone and smoking. As they entered, she shut off the player and closed her eyes. "*So-josso-aki;* you give me," she said. "*Aki-josso-so;* I give you. *So-noho-aki dokko;* you tell me how many."

They tiptoed past her and out onto the terrace. Ernst Mallin was sitting on a low hassock, with his hearing-aid on; Diamond was squatting in front of him, tying knots in a length of twine. An audiovisual recorder was set up to cover both of them. Diamond sprang to his feet and ran to meet them, crying out: "Pappy Vic! *Heeta!*" and holding up the cord to show the knots he had been learning to tie.

"Hello, Diamond. Those are very fine knots. You are a smart Fuzzy. How do I say that, Ernst?" Mallin said something, haltingly; he repeated it, patting the Fuzzy's head. "Now, how do I ask him if he's ever seen this Big One with me before?"

Mallin asked the question himself. Diamond said something; he caught *"Vov,"* a couple of times. That was negative.

"He doesn't know you, Juan. What I'm sure happened is that Herckerd and Novaes came in with you, just before the trial, then went back to Beta, probably in the aircar they stole from us, and picked up this Fuzzy. We won't know why till we catch them and question them." He turned to Mallin. "Get anything more out of him?"

Mallin shook his head. "I'm picking up a few more words, but I still can't be sure. He says two Hagga, the ones we showed him the films of, brought him here. I think they brought some other Fuzzies with him; I can't be sure. There doesn't seem to be any way of pluralizing in his language. He says they were *tosh-ki gashta*, bad people. They put him in a bad place."

"We'll put them in a bad place. Penitentiary place. I don't suppose you can find out how long ago this was? During or right after the trial, I suppose."

Sandra Glenn came out onto the terrace.

"Mr. Grego; Miss Fallada's on screen. She says representatives of all the press-services are here. They've heard about Diamond; they want the story, and pictures of him."

"That was all we needed! All right; tell her to have a policeman show them up. I'm afraid our lunch'll have to wait till we get through with them, Juan."

VIII

Coming out of the lift, Jack Holloway advanced to let the others follow and halted, looking at the three men waiting to meet them in the foyer of Victor Grego's apartment. Two he had met already: Ernst Mallin, under uniformly unpleasant circumstances culminating in the murder of Goldilocks, the beating of Leonard Kellogg and the shooting of Kurt Borch, at his camp, and Leslie Coombes, first at George Lunt's complaint court at Beta Fifteen and then in Judge Pendarvis' court during the Fuzzy Trial. As the trial had dragged out, the frigid politeness with which he and Coombes had first met had thawed into something like mutual cordiality.

But, except for news-screen appearances, he had never seen Victor Grego before. Enemy generals rarely met while the fighting was going on. It struck him that, meeting Grego for the first time as a complete stranger, he would have instantly liked him. He had to remember that Grego was the man who had wanted to treat Fuzzies as fur-bearing animals and exterminate the whole race. Well, Grego hadn't known any Fuzzies, then. It was easy enough to plan atrocities against verbal labels.

They paused for an instant, ten feet apart, Mallin and Coombes flanking Grego, and Gus Brannhard, Pancho Ybarra, Ahmed Khadra and Flora and Fauna behind him, like two gangs waiting for somebody to pull a gun. Then Grego stepped forward, extending his hand.

"Mr. Holloway? Happy to meet you." They shook hands. "You've met Mr. Coombes and Dr. Mallin. It was good of you to warn us you were coming."

Ben Rainsford hadn't thought so. He'd wanted them to descend on Company House by surprise, probably with drawn pistols, and catch Grego red-handed at whatever villainy he was up to. Brannhard and Coombes were shaking hands, so were Ybarra and Mallin. He introduced Ahmed Khadra.

"And these other people are Flora and Fauna," he added. "I brought them along to meet Diamond."

Grego stooped, and they came forward. He said, "Hello, Flora; hello, Fauna. *Aki-gazza heeta-so.*"

The accent was reasonably good, but he had to think between words. The two Fuzzies replied politely. Grego started to say that Diamond was out on the terrace, then laughed when he saw the Fuzzy peeping through the door from the living room. An instant later, Diamond saw Flora and Fauna and rushed forward, and they ran to meet him, all jabbering excitedly. A tall girl with red hair entered behind him; Grego introduced her as Sandra Glenn. And behind her came Juan Jimenez; regular Old Home Week.

"Shall we go in the living room, or out on the terrace?" Grego asked. "I'd advise the terrace; the living room might be a little crowded, with three Fuzzies getting acquainted. Sometimes it seems a trifle crowded with just one Fuzzy."

They went through the living room; the quiet and tasteful luxury of its furnishings had suffered somewhat. There was an audiovisual recorder set up, and an extra reading screen and an audiovisual screen and a tape-player; they looked more like office equipment than domestic furnishings. Evidently Fuzzies did the same things to living rooms everywhere. And another piece of furniture, surprising in any living room; a thing like an old-fashioned electric chair, with a bright metal helmet and a big translucent globe mounted above it. A polyencephalographic veridicator; Grego wasn't expecting anybody to take his unsupported word about anything. They all affected not to notice it, and passed out onto the terrace.

This had evidently been Grego's private garden; now it seemed to be mostly the Fuzzy's. An awful lot of men must have been working awfully hard up here recently. There was a lot of playground equipment—swing, slide, skeletal construction of jointed pipe for climbing-bars. A little Fuzzy-sized drinking fountain, and a bathing pool. Grego seemed to have just thought of everything he'd like if he were a Fuzzy and gotten it. Diamond led Flora and Fauna to the slide, ran up the ladder, and came shooting down. They both ran after him and tried it, too, and then ran up to try it again. Have to get some playground stuff like that for the camp. Bet Flora and Fauna would start pestering Pappy Ben to get them some things like this, as soon as they got home.

According to plan, Ahmed Khadra and Pancho Ybarra stayed on the terrace with the Fuzzies; he and Gus and Grego and Mallin and Coombes went back inside. For a while, they chatted about Fuzzies in general and Diamond in particular. One thing was obvious: Grego liked Fuzzies, and was devoted to his own.

The Fuzzies had done him all the damage they could. Now he could be friends with them.

"I suppose you want to hear how he turned up, here? If you don't mind, I'd prefer veridicating what I have to tell you, so there won't be any argument about it. Do you want to test the machine first, Mr. Brannhard?"

"It would be a good idea. Jack, you want to be the test witness?"

"If you do the questioning."

A veridicator operated by identifying and registering the distinctive electromagnetic brain-wave pattern involved in suppression of a true statement and substitution of a false one. You didn't have to do that aloud; a mere intention to falsify would turn the blue light in the globe red, and even a yogi adept couldn't control his thoughts enough to prevent it. He took his place in the chair, and Brannhard clipped on the electrodes and lowered the helmet over his head.

"What is your name?"

He answered that truthfully, and Gus nodded and asked him his place of residence.

"How old are you?"

He lied ten years off his age. The veridicator caught that at once; Gus wanted to know how old he really was.

"Seventy-four: I was born in 580. I couldn't even estimate how much to allow for on time-differential for hyperspace trips."

"That's the truth," Gus said. "I didn't think you were much over sixty."

Then he asked about the planets he'd been on. Jack named them, including one he'd never been within fifty light-years of, and the veridicator caught that. He ended in a crimson blaze of mendacity by claiming to be a teetotaler, a Gandhian pacifist, and the illegitimate son of a Satanist archbishop. Brannhard was satisfied; the veridicator worked. He unfastened Jack, and Grego took his place.

The globe stayed blue all through Grego's account of how he had found Diamond in his bedroom; it was the same story they had already gotten from newscasts while coming in from Beta. Then Grego gave place to Mallin, and Mallin to Jimenez. They were all uninvolved in bringing the Fuzzy to Mallorysport, and the veridicator supported them. They all agreed that Diamond had recognized Herckerd and Novaes as the men who had brought him and possibly other Fuzzies there.

"What do you think?" Coombes asked, when they were all back in their chairs. "Do you think they brought those Fuzzies in to sell as pets?"

"I can't see any other reason. I've been expecting something like this. Why would they bring them to Company House, though? I don't quite see the sense in that."

"I do." Grego was angry about something. What he was angry about emerged immediately; he spoke bitterly about what had been going on among the unoccupied rooms of Company House. "Chief Steefer's on the warpath, starting with his own department. We have wants out for Herckerd and Novaes, on a stolen-vehicle charge . . ."

"Forget about that," Brannhard advised. "That's petty larceny to what I'm going to charge them with."

Khadra came in from outside; he took off his beret, but left his pistol on.

"Well, there were six of them," he said. "Diamond, and five others. Herckerd and Novaes—he's positive about the identification—brought them in and kept them for a couple of days in a dark room somewhere in this building. Then the others were taken away; Diamond made a break and got away from the two *tosh-ki Hagga* while they were being put in the aircar. He doesn't know how long ago it was—three sleeps, he says. He found things to eat, and he found water to drink, and then Pappy Vic found him and gave him wonderful-food. He doesn't know what happened to his friends; he hopes they got away too."

"They didn't in here," Grego said. "Are you going to hunt for them?"

"We certainly are."

"And if anything's happened to them, we'll hunt for Herckerd and Novaes till they die of old age if we don't catch them first," Brannhard added.

"How's Diamond like it here, Ahmed?"

"Oh, wonderful. He's the happiest Fuzzy I ever saw, and I never saw any real melancholy Fuzzies. You have a mighty nice Fuzzy, Mr. Grego."

"Well, that's if I'll be allowed to keep him," Grego said.

"My report's going to be very favorable," Khadra told him.

"Of course you will, Mr. Grego. You like the Fuzzy, and he likes you, and he's happy here. That's all I'm interested in."

"I'm afraid Governor Rainsford isn't going to see it like that, Mr. Holloway."

"Governor Rainsford isn't Commissioner of Native Affairs. And he isn't the Federation Courts. The way Judge Pendarvis told me a week ago, the court will accept the advice of the Commission on Fuzzy questions."

"The Attorney-General has a little influence with the court, too," Brannhard said. "The Attorney-General will recommend granting your application for adoption." He rose to his feet. "We don't have anything more to talk about, do we? Then let's go out and see how the Fuzzies are doing."

IX

Gus Brannhard poured coffee into a cup already half full of brandy, brushed his beard out of the way with his left hand, and tasted it. It was good, but he still thought it would be better out of a tin pannikin beside a campfire on Beta. It was time to get down to business; after the bare report while hustling indecently through cocktails, they had talked all around the subject at dinner.

"Well, I can and will bring criminal charges," he assured the others who were having coffee in the drawing room at Government House. "Forcible overpowering and transportation under restraint; if that isn't kidnapping what is it?"

"Try your damnedest to make enslavement out of it, Gus," Jack Holloway said. "If you get a conviction, we can have the pair of them shot. And telecast the executions; a real memorable public example is what we want, right now."

"Well, I got the whole story out of Diamond," Pancho Ybarra said. "He and another Fuzzy met four others; the six of them went down a little stream past a waterfall, and then came to a place where there were two Hagga, the ones he was shown audiovisuals of. The Hagga gave them Extee-Three, and then gave them something out of a bottle. They all woke up with hangovers in what sounds like one of the unfinished rooms in Company House. Diamond got away from them; the two bad Big Ones took the rest away."

"So now we have five Fuzzies to hunt," Holloway said. "That'll be your job, Ahmed. You'll stay here in Mallorysport. We'll promote you to captain and chief of detectives; that'll give you a little status equality with the other enforcement heads around here. If they're trapping Fuzzies for sale, that's not just Native Commission business; that's Federation stuff."

"They probably caught them for Mallin to experiment with," Ben Rainsford said.

Jack swore. "Ben, you haven't been paying attention. All this stuff we got from them was veridicated. They don't know anything about any Fuzzies but those four Gerd and Ruth have."

"Mr. Grego has been cooperating very satisfactorily, Governor," Ahmed Khadra said, stiffly formal. "He has the whole Company police working on it, and told me to call on Chief Steefer for anything, and tomorrow Dr. Jimenez is going out to Beta to show some of our people where he was camping. From the Fuzzy's description, we think Herckerd and Novaes went back there."

"Well, what are you going to do about that Fuzzy at Company House?" he asked Jack, ignoring Khadra's words. "You aren't going to let him stay with Grego, are you?"

"Of course we are. Diamond's happy, and Grego's taking good care of him. I'm going to recommend that Judge Pendarvis issue papers of guardianship to him."

"But it isn't right! Not after all Grego did," Rainsford insisted. "Why, he was going to have all the Fuzzies trapped off for their furs. He took your own Fuzzies away from you. He had Jimenez trap those other four, and let Mallin torture them, ask Ruth about that, and then started the story about the Lurkin girl and turned them loose for the mob to kill. And look how he was trying to make out that you'd just taught your Fuzzies a few tricks and then got me to back up your claim that they were sapient beings . . ."

There, at last and obliquely, Ben had let the cat out.

What he meant was that Grego had tried to accuse him of deliberately engineering a scientific fraud. Well, a scientist would have trouble forgiving that. It was like accusing a soldier of treason or a doctor of malpractice.

"Well, it's my professional opinion," Pancho Ybarra said, "that Grego and Diamond are much attached to each other, and that it would be injustice to both to separate them, and probably psychologically harmful to the Fuzzy. I shall so advise Judge Pendarvis."

"I think that'll be official policy," Holloway said. "When we find Fuzzies and humans living happily together, we have no right to separate them, and we won't."

Rainsford, who had started to fill his pipe, looked up angrily.

"Maybe you forget I'm the Governor; I make the policy. I appointed you . . ."

Jack's white mustache was twitching at the tips; his eyes narrowed. He looked like an elderly and irascible tiger.

"That's right," he said. "You appointed me Commissioner of Native Affairs. Any time you don't like the way I do my job, get yourself a new Commissioner."

"Get yourself a new Attorney-General, too. I'm with Jack on this."

Rainsford dropped his pipe into the tobacco pouch.

"You mean you're all against me? What are you doing, bucking for jobs with the CZC?"

After a crack like that, there were those who would have insisted on continuing the discussion by correspondence and through seconds. With anybody but Ben Rainsford, he would have, himself. He turned to Pancho Ybarra.

"Doctor, as a psychiatrist what is your opinion of that outburst?" he asked.

"I'm not entitled to express an opinion," the Navy psychologist replied. "Governor Rainsford is not my patient."

"You mean, I ought to be somebody's?" Rainsford demanded.

"Well, now that you ask, you're not exactly psychotic, but you're certainly not displaying much sanity on the subject of Victor Grego."

"You think we ought to just sit back and let him do anything he pleases; run the planet the way he did before the Pendarvis Decisions?"

"He didn't do such a bad job, Ben," he said. "I'm beginning to think he did a damn sight better job than you'll do unless you stop playing Hatfields and McCoys and start governing. You have to arrange for elections for delegates, and a constitutional convention. You have to take over and operate all these public services the Company's been relieved of responsibility for when their charter was invalidated. And you'll have to stop this cattle rustling on Beta and Delta Continents, or you'll have a couple of first-class range wars on your hands. And you'd better start thinking about the immigrant rush that's going to hit this planet when the news of the Pendarvis Decisions gets around."

Rainsford, his pipe and tobacco shoved into his side pocket, was on his feet. He'd tried to interrupt a couple of times.

"Oh, to Nifflheim with you!" he cried. "I'm going out and talk to my Fuzzies."

With that, he flung out of the room. For a moment, nobody said anything, then Jack Holloway swore.

"I hope the Fuzzies talk some sense into him. Be damned if I can."

They probably would, if he'd listen to them. They had more sense than he had, at the moment. Ahmed Khadra, who had sat mumchance through the upper-echelon brawl, clattered his cup and saucer.

"Jack, you think we ought to go check in at the hotel?" he asked.

"Nifflheim, no! This isn't Ben Rainsford's private camp, this is Government House," Holloway said. "We work for the Government, too. We have work to do now."

"We'll have to talk to him again." He wasn't looking forward to it with any pleasure. "We have to get some kind of a Fuzzy Code scotchtaped together, and he'll have to okay it. We need special legislation, and till we can get a Colonial Legislature, that'll have to be by executive decree. And you'll have to figure out a way to make Fuzzies available for adoption. You can't break up a black market by shooting a few people for enslavement; you'll have to make it possible for people to get Fuzzies legally, with controls and safeguards, instead of buying them from racketeers."

"I know it, Gus," Jack said. "I've been thinking about it; a regular adoption bureau. But who can I get to handle it? I don't know anybody."

"Well, I know everybody around Central Courts Building." That ought to be enough; Central Courts was like a village, in which everybody knew everybody else. "Maybe Leslie Coombes would help me."

"My God, Gus; don't let Ben hear you say that," Jack implored. "He'd blow up about a hundred megatons. You might just as well talk about getting V-dash-R G-dash-O to help."

"He could help a lot. If we ask him, he would."

"Ruth did a lot of work with juvenile court, on her cover-job," Ybarra mentioned. "There's some kind of a Juvenile Welfare Association . . ."

"Claudette Pendarvis. The Chief Justice's wife. She does a lot about Juvenile Welfare."

"Yes," Ybarra agreed instantly. "I've heard Ruth talk about her. Very favorably, too, and Ruth has a galloping allergy for volunteer do-gooders as a rule."

"She likes Fuzzies," Jack said. "She couldn't stay away from them during the trial. I promised her a pair as soon as I got a nice couple." He got to his feet. "Let's move into one of the offices, where we have a table to work on, and some communication screens. I'll call her now and ask her about it."

"Frederic, may I interrupt?"

Pendarvis turned from the reading-screen and started to lay aside his cigar and rise. Claudette, entering the room, motioned him to keep his seat and advanced to take the low cushion-stool, clasping her hands about her knees and tilting her head back in the same girlish pose he remembered from the long ago days on Baldur when he had been courting her.

"I want to tell you something lovely, Frederic," she began. "Mr. Holloway just called me. He says he has two Fuzzies for me, a boy Fuzzy and a girl Fuzzy; he's going to have them brought in tomorrow or the next day."

"Well, that is lovely." Claudette was crazy about Fuzzies. Had been ever since the first telecasts of them, and she had watched them in court and visited them at the Hotel Mallory during the trial. Now that he considered, he would like a pair of Fuzzies too. "I think I'll enjoy having them here as much as you will. I like Fuzzies, as long as they stay out of my courtroom."

They both laughed, remembering what seventeen Fuzzies and a Baby Fuzzy had done to the dignity of the court while their sapience was being debated.

"I hope this won't be regarded as special privilege though," he added. "A great many people want Fuzzies, and . . ."

"But other people can have Fuzzies, too. That was what Mr. Holloway was calling me about. They'll be made available for adoption, and he wants me to supervise it, to make sure they don't get into wrong hands and aren't mistreated."

That was something else. They'd both have to think about that carefully.

"You think it would be proper for you to have an official position like that?" he asked.

"I can't see why not. I'm doing the same kind of work with Juvenile Welfare."

"You'll be making decisions on who should and who should not be allowed to adopt Fuzzies. When I get a Native Cases Court set up—I think Yves Janiver, for that—your decisions will be accepted."

"Whose decisions do you think Adolphe Ruiz's Juvenile Court accepts now?"

"That's right," he agreed. And she couldn't accept the Fuzzies and refuse to help with the adoption bureau; that wouldn't be right, at all. And she wanted Fuzzies so badly. "Well, go ahead, darling; do it. Whoever takes that position will have to be somebody who really loves Fuzzies. What did you tell Mr. Holloway?"

"That I'd talk to you, and then call him back. He's at Government House now."

"Well, call him and tell him you accept. I'll call Yves and talk to him about the Native Cases Court . . ."

She had left the low seat while he was speaking; she stopped to kiss him on the way out. She'd be so happy. He hoped he wouldn't be too severely criticized. Well, he'd been criticized before and survived it.

Victor Grego watched Diamond investigating the articles on top of the low cocktail table. He took a couple of salted nuts from the glass bowl, nibbled one, and put the rest back. He looked at the half-full coffee cup and the liqueur glass, and left both alone. Then he started to pick up the ashtray.

"No, Diamond. *Vov.* Don't touch."

"*Vov ninta*, Diamond," Ernst Mallin, who was a slightly more advanced Fuzzy linguist, said. "We ought to learn their language, instead of making them learn ours."

"We ought to teach them our language, so they can speak to anybody, and not just Fuzzyologists."

"I deplore that term, Mr. Grego. The suffix is Greek, from logos. Fuzzy is not a Greek word, and should not be combined with it."

"Oh, rubbish, Ernst. We're not speaking Greek; we're speaking Lingua Terra. You know what Lingua Terra is? An indiscriminate mixture of English, Spanish, Portuguese and Afrikaans, mostly English. And you know what English is? The result of the efforts of Norman men-at-arms to make dates with Saxon barmaids in the Ninth Century Pre-Atomic, and no more legitimate than any of the other results. If a little Greek suffix gets into a mess like that, it'll have to take care of itself the best way it can. And you'd better learn to like the term, because it's your new title. Chief Fuzzyologist; fifteen percent salary increase."

Mallin gave one of his tight little smiles. "For that, I believe I can condone a linguistic barbarism."

Diamond seemed, he couldn't be sure, to be wanting to know why not touch; would it hurt?

"And how do you explain that he mustn't spill ashes on the floor, in his own language? What are the Fuzzy words for 'floor,' and 'ashes?'" He leaned forward and dropped the ash from his cigarette into the tray. "Ashtray," he said.

Diamond repeated it as well as he could. Then he strolled over to where Mallin sat. Mallin regarded smoking as an act of infantile oralism; his ashtray was empty.

"*Asht'ay?*" he asked. "*Diamond vov ninta?*"

"You see. He knows that ashtray is a class-word, not just the name of a specific object," Mallin said. "And I tried so hard to prove that Fuzzies couldn't generalize. This one is empty; let's see how we can explain the difference. If we give him the word 'ashes,' and then . . ."

A bell began ringing softly; Diamond turned quickly to see what it was. It was the bell for the private communication screen, and only half a dozen people knew the call-combination. He rose and put it on. Harry Steefer looked out of it.

"We found it, sir; ninth level down." That was the one below the first reported thefts and ransackings.

"The Fuzzies were penned in a small room that looks as though it had been intended for a general toilet and washroom. It's right off a main hall, and somebody's had an aircar in and out and set it down recently. I'd say half a dozen Fuzzies for two or three days."

"Good. I want to see it. I want Diamond to see it, too. Send somebody who knows where it is up to my private stage with a car small enough to get into it."

He blanked the screen and turned to Mallin. "You heard that. Well, let's all three of us go down and look at it." Jack Holloway stopped at the head of the long escalator and looked down into the garden, now doublelighted by Darius, almost full, and Xerxes, past full and just rising. After a moment he saw Ben Rainsford reclining in a lawn-chair, with Flora and Fauna snuggled together on his lap. As he started toward them, after descending, he thought they were all asleep. Then one of the Fuzzies stirred and yeeked, and Rainsford turned his head.

"Who is it?" he asked.

"Jack. Have you been here all evening?"

"Yes, all three of us," Rainsford said. "I think it's time for Fuzzies to go to bed, now."

"Ben, we just had a screen call from Company House. They found where those Fuzzies had been kept, an empty room on one of the unfinished floors. They showed us with a portable pickup; dark, filthy place. The Company police are working on it for physical evidence to corroborate Diamond's story. And they've put out a general want for those two Company rangers, Herckerd and Novaes; kidnapping and suspicion of enslavement."

"Who called you? Steefer?"

"Grego. He says we can count on him for anything. He's really sore about this."

The Fuzzies had jumped to the ground and were trying to attract his attention. Ben shifted in his chair, and began stuffing tobacco into his pipe.

"Jack." His voice was soft; he spoke hesitantly. "I've

been talking to the kids, out here, till they got sleepy. They had a big time at Company House with Diamond. They say he's lonesome for other Fuzzies. They'd like him to come here and visit them, and they'd like to go back and visit him again."

"Well, a Fuzzy would get lonesome by himself. It didn't take Little Fuzzy long to go and bring the rest of his family into my place."

"And they say that outside that he's happy. They told me about all the nice things he had, and the garden, and the room that was fixed up for him. They say everybody's good to him, and Pappy Vic loves him. That's what they call Grego; Pappy Vic, just like they call us Pappy Ben and Pappy Jack." His lighter flared, showing a puzzled face above the pipe bowl. "I can't understand it, Jack. I thought Grego would hate Fuzzies."

"Why should he? The Fuzzies didn't know anything about the Company's charter; they don't know a Class-IV planet from Nifflheim. He doesn't even hate us; he'd have done the same thing in our place. Ben, he's willing to call the war off; why can't you?"

Rainsford puffed slowly, the smoke drifting and changing color in the double moonlight.

Do you honestly believe that Fuzzy wants to stay with Grego?" he asked.

"It'd break Diamond's heart if you took him away from Pappy Vic. Ben, why don't you invite Diamond over to play with your two? You wouldn't have to meet Grego; the girl he has helping with Diamond could bring him."

"Maybe I will. You're on speaking terms with Grego; why don't you?"

"I will, tomorrow." The Fuzzies hadn't wanted to play; they'd just wanted to be noticed. He picked Flora up and gave her to Ben, then took Fauna in his own arms. "Let's go put them to bed, and then go inside. We have a lot of things to do, in a hurry, and we need your authorization."

"Well, what?"

"Ahmed's staying here; he and Harry Steefer and Ian Ferguson and some others are having a conference tomorrow on this case and on general Fuzzy protection. And I'm setting up an Adoption Bureau; Judge Pendarvis' wife's agreed to take charge of that. We need laws, and till there's some kind of a legislature, you have to do that by decree."

"Well, all right. But there's one thing, Jack. Just because Grego's with us on this doesn't mean I'm going to let him grab back control of this planet, the way he had it before the Pendarvis Decisions. It took the Fuzzies to break the Company's monopoly; well, I'm going to see it stays broken."

X

Knowing Henry Stenson's part in the dischartering of the Zarathustra Company, Pancho Ybarra was mildly surprised to find him in the Fuzzy-room Grego had fitted up back of the kitchenette of his apartment, when Ernst Mallin, who met him on the landing stage, ushered him in. Grego's Fuzzy-sitter, Sandra Glenn, was there, and so, although in the middle of business hours, was Grego himself. And, of course, Diamond.

"Mr. Stenson," he greeted non-committally. "This is a pleasure."

Stenson laughed. "We needn't pretend to distant acquaintance, Lieutenant," he said. "Mr. Grego is quite aware of my, er, other profession. He doesn't hold it against me; he just insists that I no longer practice it on him."

"Mr. Stenson has something here that'll interest you," Grego said, picking up something that looked like a small nuclear-electric razor. "Turn off your hearing aid, if you please, Lieutenant. Thank you. Now, Diamond, make talk for Unka Panko."

"*Heyo, Unka Panko.*" Diamond said, when Grego held the thing to his mouth, very clearly and audibly. "You hear Diamond make talk like Hagga?"

"I sure do, Diamond! That's wonderful."

"How make do?" Diamond asked. "Make talk with talk-thing, talk like Hagga. Not have talk-thing, no can talk like Fuzzy, Hagga no hear. How make do?"

Fuzzies could hear all through the human-audibility

range; the race wouldn't have survived the dangers of the woods if they hadn't been able to. They could hear beyond that, to about 40,000 cycles. None of the other Zarathustran mammals could; that supported Gerd van Riebeek's theory that Fuzzies were living fossils, the sole survivors of a large and otherwise extinct order of Zarathustran quasi-primates. Gerd thought they had developed ultrasonic hearing to meet some ancient survival-problem long before they had developed the power of symbolizing ideas in speech, and had always conversed ultrasonically with one another, probably to avoid betraying themselves to their natural enemies.

"Fuzzies hear Big Ones talk. Fuzzies little, Hagga big, make big talk. Hagga not hear Fuzzy talk, Fuzzies little, make little talk. So, Big Ones make ear-things, make Fuzzy talk big in ears, can hear. Now, Hagga make talk-things, so Fuzzies make big talk like Hagga, everybody hear, have ear-things, not have ear-things."

That wasn't the question. Diamond had gotten that far, himself, already. The question, which he repeated, was, "How make do?"

Grego was grinning at him. "You're doing fine, Lieutenant. Now, go ahead and give him a lecture on ultrasonics and electronics and acoustics."

"Has your Chief Fuzzyologist done anything on that yet?"

"I haven't even tried," Mallin said. "You know much more of the language than I do; what Fuzzy words would you use to explain anything like that?"

That was right. Any race—*Homo sapiens terra*, or *Fuzzy fuzzy holloway zarathustra*—thought just as far as their verbal symbolism went, and no further. And they could only comprehend ideas for which they had words.

"Just tell him it's Terran black magic," Sandra Glenn suggested.

That would work on planets like Loki or Thor or Yggdrasil; on Shesha or Uller, you could also mention the mysterious ways of the gods. The Fuzzies had just about as much conception of magic or religion as they had of electronics or nucleonics or the Abbot lift-and-drive.

He stooped forward and held out his hand. "*So-josso-aki*, Diamond. *So-pokko* Unka Panko."

The Fuzzy gave him the thing, which he had been holding in both hands. The resemblance to an electric razor was more than coincidental; the mechanism was enclosed in the plastic case of one. The end that would have done the shaving was open; the Fuzzy talked into that. There was a circular screened opening on the side from which the transformed sound emerged. It still had the original thumb-switch.

"Still has the original power-unit, too," Stenson said. That would be a little capsule the size of a 6-mm short pistol cartridge. "A lot of the parts are worked over from ultrasonic hearing-aid parts. I'm going to have to do something better than that switch, too. A little handle, maybe like a pistol grip, with a grip-squeeze switch, so that the Fuzzy will turn it on when he takes hold of it, and turn it off when he lets go. And it'll have to be a lot lighter and a lot smaller." He gestured toward some sheets of paper on which he had been making diagrams and schematics and notes. "I have some people at my shop working on that now. We'll have production prototypes in about a week. The Company's factory will start production as soon as they can tool up for it."

"We're getting a patent," Grego said. "We're calling it the Stenson Fuzzyphone."

"Grego-Stenson; it was your original idea."

"Hell, I just told you what I wanted; you invented it," Grego argued. "As soon as we have all the bugs chased out, we'll be in production. We don't know how much we'll have to ask for them. Not more than twenty sols, I don't suppose."

Flora and Fauna were puzzled. They sat on the floor at Pappy Ben's feet, looking up at the funny people that came and went in the picture-thing on the wall and spoke out of it. Long ago they had found out that nothing in the screen could get out of it, and they couldn't get in. It was just one of the strange things the Big Ones had, and they couldn't understand it, but it was fun.

But then, all of a sudden, there was Pappy Ben, right in the screen. They looked around, startled, thinking he had left them, but no, there he was, still in the chair smoking his pipe. They both felt him to make sure he was really there, then they both climbed onto his lap and pointed at the Pappy Ben in the screen.

Flora and Fauna didn't know about audiovisual recordings; they couldn't understand how Pappy Ben could be in two places at the same time. That bothered them. It just couldn't happen.

"It's all right, kids," he assured them. "I'm really here. That isn't me, there."

"Is," Flora contradicted. "I see it."

"Is not," Fauna told her. "Pappy Ben here."

Maybe Pancho Ybarra or Ruth van Riebeek could explain it; he couldn't.

"Of course I'm here," he said, hugging both of them. "That is just not-real look-like."

"It will be illegal," the Pappy Ben in the screen was saying, "to capture any Fuzzy in habitat by any other means, including the use of intoxicants, narcotics, sleepgas, sono-stunners or traps. This will constitute kidnapping. It will be illegal to keep any Fuzzy chained, tied or otherwise physically restrained. It will be illegal to transport any Fuzzy from Beta Continent to any other part of this planet without a permit from the Native Affairs Commission, each permit to bear the fingerprints of the Fuzzy for whom it is issued. It will be illegal knowingly to deliver any Fuzzy to anybody intending to so transport him. This will constitute kidnapping, also, and will be punished accordingly."

The Pappy Ben in the screen was scowling menacingly. Flora and Fauna looked quickly around to see if the real Pappy Ben was mad about something too.

Flora said: "Make talk about Fuzzy."

"Yes. Talk about what Big Ones do to bad Big Ones who hurt Fuzzies," he told her.

"Make dead, like bad Big One who make Goldilocks dead?" Fauna asked.

"Something like that."

That was what all the Fuzzies who had been in court during the trial thought had happened. Suicide while of unsound mind due to remorse of conscience was a little too complicated to explain to a Fuzzy, at least at present.

All the Fuzzies who knew what had happened to Goldilocks thought that had been no more than the bad Big One deserved.

Captain Ahmed Khadra, chief of detectives, ZNPF, and Colonel Ian Ferguson, Commandant, Colonial Constabulary, were listening to the telecast with Max Fane, the Colonial Marshal, in the latter's office. In the screen, Governor Rainsford was saying:

"And any person capturing or illegally transporting or illegally holding in restraint any Fuzzy for purposes of sale will be guilty of enslavement."

"Aah!" Max Fane set a stiffly extended index finger against the base of his skull, cocked his thumb and clicked his tongue. "Death's mandatory; no discretion-of-the-court about it."

"Yves Janiver'll try all the Fuzzy cases. He likes Fuzzies," Ferguson said: "He won't like people who mistreat them."

"I know Janiver's attitude on death penalties," Fane said. "He doesn't think people should be shot for committing crimes; he thinks they should be shot for being the kind of people who commit them. He thinks shooting criminals is like shooting diseased veldbeest. A sanitation measure. So do I."

"If Herckerd and Novaes are smart, they'll come in and surrender now," Ferguson said. "You think they still have the other five?"

Khadra shook his head. "I think they sold them to somebody in Mallorysport as soon as they moved them out of Company House. If we could find out who that is..."

"I could name a dozen possibilities," Max Fane told him. "And back of each one of them is Hugo Ingermann."

"I wish we could haul Ingermann in and veridicate him," Ferguson said.

"Well, you can't. Ingermann's a lawyer, and the only way you can question a lawyer under veridication is catch him standing over a corpse with a bloody knife in his hand. And you have a Nifflheim of a time doing it, even then."

"A great many people want Fuzzies; we know that," the Governor was saying. "Many of them should have them; they would make Fuzzies happy, and would be made happy by them. We are not going to deny such people an opportunity to adopt these charming little persons. An adoption bureau has been set up already; Mrs. Frederic Pendarvis, the wife of the Chief Justice, will be in charge of it, and the offices have already been set up in the Central Courts Building, and will open tomorrow morning..."

"Oh, Daddy; Mother!" the little girl cried. "You hear that, now. The Governor says people can have Fuzzies of their own. Won't you get me a Fuzzy? I'll be as good as good to it—him, I mean, or her, whichever."

The parents looked at one another, and then at their twelve-year-old daughter.

"What do you think, Bob?"

"You'll have to take care of it, Marjory, and that will be a lot of work. You'll have to feed it, and give it baths, and..."

"Oh, I will; I'll do anything, just if I can have one. And people mustn't call Fuzzies 'it,' Daddy; Fuzzies are people, too, like us. You didn't call me 'it,' when

I was a little baby, did you?"

"I'm afraid your father did, my dear. Just at first. And you'll have to study and learn the language, so you can talk to the Fuzzy, because Fuzzies don't speak Lingua Terra. You know, Bob, I think I'd enjoy having a Fuzzy around, myself."

"You know, I believe I would, too. Well, let's get around to this adoption bureau the first thing tomorrow . . ."

XI

They were having a party at the Pendarvis home. Jack Holloway sat on his heels on the floor, smoking his pipe and interpreting, while the judge and his wife, in a low easy-chair and on a drum-shaped hassock respectively, were getting acquainted with the guests of honor, the two Fuzzies Juan Jimenez had brought in from Beta Continent that evening. Gus Brannhard, who had come along from Government House, was sprawled in one of the larger chairs, chuckling in his beard. Juan Jimenez and Ahmed Khadra had removed their hearing-aids and carried their drinks to the other side of the room, where they were talking about Jimenez's visit, with a couple of George Lunt's troopers, to the site of his former camp.

"They were back, after we left," Jimenez was saying. "We could see where they'd set a car down. There wasn't much to see; they policed everything up very neatly after they left, the second time. Didn't leave any litter around."

"Or any evidence," Khadra added.

"That was what Yorimitsu and Calderon said when they saw it. I gather they take a dim view of neatness."

"Around where they're investigating, sure. Tidying up around the scene of a crime's gotten more criminals off than all the crooked lawyers in the Galaxy. In this case it doesn't matter. Herckerd and Novaes brought those Fuzzies in; we know that. We have a witness."

"Can you veridicate a Fuzzy?" Brannhard asked,

over his shoulder. "If you can't, the defense'll object."

Pendarvis looked up and around. "Mr. Brannhard, I'm afraid I'd have to sustain such an objection. I suspect that Judge Janiver, who'd be hearing the case, would, too. If I were you, I'd find out. Have you ever been veridicated?" he asked the Fuzzy on his lap.

The Fuzzy—the male member of the couple, who was trying to work the zipper of his jacket—said, "Unnh?" The judge scratched the back of his head, which the Fuzzy, like most furry people, liked, and wondered how long it would take to learn the language.

"Not too long," Jack told him. "It only took me a day to learn everything the people on Xerxes learned; by the time we were starting for home, after the trial, I could talk to them. What are you going to call them?"

"Don't they have names of their own, Mr. Holloway?" the judge's wife asked.

"They don't seem to. In the woods, there are never more than six or eight in a family, if that's what the groups are. I guess all the natives names are things like 'me,' and 'you,' and 'this one,' and 'that one.'"

"You'll have to have names for them, for the adoption papers," Brannhard said.

"At the camp, we just called them 'the Newlyweds,'" Khadra said.

"How about Pierrot and Columbine?" Mrs. Pendarvis asked.

Her husband nodded. "I think that would be fine." He pointed to himself. "*Aki Pappy Frederic. So Pierrot.*"

"*Aki Py'hot? Py'hot siggo Pappy F'ed'ik.*"

"He accepts the name. He says he likes you. What are you going to do with them tomorrow, Mrs. Pendarvis? Do you have any human servants here?"

"No, everything's robotic, and I oughtn't to leave them alone with robots. Not till they get used to them."

"Drop them off at Government House; they can play with Flora and Fauna," Brannhard suggested. "And

I'll call Victor Grego and invite his Diamond over, and they can have a real party. First Fuzzy social event of the season."

A mellow-toned bell began chiming. The Judge set Pierrot on the floor and excused himself; Pierrot trotted after him. In a moment, both were back.

"Chief Earlie's on screen," he said. "He wants to talk either to Captain Khadra or Mr. Holloway."

That was the new Mallorysport chief of police. Jack nodded to Khadra, who left the room.

"Probably found something out about Herckerd and Novaes," Brannhard said.

"Will you really charge them with enslavement?" Mrs. Pendarvis asked. "That's mandatory death."

"You catch people, deprive them of their freedom, make property of them," Brannhard said. "What else can you call it? A pet slave is still a slave, if he belongs to somebody else. I don't know how a Fuzzy could be made to work . . ."

"Nightclub entertainers, attractions in bars, sideshow acts . . ."

Khadra came back; he had his beret on, and was buckling on his pistol.

"Earlie says he has a report on a Fuzzy being seen in an apartment-unit over on the north side of the city," he said. "Informant says a Fuzzy is being kept by a family on one of the upper floors. He's sending men there now."

That would probably be one of the five Herckerd and Novaes had brought in. He could see what had happened. The two former Company employees had sold them all to somebody here in Mallorysport, some racketeer who was selling them individually. There was somebody who really did need shooting. And by this time, Herckerd and Novaes would be back on Beta Continent, trapping more. Get the people who had bought this Fuzzy under veridication, the police had plenty of ways to make people want to talk, and work back from there.

"I'll go see what it is," Khadra was saying. "I'll call in as soon as I can. I don't know how long I'll be gone. In case I don't get back, thanks for a nice evening, Judge, Mrs. Pendarvis."

He hurried out, and for a moment nobody said anything. Then Jimenez suggested that if this were one of the Herckerd-Novaes lot, Diamond ought to see him as soon as possible; he'd be able to identify him. Khadra would think of that. Mrs. Pendarvis hoped there wouldn't be any shooting. Mallorysport city police were notoriously trigger-happy. The conversation continued by jerks and starts; the two Fuzzies seemed to be the only ones unconcerned.

After about an hour, Khadra returned; he had left his belt and beret in the hall.

"What was it?" Brannhard asked. Jack was wanting to know if the Fuzzy was all right.

"It wasn't a Fuzzy," Khadra said disgustedly. "It was a Terran marmoset; these people have had it for a couple of years; brought it from Terra. The people who own it have had a wire screen around their terrace to keep it, ever since they moved in. Somebody in an aircar saw it outside and thought it was a Fuzzy. I wonder how much more of this we're going to get."

It was a wonder he hadn't gotten that, himself, when his own family were lost and he was hunting for them.

XII

The air traffic around Central Courts Building the next morning seemed normal to Jack Holloway. There were quite a few cars on the landing stage above the sixth level down when he came in, but no more than he remembered from the time of the Fuzzy Trial. It was not until he left the escalator on the fourth floor below, where the Adoption Bureau offices were, that he began to suspect that there was a Fuzzy rush on.

The corridor leading back from the main hall to the suite that had been taken over yesterday was jammed. It was a well behaved, well dressed, crowd, mostly couples clinging to each other to avoid being jostled apart. Everybody seemed to be happy and excited; it was more like a Year-End Holidays shopping crowd than anything else.

A uniformed deputy-marshal saw him and approached, touching his cap-brim in a half salute.

"Mr. Holloway; are you trying to get in to your offices? You'd better come this way, sir; there's a queue down at the other end."

There must be five or six hundred of them. Cut that in half; most of them were couples.

"How long's this been going on?" he asked, noticing that several more couples and individuals were coming behind him.

"Since about 0700. There were a few here before then; the big rush didn't start till 0830."

Some of the people in the rear of the jam saw and

recognized him. "Holloway." "Jack Holloway; he's the Commissioner." "Mr. Holloway; are there Fuzzies here now?"

The deputy took him down the hall and unlocked the door of an office; it was empty, and the desks and chairs and things shrouded in dust-covers. They went through and out into a back hall, where another deputy-marshal was arguing with some people who were trying to get in that way.

"Well, why are they letting him in; who's he?" a woman demanded.

"He works here. That's Jack Holloway."

"Oh! Mr. Holloway! Can you tell us how soon we can get Fuzzies?"

His guide rushed him, almost as though he were under arrest, along the hall, and opened another door.

"In here, Mr. Holloway; Mrs. Pendarvis' office. I'll have to get back and keep that mob in front straightened out." He touched his cap-brim again and hastened away.

Mrs. Pendarvis sat at a desk, her back to the door, going over a stack of forms in front of her. Beside her, at a smaller desk, a girl was taking them as she finished with them, and talking into the whisper-mouthpiece of a vocowriter. Two more girls sat at another desk, one talking to somebody in a communication screen. Mrs. Pendarvis said, "Who is it?" and turned her head, then rose, extending her hand. "Oh; Mr. Holloway. Good morning. What's it like out in the hall, now?"

"Well, you see how I had to come in. I'd say about five hundred, now. How are you handling them?"

She gestured toward the door to the front office, and he opened it and looked through. Five girls sat at five desks; each was interviewing applicants. Another girl was gathering up application-forms and carrying them to a desk where they were being sorted to be passed on to the back office.

"I arrived at 0830," Mrs. Pendarvis said. "Just after I dropped Pierrot and Columbine off at Government

House. There was a crowd then, and it's been going on ever since. How many Fuzzies have you, Mr. Holloway?"

"Available for adoption? I don't know. Beside mine and Gerd and Ruth van Riebeek's and the Constabulary Fuzzies, there were forty day-before yesterday. That had gotten up to a hundred and three by last evening."

"We have, to date, three hundred and eleven applications; there are possibly twenty more that haven't been sent back to me yet. By the time we close, it'll be five or six hundred. How are we going to handle this, anyhow? Some of these people want just one Fuzzy, some of them want two, some of them will take a whole family. And we can't separate Fuzzies who want to stay together. If you'd separate Pierrot and Columbine, they'd both grieve themselves to death. And there are families of five or six who want to stay together, aren't there?"

"Well, not permanently. These groups aren't really families; they're sort of temporary gangs for mutual assistance. Five or six are about as many as can make a living together in the woods. They're hunters and food-gatherers, low Paleolithic economy, and individual smallgame hunters at that. When a gang gets too big to live together, they split up; when one couple meets another, they team up to hunt together. That's why they have such a well-developed and uniform language, and I imagine that's how the news about the zatku spread all over the Fuzzy country as fast as it did. They don't even mate permanently. Your pair are just young, first mating for both of them. They think each other are the most wonderful ever. But you will have others that won't want to be separated; you'll have to let them be adopted together." He thought for a moment. "You can't begin to furnish Fuzzies for everybody; why don't you give them out by lot? Each of those applications is numbered, isn't it? Draw numbers."

"Like a jury-drawing, of course. Let the jury-commissioners handle that," the Chief Justice's wife said.

"Fair enough. You'll have to investigate each of these applicants, of course; that'll take a little time, won't it?"

"Well, Captain Khadra's taking charge of them. He's borrowed some people from the schools, and some from the city police juvenile squad and some from the Company personnel division. I've been getting my staff together the same way—parent-teacher groups, Juvenile Welfare. I'm going to get a paid staff together, as soon as I can. I think they'll come from the Company's public-service division; I'm told that Mr. Grego's going to suspend all those activities in ninety days."

"That's right. That includes the schools, and the hospitals. Why don't you talk to Ernst Mallin? He'll find you all the people you want. He's joined the Friends of Little Fuzzy, too, now."

"Well, after we've allocated Fuzzies to these people, what then? Do they come out to your camp and pick their own?"

"Good Lord, no! We have enough trouble, without having the place overrun with human people." He hadn't given that thought until now. "What we'll need will be a place here in Mallorysport where a couple of hundred Fuzzies can stay and where the people who have been endorsed for foster-parents can come and select the ones they want."

That would have to be a big place, with a park all around it, that could be fenced in to keep them from wandering off and getting lost. A nice place, where they could all have fun together. He didn't know of any such place, and asked her about it.

"I'll talk to Mr. Urswick, he's the Company Chief of Public Services. He'll know about something. You know, Mr. Holloway, I didn't have any idea, when I took this job, that it was going to be so complicated."

"Mrs. Pendarvis, I've been saying that every hour

on the hour since I let Ben Rainsford talk me into taking the job I have. You're going to have to do something about information, too—Fuzzies, care and feeding of; Fuzzies, psychology of; language. We'll try to find somebody to prepare booklets and language-learning tapes. And hearing-aids."

The door at the side of the room was marked INVESTIGATION. He found Ahmed Khadra in the room behind it, talking to somebody in a city police uniform by screen.

"Well, have you gotten anything from any of them?" he was asking.

"Damn little," the city policeman told him. "We've been pulling them in all day, everybody in town who has a record. And Hugo Ingermann's been pulling them away from us as fast as they come in. He had a couple of his legmen and assistants here with portable radios, and as fast as we bring some punk in, they call somebody at Central Courts and he gets a writ; order to show grounds for suspicion. Most of them we can't question at all; it takes an hour to an hour and a half from the time they're brought in before we can veridicate those we can. And none of them knows a damn thing when we do."

"Well, how about known associates? Didn't either of them have any friends?"

"Yes. All middle-salary Company people; they've been cooperating, but none of them know anything."

The conversation went on for a few more minutes, then they blanked screens. Khadra turned in his chair and lit a cigarette.

"Well, you heard it, Jack," he said. "They just vanished, and the Fuzzies with them. I'm not surprised we're not getting anything out of their friends in the Company. They wouldn't know. We searched their rooms; they seem to have cleaned out everything they had when they disappeared. And we can't get anything from underworld sources. None of the city police stool-pigeons know anything."

"You know, Ahmed, I'm worried about that. I wonder what's happened to those Fuzzies..." He sat down on the edge of the desk and got out his pipe and tobacco. "How soon will you be able to start investigating these people who want Fuzzies?"

Gerd van Riebeek refilled his cup and shoved the coffee across the table to George Lunt. He ought to be getting back to work; they both ought to. Work was piling up, with both Jack and Pancho away and Ahmed Khadra permanently detached from duty at the camp.

"Eighty-seven," Lunt said. "That's not counting yours and mine and Jack's."

"The Extee Three's getting low." They'd had to start rationing it; tomorrow, they'd not be able to issue any, or on alternate days thereafter. The Fuzzies wouldn't like that. "Jack says he thinks speculators are buying it and holding it off the market. They'll get big prices for it when the Fuzzies start coming in to Mallorysport."

There wasn't much Extee Three on Zarathustra. People kept a tin or so in their aircars, in case of forced landings in the wilderness which was ninety percent of the planet's land surface, but until the Fuzzies found out about it, the consumption had been practically zero. There was a supply on Xerxes, for emergency ships' stores, individual survival kits and so on, but that wouldn't last. It was on order, but it would be four months till any could get in from the nearest Federation planet. And the supply on hand wouldn't last that long.

"Personally, I wish there was eighty-seven hundred of them," Lunt said. "No, I'm not crazy, and I mean it. The ones we have here aren't getting into deviltry down in the farming country. So far, I haven't heard of any of them getting that far, except that one family that's moved in on the backwoods farm, and they're behaving themselves. But wait till they get down in the real farm-country, and among the sugar plantations. You know, Jack and I thought, at first, that our big job was going to be protecting Fuzzies from humans. It looks to me, now, like it's going to be the other way round too."

"That's right. They won't mean any harm; the only malicious thing I ever heard of Fuzzies doing was the time Jack's family wrecked Juan Jimenez's office, after they broke out of the cages he put them in, and I don't blame them for that. But they just don't understand about what they mustn't do among humans. They don't seem to have any idea at all of property in the absence of a visible owner."

"That's what I'm talking about. Crops; they won't understand that somebody's planted them, they'll think they're just there. And I never saw a farmer that wouldn't shoot first and argue afterward to protect his crops."

"Education," Gerd said.

"Recipe for roast turkey—first catch a turkey," Lunt said. "We're educating this crowd. How in Nifflheim are we going to catch all the other ones?"

"Educate the farmers. What do Fuzzies eat, beside Extee Three?"

"Zatku, and they've cleaned all of them out around the camp. That's why we have to have one car patroling a couple of miles out to shoot harpies off."

"And do you know any kind of crops land-prawns don't destroy? I was making a study of them, for a while. I don't. That's what I mean by educating the farmers. A Fuzzy does X-much damage to crops. He kills half a dozen land-prawns a day, and among them they do about X-times-ten damage."

"Write up a script about it, and we'll put it on the air this evening. 'Be good to Fuzzies; Fuzzies are the farmer's best friend.' Maybe that'll help some."

Gerd nodded. "Eighty-seven, we have now. How many little ones?"

"Beside Baby Fuzzy? Four. Why?"

"And we think we have five pregnancies. That's all Lynne Andrews is sure of; the only way she can tell is listening with a stethoscope for fetal movements. They seem to be too small to make any conspicuous visible difference. This is out of eighty seven. What kind of a birthrate do you call that, George?"

George Lunt poured more coffee into his cup and blew on it automatically. Somewhere, maybe Constabulary School, the coffee had always been too hot to drink right away. Across the messhall, half a dozen Fuzzies tagged behind a robot, watching it clear the tables.

"It sure to Nifflheim isn't any population explosion," he said.

"Race extinction, George. I don't know what the normal life expectancy is in the woods, but I'd say four out of five of them die by violence. When the birthrate curve drops below the deathrate curve, a race is dying out."

"A hundred and two Fuzzies, and four children. Hey, you said five of the girls were pregnant, didn't you? And you admit that's not complete, if Doc Andrews has to use a stethoscope for a pregnancy-test."

"I wondered if you'd notice that. That's not a bad ratio, for females who have a monthly cycle instead of an annual mating season. And these four children; we don't know anything about the maturation period, but in the three months we've been checking on him, Baby Fuzzy's only gained six ounces and an inch. I'd make it about fifteen years, ten at very least."

"Then," Lunt said, "it isn't birthrate at all. It's infant mortality. They just don't live."

"That's it, George. That's what I'm worried about. And Ruth and Lynne, too. If we don't find out what causes it, and how to stop it, there won't be any Fuzzies after a while."

"This is like old times, Victor," Coombes said, stretching in one of the chairs. "Nobody here but us humans."

"That's right." He brought the jug and the two glasses over and put them on the low table, careful not to disturb a pattern of colored tiles laid on one end of it. "That thing there is a Fuzzy work of art. It is unfinished, but just see the deep symbolic significance."

"You see it. I can't." Coombes accepted his glass with mechanical thanks and sipped. "Where is everybody?"

"Diamond is a guest, at a place where I'm not welcome. Government House. He and Flora and Fauna are meeting Pierrot and Columbine, Judge and Mrs. Pendarvis' Fuzzies. Sandra is chaperoning the affair, and Ernst is conferring with Mrs. Pendarvis about quarters for a couple of hundred Fuzzies who are coming to town in about a week to be adopted."

"I'll say this: your Fuzzy and Fuzzyologists are getting in with the right people. Did you hear Hugo Ingermann's telecast this afternoon?"

"I did not. I pay people to do that kind of work for me. I went over a semantically correct summary, with a symbolic-logic study. As nearly as I can interpret it, it reduces to the propositions that, A) Ben Rainsford is a bigger crook than Victor Grego, and, B) Victor Grego is a bigger crook than Ben Rainsford, and, C) between them, they are conspiring to rob and enslave everybody on the planet, Fuzzies included."

"I listened to it very carefully, and recorded it, in the hope that he might forget himself and say something actionable. He didn't; he's lawyer enough to know what's libel and what isn't. Sometimes I dream of being able to sue that bastard for something, so that I can get him in the stand under veridication, but . . ." He shrugged.

"I noticed one thing. He's attacking the Company, and he's attacking Rainsford, but at the same time he's trying to drive wedges between us, so we won't gang up on him."

"Yes. That spaceport proposition. Why doesn't our honest and upright Governor do something to end this infamous space-transport monopoly of the Company's, which is strangling the economy of the planet?"

"Well, why doesn't he? Because it would cost about fifty million sols, and ships using it would have to load and unload from orbit. But that sounds like a real live issue to the people who don't think and have nothing to think with, which means a large majority of the voters. You know what I'm worried about, Leslie? Ingermann attacking Rainsford for collusion with the Company. He hammers at that point long enough, and Rainsford's going to do something to prove he isn't, and what ever it is, it'll hurt us."

"That's the way it looks to me, too," Coombes agreed. "You know, among the many benefits of the Pendarvis Decisions, we now have a democratic government on Zarathustra. That means, we now have politics here. Ingermann controls all the other rackets, and politics is the biggest racket there is. Hugo Ingermann is running himself for political boss of Zarathustra."

XIII

The aircar settled to the ground; the Marine sergeant at the controls, who had been expecting to smash a dozen or so Fuzzies getting down, gave a whoosh of relief. Pancho Ybarra opened the door and motioned his companion, in Marine field-greens, to precede him, then stepped to the ground. George Lunt, still in his slightly altered Constabulary uniform, and Gerd van Riebeek, in bush-jacket and field-boots, advanced to meet them, accompanied by a swarm of Fuzzies. They all greeted him enthusiastically, and then wanted to know where Pappy Jack was.

"Pappy Jack in Big House Place; not come this place with Unka Panko. Pappy Jack come this place soon; two lights-and-darks," he told them. "Pappy Jack have to make much talk with other Big Ones."

"Make talk about Fuzzies?" Little Fuzzy wanted to know. "Find Big Ones for all Fuzzies?"

"That's right. Find place for Fuzzies to go in Big House Place," he said.

"He's been on that ever since Jack went away," Gerd said. "All the Fuzzies are going to have Big Ones of their own, now."

"Well, Jack's working on it," he said. "You've both met Captain Casagra, haven't you? Gerd van Riebeek; Major Lunt. The captain's staying with us a couple of days; tomorrow Lieutenant Paine and some reinforcements are coming out; fifty men and fifteen combat-cars, to help out with the patroling till we can get men and vehicles of our own."

"Well, I'm glad to hear that, Captain!" Lunt said. "We're very short of both."

"You have a lot of country to patrol, too," Casagra said. "As Navy-Lieutenant Ybarra says, I'll only stay a few days, to get the feel of the situation. Marine-Lieutenant Paine will stay till you can get your own force recruited up and trained. That is, if things don't blow up again in the veldbeest country."

"Well, I hope they don't," Lunt said. "The vehicles are as welcome as the men; we have very few of our own."

"The Company's making some available," he said. "And along with his other work, Ahmed Khadra's starting a ZNPF recruiting drive."

"Has Jack been able to get his hands on any more Extee Three?" Gerd wanted to know.

He shook his head. "He hasn't even been able to get any for the reception center, when the Fuzzies start coming in to town. The Company's going to start producing it, but that'll take time. After they get the plant set up, they'll probably be running off test batches for a couple of weeks before they get one right."

"The formula's very simple," Casagra said.

"Some of the processes aren't; I was talking to Victor Grego. His synthetics people aren't optimistic, but Grego's whip-cracking at them to get it down yesterday morning."

"Isn't that something?" Gerd asked. "Victor Grego, Fuzzy-lover. And Jimenez, and Mallin; you ought to have heard the language my refined and delicate wife used when she heard about that."

"Last war's enemies, next war's allies," Casagra laughed. "I spent a couple of years on Thor; clans that'd be shooting us on sight one season would be our bosom friends the next, and planning to double-cross us the one after."

An aircar rose from behind the ZNPF barracks across the run and started south; another, which had been circling the camp five miles out, was coming in.

"Happy patrol," Lunt was explaining to Casagra. "The Fuzzies cleaned out all the zatku, land-prawns, around the camp, and they've been hunting farther out each day. Harpies like Fuzzies the way Fuzzies like zatku, so we have to give them air-cover. That's been since you left, Pancho; we've shot about twenty harpies since then. Four up to noon today; I don't know how many since."

"Lost any Fuzzies yet?"

"Not to harpies, no. We almost had a lot of them massacred yesterday; two of these families or whatever they are got into a *shoppo-diggo* fight about some playthings. A couple got chopped up a little; there's one." He pointed to a Fuzzy with a white bandage turbaned about his head; he seemed quite proud of it. "One got a broken leg; Doc Andrews has him in the hospital with his leg in a cast. Before I could get to the fight, Little Fuzzy and Ko-Ko and Mamma Fuzzy and a couple of my crowd had broken it up; just waded in with their flats as if they'd been doing riot-work all their lives. And you ought to have heard Little Fuzzy chewing them out afterward. Talked to them like an old sergeant in boot-camp."

"Oh, they fight among themselves?" Casagra asked.

"This is the first time it's happened here. I suppose they do, now and then, in the woods, with their wooden *zatku-hodda*. They have a regular fencing system. Nothing up to Interstellar Olympic epée standards, but effective. That's why half of them weren't killed in the first five seconds." Lunt looked at his watch. "Well, Captain, suppose you come with me; we'll go to Protection Force headquarters and go over what we've been doing and how your Lieutenant Paine and his men can help out."

Casagra went over to the car and spoke to the sergeant at the controls, then he and Lunt climbed in. Ybarra fell in with Gerd and they started in the direction of the lab-hut.

"One of the pregnancy cases lost her baby," Gerd said. "It was born prematurely and dead. We have the baby, fetus rather, under refrigeration. It seems to be about equivalent to human six-month stage. It wouldn't have survived in any case. Malformed, visibly and I suppose internally as well. We haven't done anything with it, yet; Lynne wanted you to see it. The Fuzzies were all sore; they thought it rated a funeral. We managed to explain to Little Fuzzy and a couple of others what we wanted to do with it, and they tried to explain to the others. I don't know how far any of it got."

The Fuzzies with them ran ahead, shouting "Mummy Woof! Auntie Lynne! Unka Panko bizzo do-mitto!" They were all making a clamor inside the lab-hut when he and Gerd entered, and Ruth, who was working at one of the benches making some kind of a test, was trying to shush them.

"Heyo, Unka Panko," she greeted him, hastening through with what she had at hand. "I'll be loose in a jiffy." She made a few notes, set a test-tube in a rack and made a grease-pencil number on it, and then pulled down the cover and locked it. "I haven't done this since med-school. Lynne's back in the dispensary with a couple of volunteer native nurses, looking after the combat-casualty." She got cigarettes out of her smock-pocket and lit one, then dropped into a chair. "Pancho, what *is* this about Ernst Mallin?" she asked. "Do you believe it?"

"Yes. He's really interested, now that he doesn't have to prove any predetermined Company-policy points about them. And he really likes Fuzzies. I've seen him with that one of Grego's, and with Ben's Flora and Fauna, and Mrs. Pendarvis' pair."

"I wouldn't believe it, even if I saw it. I saw what he did to Id and Superego and Complex and Syndrome. It's a wonder all four of them aren't incurably psychotic."

"But they aren't; they're just as sane as any other Fuzzies. Mallin's sorry for doing what he did with them, but he isn't sorry about what he learned from them. He says Fuzzies are the only people he's ever seen who are absolutely sane and can't be driven out of sanity. He says if humans could learn to think like Fuzzies, it would empty all the mental hospitals and throw all the psychiatrists out of work."

"But they're just like little children. Dear, smart little children, but . . ."

"Maybe children who are too smart to grow up. Maybe we'd be like Fuzzies, too, if we didn't have a lot of adults around us from the moment we were born, infecting us with non-sanity. I hope we don't begin infecting the Fuzzies, now. What was this fight all about, the other day?"

"Well, it was about some playthings, over in the big Fuzzy-shelter. This new crowd that came in that day saw them and wanted to take them. They were things that were intended for everybody to play with, but they didn't know that. There was an argument, and the next thing the *shoppo-diggo* were going. The crowd who started it are all sorry, now, and everybody's friends."

Lynne came through the door from the dispensary at the end of the hut. A couple of Fuzzies were running along with her. Some of the Fuzzies who had come in from outside with them drifted in through the dispensary door, to visit their wounded friend. Lynne came over and joined them. Gerd asked about the patient; the patient was doing well, and being very good about staying in bed.

"How about the girl who lost her baby?" he asked.

"She's running around as though nothing had happened. It was heartbreaking, Pancho. The thing—it was so malformed that I'm not sure it was male or female—was born dead. She looked at it, and touched it, and then she looked up at me and said, '*Hudda. Shi-nozza.*' "

"Dead. Like always," Gerd said. "She acted as though it were only what she'd expected. I don't think more than ten percent of them live more than a few days. You want to see it, Pancho?"

He didn't, particularly; it wasn't his field. But then, Fuzzy embryology wasn't anybody's field, yet. They went over to one of the refrigerators, and Gerd got it out and unwrapped it. It was smaller than a mouse, and he had to use a magnifier to look at it. The arms and legs were short and under-developed; the head was malformed, too.

"I can't say anything about it," he said, "except that it's a good thing it was born dead. What are you going to do with it?"

"I don't want to dissect it myself," Lynne said. "I'm not competent. That's too important to bungle with."

"I'm no good at dissection. Take it in to Mallorysport Hospital; that's what I'd do." He re-wrapped the tiny thing and put it back. "The more of you work on it, the less you'll miss. You want to find everything out you can."

"That's what I'm going to do. I'll call them now, and see who all can help, and when."

Half a dozen Fuzzies came in from outside; they were carrying a dead land-prawn. Some of the Fuzzies already in the hut ran ahead of them, into the dispensary.

"Come on, Pancho; let's watch," Gerd said. "They're bringing a present for their sick friend. They must have dragged that thing three or four miles."

There were five Fuzzies and two other people in the west lower garden of Government House, as the aircar came in. The other people were Captain Ahmed Khadra, ZNPF, and Sandra Glenn, so the five Fuzzies would be the host and hostess, Fauna and Flora, and Pierrot and Columbine Pendarvis and Diamond Grego. They had a red and gold ball, two feet, or one Fuzzy-height, in diameter, and they were pushing and chasing it about the lawn. Every once in a while, they would push it to where Khadra was standing, and then he would give it a kick and send it bounding. Jack Holloway chuckled; it looked like the kind of romping he and his Fuzzies had done on the lawn beside his camp, when there had been a lawn there and when there had just been his own Fuzzies.

"Ben, drop me down there, will you?" he said. "I feel like a good Fuzzy-romp, right now."

"So do I," Rainsford said. "Will, set us down, if you please."

The pilot circled downward, holding the car a few inches above the grass while they climbed out. The Fuzzies had seen the car descend and came pelting over. At first, he thought they were carrying pistols; at least, they wore belts and small holsters. The things in the holsters had pistol-grips, but when they drew them, he saw that they were three-inch black discs, which the Fuzzies held to their mouths.

"Pappy Ben; Pappy Jack!" they were all yelling. "Listen; we talk like Big Ones, now!"

He snapped off his hearing-aid. It was true; they were all speaking audibly.

"Pappy Vic make," Diamond said proudly.

"Actually, Henry Stenson made them," the girl said. "At least, he invented them. All Mr. Grego did was tell him what he wanted. They are Fuzzyphones."

"*Heeta*, Pappy Jack." Diamond held his up. "Yeek-yeek. *Yeeek!*" He was exasperated, and then remembered he'd taken it away from his mouth. "Fuzzy-talk go in here, this side. Inside, grow big. Come out this side, big like Hagga-talk," he said, holding the device to his mouth.

"That good, Diamond. Good-good," he commended. "What do you think of this, Ben?"

Rainsford squatted in front of his own Fuzzies, holding out a hand. "So-*pokko-aki*, Flora," he said, and the Fuzzy handed him hers, first saying, "*Keffu*, Pappy Ben; *do' brek.*"

"I won't." Rainsford looked at it curiously, and handed it back. "That thing's good. Little switch on the grip, and it looks as though the frequency-transformer's in the middle and they can talk into either side of it."

It would have to work that way; Fuzzies were ambidextrous. Gerd had a theory about that. Fuzzies weren't anatomists, mainly because they didn't produce fire and didn't cut up the small animals they killed for cooking, and only races who had learned the location and importance of the heart fought with their hearts turned away from the enemy. *Homo sapiens terra's* ancestors in the same culture-stage were probably ambidextrous too. Like most of Gerd's theories, it made sense.

"Who makes these things?" he asked. "Stenson?"

"He made these, in his shop. The CZC electronics equipment plant is going to manufacture them," the girl said, adding: "Advertisement."

"You tell Mr. Grego to tell his electronics plant to get cracking on them. The Native Affairs Commission wants a lot of them."

"You staying for dinner with us, Miss Glenn?" Rainsford asked.

"Thank you, Governor, but I have to take Diamond home."

"I have to take Pierrot and Columbine home, too," Khadra said. "What are you doing this evening?"

"I have my homework to do. Fuzzy language lessons."

"Well, why can't I help you with your homework?" Khadra wanted to know. "I speak Fuzzy like a native, myself."

"Well, if it won't be too much trouble . . ." she began.

Holloway laughed. "Who are you trying to kid, Miss Glenn? Look in the mirror if you think teaching you Fuzzy would be too much trouble for anybody Ahmed's age. If I was about ten years younger, I'd pull rank on him and leave him with the Fuzzies."

Pierrot and Columbine thought all this conversation

boring and irrelevant. They trundled the ball over in front of Khadra and commanded: *"Mek kikko!"*

Khadra kicked the ball, lifting it from the ground and sending it soaring away. The Fuzzies ran after it.

"Dr. Mallin says you were looking at the sanatorium," Sandra said.

"Yes. That's going to be a good place. You know about it?" he asked Khadra.

"Well, it's a big place," Khadra said. "I've seen it from the air, of course. They only use about ten percent of it, now."

"Yes. We're taking a building, intended for a mental ward; about a half square mile of park around it, with a good fence, so the Fuzzies won't stray off and get lost. We could put five-six hundred Fuzzies in there, and they wouldn't be crowded a bit. And it'll be some time before we get that many there at one time. I expect there'll be about a hundred to a hundred and fifty this time next week."

"There were precisely eight hundred and seventy-two applications in when the office closed this evening," Khadra said. "When are you going back, Jack?"

"Day after tomorrow. I want to make sure the work's started on the reception center, and I'm still trying to locate some Extee-Three. I think a bunch of damn speculators have cornered the market and are holding it for high prices."

The Fuzzies had pushed the ball into some shrubbery and were having trouble dislodging it. Sandra Glenn started off to help them, Ben Rainsford walking along with her. Khadra said:

"That'll probably be some of Hugo Ingermann's crowd, too."

"Speaking about Ingermann; how are you making out about Herckerd and Novaes?" he asked. "And the five Fuzzies."

"Jack, I swear. I'm beginning to think Herckerd and Novaes and those Fuzzies all walked into a mass-energy converter together. That's how completely all of them have vanished."

"They hadn't sold them before Ben's telecast, evening before last. After that, with the Adoption Bureau opening all that talk about kidnapping and enslavement and so on, nobody would buy a bootleg Fuzzy. So they couldn't sell them, so they got rid of them." How? That was what bothered him. If they'd used sense, they'd have flown them back to Beta and turned them loose. He was afraid, though, that they'd killed them. By this time everybody knew that live Fuzzies could tell tales. "I think those Fuzzies are dead."

"I don't know. Eight hundred and seventy-two applications, and a hundred and fifty Fuzzies at most," Khadra said. "There'll be a market for bootleg Fuzzies. Jack, you know what I think? I think those Fuzzies weren't brought in for sale. I think this gang—Herckerd and Novaes and whoever else is in with them— are training those Fuzzies to help catch other Fuzzies. Do you think a Fuzzy could be trained to do that?"

"Sure. To all intents and purposes, that's what our Fuzzies are doing out at the camp. You know how Fuzzies think? Big Ones are a Good Thing. Any Fuzzy who has a Big One doesn't need to worry about anything. All Fuzzies ought to have Big Ones. That's what Little Fuzzy has been telling the ones from the woods, out at camp. Ahmed, I think you have something."

"I thought of something else, too. If this gang can make a deal with some tramp freighter captain, they could ship Fuzzies off-planet and make terrific profits on it. You wait till the news about the Fuzzies gets around. There'll be a sale for them everywhere—Terra, Odin, Freya, Marduk, Aton, Baldur, planets like that. Anybody can bring a ship into orbit on this planet, now, if he has his own landing-craft and doesn't use the CZC spaceport. In a month, word will have gotten to Gimli, that's the nearest planet, and in two more months a ship can get here from there."

"Spaceport. That could be why Ingermann's been harping on this nefarious CZC space-terminal monopoly. If he had a little spaceport of his own, now..."

"Any kind of smuggling you can think of," Khadra said. "Hot sunstones. Narcotics. Or Fuzzies."

Rainsford and Sandra Glenn were approaching; Sandra carried Diamond, Pierrot and Columbine ran beside her, and Flora and Fauna were trundling the ball ahead of them. He wanted to talk to Rainsford about this. They needed more laws, to prohibit shipping Fuzzies off-planet; nobody'd thought of that possibility before. And talk to Grego; the company controlled the only existing egress from the planet.

Lynne Andrews straightened and removed the binocular loop and laid it down, blinking. The others, four men and two women in lab-smocks, were pushing aside the spotlights and magnifiers and cameras on their swinging arms and laying down instruments.

"That thing wouldn't have lived thirty seconds, even if it hadn't been premature," one man said. "And it doesn't add a thing to what we don't know about Fuzzy embryology." He was an embryologist, human-type, himself. "I have dissected over five hundred aborted fetuses and I never saw one in worse shape than that."

"It was so tiny," one of the women said. She was an obstetrician. "I can't believe that that's human six-months equivalent."

"Well, I can," somebody else said. "I know what a young Fuzzy looks like; I spent a lot of time with Jack Holloway's Baby Fuzzy, during the trial. And I don't suppose a fertilized Fuzzy ovum is much different from one of ours. Between the two, there has to be a regular progressive development. I say this one is two-thirds developed. Misdeveloped, I should say."

"Misdeveloped is correct, Doctor. Have you any idea why this one misdeveloped as it did?"

"No, Doctor, I haven't."

"They come from northern Beta; that country's never been more than air-scouted. Does anybody know what radioactivity conditions are, up there? I've seen pictures of worse things than this from nuclear bomb radiations on Terra during and after the Third and Fourth World Wars, at the beginning of the First Federation."

"The country hasn't been explored, but it's been scanned. Any natural radioactivity strong enough to do that would be detectable from Xerxes."

"Oh, Nifflheim; that fetus could have been conceived on a patch of pitchblende no bigger than this table . . ."

"Well, couldn't it be chemical? Something in the pregnant female's diet?" the other woman asked.

"The Thalidomide Babies!" somebody exclaimed. "First Century, between the Second and Third World Wars. That was due to chemicals taken orally by pregnant women."

"All right; let's get the biochemists in on this, then."

"Chris Hoenveld," somebody else said. "It's not too late to call him now."

Fuzzies didn't have Cocktail Hour; that was for the Big Ones, to sit together and make Big One talk. Fuzzies just came stringing in before dinner, more or less interested in food depending on how the hunting had been, and after they ate they romped and played until they were tired, and then sat in groups, talking idly until they became sleepy.

In the woods, it had not been like that. When the sun began to go to bed, they had found safe places, where the big animals couldn't get at them, and they had snuggled together and slept, one staying awake all the time. But here the Big Ones kept the animals away, and killed them with thunder-things when they came too close, and it was safe. And the Big Ones had things that made light even when the sky was dark, and there were places where it was always bright as day. So here, there was more fun, because there was less danger, and many new things to talk about. This was the *Hoksu-Mitto*, the Wonderful Place.

And today, they were even happier, because today Pappy Jack had come back.

Little Fuzzy got out his pipe, the new one Pappy Jack had brought from the Big House Place, and stuffed it with tobacco, and got out the little fire-maker. Some of the Fuzzies around him, who had just come in from the woods, were frightened. They were not used to fire; when fire happened in the woods, it was bad. That was wild fire, though. The Big Ones had tamed fire, and if a person were careful not to touch it or let it get loose, fire was nothing to be afraid of.

"We go other places, and all have Big Ones, tomorrow?" one asked. "Big Ones for us, like Pappy Jack for you?"

"Not tomorrow. Not next day. Day after that." He help up three fingers. "Then go in high-up-thing, to place like this. Big Ones come, make talk. You like Big One, Big One like you, you go with Big One, you live in Big One place."

"Nice place, like this?"

"Nice place. Not like this. Different place."

"Not want to go. Nice place here, much fun."

"Then you not go. Pappy Jack not make you go. You want to go, Pappy Jack find nice Big One for you, be good to you."

"Suppose not good. Suppose bad to us?"

"Then Pappy Jack come, Pappy Jorj, Unka Ahmed, Pappy Ge'hd, Unka Panko; make much trouble for bad Big One, *bang, bang bang!*"

XIV

Myra was vexed. "It's Mr. Dunbar. The chief chemist at Synthetic Foods," she added, as though he didn't know that. "He is here himself; he has something he insists he must give to you personally."

"That's what I told him to do, Myra. Send him in."

Malcolm Dunbar pushed through the door from Myra's office with an open fiberboard carton under his arm. That had probably helped vex Myra; Dunbar was an executive, and executives ought not to carry their own parcels; it was *infra dignitatem*. He set it on the corner of the desk.

"Here it is, Mr. Grego; this is the first batch. We just finished the chemical tests on it. Identical with both the Navy stuff and the stuff we imported ourselves."

He rose and went around the desk, reaching into the carton and taking out a light brown slab, breaking off a corner and tasting it. It had the same slightly rancid, slightly oily and slightly sweetish flavor as the regular product. It tasted as though it had been compounded according to the best scientific principles of dietetics, by somebody who thought there was something sinful about eating for pleasure. He yielded to no one in his admiration of *Fuzzy fuzzy holloway*, but anybody who liked this stuff was nuts.

"You're sure it's safe?"

Dunbar was outraged. "My God, would I bring it here for you to feed your Fuzzy if I didn't know it was? In the first place, it's made strictly according to

Terran Federation Armed Forces specifications. The bulk-matter is pure wheat farina, the same as Argentine Syntho-Foods and Odin Dietetics use. The rest is chemically pure synthetic nutrients. We have a man at the plant who used to be a chemical engineer at Odin Dietetics; he checked all the processes and they're identical. And we tried it on all the standard lab-animals; Terran hamsters and Thoran tilbras, and then on Freyan kholphs and Terran rhesus monkeys. The kholphs," he footnoted, "didn't like it worth a damn. It harmed none of them. And I ate a cake of the damned stuff myself, and it took a couple of hours and a pint of bourbon to get rid of the taste," the martyr to science added.

"All right. I will accept that it is fit for Fuzzy consumption. Fortunately, the whole Fuzzy population of Mallorysport, all five of them, are up on my terrace now. Let's go."

Ben Rainsford's Flora and Fauna, and Mrs. Pendarvis' Pierrot and Columbine were with Diamond in the Fuzzy-room. Outside on the terrace it was raw and rainy, one of Mallorysport's rare unpleasant days. They had a lot of colored triangular tiles on the floor, and were making patterns with them. Sandra Glenn was watching them with one eye and reading with the other. They all sprang to their feet and began yeeking, then remembered the Fuzzy phones on their belts, whipped them out, and began shouting, "*Heyo, Pappy Vic!*" He'd tried to explain that he was Diamond's Pappy Vic, and just Uncle Vic to the rest, but they refused to make the distinction. Pappy to one Fuzzy, pappy to all.

"Pappy Vic give *esteefee*," he told them. "New *estefee*, very good." He set the box down and got out one of the slabs, breaking and distributing it. The Fuzzies had nice manners; the two most recent guests, Pierrot and Columbine, served first, held theirs till the others were served. Then they all nibbled together.

They each took one nibble and stopped.

"Not good," Diamond declared. "Not *esteefee*. Want *esteefee*."

"Bad," Flora pronounced it, spitting out what she had in her mouth and carrying the rest to the trashbin. "*Esteefee* good; this not."

"*Esteefee* for look; not *esteefee* in mouth," Pierrot said.

"What are they saying?" Dunbar wanted to know.

"They say it isn't Extee Three at all, and they want to know how dumb I am to think it is."

"But look, Mr. Grego; this *is* Extee Three. It is chemically identical with the stuff they've been eating all along."

"The Fuzzies aren't chemists. They only know what it tastes like, and it doesn't taste like Extee Three to them."

"It tastes like Extee Three to me . . ."

"You," Sandra told him, "are not a Fuzzy." She switched languages and explained that Pappy Vic and the other Big One really thought it was *esteefee*.

"Pappy Vic feel bad," he told them. "Pappy Vic want to give real esteefee."

He gathered up the offending carton and carried it into the kitchenette, going to one of the cupboards and getting out a tin of the genuine article. Only a dozen left; he'd have to start rationing it himself. He cut it into six pieces, put by a piece for Diamond after the company was gone, and distributed the rest.

Dunbar was still arguing with Sandra that the stuff he'd brought was chemically Extee Three.

"All right, Malcolm, I believe you. The point is, these Fuzzies don't give a hoot on Nifflheim what the chemical composition is." He looked at the label on the tin. "The man you have at the plant worked for Odin Dietetics, didn't he? Well, this stuff was made on Terra by Argentine Syntho-Foods. What do they use for cereal bulk-matter at Odin Dietetics, some native grain?"

"No, introduced Terran wheat, and Argentine uses

wheat from the pampas and from the Mississippi Valley in North America."

"Different soil-chemicals, different bacteria; hell, man, look at tobacco. We've introduced it on every planet we've ever colonized, and no tobacco tastes just like the tobacco from anywhere else."

"Do we have any Odin Extee Three?" Sandra asked.

"Smart girl; a triple A for good thinking. Do we?"

"Yes. The stuff we import's Argentine, and the stuff the Navy has on Xerxes is Odin."

"And the Fuzzies can't tell the difference? No, of course they can't. Jack Holloway bought his Extee Three from us and gave it to his Fuzzies, and when they got on Xerxes, the Navy fed them theirs. What did you use in this stuff, local wheat?"

"Introduced wheat; seed came from South America. Grown on Gammz Continent."

"Well, Mal, we're going to find out what's the matter with this stuff. Real all-out study, tear it apart molecule by molecule. Who's our best biochemist?"

"Hoenveld."

"Well, put him to work on it. There's some difference, and the Fuzzies know it. You say this stuff's Government specification standard?"

"It meets the Government tests."

"Well; Napier has a lot of Extee Three on Xerxes he won't release because it's regulation-required emergency stores. We'll see if we can trade this for it . . ."

"Well, you goofed on it somehow!" the superintendent of the synthetics plant was insisting. "The Fuzzies eat regular Extee Three; they're crazy about it. If they won't eat your stuff, it isn't Extee Three."

"Listen, Abe, goddamit, I know it *is* Extee Three! We followed the formula exactly. Ask Joe Vespi, here; he used to work at Odin Dietetics . . ."

"That's correct, Mr. Fitch; every step of the process is exactly as I remember it from Odin—"

"As you remembered it!" Fitch pounced trium-

phantly. "What did you remember wrong?"

"Why, nothing, Mr. Fitch. Look, here's the schematic. The farina, that's the bulk-matter, comes in here, to these pressure-cookers . . ."

Dr. Jan Christiaan Hoenveld was annoyed, and because he was an emminent scientist and Victor Grego was only a businessman, he was at no pains to hide it.

"Mr. Grego, do you realize how much work is piled up on me now. Dr. Andrews and Dr. Reynier and Dr. Dosihara are at me to find out whether there is any biochemical cause of premature and defective births among Fuzzies. And now you want me to drop that and find out why one batch of Extee Three tastes differently to a Fuzzy from another. There is a gunsmith here in town who has a sign in his shop, *There are only twenty-four hours in a day and there is only one of me.* I have often considered copying that sign in my laboratory." He sat frowning into his screen from Science Center, across the city, for a moment. "Mr. Grego, has it occurred to you or any of your master-minds at Synthetics that difference may be in the Fuzzies' taste-perception?"

"It has occurred to me that Fuzzies must have a sense of taste that would shame the most famous winetaster in the Galaxy. But I question if it is more accurate than your chemical analysis. If those Fuzzies tasted a difference between our Extee Three and Argentine Syntho-Food's, the difference must be detectable. I don't know anybody better able to detect it than you, Doctor; that's why I'm asking you to find out what it is."

Dr. Jan Christiaan Hoenveld said, "Hunnh!" ungraciously. Flattered, and didn't want to show it.

"Well, I'll do what I can, Mr. Grego . . ."

XV

I must be very nice to Dr. Ernst Mallin. I must be very nice to Dr. Ernst Mallin. I must be . . . Ruth van Riebeek repeated it silently, as though writing it a hundred times on a mental blackboard, as the airboat lost altitude and came slanting down across the city, past the high crag of Company House, with the lower, broader, butte of Central Courts Building in the distance to the left. Ahead, the sanatorium area drew closer, wide parklands scattered with low white buildings. She hadn't seen Mallin since the trial, and even then she had avoided speaking to him as much as possible. Part of it was because of the things he had done with the four Fuzzies; Pancho Ybarra said she also had a guilt-complex because of the way she'd fifth-columned the company. Rubbish! That had been intelligence-work; that had been why she'd taken a job with the CZC in the first place. She had nothing at all to feel guilty about . . .

"I must be very nice to Dr. Ernst Mallin," she said, aloud. "And I'm going to have one Nifflheim of a time doing it."

"So am I," her husband, standing beside her, said. "He'll have to make an effort to be nice to us, too. He'll still remember my pistol shoved into his back out at Holloway's the day Goldilocks was killed. I wonder if he knows how little it would have taken to make me squeeze the trigger."

"Pancho says he is a reformed character."

"Pancho's seen him since we have. He could be right. Anyhow, he's helping us, and we need all the help we can get. And he won't hurt the Fuzzies, not with Ahmed Khadra and Mrs. Pendarvis keeping an eye on him."

The Fuzzies, crowded on the cargo-deck below, were becoming excited. There was a forward-view screen rigged where they could see it, and they could probably sense as well as see that the boat was descending. And this place ahead must be the place Pappy Jack and Pappy Gerd and Unka Panko and Little Fuzzy had been telling them about, where the Big Ones would come and take them away to nice places of their own.

She hoped too many of them wouldn't be too badly disappointed. She hoped this adoption deal wouldn't be too much of a failure.

The airboat grounded on the vitrified stone apron beside the building. It looked like a good place; Jack said it had been intended for but never used as a mental ward-unit; four stories high, each with its own terrace, and a flat garden-planted roof. High mesh fences around each level; the Fuzzies wouldn't fall off. Plenty of trees and bushes; the Fuzzies would like that.

They got the Fuzzies off and into the building, helped by the small crowd who were waiting for them. Mrs. Pendarvis; she and the Chief Justice's wife were old friends. And a tall, red-haired girl, Grego's Fuzzy-sitter, Sandra Glenn. And Ahmed Khadra, in a new suit of civvies but bulging slightly under the left arm. And half a dozen other people whom she had met now and then—school department and company public health section. And Ernst Mallin, pompous and black-suited and pedantic-looking. *I must be very nice* . . . She extended a hand to him.

"Good afternoon, Dr. Mallin."

Maybe Gerd was right; maybe she did feel guilty about the way she'd tricked him. She was, she found, being counter-offensively defensive.

"Good afternoon, Ruth. Dr. van Riebeek," he corrected himself. "Can you bring your people down this way?" he asked, nodding to the hundred and fifty Fuzzies milling about in the hall, yeeking excitedly. People, he called them. He must be making an effort, too. "We have refreshments for them. Extee Three. And things for them to play with."

"Where do you get the Extee Three?" she asked. "We haven't been able to get any for almost a week, now."

Mallin gave one of his little secretive smiles, the sort he gave when he was one up on somebody.

"We got it from Xerxes. The company's started producing it, but unfortunately, the Fuzzies don't like it. We still can't find out why; it's made on exactly the same formula. And as it's entirely up to Government specifications, Mr. Grego was able to talk Commodore Napier into accepting it in exchange for what he has on hand. We have about five tons of it. How much do you need at Holloway's Camp? Will a couple of tons help you any?"

Would a couple of tons help them any? "Why, I don't know how to thank you, Dr. Mallin! Of course it will; we've been giving it to our Fuzzies, a quarter-cake apiece on alternate days." *I must be very, VERY, nice to Dr. Mallin!* "Why don't they like the stuff you people have been making? What's wrong with it?"

"We don't know. Mr. Grego has been raging at everybody to find out; it's made in exactly the same way..."

When Malcolm Dunbar lighted his screen, Dr. Jan Christiaan Hoenveld appeared in it. He didn't waste time on greetings or other superfluities.

"I think we have something, Mr. Dunbar. There is a component in both the Odin Dietetics and the Argentine Syntho-Foods products that is absent from our own product. It is not one of the synthetic nutrient or vitamin or hormone compounds which are part of the fieldration formula; it is not a compound regularly synthesized either commercially or experimentally in any laboratory I know of. It's a rather complicated longchain organic molecule; most of it seems to be oxygen-hydrogen-carbon, but there are a few atoms of titanium in it. If that's what the Fuzzies find lacking in our products, all I can say is that they have the keenest taste perception of any creature, sapient or non-sapient, that I have ever heard of."

"All right, then; they have. I saw them reject our Extee Three in disgust, and then Mr. Grego gave them a little of the Argentine stuff, and they ate it with the greatest pleasure. How much of this unknown compound is there in Extee Three?"

"About one part in ten thousand," Hoenveld said.

"And the titanium?"

"Five atoms out of sixty-four in the molecule."

"That's pretty keen tasting." He thought for a moment. "I suppose it's in the wheat; the rest of that stuff is synthesized."

"Well, naturally, Mr. Dunbar. That would seem to be the inescapable conclusion," Hoenveld said, patronizingly.

"We have quite a bit of metallic titanium, imported in fabricated form before we got our own steel-mills working. Do you think you could synthesize that molecule, Dr. Hoenveld?"

Hoenveld gave him a look of undisguised contempt. "Certainly, Mr. Dunbar. In about a year and a half to two years. As I understand, the object of manufacturing the stuff here is to supply a temporary shortage which will be relieved in about six months, when imported Extee Three begins coming in from Marduk. Unless I am directly and specifically ordered to do so by Mr. Grego, I will not waste my time on trying."

Of course, it was ending in a cocktail party. Wherever Terran humans went, they planted tobacco and coffee, to have coffee and cigarettes for breakfast, and wherever they went they found or introduced something that would ferment to produce C_2H_5OH, and around 1730-ish each day, they had Cocktail Hour. The natives on planets like Loki and Gimli and Thor and even Shesha and Uller thought it was a religious observance.

Maybe it was, at that.

Sipping his own cocktail, Gerd van Riebeek ignored, for a moment, the conversation in which he had become involved and eavesdropped on his wife and Claudette Pendarvis and Ernst Mallin and Ahmed Khadra and Sandra Glenn.

"Well, we want to keep them here for at least a week before we let people take them away," the Chief Justice's wife was saying. "You'll have to stay with us for a day or so, Ruth, and help us teach them what to expect in their new homes."

"You're going to have to educate the people who adopt them," Sandra Glenn said. "What to expect and what not to expect from Fuzzies. I think, evening classes. Language, for one thing."

"You know," Mallin said, "I'd like to take a few Fuzzies around through the other units of the sanatorium, to visit the patients. The patients here would like it. They don't have an awful lot of fun, you know."

That was new for Ernst Mallin. He never seemed to recall that Mallin had thought having fun was important, before. Maybe the Fuzzies had taught him that it was.

The group he was drinking with were Science Center and Public Health people. One of them, a woman gynecologist, was wondering what Chris Hoenveld had found out, so far.

"What can he find out?" Raynier, the pathologist asked. "He only has the one specimen, and it probably isn't there at all, it's probably something in the mother's metabolism. It might be radioactivity, but that would only produce an occasional isolated case, and from what you've seen, it seems to be a racial characteristic. I think you'll find it in the racial dietary habits."

"Land-prawns," somebody suggested. "As far as I know, nothing else eats them but Fuzzies; that right, Gerd?"

"Yes. We always thought they had no natural enemies at all, till we found out about the Fuzzies. But it's been our observation that Fuzzies won't take anything that'll hurt them."

"They won't take anything that gives them a bellyache or a hangover, no. They can establish a direct relationship there. But whatever caused this defective birth we were investigating, and I agree that that's probably a common thing with Fuzzies, was something that acted on a level the Fuzzies couldn't be aware of. I think there's a good chance that eating land-prawns may be responsible."

"Well, let's find out. Put Chris Hoenveld to work on that."

"You put him to work on it. Or get Victor Grego to; he won't throw Grego out of his lab. Chris is sore enough about this Fuzzy business as it is."

"Well, we'll have to study more than one fetus. We have a hundred and fifty Fuzzies here, we ought to find something out . . .

"Isolate all the pregnant females; get Mrs. Pendarvis to withhold them from adoption . . ."

". . . may have to perform a few abortions . . ."

". . . microsurgery; fertilized ova . . ."

That wasn't what he and Ruth and Jack Holloway had had in mind, when they'd brought this lot to Mallorysport. But they had to find out; if they didn't, in a few more generations there might be no more Fuzzies at all. If a few of them suffered, now . . .

Well, hadn't poor Goldilocks had to be killed before the Fuzzies were recognized for the people they were?

"Titanium," Victor Grego said. "Now that's interesting."

"Is that all you can call it, Mr. Grego?" Dunbar, in the screen, demanded. "I call it impossible. I was checking up. Titanium, on this planet, is damn near as rare as calcium on Uller. It's present, and that's all; I'll bet most of the titanium on Zarathustra was brought here in fabricated form between the time the planet was discovered and seven years ago when we got our steel-mill going."

That was a big exaggeration, of course. It existed, but it was a fact that they'd never been able to extract it by any commercially profitable process, and on Zarathustra they used light-alloy steel for everything for which titanium was used elsewhere. So a little of it got picked up, as a trace-element, in wheat grown on Terra or on Odin, but it was useless to hope for it in Zarathustran wheat.

"It looks," he said, "as though we're stuck, Mal. Do you think Chris Hoenveld could synthesize that molecule? We could add it to the other ingredients . . ."

"He says he could—in six months to a year. He refuses to try unless you order him categorically to."

"And by that time, we'll have all the Extee Three we want. Well, a lot of Fuzzies, including mine, are going to have to do without, then."

He blanked the screen and lit a cigarette and looked at the globe of Zarathustra, which Henry Stenson had running on time again and which he could interpret like a clock. Be another hour till Sandra got back from the new Adoption Center; she'd have to pick up Diamond at Government House. And Leslie wouldn't be in for cocktails this evening; he was over on Epsilon Continent, talking to people about things he didn't want to discuss by screen. Ben Rainsford had finally gotten around to calling for an election for delegates to a constitutional convention, and they wanted to line up candidates of their own. It looked as though Mr. Victor Grego would have cocktails with the manager-in-chief of the Charterless Zarathustra Company, this evening. Might as well have them here.

Titanium, he thought disgustedly. It would be something like that. What was it they called the stuff? Oh, yes; the nymphomaniac metal; when it gets hot it combines with anything. An idea suddenly danced just out of reach. He stopped, half way from the desk to the cabinet, his eyes closed. Then he caught it, and dashed for the communication screen, punching Malcolm Dunbar's call-combination.

It was a few minutes before Dunbar answered; he had his hat and coat on.

"I was just going out, Mr. Grego."

"So I see. That man Vespi, the one who worked for Odin Dietetics; is he still around?"

"Why, no. He left twenty minutes ago, and I don't know how to reach him, right away."

"No matter; get him in the morning. Listen, the pressure cookers, the ones you use to cook the farina for bulk-matter. What are they made of?"

"Why, light nonox-steel; our manufacture. Why?"

"Ask Vespi what they used for that purpose on Odin. Don't suggest the answer, but see if it wasn't titanium."

Dunbar's eyes widened. He'd heard about the chemical nymphomania of titanium, too.

"Sure; that's what they'd use, there. And at Argentine Syntho-Foods, too. Listen, suppose I give the police an emergency-call request; they could find Joe in half an hour."

"Don't bother; tomorrow morning's good enough. I want to try something first."

He blanked the screen, and called Myra Fallada. She never left the office before he did.

"Myra; call out and get me five pounds of pure wheat farina, and be sure it's made from Zarathustran wheat. Have it sent up to my apartment, fifteen minutes ago."

"Fifteen minutes from now do?" she asked. "What's

it for; the Little Monster? All right, Mr. Greg ."

He forgot about the drink he was going to have with Mr. Victor Grego. You had a drink when the work was done, and there was still work to do.

There was clattering in the kitchenette when Sandra Glenn brought Diamond into the Fuzzy-room. She opened the door between and looked through, and Diamond crowded past her knees for a look, too. Mr. Grego was cooking something, in a battered old stewpan she had never seen around the place before. He looked over his shoulder and said, "Hi Sandra. *Heyo,* Diamond; use Fuzzyphone, Pappy Vic no got earthing."

"What make do, Pappy Vic?" Diamond asked.

"That's what I want to know, too?"

"Sandra, keep your fingers crossed; when this stuff's done and has cooled off, we're going to see how Diamond likes it. I think we have found out what's the matter with that Extee Three."

"*Esteefee?* You make *esteefee?* Real? Not like other?" Diamond wanted to know.

"You eat," Pappy Vic said. "Tell if good. Pappy Vic not know."

"Well, what is it?" she said.

"Hoenveld found what was different about it." The explanation was rather complicated; she had been exposed to, rather than studied, chemistry. She got the general idea; the Extee Three the Fuzzies liked had been cooked in titanium.

"That's what this stewpan is; part of a camp cooking kit I brought here from Terra." He gave the white mess in the pan a final stir and lifted it from the stove, burning his finger and swearing; just like a man in a kitchen. "Now, as soon as this slop's cool . . ."

Diamond smelled it, and wanted to try it right away. He had to wait, though, until it was cool. Then they carried the pan, it had a treacherous-looking folding handle, out to the Fuzzy-room, and Mr. Grego spooned some onto Diamond's plate, and Diamond took his little spoon and tasted, cautiously. Then he began shoveling it into his mouth ravenously.

"The Master Mind crashes through again," she said. "He really likes it." Diamond had finished what was on his plate. "You like?" she asked, in Fuzzy. "Want more?"

"Give him the rest of it, Sandra. I'm going to call Dr. Jan Christiaan Hoenveld, and suggest an experiment for him to try. And after that, Miss Glenn, will you honor me by having a cocktail with me?"

Jack Holloway laughed. "So that's it. When did you find out?"

"Mallin just screened me; he just got it from Grego," Gerd van Riebeek, in the screen, said. "They're going to start tearing out all the stainless-steel cookers right away, and replace them with titanium. Jack have you any titanium cooking utensils?"

"No. Everything we have here is steel. We have sheet titanium; the house and the sheds and the old hangar are all sheet-titanium. We might be able to make something..." He stopped short. "Gerd, we don't have to cook the food in titanium. We can cook titanium in the food. Cut up some chunks and put them in the kettles. It would work the same way."

"Well, I'll be damned," Gerd said. "I never thought of that. I'll bet nobody else did, either."

Dr. Jan Christiaan Hoenveld was disgusted and chagrined and embarrassed, and mostly disgusted.

It had been gratifying to discover a hitherto unknown biochemical, especially one existing unsuspected in a well known, long manufactured, and widely distributed commercial product. He could understand how it had happened; a by-effect in one of the manufacturing processes, and since the stuff had been proven safe and nutritious for humans and other life-forms having similar biochemistry and metabolism, nobody had bothered until some little animals—no, people, that had been scientifically established—had detected its absence by taste. Things like that happened all the time. He had been proud of the accomplishment; he'd been going to call the newly discovered substance hoenveldine. He could have worked out a way of synthesizing it, too, but by proper scientific methods it would have taken over a year, and he knew it, and he'd said so to everybody.

And now, within a day, it had been synthesized, if that were the word for it, by a rank amateur, a layman, a complete non-scientist. And not in a laboratory in a kitchen, with no equipment but a battered old stewpan!

And the worst of it was that this layman, this empiric, was his employer. The claims of the manager-in-chief of the Zarathustra Company simply couldn't be brushed off. Not by a company scientist.

Well, Grego had found out what he wanted; he could stop worrying about that. He had important work to do; an orderly, long-term study of the differences between Zarathustran and Terran biochemistry. The differences were minute, but they existed, and they had to be understood, and they had to be investigated in an orderly, scientific manner.

And now, they wanted him to go haring off, hit-or-miss, after this problem about Fuzzy infant mortality and defective births, and they didn't even know any such problem existed. They had one, just one, case—that six-month fetus the Andrews girl had brought in—and they had a lot of unsubstantiated theorizing by Gerd van Riebeek, pure conclusion-jumping. And now they wanted him to find out if eating land-prawns caused these defective births which they believed, on the basis of one case and a lot of supposition, to exist. Maybe after years of observation of hundreds of cases they might have some justifications, but . . .

He rose from the chair at the desk in the corner of

the laboratory and walked slowly among the workbenches. Ten men and women, eight of them working on new projects that had been started since young van Riebeek had started after this mare's-nest of his, all of them diverted from serious planned research. He stopped at one bench, where a woman was working.

"Miss Tresca, can't you keep your bench in better order than this?" he scolded. "Keep things in their places. What are you working on?"

"Oh, a hunch I had, about this hokfusine."

Hunch! That was the trouble, all through Science Center; too many hunches and not enough sound theory.

"Oh, the titanium thing. It's a name Mr. Grego suggested, from a couple of Fuzzy words, *hoku fusso,* wonderful food. It's what the Fuzzies call Extee Three."

Hokfusine, indeed. Now they were getting the Fuzzy language into scientific nomenclature.

"Well, just forget about your hunch," he told her. "There are a lot of samples of organic matter, blood, body-secretions, hormones, tissue, from pregnant female Fuzzies that they want analyzed. I don't suppose it makes any more sense than your hunch, but they want analyses immediately. They want everything immediately, it seems. And straighten up that clutter on your bench. How often do I have to tell you that order is the first virtue in scientific work?"

XVI

They were in Jack's living room, and it looked almost exactly as it had the first night Gerd van Riebeek had seen it, when he and Ruth and Jaua Jimenez had come out to see the Fuzzies, without the least idea that the validity of the company's charter would be involved. All the new office equipment that had cluttered it had gone, in the two weeks he and Ruth had been in Mallorysport, and there was just the sturdy, comfortable furniture Jack had made himself, and the damnthing and the bush-goblin and verdbeest skins on the floor, and the gunrack with the tangle of bedding under it.

There were just five of them, as there had been that other evening, three months, or was it three ages, ago. Juan Jimenez and Ben Rainsford were absent, in Mallorysport, but they had been replaced by Pancho Ybarra, lounging in one of the deep chairs, and Lynne Andrews, on the couch beside Ruth. Jack sat in the armchair at his table-desk, trying to keep Baby Fuzzy, on his lap, from climbing up to sit on his head. On the floor, the adult Fuzzies—just Jack's own family; this was their place, and the others didn't intrude here—were in the middle of the room, playing with the things that had been brought back from Mallorysport. The kind of playthings Fuzzies liked; ingenuity; challenging toys for putting together shapes and colors.

He was glad they weren't playing with their molecule-model kit. He'd seen enough molecule models in the last two weeks to last him a lifetime.

"And there isn't anything we can do about it, at all?" Lynne was asking.

"No. There isn't anything anybody can do. The people in Mallorysport have given up trying. They're still investigating, but that's only to be able to write a scientifically accurate epitaph for the Fuzzy race."

"Can't they do something to reverse it?"

"It's irreversible," Ruth told her. "It isn't a matter of diet or environment or anything external. It's this hormone, NFMp, that they produce in their own bodies, that inhibits normal development of the embryo. And we can't even correct it in individual cases by surgery; excising the glands that secrete it would result in sterility."

"Well, it doesn't always work," Jack said, lifting Baby Fuzzy from his shoulder. "It didn't work in Baby's case."

"It works in about nine cases out of ten, apparently. We've had ten births so far; one normal and healthy, and the rest premature and defective, stillbirths, or live births that die within hours."

"But there are exceptions, Baby here, and the one over at the Fuzzy-shelter," Lynne said. "Can't we figure out how the exceptions can be encouraged?"

"They're working on that, in a half-hearted way," he told her. "Fuzzies have a menstrual cycle and fertility rhythm, the same as *Homo s. terra*, and apparently the NFMp output is also cyclic, and when the two are out of phase there is a normal viable birth, and not otherwise. And this doesn't happen often enough, and any correction of it would have to be done individually in the case of each female Fuzzy, and nobody even knows how to find out how it could be done."

"But, Gerd, the whole thing doesn't make sense to me," Pancho objected. "I know, 'sense' is nothing but ignorance rationalized, and this isn't my subject, but if this NFMp thing is a racial characteristic, it must be hereditary, and a hereditary tendency to miscarriages premature and defective births, and infant mortality, now; what kind of sense does that make?"

"Well, on the face of it, not much. But we know nothing at all about the racial history of the Fuzzies, and very little about the history of this planet. Say that fifty thousand years ago there were millions of Fuzzies, and say that fifty thousand years ago environmental conditions were radically different. This NFMp hormone was evolved to meet some environmental survival demand, and something in the environment, some article of diet that has now vanished, kept it from injuriously affecting the unborn Fuzzies. Then the environment changed—glaciation, glacial recession, sealevel fluctuation, I can think of dozens of reasons—and after having adapted to original conditions, they couldn't re-adapt to the change. We've seen it on every planet we've ever studied; hundreds of cases on Terra alone. The Fuzzies are just caught in a genetic trap they can't get out of, and we can't get them out of it."

He looked at them; six happy little people, busily fitting many-colored jointed blocks together to make a useless and delightful pretty-thing. Happy in ignorance of their racial doom.

"If we knew how many children the average female has in her lifetime, and how many child-bearers there are, we could figure it out mathematically, I suppose. Ten little Fuzzies, nine little Fuzzies, eight little Fuzzies, and finally no little Fuzzies."

Little Fuzzy thought he was being talked about; he looked up inquiringly.

"Well, they won't all just vanish in the next minute," Jack said. "I expect this gang'll attend my funeral, and there'll be Fuzzies as long as any of you live, and longer. In a couple of million years, there won't be any more humans, I suppose. Let's just be as good to the Fuzzies we have as we can, and make them as happy as possible. "Yes, Baby; you can sit on Pappy's head if you want to."

XVII

The best time for telecast political speeches was between 2000 and 2100, when people were relaxing after dinner and before they started going out or before guests began to arrive. That was a little late for Beta Continent and impossibly so for Gamma, but Delta and Epsilon, to the west, could be reached with late night repeats and about eighty percent of the planetary population was concentrated here on Alpha Continent. Of late, Hugo Ingermann had been having trouble getting on the air at that time. The 2000-2100 spot, he was always told, was already booked, and it would usually turn out to be by the Citizen's Government League which everybody knew but nobody could prove was masterminded by Leslie Coombes and Victor Grego, or it would be Ben Rainsford trying to alibi his Government, or by a lecture on the care and feeding of Fuzzies. But this time, somebody had goofed. This time, he'd been able to get the 2000-2100 spot himself. The voice of the announcer at the telecast station came out of the sound-outlet:

". . . an important message, to all the citizens of the Colony, now, by virtue of the Pendarvis Decisions, enjoying, for the first time, the right of democratic self-government. The next voice you will hear will be that of the Honorable Hugo Ingermann, organizer and leader of the Planetary Prosperity Party. Mr. Ingermann."

The green light came on, and the showback lightened; he lifted his hand in greeting.

"My . . . *friends*" he began.

Frederic Pendarvis was growing coldly angry. It wasn't an organizational abstraction, the Native Adoption Bureau, that was being attacked; it was his wife, Claudette, and he was taking it personally, and a judge should never take anything personally. Why, he had actually been looking at the plump, bland-faced man in the screen, his blue eyes wide with counterfeit sincerity, and wondering whom to send to him with a challenge. Dueling wasn't illegal on Zarathustra, it wasn't on most of the newer planets, but judges did not duel.

And the worst of it, he thought, was that the next time he had to rule against Ingermann in court, Ingermann would be sure, by some innuendo which couldn't be established as overt contempt, to create an impression that it was due to personal vindictiveness.

"It is a disgraceful record," Ingermann was declaring. "A record reeking with favoritism, inequity, class prejudice. In all, twelve hundred applications have been received. Over two hundred have been rejected outright, often on the most frivolous and insulting grounds . . ."

"Mental or emotional instability, inability to support or care for a Fuzzy, irresponsibility, bad character, undesirable home conditions," Claudette, who was beginning to become angry herself, mentioned.

Pierrot and Columbine, on the floor, with a big Mobius strip somebody had made from a length of tape, looked up quickly and then, deciding that it was the man in the wall Mummy was mad at, went back to trying to figure out where the other side always went.

"And of the thousand applications, only three hundred and forty-five have been filled, although five hundred and sixty-six Fuzzies have been brought to this city since the Adoption Bureau was opened. One hundred and seventy-two of these applicants have received a Fuzzy each. One hundred and fifty-five have received two Fuzzies each. And eighteen especially favored ones have received a total of eighty-four Fuzzies.

"And almost without exception, all these Fuzzies have gone to socially or politically prominent persons, persons of wealth. You might as well make up your mind to it, a poor man has no chance whatever. Look who all have gotten Fuzzies under the Fuzzy laws, if one may so term the edicts of a bayonet-imposed Governor. The first papers of adoption were issued to— guess who now?—Victor Grego, the manager-in-chief of the now Charterless Zarathustra Company. And the next pair went to Mrs. Frederic Pendarvis, and beside being the Chief Justice's wife, who is she? Why, the head of the Adoption Bureau, of course. And look at the rest of these names! Nine tenths of them are Zarathustra Company executives." He help up his hands, as though to hush an outburst of righteous indignation. "Now I won't claim, I won't even suppose, that there is any actual corruption or any bribery about this . . ."

"You damned well better hadn't! If you do, I won't sue you, I'll shoot you," Pendarvis barked.

"I won't do either," his wife told him calmly. "But I will answer him. Under veridication, and that's something Hugo Ingermann would never dare do."

"Claudette!" He was shocked. "You wouldn't do that? Not on telecast?"

"On telecast. You can't ignore this sort of thing. If you do, you just admit it by default. There's only one answer to slander, and that's to prove the truth."

"And who's paying for all this?" Ingermann demanded out of the screen. "The Government? When Space Commodore Napier presented us with this Government, and this Governor, at pistol point, there was exactly half a million sols to the account of the Colony in the Bank of Mallorysport. Since then, Governor Rainsford has borrowed approximately half a *billion* sols from the Banking Cartel. And how is Ben Rainsford going to repay them? By taking it out of you and me and all of us, as soon as he can get a Colonial Legislature to rubberstamp his demands for him. And now, do you know what he is spending millions of your money on? On a project to increase the Fuzzy birthrate, so that you'll have more and more Fuzzies for his friends to make pets of and for you to pay the bills for . . ."

"He is a God damned unmitigated liar!" Victor Grego said. "Except for a little work Ruth Ortheris and her husband and Pancho Ybarra and Lynne Andrews are doing out at Holloway's, the company's paying for all that infant mortality research, and I'll have to justify it to the stockholders."

"How about some publicity on that?" Coombes asked.

"You're the political expert; what do you think?"

"I think it would help. I think it would help us, and I think it would help Rainsford. Let's not do it ourselves, though. Suppose I talk to Gus Brannhard, and have him advise Jack Holloway to leak it to the press?"

"Press is going to be after Mrs. Pendarvis for a statement. She knows what the facts are. Let her tell it."

"He make talk about Fuzzies?" Diamond, who had been watching Hugo Ingermann fascinatedly, inquired.

"Yes. Not like Fuzzies. Bad Big One; *tosh-ki Hagga*. Pappy Vic not like him."

"Neither," Coombes said, "does Unka Leslie."

Ahmed Khadra blew cigarette smoke insultingly at the face in the screen. Hugo Ingermann was saying:

"Well, if few politicians and company executives are getting all the Fuzzies, why not make them pay for it, instead of the common people of the planet? Why not charge a fee for adoption papers, say five hundred to a thousand sols? Everybody who's gotten Fuzzies so far could easily pay that. It wouldn't begin to meet the cost of maintaining the Native Affairs Commission, but it would be something . . ."

So that was what the whole thing had been pointed toward. Make it expensive to adopt Fuzzies legally. A black market couldn't compete with free Fuzzies, but let the Adoption Bureau charge five hundred sols apiece for them . . .

"So that's what you're after, you son of a Khooghra? A competitive market."

XVIII

"You got this from one of my laboratory workers," Jan Christiaan Hoenveld accused. "Charlotte Tresca, wasn't it?"

He was calling from his private cubical in the corner of the biochemistry lab; through the glass partition behind him Juan Jimenez could see people working at benches, including, he thought, his informant. For the moment, he disregarded the older man's tone and manner.

"That's correct, Dr. Hoenveld. I met Miss Tresca at a cocktail party last evening. She and some other Science Center people were discussing the different phases of the Fuzzy research, and she mentioned having found hokfusine, or something very similar to it, in the digestive tracts of land-prawns. That had been a week ago; she had reported her findings to you immediately, and assumed that you had reported them to me. Now, I want to know why you didn't."

"Because it wasn't worth reporting," Hoenveld snapped. "In the first place, she wasn't supposed to be working on land-prawns, or hokfusine,"—he almost spat the word in contempt—"at all. She was supposed to be looking for NFMp in this mess of guts and tripes you've been dumping into my laboratory from all over the planet. And in the second place, it was merely a trace-presence of titanium, with which she had probably contaminated the test herself. The girl is an incurably careless and untidy worker. And finally," Hoenveld raged, "I want to know by what right you question my laboratory workers behind my back..."

"Oh, you do? Well, they are not your laboratory workers, Dr. Hoenveld; they are employees of the Zarathustra Company, the same as you. Or I. And the biochemistry laboratory is not your private empire. It is a part of Science Center, of which I am division chief, and from where I sit the difference between you and Charlotte Tresca is barely perceptible to the naked eye. Is that clear, Dr. Hoenveld?"

Hoenveld was looking at him as though a pistol had blown up in his hand. He was, in fact, mildly surprised at himself. A month ago, he wouldn't have dreamed of talking so to anybody, least of all a man as much older than himself as Hoenveld, and one with Hoenveld's imposing reputation.

But as division chief, he had to get things done, and there could be only one chief in the division.

"I am quite well aware of your recent and sudden promotion, Dr. Jimenez," Hoenveld retorted acidly. "Over the heads of a dozen of your seniors."

"Including yourself; well, you've just demonstrated the reason why you were passed over. Now, I want some work done, and if you can't or won't do it, I can promote somebody to replace you very easily."

"What do you think we've been doing? Every ranger and hunter on the company payroll has been shooting everything from damnthings and wild veldbeest to ground-mice and dumping the digestive and reproductive tracts in my—I beg your pardon, I mean the Charterless Zarathustra Company's—laboratory."

"Have you found any trace of NFMp in any of them?"

"Negative. They don't have the glands to secrete it; I have that on the authority of the comparative mammalian anatomists."

"Then stop looking for it; I'll order the specimen collecting stopped at once. Now, I want analyses of land-prawns made, and I want to know just what Miss Tresca found in them; whether it was really hokfusine, or anything similar to it, or just trace-presences of titanium, and I want to know how it gets into the land-prawns' systems and where it concentrates there. I would suggest—correction, I direct—that Miss Tresca be put to work on that herself, and that she report directly to me."

"What's your opinion of Chris Hoenveld, Ernst?" Victor Grego asked.

Mallin frowned—his standard think-seriously-and-weigh-every-word frown.

"Dr. Hoenveld is a most distinguished scientist. He has an encyclopediac grasp on his subject, an infallible memory, and an infinite capacity for taking pains."

"Is that all?"

"Isn't that enough?"

"No. A computer has all that, to a much higher degree, and a computer couldn't make an original scientific discovery in a hundred million years. A computer has no imagination, and neither has Hoenveld."

"Well, he has very little, I'll admit. Why do you ask about him?"

"Juan Jimenez is having trouble with him."

"I can believe it," Mallin said. "Hoenveld has one characteristic a computer lacks. Egotism. Has Jimenez complained to you?"

"Nifflheim, no; he's running Science Center without yelling to Big Brother for help. I got this off the powder-room and coffee-stand telegraph, to which I have excellent taps. Juan cut him down to size; he's doing all right."

"Well, how about the NFMp problem?"

"Nowhere, on hyperdrive. The Fuzzies just manufacture it inside themselves, and nobody knows why. It seems mainly to be associated with the digestive system, and gets from there into the blood-stream, and into the gonads, in both sexes, from there. Thirty-six births, so far; three viable."

From the terrace outside came the happy babble of Fuzzy voices. They were using their Fuzzyphones to talk to one another; wanted to talk like the Hagga. Poor little tail-enders of a doomed race.

The whole damned thing was getting too big for comfort, Jack Holloway thought. A month ago, there'd only been Gerd and Ruth and Lynne Andrews and Pancho Ybarra, and George Lunt, and the men George had brought when he'd transferred from the Constabulary. They all had cocktails together before dinner, and ate at one table, and had bull-sessions in the evenings, and everybody had known what everybody else was doing. And there had only been forty or fifty Fuzzies, beside his and George's and Gerd's and Ruth's.

Now Gerd had three assistants, and Ruth had dropped work on Fuzzy psychology and was helping him with whatever he was doing, and what that was he wasn't quite sure. He wasn't quite sure what anybody was doing, any more. And Pancho was practically commuting to and from Mallorysport, and Ernst Mallin was out at least once a week. Funny, too; he used to think Mallin was a solid, three-dimensional bastard, and now he found he rather liked him. Even Victor Grego was out, one week-end, and everybody liked him.

Lynne had a couple of helpers, too, and a hospital and clinic, and there was a Fuzzy school, where they were taught Lingua Terra and how to use Fuzzyphones and about the strange customs of the Hagga. Some old hen Ruth had kidnapped from the Mallorysport schools was in charge of it, or thought she was; actually Little Fuzzy and Ko-Ko and Cinderella and Lizzie Borden and Dillinger were running it.

And he and George Lunt couldn't yell back and forth to each other any more, because their offices, at opposite ends of the long hut, were partitioned off and separated by a hundred and twenty feet of middle office, full of desks and business machines and roboclerks, and humans working with them. And he had a secretary, now, and she had a secretary, or at least a stenographer, of her own.

Gerd van Riebeek came in from the outside, tossing his hat on top of a microbook-case and unbuckling his pistol.

"Hi, Jack. Anything new?" he asked.

Gerd and Ruth had been away for a little over a week, in the country to the south. It must have been fun, just the two of them and Complex and Superego and Dr. Crippen and Calamity Jane, camping in Gerd's airboat and visiting the posts Lunt had strung out along the edge of the big woods.

"I was going to ask you that. Where's Ruth?"

"She's staying another week, at the Kirtland plantation, with Superego and Complex; there must be fifty to seventy-five Fuzzies there; she's helping the Kirtland people with them, teaching them not to destroy young sugarplant shoots. Kirtland's been taking a lot of damage to his shoots from zatku. What's the latest from Mallorysport?"

"Well, nowhere on the NFMp, but they seem to have found something interesting about the land-prawns."

"More on that?" Gerd had heard about the alleged hokfusine. "Have they found out what it is?"

"It isn't hokfusine, it's just a rather complicated titanium salt. The land-prawns eat titanium, mostly in moss and fungus and stuff like that. It probably grades about ten atoms to the ton on what they eat. But they fix it, apparently in that middle intestine that they have. I have a big long writeup on what it does there. The Fuzzies seem to convert it to something else in their own digestive system. Whatever it does, hokfusine seems to do it a lot better. They're still working on it."

"They ate land-prawns all along, but it was only since this new generation hatched, this Spring, that they really got all they wanted of them. I wonder what they ate before, up north."

"Well, we know what all they eat beside zatku and the stuff we give them. Animals small enough to kill with those little sticks, fruit, bird-eggs, those little yellow lizards, grubs."

"What are Paine's Marines doing up north now, beside looking for non-existent Fuzzy-catchers?"

"That's about all. Flying patrol, taking photos, mapping. They say there are lots of Fuzzies north of the Divide that haven't started south yet, probably haven't heard about the big zatku bonanza yet."

"I'm going up there, Jack. I want to look at them, see what they live on."

"Don't go right away; wait a week, and I'll go along with you. I still have a lot of this damn stuff to clear up, and I have to go in to Mallorysport tomorrow. Casagra's talking about recalling Paine and his men and vehicles. You know where that would put us."

Gerd nodded. "We'd have to double the ZNPF. It's all George can do to maintain those posts along the edge of the big woods and fly inspections in the farm country, without having to patrol in the north too."

"I don't know how we could pay or equip them, even if we could recruit them. We're operating on next year's budget now. That's another thing I'll have to talk to Ben about. He'll have to allocate us more money."

"God damn it, there's no money to give him!"

Ben Rainsford spoke aloud and bitterly, and then caught himself and puffed furiously on his pipe, the smoke reddening in the sunset afterglow. Have to watch that; people hear him talking to himself, it would be all over Government House, and all over Mallorysport in the next day, that Governor Rainsford was going crazy. Not that it would be any wonder if he were.

The three Fuzzies, Flora and Fauna and their friend

Diamond, who had gotten hold of a lot of wooden strips of the sort the gardeners used for trelliswork and were building a little arbor of their own, looked up quickly and then realized that he wasn't speaking to them and went on with what they were doing. The sun had gone to bed already, and the sky-light was fading, and they wanted to get whatever it was they were making finished before it got dark. Fuzzies, like Colonial Governors, found time running out on them occasionally.

Time was running out fast for him. The ninety days the CZC had allowed him to take over all the public services they were no longer obliged to maintain were more than half gone now, and nothing had been done. The election for delegates to a constitutional convention was still a month in the future, and he had no idea how long it would take the elected delegates, whoever they'd be, to argue out a constitution, and how long thereafter it would take to get a Colonial Legislature set up, and how long after tax laws were enacted it would be before the Government would begin collecting money.

He wished he'd been able to borrow that half billion sols from the Banking Cartel that Hugo Ingermann had been yakking about. Ingermann had later been forced to back down to something closer the actual figure of fifty million, just as he had been forced to retreat from some of his exaggerated statements about the Adoption Bureau, but it seemed that the public still believed his original statements and were disregarding the hedging and weasel-worded retractions. Fifty million sounded like a lot of money, too—till you had to run a planetary government on it, and everything was going to cost so much more than he had expected.

The Native Affairs Commission, for instance. He and Jack had both believed that a hundred and fifty men would be ample for the Native Protection Force; now they were finding that three times that number wouldn't be enough. They had thought that Gerd and

Ruth van Riebeek and Lynne Andrews, and Pancho Ybarra, on loan from the Navy, would be able to do all the study and research work; now that was spread out to Mallorysport Hospital and Science Center, for which the CZC was paying and would expect compensation. And the Adoption Bureau was costing as much, now, as the whole original Native Affairs Commission estimate.

At least, he'd been able to do one thing for Jack. Alex Napier had agreed that protection and/or policing of natives on Class-IV planets was a proper function of the Armed Forces, and instead of recalling his fifty men, Casagra had been ordered to reenforce them with twenty more.

The Fuzzies suddenly stopped what they were doing and turned. Diamond drew his Fuzzyphone. "Pappy Vic!" he called, in delighted surprise. "Come; look what we make!" Flora and Fauna were whooping greetings, too.

He rose, and saw behind him the short, compactly-built man, familiar from news-screen views, whom he had so far avoided meeting personally. Victor Grego greeted the Fuzzies, and then said, "Good evening, Governor. Sorry to intrude, but Miss Glenn has a dinner-and-dancing date, and I told her I'd get Diamond myself."

"Good evening, Mr. Grego." Somehow, he didn't feel the hostility to the man that he had expected. "Could you wait a little while? They have an important project, here, and they want to finish it while there's still daylight."

"Well, so I see." Grego spoke to the Fuzzies in their own language, and listened while they explained what they were doing. "Of course; we can't interfere with that."

The Fuzzies went back to their trellis-building. He and Grego sat down in lawn-chairs; Grego lit a cigarette. He watched the CZC manager-in-chief as the latter sat watching the Fuzzies. This couldn't be Victor

Grego; "Victor Grego" was a label for a personification of black-hearted villainy and ruthless selfishness; this was a pleasant-spoken, courteous gentleman who loved Fuzzies, and was considerate of his employees.

"Miss Glenn's date was with Captain Ahmed Khadra," Grego was saying, to make conversation. "The fifth in the last two weeks. I'm afraid I'm just before losing a good Fuzzy-sitter by marriage."

"I'm afraid so; they seem quite serious about each other. If so, she'll be getting a good husband. I've known Ahmed for some time; he was at the Constabulary post near my camp, on Beta. It's too bad," he added, "that he seems to be getting nowhere on this Herckerd-Novaes investigation. It's certainly not from lack of trying."

"My police chief, Harry Steefer, is getting nowhere just as rapidly," Grego said. "He's ready to give the whole thing up, and when Harry Steefer gives up, it's hopeless."

"Do you think there is anything to this theory that somebody is training those Fuzzies to help catch other Fuzzies?"

Grego shook his head. "You know Fuzzies at least as well as I do, Governor. Almost two months; anything you can train a Fuzzy to do, you can train him to do it in less than that," he said. "And I don't see why anybody would try to catch wild Fuzzies, not with the bloodthirsty laws you've enacted. Criminals only take chances in proportion to profits, and almost anybody who wants a Fuzzy can get one free."

That was true. And there was no indication of any black market in Fuzzies here, and Jack's patrols over northern Beta Continent hadn't found any evidence that anybody was live-trapping Fuzzies there.

"Ahmed had an idea, for a while, that they were going into the export business; catching Fuzzies to smuggle out for sale off-planet."

"He mentioned that to Harry Steefer. Jack Holloway was talking to me about that, too; wanted to know what could be done to prevent it. I told him it would be impossible to get Fuzzies onto a ship from Darius, or onto Darius from Mallorysport Space Terminal. As long as we keep our 'flagrant and heinous space-traffic monopoly,' you can be sure no Fuzzies are going to be shipped off-planet."

"You think Ingermann really has anything to do with it?" he asked hopefully, recognizing the source of the quotation.

"If there is a black market in Fuzzies, Ingermann's back of it," Grego said, as though stating a natural law. "In the six or so years he's infected this planet, I've learned a lot about the *soi-disant* Honorable Hugo Ingermann, and none of it's been good."

"Ahmed Khadra thinks his attacks on the CZC space-monopoly may stem from a desire to get some way around your controls at the ground terminal here and on Darius. Of course, he's talking about a Government spaceport, and that would be just as tightly controlled . . ."

Grego hesitated for a moment, then dropped his cigarette to the ground and heeled it out. He leaned toward Rainsford in his chair.

"Governor, you know, yourself, that as things stand you can't build a second spaceport here," he said. "Ingermann knows that, too. He's making that issue to embarrass you and to attack the CZC at the same time. He has no expectation that your Government would build any spaceport facilities here. He certainly hopes not; he wants to do that himself."

"Where the devil would he get the money?"

"He could get it. Unless I miss my guess, he's getting it now, or as soon as a ship can get in, on Marduk. There are a number of shipping companies who would like to get in here in competition with Terra-Baldur-Marduk Spacelines, and there are quite a few import-export houses there who would like to trade on Zarathustra in competition with CZC. Inside six months somebody will be trying to put in a spaceport here.

If they can get land to set it on. And due to a great error in my judgment eight years ago, the land's available."

"Where?"

"Right here on Alpha Continent, less than a hundred miles from where we're sitting. A wonderful place for a spaceport. You weren't here, then, were you, Governor?"

"No. I came here, I blush to say, on the same ship that brought Ingermann, six and a half years ago."

"Well, you got here, and do did he, after it was over, but just before that we had a big immigration boom. At that time, the company wasn't interested in local business, just off-planet trade in veldbeest meat. A lot of independent concerns started, manufacturing, food-production, that sort of thing that we didn't want to bother with. We sold land north of the city, in mile and two-mile square blocks, about two thousand square miles of it. Then the immigrants stopped coming, and a lot of them moved away. There simply wasn't employment for them. Most of the companies that had been organized went broke. Some of the factories that were finished operated for a while; most of them were left unfinished. The banks took over some of the land; most of it got into the hands of the shylocks; and since the Fuzzy Trial Ingermann has been acquiring title to a lot of it. Since the Fuzzy Trial, nobody else has been spending money for real-estate; everybody expects to get all the free land they want."

"Well, he'll probably make some money out of that, but the people who come in here with the capital will be the ones to control it, won't they?"

"Of course they will, but that's honest business; Ingermann isn't interested. He's expecting an increase of about two to three hundred percent in the planetary population in the next five years. With eighty percent of the land-surface in public domain, that's probably an under-estimate. Most of them will be voters; Ingermann's going to try to control that vote."

And if he did ... His own position was secure; Colonial Governors were appointed, and it took something like the military intervention which had put him into office to unseat one. But a Colonial Governor had to govern through and with the consent of a Legislature. He wasn't looking forward happily to a Legislature controlled by Hugo Ingermann. Neither, he knew, was Grego.

He'd have to be careful, though. Grego wanted to put the company back in its old pre-Fuzzy position of planetary dominance. He was still violently opposed to that.

It was almost dark, now. The Fuzzies had put the final touches to the lacy trellis they had built, and came crowding over, wanting Pappy Ben and Pappy Vic to come look. They went and examined it, and spoke commendation. Grego picked up Diamond; Flora and Fauna were wanting him to go and sit down and furnish them a lap to sit on.

"I've been worrying about just that," he said, when he was back in his chair, with the Fuzzies climbing up onto him. "A lot of the older planets are beginning to overpopulate, and there's never room enough for everybody on Terra. There'll be a rush here in about a year. If I can only get things stabilized before then ..."

Grego was silent for a moment. "If you're worried about all those public-health and welfare and service functions, forget about them for a while," he said. "I know, I said the company would discontinue them in ninety days, but that was right after the Pendarvis Decisions, and nobody knew what the situation was going to be. We can keep them going for a year, at least."

"The Government won't have any more money a year from now," he said. "And you'll expect compensation."

"Of course we will, but we won't demand gold or Federation notes. Tax-script, bonds, land-script ..."

Land-script, of course; the law required a Colonial Government to make land available to Federation citizens, but it did not require such land to be given free. That might be one way to finance the Government.

It could also be a way for the Zarathustra Company, having gotten the Government deeply into debt, to regain what had been lost in the aftermath of the Fuzzy Trial.

"Suppose you have Gus Brannhard talk it over with Leslie Coombes," Grego was suggesting. "You can trust Gus not to stick the Government's foot into any bear-trap, can't you?"

"Why, of course, Mr. Grego. I want to thank you, very much, for this. That public services takeover was worrying me more than anything else."

Yet he couldn't feel relieved, and he couldn't feel grateful at all. He felt discomfited, and angry at himself more than at Grego.

XIX

Gerd van Riebeek crouched at the edge of the low cliff, slowly twisting the selector-knob of a small screen in front of him. The view changed; this time he was looking through the eye of a pickup fifty feet below and five hundred yards to the left. Nothing in it moved except a wind-stirred branch that jiggled a spray of ragged leaves in the foreground. The only thing from the sound-outlet was a soft drone of insects, and the *tweet-twonk, tweet-twonk* of a presumably love-hungry banjo-bird. Then something just out of sight scuffled softly among the dead leaves. He turned up the sound-volume slightly.

"What do you think it is?"

Jack Holloway, beside him, rose to one knee, raising his binoculars.

"I can't see anything. Try the next one."

Gerd twisted the knob again. This pickup was closer to the ground; it showed a vista of woods lit by shafts of sunlight falling between trees. Now he could hear rustling and scampering, and with ultrasonic earphone, Fuzzy voices:

"This way. Not far. Find *hatta-zosa*."

Jack was looking down at the open slope below the cliff.

"If that's what they call goofers, I see six of them from here," he said. "Probably a dozen more I can't see." He watched, listening. "Here they come, now."

The Fuzzies had stopped talking and were making

very little noise; then they came into view; eight of them, in single file. The weapons they carried were longer and heavier than the prawn-killers of the southern Fuzzies, knobbed instead of paddle-shaped, and sharp-pointed on the other end. All of them had picked up stones which they carried in their free hands. They all stopped, then three of them backed away into the brush again. The other five spread out in a skirmish line and waited. He shut off the screen and crawled over beside Jack to peep over the edge of the cliff.

There were seven goofers, now; rodent-looking things with dark gray fur, a foot and a half long and six inches high at the shoulder, all industriously tearing off bark and digging at the roots of young trees. No wonder the woods were so thin, around here; if there were any number of them it was a wonder there were any trees at all. He picked up a camera and aimed it, getting some shots of them.

"Something else figuring on getting some lunch here," Jack said, sweeping the sky with his glasses. "Harpy, a couple of miles off. Ah, another one. We'll stick around a while; we may have to help our friends out."

The five Fuzzies at the edge of the brush stood waiting. The goofers hadn't heard them, and were still tearing and chewing at the bark and digging at the roots. Then, having circled around, the other three burst out suddenly, hurling their stones and running forward with their clubs. One stone hit a goofer and knocked it down; instantly, one of the Fuzzies ran forward and brained it with his club. The other two rushed a second goofer, felling and dispatching it with their clubs. The other fled, into the skirmish line on the other side. Two were hit with stones, and finished off on the ground. The others got away. The eight Fuzzies gathered in a clump, seemed to debate pursuit for a moment, and then abandoned the idea. They had four goofers, a half-goofer apiece. That was a good meal for them.

They dragged their game together and began tearing the carcasses apart, using teeth and fingers, helping one another dismember them, tearing off skin and pulling meat loose, using stones to break bones. Gerd kept his camera going, filming the feast.

"Our gang's got better table-manners," he commented.

"Our gang have the knives we make for them. Beside, our gang mostly eat zatku, and they break off the manibles and make little lobster-picks out of them. They're ahead of our gang in one way, though. The Fuzzies south of the Divide don't hunt cooperatively," Jack said.

The two dots in the sky were larger and closer; a third had appeared.

"We better do something about that," he advised, reaching for his rifle.

"Yes." Jack put down the binoculars and secured his own rifle, checking it. "Let them eat as long as they can; they'll get a big surprise in a minute or so."

The Fuzzies seemed to be aware of the presence of the harpies. Maybe there were ultrasonic wing-vibration sounds they could hear; he couldn't be sure, even with the hearing aid. There was so much ultrasonic noise in the woods, and he hadn't learned, yet, to distinguish. The Fuzzies were eating more rapidly. Finally, one pointed and cried, *"Gotza bizzo!" Gotza* was another native zoological name he had learned, though the Fuzzies at Holloway's Camp mostly said, "Hah'py," now. The diners grabbed their weapons and what meat they could carry and dashed into the woods. One of the big pterodactyl-things was almost overhead, another was within a few hundred yards, and the third was coming in behind him. Jack sat up, put his left arm through his rifle-sling, cuddled the butt to this cheek and propped his elbows on his knees. The nearest harpy must have caught a movement in the brush below; it banked and started to dive.

Jack's 9.7 magnum bellowed. The harpy made a graceless flop-over in the air and dropped. The one behind banked quickly and tried to gain altitude; Gerd shot it. Jack's rifle thundered again, and the third harpy thrashed leathery wings and dropped.

From below, there was silence, and then a clamor of Fuzzy voices:

"Harpies dead; what make do?"

"Thunder; maybe kill harpies! Maybe kill us next!"

"Bad place, this! *Bizzo, fazzu!*"

Roughly, *fazzu* meant, "Scram."

Jack was laughing. "Little Fuzzy took it a lot calmer the first time he saw me shoot a harpy," he said. "By that time, though, he'd seen so much he wasn't surprised at anything." He replaced the two fired rounds in the magazine of his rifle. "Well, *bizzo, fazzu*; we won't get any more movies around here."

They went around with the car, collecting the pickups they had planted, then lifted out, turning south toward the horizon-line of the Divide, the mountain range that stretched like the cross-stroke of an H between the West Coast Range and the Eastern Cordilleras. Evidently the Fuzzies never crossed it much; the language of the northern Fuzzies, while comprehensible, differed distinguishably from that spoken by the ones who had come in to the camp. Apparently the news of the bumper crop of zatku hadn't gotten up here at all.

They talked about that, cruising south at five thousand feet, with the foothills of the Divide sliding away under them and the line of sheer mountains drawing closer. They'd have to establish a permanent camp up here; contact these Fuzzies and make friends with them, give them tools and weapons, learn about them.

That was, if the Native Commission budget would permit. They talked about that, too.

Then they argued about whether to stay up here for another few days, or start back to the camp.

"I think we'd better go back," Jack said, somewhat

regretfully. "We've been away for a week. I want to see what's going on, now."

"They'd screen us if anything was wrong."

"I know. I still think we'd better go back. Let's cross the Divide and camp somewhere on the other side, and go on in tomorrow morning."

"*Hokay; bizzo.*" He swung the aircar left a trifle. "We'll follow that river to the source and cross over there."

The river came down through a wide valley, narrowing and growing more rapid as they ascended it. Finally, they came to where it emerged, a white mountain torrent, from the mouth of a canyon that cut into the main range of the Divide. He took the car down to within a few hundred feet and cut speed, entering the canyon. At first, it was wide, with a sandy beach on either side of the stream and trees back to the mountain face and up the steep talus at the foot of it. Granite at the bottom, and then weathered sandstone, and then, for a couple of hundred feet, gray, almost unweathered flint.

"Gerd," Jack said, at length, "take her up a little, and get a little closer to the side of the canyon." He shifted in his seat, and got his binoculars. "I want a close look at that."

He wondered why, briefly. Then it struck him.

"You think that's what I think it is?" he asked.

"Yeah. Sunstone-flint." Jack didn't seem particularly happy about it. "See that little bench, about half way up? Set her down there. I'm going to take a look at that."

The bench, little more than a wide ledge, was covered with thin soil; a few small trees and sparse brush grew on it. A sheer face of gray flint rose for a hundred feet above it. They had no blasting explosives, but there was a microray scanner and a small vibrohammer in the toolkit. They set the aircar down and went to work, cracking and scanning flint, and after two hours they had a couple of sunstones. They were nothing spectacular—an irregular globe seven or eight millimeters in diameter and a small elipsoid not quite twice as big. However, when Jack held them against the hot bowl of his pipe, they began to glow.

"What are they worth, Jack?"

"I don't know. Some of these freelance gem-buyers would probably give as much as six or eight hundred for the big one. When the company still had the monopoly, they'd have paid about four-fifty. Be worth twenty-five hundred on Terra. But look around. This layer's three hundred feet thick; it runs all the way up the canyon, and probably for ten or fifteen miles along the mountain on either side." He knocked out his pipe, blew through the stem, and pocketed it. "And it all belongs to the Fuzzies."

He started to laugh at that, and then remembered. This was, by executive decree, the Fuzzy Reservation. The Fuzzies owned it and everything on it, and the Government and the Native Commission were only trustees. Then he began laughing again.

"But, Jack! The Fuzzies can't mine sunstones, and they wouldn't know what to do with them if they could."

"No. But this is their country. They were born here, and they have a right to live here, and beside that, we gave it to them, didn't we? It belongs to them, sunstones and all."

"But Jack . . ." He looked up and down the canyon at the gray flint on either side; as Jack said, it would extend for miles back into the mountain on either side. Even allowing one sunstone to ten cubic feet of flint, and even allowing for the enormous labor of digging them out . . . "You mean, just let a few Fuzzies scamper around over it and chase goofers, and not do anything with it?" The idea horrified him. "Why, they don't even know this is the Fuzzy Reservation."

"They know it's their home. Gerd, this has happened on other Class-IV planets we've moved in on. We give the natives a reservation; we tell them it'll be theirs forever, Terran's word of honor. Then we find something valuable on it—gold on Loki, platinum on Thor, vanadium and wolfram on Hathor, nitrates on Yggdrasil, uranium on Gimli. So the natives get shoved off onto another reservation, where there isn't anything anybody wants, and finally they just get shoved off, period. We aren't going to do that here, to the Fuzzies."

"What are you going to do? Try to keep it a secret?" he asked. "If that's what you want, we'll just throw those two sunstones in the river and forget about it," he agreed. "But how long do you think it'll be before somebody else finds out about it?"

"We can keep other people out of here. That's what the Fuzzy Reservation's for, isn't it?"

"We need people to keep people out; Paine's Marines, George Lunt's Protection Force. I think we can trust George. I wouldn't know about Paine. Anybody below them I wouldn't trust at all. Sooner or later somebody'll fly up this canyon and see this, and then it'll be out. And you know what'll happen then." He thought for a moment. "Are you going to tell Ben Rainsford?"

"I wish you hadn't asked me that, Gerd." Jack fumbled his pipe and tobacco out of his pocket. "I suppose I'll have to. Have to give him these stones; they're Government property. Well, bizzo; we'll go straight to camp." He looked up at the sun. "Make it in about three hours. Tomorrow I'll go to Mallorysport."

"I'm afraid to believe it, Dr. Jimenez," Ernst Mallin said. "It would be so wonderful if it were true. Can you be certain?"

"We're all certain, now, that this hormone, NFMp, is what prevents normal embryonic development," Juan Jimenez, in the screen, replied. "We're certain, now, that hokfusine combines destructively with NFMp; even Chris Hoenveld, he's seen it happen in a test tube, and he has to believe it whether he wants to or not. It appears that hokfusine also has an inhibitory effect on the glands secreting NFMp. But to be certain, we'll have to wait four more months, until the infants conceived after the mothers began eating Extee Three are born. Ideally, we should wait until the females we have begun giving daily doses of pure hokfusine conceive and bear children. But if I'm not certain now, I'm confident."

"What put your people onto this, Dr. Jimenez?"

"A hunch," the younger man smiled. "A hunch by the girl in Dr. Hoenveld's lab, Charlotte Tresca." The smile became an audible laugh. "Hoenveld is simply furious about it. No sound theoretical basis, just a lot of unsupported surmises. You know how he talks. He did have to grant her results; they've been duplicated. But he rejects her whole line of reasoning."

He would; Jan Christiaan Hoenveld's mind plodded obstinately along, step by step, from A to B to C to D; it wasn't fair for somebody suddenly to leap to W or X and run from there to Z. For his own part, Ernst Mallin respected hunches; he knew how much mental activity went on below the level of consciousness and with what seeming irrationality fragments of it rose to the conscious mind. His only regret was that he had so few good hunches, himself.

"Well, what was her reasoning?" he asked. "Or was it pure intuition?"

"Well, she just got the idea that hokfusine would neutralize the NFMp hormone, and worked from there," Jimenez said. "As she rationalizes it, all Fuzzies have a craving for land-prawn meat, without exception. This is a racial constant with them. Right?"

"Yes, as far as we can tell. I hate to use the word loosely, but I'd say, instinctual."

"And all Fuzzies, for which read, all studied individuals, have a craving for Extee Three. Once they taste the stuff, they eat it at every opportunity. This isn't a learned taste, like our taste for, say, coffee or tobacco or alcohol; every human has to learn to like all three. The Fuzzy's response to Extee Three is immediate and automatic. Still with it, Doctor?"

"Oh, yes; I've seen quite a few Fuzzies taking their first taste of Extee Three. It's just what you call it; a physical response." He gave that a moment's thought, adding: "If it's an instinct, it's the result of natural selection."

"Yes. She reasoned that a taste for the titanium-molecule compound present both in land-prawns and Extee Three contributed to racial survival; that Fuzzies lacking it died out, and Fuzzies having it to a pronounced degree survived and transmitted it. So she went to work—over Hoenveld's vehement objections that she was wasting her time—and showed the effect of hokfusine on the NFMp hormone. Now, the physiologists who had that theory about cyclic production of NFMp getting out of phase with the menstrual cycle and permitting an occasional viable birth are finding that the NFMp fluctuations aren't cyclic at all but related to hokfusine consumption."

"Well, you have a fine circumstantial case there. Everything seems to fit together with everything else. As you say, you'll have to wait about a year before you can really prove a one-to-one relationship between hokfusine and viable births. but if I were inclined to gamble I'd risk a small wager on it."

Jimenez grinned. "I have, already, with Dr. Hoenveld. I think it's money in the bank now."

Bennett Rainsford warmed the two sunstones between his palms, then rolled them, like a pair of dice, on the desk in front of him. He had been so happy, ever since Victor Grego had called him to tell him what had been discovered at Science Center about the hokfusine and the NFMp hormone. They were on the right track, he was sure of it, and in a few years all the Fuzzy children would be born alive and normal.

And then, just after lunch, Jack Holloway had come dropping out of the sky from Beta Continent with this.

"You can't keep it a secret, Jack. You can't keep any discovery a secret, because anything anybody discovers, somebody else can, and will, discover later. Look how the power interests tried to suppress the discovery of direct conversion of nuclear energy to electric current, back in the First Century. Look how they tried to suppress the Abbot Drive."

"This is different," Jack Holloway argued, bullheadedly. "This isn't a scientific principle anybody, anywhere, can discover. This is something at a certain place, and if we can keep people away from it . . ."

"*Quis custodiet ipsos custodes?*" Then, realizing that Latin was *terra incognita* to Jack, he translated: "Who'll watch the watchmen?"

Jack nodded. "That's what Gerd said. A thing like that would be an awful strain on anybody's moral fiber. And you know what'll happen as soon as it gets out."

"There'd be pressure on me to open the Fuzzy Reservation. Hugo Ingermann's John Doe and Richard Roe and all. I suppose I could stall it off till a legislature was elected, but after that . . ."

"I wasn't talking about political pressure. I was talking about a sunstone rush. There'd be twenty thousand men stampeding up there, with everything they could put onto contragravity. And everything they could find to shoot with, too. And the longer it's stalled off, the worse it'll be, because in six months the off-planet immigrants'll start coming in."

He hadn't thought of that. He should have; he'd been on other frontier planets where rich deposits of mineral wealth had been discovered. And there was nothing in the Galaxy that concentrated more value in less bulk than sunstones.

"Ben, I've been thinking," Jack continued. "I don't like the idea, but it's the only idea I have. Those sunstones are in a little section about fifty miles square on the north side of the Divide. Suppose the Government makes that a sort of reservation-inside-the-reservation, and operates the sunstone mines. You do it before anything leaks out—announce that the Government has discovered sunstones on the Fuzzy Reservation, that the Government claims all the sunstones on Fuzzy land in the name of the Fuzzies, and that the Government is operating all sunstone mines, and it'll head off the rush, or the worst of it. And the Fuzzies'll get out of that immediate area; they won't stay around where there's underground blasting. And the money the Government gets out of it can go to the Fuzzies in protection and welfare and medical aid and *shoppo-diggo* and *shodda-bag* and *esteefee*."

"Have you any idea what it would cost to start an operation like that, before we could even begin getting out sunstones in paying quantities?"

"Yes. I've been digging sunstones as long as anybody knew there were sunstones. But this is a good thing, Ben, and if you have a good thing you can always finance it."

"It would protect the Fuzzies' rights, and they'd benefit enormously. But the initial expense..."

"Well, lease the mineral rights to somebody who could finance it. The Government would get a royalty, the Fuzzies would benefit, the Reservation would be kept intact."

"But who? Who would be able to lease it?"

He knew, even as he asked the question. The Charterless Zarathustra Company; they could operate that mine. Why, that mine would be something on the odd-jobs level, compared to what they'd done on the Big Blackwater Swamp. Lease them the entire mineral rights for the Reservation; that would keep everybody else out.

But it would put the Company back where they'd been before the Pendarvis Decisions; it would give them back their sunstone monopoly; it would... Why, it was unthinkable!

Unthinkable, hell. He was thinking about it now, wasn't he?

Victor Grego crushed out his cigarette and leaned back in his relaxer-chair, closing his eyes. From the Fuzzyroom, he could hear muted voices, and the frequent popping of shots. Diamond was enjoying a screen-play. He was very good about keeping the volume turned down, so as not to bother Pappy Vic, but he'd get some weird ideas about life among the Hagga from some of those shows. Well, the good Hagga always licked the bag Hagga in the end, that was one thing.

He went back to thinking about bad Hagga, four of them in particular. Ivan Bowlby, Spike Heenan, Raul Laporte, Leo Thaxter.

Mallorysport was full of bad Hagga, on the lower echelons, but those four were the General Staff. Bowlby was the entertainment business. Beside the telecast show which Diamond was watching at the moment, that included prize-fights, nightclubs, prostitution and, without doubt, dope. Maybe he'd like to get Fuzzies as attractions at his night-spots, and through that part of his business he could make contacts with well to do people who wanted Fuzzies, couldn't adopt them, and would pay fancy prices for them. If there really were a black market, he'd be in it.

Spike Heenan was gambling; crap-games, numbers racket, bookmaking. On sport-betting, his lines and Bowlby's would cross with mutual profit. Laporte was racketeering, extortion, plain old-fashioned country-style crime. And stolen goods, of course, and, while there'd been money in it, illicit gem-buying.

Leo Thaxter was the biggest, and the most respectably fronted, of the four. L. Thaxter, Loan Broker & Private Financier. He loaned money publicly at a righteously legal seven percent; he also loaned, at much higher rates, to all the shylocks in town, who, in turn, loaned it at six-for-five to people who could not borrow elsewhere, including suckers who went broke in Spike Heenan's crap-games, and he used Raul

Laporte's hoodlums to do his collecting.

And, notoriously but unprovably, behind them stood Hugo Ingermann, Mallorysport's unconvicted underworld generalissimo.

Maybe they were just before proving it, now. Leslie Coombes' investigators had established that all four of them, and especially Thaxter, were the dummy owners behind whom Ingermann controlled most of the land the company had unwisely sold eight years ago, the section north of Mallorysport that was now dotted with abandoned factories and commercial buildings. And it was pretty well established that those four had been the John Doe, Richard Roe, *et alii*, who had been represented in court by Ingermann just after the Pendarvis Decisions.

Strains of music were now coming from the Fuzzyroom; the melodrama was evidently over. He opened his eyes, lit another cigarette, and began going over what he knew about Ingermann's four chief henchmen. Thaxter; he'd come to Zarathustra a few years before Ingermann. Small-time racketeer, at first, and then he'd tried to organize labor unions, but labor unions organized by outsiders had been frowned upon by the company, and he'd been shown the wisdom of stopping that. Then he'd organized an independent planters' marketing cooperative, and from that he'd gotten into shylocking. There'd been some woman with him, at first, wife or reasonable facsimile. Maybe she was still around; have Coombes look into that. She might be willing to talk.

Diamond strolled in from the Fuzzy-room.

"Pappy Vic! Make talk with Diamond, *plis.*"

Lieutenant Fitz Mortlake, acting-in-charge of company detective bureau for the 1800-2400 shift, yawned. Twenty more minutes; less than that if Bert Eggers got in early to relieve him. He riffled through the stack of complaint-sheet copies on the desk and put a paperweight on them. In the squadroom outside the mechanical noises of card-machines and teleprinters and the occasional howl of a sixty-speed audiovisual transmission were being replaced by human sounds, voices and laughter and the scraping of chairs, as the midnight-to-six shift began filtering in. He was wondering whether to go home and read till he became sleepy, or drift around the bars to see if he could pick up a girl, when Bert Eggers pushed past a couple of sergeants at the door and entered.

"Hi, Fitz; how's it going?"

"Oh, quiet. We found out where Jayser hid that stuff; we have all of it, now. And Millman and Nogahara caught those kids who were stealing engine parts out of Warehouse Ten. We have them in detention; we haven't questioned them yet."

"We'll take care of that. They work for the company?"

"Two of them do. The third is just a kid, seventeen. Juvenile Court can have him. We think they were selling the stuff to Honest Hymie."

"Uhuh. I'll suspect anybody they all call Honest Anybody or anything," Eggers said, sitting down as he vacated the chair.

He took off his coat, pulled his shoulder holster and pistol from the bottom drawer and put it on, resuming the coat. He gathered up his lighter and tobacco pouch, and then discovered that his pipe was missing, and hunted the desk-top for it, unearthing it from under some teleprinted photographs.

"What are these?" Eggers asked, looking at them.

"Herckerd and Novaes, false alarm number steen thousand. A couple of woods-tramps who turned up on Epsilon."

Eggers made a sour face. "Those damn Fuzzies have made more work for us," he began. "And now, my kids are after me to get them one. So's my wife. You know what? Fuzzies are a status-symbol, now. If you don't have a Fuzzy, you might as well move to Junktown with the rest of the bums."

"I don't have a Fuzzy, and I haven't moved to Junktown yet."

"You don't have kids in high school."

"No, thank God!"

"Bet he doesn't have finance-company trouble, either," one of the sergeants in the doorway said.

Bert was going to make some retort to that. Before he could, another voice spoke up:

"*Yeeek!*"

"Speak of the devil," somebody said.

"You have that Fuzzy in here, Fitz?" Eggers demanded. "Where the hell . . . ?"

"There he is," one of the men in the doorway said, pointing.

The Fuzzy, who had been behind the desk-chair, came out into view. He pulled the bottom of Eggers' coat, yeeking again. He looked like a hunchback Fuzzy.

"What's he got on his back?" Eggers reached down. "Whatta you got there, anyhow?"

It was a little rucksack, with leather shoulder-straps and a drawstring top. As soon as Eggers displayed an interest in it, the Fuzzy climbed out of it as though glad to be rid of it. Mortlake picked it up and put it on the desk; over ten pounds, must weigh almost as much as the Fuzzy. Eggers opened the drawstrings and put his hand into it.

"It's full of gravel," he said, and brought out a handful.

The gravel was glowing faintly. Eggers let go of it as though it were as hot as it looked.

"Holy God!" It was the first time he ever heard anybody screaming in baritone. "The damn things are sunstones!"

XX

"But what for?" Diamond was insisting. "What for Big Ones first, bang, bang, make dead? Not good. What for not make friend, make help, have fun?"

"Well, some Big Ones bad, make trouble. Other Big Ones fight to stop trouble."

"But what for Big Ones be bad? Why not everybody make friend, have fun, make help, be good?"

Now how in Nifflheim could you answer a question like that? Maybe that was what Ernst Mallin meant when he said Fuzzies were the sanest people he'd ever seen. Maybe they were too sane to be bad, and how could a non-sane human explain to them?

"Pappy Vic not know. Maybe Unka Ernst, Unka Panko, know."

The bell of the private communication screen began its slow tolling. Diamond looked around; this was something that didn't happen often. He rose, taking Diamond from his lap and setting him on the chair, then went to the wall and put the screen on. It was Captain Morgan Lansky, at Chief Steefer's desk. He looked as though a planetbuster had just dropped in front of him and hadn't exploded yet.

"Mr. Grego; the gem vault! Fuzzies in it, robbing it!"

He conquered the impulse to ask Lansky if he were drunk or crazy. Lansky was neither; he was just frightened.

"Take it easy, Morgan. Tell me about it. First, what

you know's happened, and then what you think is happening."

"Yes, sir." Lansky got hold of himself; for an instant he was silent. "Ten minutes ago, in the captain's office at detective bureau; the shifts were changing, and both lieutenants were there. A Fuzzy came out of a storeroom in back of the office; he had a little knapsack on his back, with about twelve pounds of sunstones in it. The Fuzzy's here now, so are the sunstones. Do you want to see them?"

"Later; go ahead." Then, before Lansky could speak, he asked: "Sure he came out of this storeroom?"

"Yes, sir. There was five-six men in the doorway to the squadroom, he couldn't of come through that way. And the only way he could of got into this storeroom was out a ventilation duct there. The grating over it was open."

"That sounds reasonable. He could have gotten into the gem-vault through the ventilation system too."

The entrance to the gem-vault stairway was on the same floor as the detective bureau. The inlet and outlet screens were hinged, and the latch worked from either side to allow any outlet-screen to be put on anywhere. And the sunstones couldn't have come from anywhere else; just yesterday he'd had to go down and let Evins in to put away what had accumulated in his office safe.

"Ten minutes; what's been done since?"

"Carlos Hurtado's here, he hadn't gone home. He's staying, and so are most of the pre-midnight men. We put out a quiet alert to all the police in the building. We're blocking off everything from the top of the fourteenth level down, and a second block around the fifteenth. I called the Chief; he's coming in. Hurtado's calling the Constabulary and the Mallorysport police for men and vehicles to blockade the building from the outside. I've sent calls out for Dr. Mallin, and for Mr. E. Evins, and I've sent out for as many hearing-aids as I can get."

"That was good. Now, have a jeep or something up here for me right away; I'll have to open the gem-vault. And have men there to meet me. With sono-stunners; there may be more Fuzzies inside. And get hold of the building superintendent and the ventilation engineer, and get plans of the ventilation system."

"Right. Anything else, Mr. Grego?"

"Not that I can think of now. Be seeing you."

He blanked the screen. Diamond, in the chair, was looking at him wide-eyed.

"Pappy Vic; what make do?"

He looked at Diamond for a moment. "Diamond, you remember when bad Big Ones bring you, other Fuzzies, here?" he asked. "You know other Fuzzies again, you see them?"

"Yeh, tsure. Good friend; know again."

"Hokay. Stay put; Pappy Vic be back."

He ran into the kitchenette and gathered a couple of tins of Extee Three. Returning, he found a hearing-aid—Diamond was using his Fuzzyphone, and he hadn't needed it— and pocketed it. Then, swinging Diamond to his shoulder, he went outside. Just as he emerged onto the terrace, a silver-trimmed maroon company airjeep, lettered POLICE, lifted above the edge of the terrace, turned, and glided down. He thought, again, that police vehicles should have some distinctive color-scheme to distinguish them from ordinary company cars. Talk about that with Harry Steefer, some time. Then the jeep was down and the pilot had opened the door. He climbed in and held Diamond on his lap, while the pilot reported him aboard. Then he took the radio handphone himself.

"Grego; who's there?" he asked.

"Hurtado. We have everything from the fourteenth level down to the sixteenth sealed off, inside and out. Captain Lansky and Lieutenant Eggers have gone to meet you at the gem-vault. Dr. Mallin's coming in; so's Miss Glenn and Captain Khadra of the ZNPF. Maybe they can get something out of this Fuzzy." He mut-

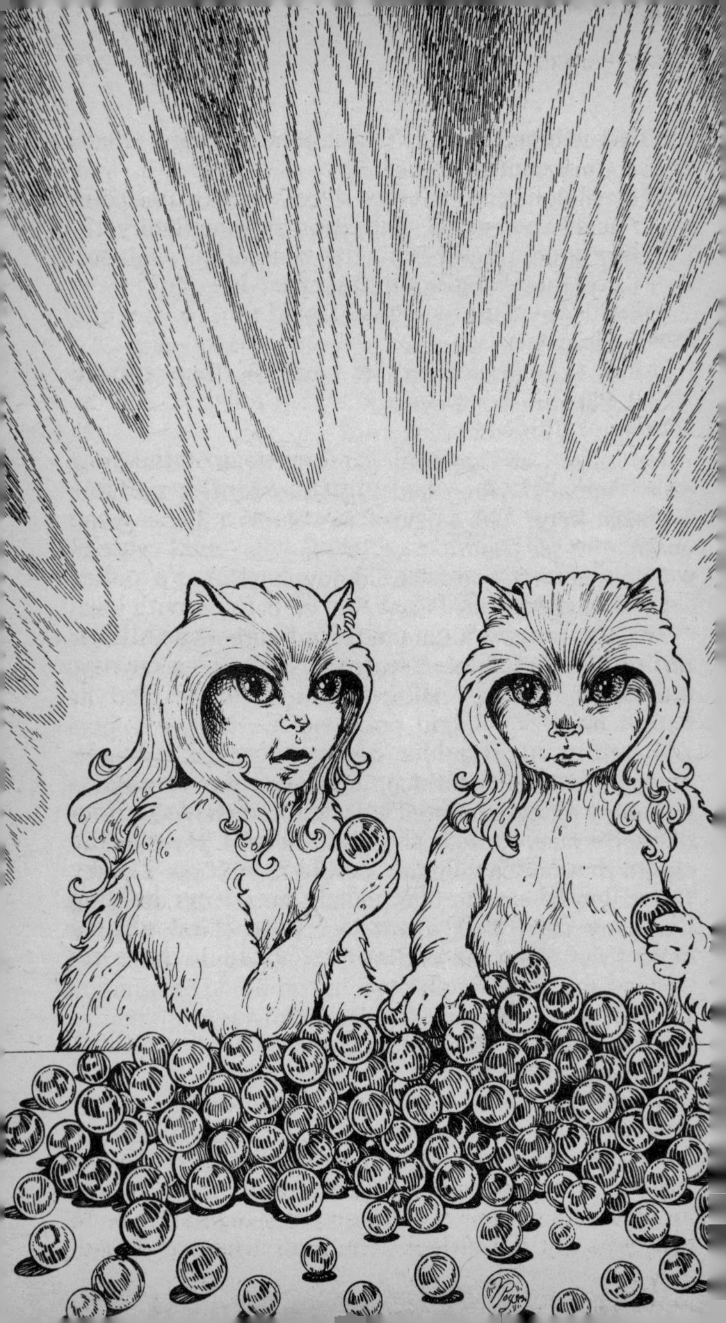

tered something bitterly. "Questioning Fuzzies; what's police work coming to next?"

"Teaching Fuzzies to crack safes; what's crime coming to next? You get the ventilation-system plans yet?"

"They're coming up; so's the ventilation engineer. You think there's more Fuzzies than this one?"

"Four more. And two men, named Phil Novaes and Moses Herckerd."

Hurtado was silent for a moment, then cursed. "Now why in Nifflheim didn't I think of that?" he demanded. "Sure!"

They went inside from a landing-stage on the third level down. There were police there, with portable machine guns, and a couple of cars. Work was going on in some of the offices along the horizontal vehicleway, but no excitement. They encountered a police car in the vertical shaft just above the fourteenth level down; the jeep pilot put on his red-and-white blinker and picked up the handphone of his loudspeaker, saying, "Mr. Grego here; please don't delay us." The car moved out of the way.

The fifteenth level down was police country. Everything was superficially quiet, but a number of vehicles were concentrated around the horizontal ways from the vertical shaft. The pilot set the jeep down at the entrance to the gem-buyer's offices. Morgan Lansky and a detective were waiting there. He got out, holding Diamond, and the pilot handed the tins of Extee Three to the detective. Lansky, who seemed to have recovered his aplomb, grinned.

"Interpreter, Mr. Grego?" he asked.

"Yes, and maybe he can make identification. I think he knows these Fuzzies."

It took Lansky two seconds to get that. Then he nodded.

"Sure. That would explain everything."

They went through the door, and, inside, it was immediately evident that the security-regulation book had gone out the airlock. The portcullis was raised, though a couple of submachine-gunners loitered watchfully in front of it. Half a dozen men, all carrying sono-stunners, short carbines with flaring muzzles like ancient blunderbusses, fell in behind them. The door at the end of the short hall was open, too, and nobody was bothering with identity-checks.

Nobody was supposed to be within sight of him when he opened the vault, but he ignored that, too. Lansky, Eggers, the man who was carrying the two tins of Extee Three, and the men with the stunners all crowded down the stairway after him. Quickly he punched the nonsense sentence out on the keyboard. Ten seconds later the door receded and slid aside.

Inside, the lights were on, as always; bright as they were, they could not dim the many-colored glow on the black velvet table-top, where two Fuzzies were playing concentratedly with a thousand or so sun-stones. A little rope ladder, just big enough for a Fuzzy, dangled past the light-shade from the air-outlet above.

Both Fuzzies looked up, startled. One said in accusing complaint, "You not say stones make shine; you say just stones, like always." His companion looked at them for a moment, and then cried: "Not know these Big Ones! How come this place?"

Lansky, who had been holding Diamond while he had been using the keyboard, followed him in. Diamond saw the two on the table and jabbered in excited recognition. He took Diamond and set him on the table with the others.

"Not be afraid," he said. "I not hurt. He friend; show him pretty things."

Recognition was mutual; the other Fuzzies were hugging Diamond and talking rapidly. Lansky had gone to a communication screen and was punching a call-number.

"You get away from bad Big Ones, too?" Diamond was asking. "How you come this place?"

"Big Ones bring us. Make us go through long little

hole. Tell us, get stones, like at other place."

What other place, he wondered. The other strange Fuzzy was saying:

"All-time, Big Ones make us go through long little holes, get stones. We get stones, Big Ones give us good things to eat. Not get stones, Big Ones angry. Make hurt, put us in dark place, not give anything to eat, make us do again."

"Who has the Extee Three?" he asked. "Open a tin for me."

"*Esteefee!*" Diamond, hearing him, repeated. "Pappy Vic give *esteefee; hoksu-fusso.*"

Lansky had Hurtado in the screen; he was standing aside to allow the latter to see what was going on in the gem-vault. Hurtado was swearing.

"Now, we gotta make everything in the building Fuzzy-proof," he was saying. "The Chief's just come in." He turned. "Hey, Chief, come and look at this!"

Eggers had the Extee Three; he got the tin open. Taking the cake from him, he broke it in three, then shoved a couple of million sols in sunstones out of the way and gave a piece to each of the Fuzzies. The two little jewel-thieves knew just what it was, and began eating at once. Telling Eggers to keep an eye on them, he went to the screen. In it, Harry Steefer was cursing even more fluently than Hurtado. He broke off and greeted:

"Hello, Mr. Grego. Beside what's on the table, are there any sunstones left?"

"I haven't checked, yet."

He looked around. All the drawers had been pulled out of the cabinet; the Fuzzies had evidently gotten at the upper rows by stacking and standing on the ones from below. Lansky was examining a couple of small canvas rucksacks he had found.

"What's it look like, Captain?"

"Don't come around the table, anybody," Lansky warned. "The floor's all over stones, here."

"Then we have some left. Has Conrad Evins come

in, yet?"

"We're still trying to contact him," Steefer said. "Dr. Mallin's here, and Captain Khadra and Miss Glenn are on the way here. I'm going over to operation-command room, now; I'll leave somebody here."

"Suppose you leave the Fuzzy in your office, too. I'll bring this pair up, and Diamond can help question them all."

Steefer assented, then excused himself to talk to somebody in the room with him. One of the detectives, who had gone out, returned with a broom and dustpan; he held the pan while Lansky swept the scattered sunstones up. There were more than he had expected, perhaps as many as half of them. He poured them into drawers, regardless of size or grade; they could be sorted out later. All the Fuzzies protested strenuously when he began gathering up the ones on the table; even Diamond wanted to play with them. He consoled them with the other cake of Extee Three, and assured Diamond, who assured his friends, that Pappy Vic would provide other pretties.

"Captain, you and Lieutenant Eggers and a couple of men stay here," he said. "I think we have two more Fuzzies, and they may be back for more stones. Catch them by hand if you can, stun them if you have to. Try not to hurt them, but get them, and bring them to the Chief's office. That's where I'm going now."

"Christ, I wish they'd hurry! What do you think's keeping them?"

That was the tenth or twelfth time Phil Novaes had said that in the last twenty minutes. Phil was getting on edge. Been on edge ever since they'd come here, and getting edgier every minute. Moses Herckerd was beginning to worry just a little about that. Losing your nerve was the surest way to disaster in a spot like this, and it would be disaster to both of them. Phil had been a little overconfident, at the beginning; that had been bad, too.

Getting the car hidden, on the unoccupied ninth level down, had been easy enough; they'd stowed it in one of the unfinished main office rooms close to where they'd kept the Fuzzies, two months ago. He knew the company police had started patrolling the unoccupied levels after that one damned Fuzzy had gotten away from them and, of all places, into Victor Grego's own apartment. Still, the place where they'd left the car was safe enough.

The long descent, nearly a thousand feet, among the water mains and ventilation mains to the fifteenth level down, had been hard and dangerous, clinging to the contragravity lifter with the Fuzzies jostling about in the box. Once this was over, he hoped he'd never see another damned Fuzzy as long as he lived. Phil had been all right then; he'd had to keep his mind on what he was doing, keep the lifter from swinging out and carrying them away from the hand-holds. It had been after they had gotten onto this ledge at the ventilation-duct outlet that Phil's nerves had begun to get away from him.

"Take it easy, Phil," he whispered. "They have half a mile, coming and going, through those ducts. And they have to fill their packs in the vault, and they always poke around doing that. Never can teach the buggers to hurry."

"Well, something could have happened. Maybe they took a wrong turn and got lost. That place is a lot more complicated than the practice setup."

"Oh, they'll get out all right. They all made three trips already without anything going wrong, didn't they?" he said. "And don't talk so damned loud."

That was what he was worried about, as much as anything. The whole company police force was concentrated around the place where he and Novaes were waiting. They were outside the actual police zone, but all the other emergency services—fire protection, radiation safety, the first-aid dispensaries and the ambulance hangars—were all around them, and sound carried an incredible distance through these shafts and air ducts and conduits.

"We have enough, now," Phil said. "Let's just pick up and go, now. Why, we must have fifty million already."

"But out and leave the Fuzzies?"

"Hell with the Fuzzies," Phil said.

"Hell with the Fuzzies, hell! Haven't you found out yet that Fuzzies can talk. We've spent two months, now, cooped up indoors, because that Fuzzy Grego found put the finger on us. We've got to get all five back, and we've got to finish them off. If we don't and the police get hold of them, they'll finish us."

Phil, who was stooping by the rectangular outlet, looked up.

"I hear something. A couple of them, talking."

He turned on his hearing-aid and put his head to the opening beside Phil's. Yes, a couple of Fuzzies talking; arguing about how far it was yet.

"As soon as they come out, let's shove them into the chute," Phil argued, nodding toward the access-port to the trash-chute, that went seven hundred feet down to the mass-energy converters.

That was where the Fuzzies would go, all of them, when the sunstones were all out of the vault. But the sunstones weren't all out. He doubted if they had more than half of them, yet.

"No, not yet. Here they come; grab the first one."

Novaes caught the Fuzzy as he came out. He caught the second. They were both carrying loaded packs. He slipped the straps down over the Fuzzy's arms and gave him to Novaes to hold, then loosened the drawstrings, emptying the stones into the open suitcase along with the other gems. Then he put the rucksack onto the Fuzzy's back.

"All right. In with you. Go get stones."

The Fuzzy said something, he wasn't sure what, in a complaining tone. *Fusso*; that meant food, or eat. Important word to a Fuzzy.

"No. You get stone; then I give *fusso"* He shoved the Fuzzy back into the ventilation duct. "Let's unload yours and send him back. As long as there's sunstones in there, we want them."

A uniformed sergeant was holding down Chief Steefer's desk, smoking what was probably one of the Chief's cigars and talking to a girl in another screen. Across the room, Ernst Mallin, Ahmed Khadra and Sandra Glenn were talking to a Fuzzy who sat on the edge of a table, contentedly munching Extee Three. Khadra was in evening clothes, and Sandra was wearing something glamorous with a lot of black lace. She was also wearing a sunstone which he hadn't noticed before, on the third finger of her left hand. *Wanted, Fuzzy Sitter. Apply Victor Grego.*

They set Diamond and his friends on the floor; he thanked and dismissed the men who had helped him with them. As soon as they saw the Fuzzy on the table, they raised an outcry and ran forward; the Fuzzy on the table dropped to the floor and hurried to meet them.

"What did you get from him?" he asked.

"Herckerd and Novaes, natch," Khadra said, disgustedly. "All the time I was looking for a black market that wasn't there, they were right here in town somewhere, being taught to steal sunstones. Fagin-racket, by God!"

"Herckerd and Novaes and who else?"

"Two other men, and one woman. And just the five Fuzzies Herckerd and Novaes brought in along with Diamond. They were somewhere not more than fifteen minutes by air from Company House all the time. This gang taught them to go through ventilator ducts, and open the screen-covers on the inlets, and use rope ladders and get stones out of cabinets. They must have had a mockup of the gem-vault and the ventilation system. They had to practice all the time. If they cleaned out the cabinets and brought the stones, river-gravel, I suppose, out, they got Extee Three. If they goofed, they were punished, electric shock, I suppose, and shoved in a dungeon with nothing to eat. You know, they could be shot for that."

"They oughtn't to be shot; they ought to be burned at the stake!" Sandra cried angrily.

Gentler sex, indeed! "Well, I'll settle for shooting, if we can catch them. Done anything in aid of that yet?"

"Not too much," Mallin regretted. "His vocabulary is limited, and he hasn't words for much that he experienced. We've been trying to learn his route through the ventilation system. He knows how he went in to the gem-vault, but he simply can't verbalize it."

"Diamond; you help Pappy Vic. Make talk for Unka Ernst, Unka Ahmed, Auntie Sandra; help other Fuzzies make talk about bad Big Ones, about place where were, about what make do, about how go through long little holes." He turned to Khadra. "Has he seen Herckerd and Novaes on screen?"

"Not yet; we've just been talking to him, so far."

"Better let all three of them see those audiovisuals; get identifications made. And keep on about the ventilation ducts. See if any of them can tell which way they went toward the gem-vault, and what kind of a place they went in at."

XXI

Crossing the hall, he found the operation-command room busy, in a quiet and almost leisurely manner. Everybody knew what to do, and was getting it done with a minimum of fuss. A group of men, policemen and engineers, were huddled at a big table, going over plans, on big sheets and on photoprint screens. More men, police and maintenance people, gathered around a big solidigraph model of the fourteenth, fifteenth and sixteenth levels, projected in a tri-di screen. The thing was transparent, and looked almost anatomical; well, Company House was an organism of a sort. Respiratory system; the ventilation, in which everybody was interested. Circulatory system; the water-lines. Excretory system; sewage disposal.

And now it had been invaded by a couple of inimical microbes, named Phil Novaes and Moses Herckerd, whom the police leucocytes were seeking to neutralize.

He looked at it for a while, then strolled on to the banks of viewscreens. Views of halls and vehicleways, mostly empty, patrolled here and there by police or hastily mobilized and armed maintenance workers. Views of landing-stages, occupied by police and observed from aircars. A view from a car a thousand feet over the building, in which a few Constabulary and city police vehicles circled slowly, blockading the building from outside. He nodded in satisfaction; they couldn't get out of the building, and as soon as enough of the fifty-odd widely scattered locations from which they might be operating could be eliminated, the police would close in on them.

In one screen from a pickup installed over the door in the gem-vault, he could see Morgan Lansky, Bert Eggers and two detectives, coatless and perspiring, around the electrically warmed table-top, staring at the little rope ladder that dangled down around the light-shade. In another screen, from a high pickup in a corner of Harry Steefer's office, the uniformed sergeant at the desk watched Ernst Mallin and Ahmed Khadra fussing with a screen, while Sandra Glenn sat on the floor talking to Diamond and his three friends.

Harry Steefer sat alone at the command-desk, keeping track of everything at once. He went over and sat down beside him.

"Mr. Grego. We don't seem to be making too much progress," the Chief said. "Everything's secure so far, though."

"Have the news services gotten hold of it yet?"

"I don't believe. Planetwide News called the city police to find out what all the cars were doing around Company House; somebody told them that it was a shipment of valuables being taken under guard to the space terminal. They seemed to accept that."

"We can't sit on it indefinitely."

"I hope we can till we catch these people."

"Have you contacted Conrad Evins yet?"

"No. He's not at home; here, I'll show you."

Steefer punched out a call on one of his communication screens. When it lighted, the chief gem-buyer's wide-browed, narrow chinned face looked out of it.

"This is a recording, made at 2100, Conrad Evins speaking. Mrs. Evins and I are going out; we will not be home until after midnight," Evins' voice said. Then the screen flickered, and the recording began again.

"I could put out an emergency call for him, but I don't want to," Steefer said. "We don't know how many people outside the building are involved in this, and we don't want to alarm them."

"No. Four men and one woman; the Fuzzies say there were only two men, presumably Herckerd and Novaes, brought them here. That means two men and a woman somewhere outside waiting for them. And we don't really need Evins, at present. It's after midnight now; we can keep calling at his home."

Evins and his wife had probably gone to a show, or visiting. Evins' wife; he couldn't seem to recall ever having met her. He'd heard something or other about her . . . He shoved that aside.

"Don't they have little robo-snoopers they use to go through the ventilation ducts?" he asked.

"Yes. Mr. Guerrin, the ventilation engineer, has a dozen of them. He suggested using them, but I vetoed it till I could see what you thought. Those things float on contragravity, and even a miniature Abbott drive generator makes quite an ultrasonic noise. We still have two Fuzzies loose in the ventilation system; we don't want to scare them, do we?"

"No. Let them carry on. There's a chance they may come out in the gem-vault, if we don't frighten them."

He looked across the room at the view-screens. Khadra and Mallin had their screen set up, Sandra had brought the Fuzzies over in front of it, and Diamond seemed to be explaining about view-screens and audiovisual screens to the others. In the gem-vault screen, Lansky and the others were leaning forward across the table, listening. They had a couple of hearing-aids, now, which Eggers and one of his detectives were using. Lansky turned to make frantic gestures at the pickup. Steefer picked up a speaker-phone and advised everybody to pay attention to the gem-vault screen.

For one of those ten-second eternities, nothing happened in the screen. A moment later, a Fuzzy came climbing down the ladder. One of the detectives would have grabbed him; Eggers stopped him. A moment later, another Fuzzy appeared.

Eggers caught him by the feet with both hands and pulled him off the ladder; the Fuzzy hit Eggers in the face with his fist. The first Fuzzy, having dropped to the table, tried to get up the ladder again; Lansky grabbed him. One of the detectives came to Egger's assistance. Then the struggle was over, and the two prisoners had been secured. Lansky was yelling:

"We got them both! We're bringing them up."

Steefer yelled to the girl who was monitoring the screen to cut in sound transmission and tell Lansky and one man to remain on guard; Lansky acknowledged, and Eggers and one of the detectives left the vault, each carrying a Fuzzy. In the screen from Steefer's office, they had an audiovisual of Moses Herckerd on the screen; it was the employment interview film, and Herckerd was talking about his educational background and former job experience. Steefer was talking to the sergeant at his desk; the latter beckoned Ahmed Khadra over.

"Good," Khadra said, when Steefer told him what had happened. "That's all of them. We'll run Herckerd over for them when they come up, and show them Novaes. They're the two who brought them here tonight, the three we have here all say so."

"They're still in here," Steefer said. "That leaves two men and a woman outside. I wonder . . ."

"I think I know who they are, Chief."

It was just a guess, of course, but it fitted. He had suddenly remembered what he knew about Mrs. Conrad Evins.

When Leo Thaxter, now Loan Broker & Private Financier, first came to Zarathustra ten years ago, a woman had come with him, but she hadn't been a wife or reasonable facsimile, she had been a sister or reasonable facsimile. Rose Thaxter. After a while, she had left Thaxter and married a company minerologist named Conrad Evins, who, after the discovery of the sunstones, had become chief company gem-buyer.

"What's that call-number of Evins'?" he asked Steefer, and when Steefer gave it, he repeated it to Khadra. "When those other Fuzzies come in, call it. It'll be answered by an audiovisual recording. See if the kids recognize him."

Steefer looked at him, more amused than surprised. "'I wouldn't have thought of that, myself, Mr. Grego. It seems to fit, though."

"Hunch." If anybody respected hunches, it would be a cop. "I just remembered who Evins was married to. Rose Thaxter."

"Yeh!" Steefer muttered something else. "I know that, too; I just never connected it. It all hangs together, too."

For a couple of minutes, they were both talking at the same time, telling one another just how it did hang together, and watching the screen from Steefer's office. Eggers and the detective were coming in, still coatless, carrying a Fuzzy apiece; the one Eggers was carrying was trying to get the gun out of the lieutenant's shoulder holster.

Of course it hung together. Somebody in the gang had to have exact knowledge of the layout of the gem-vault, which Evins, and very few others, could provide. The arrangement of the ventilation-ducts wasn't classified top-secret; anybody in Evins' position could have gotten that. They had to have a place to keep the Fuzzies, big enough to build a replica of the gem-vault and of the ventilation system. Well, there were all those vacant factories and warehouses out in the district everybody called Mortgageville. The ones Hugo Ingermann had been acquiring title to, with Thaxter as dummy buyer. How Herckerd and Novaes had been roped in wasn't immediately important; catch them and question them and that would emerge. Ten to one, Rose Thaxter, Mrs. Conrad Evins, was the connecting-link and mainspring.

The Fuzzies in Steefer's office were having a reunion. Khadra and Mallin and Sandra were trying to get them to look at the communication-screen. He turned to Steefer.

"Get some men to Conrad Evins' place; make a thorough search, for anything that might look like evidence of anything."

"They won't be there."

"No. They'll be in one of those buildings over in Mortgageville, and we don't know which one. I'm going to call Ian Ferguson."

He told Ferguson quickly what he suspected. The Constabulary commandant nodded.

"Reasonable," he agreed. "I'll call the city police for help; we'll close the place off so nobody can get in or out and then we'll start making a search. It's only about two thousand square miles, and there are only about three hundred buildings on it," he added. "I think I'll call Casagra, too, and see how many Marines he can give me."

"Well, take your time searching; just make sure anybody who's there now stays there. We'll give you what help we can as soon as we can."

He looked up at the screen from Steefer's office. Khadra had called Evins' home, now, and he could hear Evins' recorded voice stating that he wouldn't be home before midnight. The Fuzzies evidently recognized him. It was also evident that they didn't like him.

"And put out a general alert to pick up Evins, Mrs. Evins, and Leo Thaxter, and I don't think you need to worry about how much noise you make doing it."

"And Ivan Bowlby, and Raul Laporte, and Spike Heenan," Ferguson added. "And any or all of their hoods." He thought for a moment. "And Hugo Ingermann. We may finally have grounds for interrogating him as a suspect. I'll call Gus Brannhard, too."

"And Leslie Coombes; he'll be a help."

"All right, everybody!" Steefer was calling out with his loudspeaker. "We have all the Fuzzies out; now let's get the show started!" Then he rose and went around the desk.

Khadra was on the communication screen from the Chief's desk:

"They made that fellow Evins, all right. He was one of the gang. Who is he?"

"Well, he used to be the Company's chief gem-buyer, up to fifteen minutes ago, but now he has been discharged, without notice, severance-pay or recommendation." He thought for a moment. "Captain, are those Fuzzies' feet dirty?" he asked.

"Huh?" Khadra stared at him for an instant, then nodded. "Yes, they are; gray-brown dust. Same kind of dust on their fur."

"Uhuh; that's good." He rose and went to the big table and the solidigraph, where Steefer was already talking to a dozen or so men. He saw Niles Guerrin, the ventilation engineer, and pulled him aside.

"Niles, the insides of those ducts are dusty?" he asked.

"The ones that carry stale air to the reconditioners," Guerrin replied. "Dust from the air in the rooms . . ."

"They're the ones we're interested in. Now, these snoopers, robo-inspectors; could they pick up tracks the Fuzzies make, or traces where they've brushed against the sides of the ducts?"

"Yes, sure. They have a full optical reception and transmission system for visible light and infra-red light, and controllable magnifying vision . . ."

"How soon can you get them started, from the gem-vault and from the captain's office in detective headquarters?"

"Right away; we've set up screens and controls for them in here; did that right at the start."

"Good." He raised his voice. "Chief! Captain Hurtado, Lieutenant Mortlake; *do-bizzo*. We're going to fill the ventilation system with snoopers, now."

Phil Novaes looked at his watch. It was still 0130, the damned thing must have stopped, and he was sure he'd wound it. Holding his wrist to catch the dim light from above he squinted at the second-hand. It was still making its slow circuit around the dial. It must have been only a few seconds since he had looked at it last.

"Herk, let's get the hell out of here," he urged. "They aren't coming out at all. It's been an hour since the last two went in."

"Thirty-five minutes," Herckerd said.

"Well, it's been over an hour since the other three went in. Something's gone wrong; we'll wait here till hell freezes over . . ."

"We'll wait here a little longer, Phil. We still have fifty million in sunstones to wait for, and we want to get those Fuzzies and shut them up for good."

"We have better than fifty million already. All we'll get'll be a hole in the head if we stay around here any longer. I know what's happened, those Fuzzies have gone out some other way; they're running around loose, packing sunstones . . ."

"Be quiet, Phil." Herckerd reached to his shirt pocket to turn on his hearing-aid and put his head to the ventilation duct opening. "I hear something in there." He snapped off the hearing-aid, listened, and snapped it on again. "It's ultrasonic, whatever it is. Probably vibration in the walls of the duct. Now just take it easy, Phil. Nobody knows there's anything happening at all. Grego's the only man in Company House that can open that vault, and he won't open it for a couple of weeks, at least. All the stones from Evins' office were put away yesterday. It'll take that long before anybody knows they're gone."

"Suppose those Fuzzies got out somewhere else. My God, they could have come out right in the police area." That could have happened; he wished he hadn't thought of it, but now that he had, he was sure that was what had happened. "If they did, everybody in the building's looking for us."

Herckerd wasn't listening to him. He'd turned off

his hearing-aid, and was squatting by the intake port, peeling the wrapper from a chewing-gum stick and putting the wrapper carefully in his pocket. Another piece of foolishness; no reason at all why they couldn't smoke here. He listened with his hearing-aid again. The noise, whatever it was, was louder.

"There's something in there." He pulled the goggles down from his cap and took out his infra-red flashlight.

"Don't do that," Herckerd said sharply.

He disregarded the warning and turned the invisible light into the duct. There was something moving forward toward the opening; it wasn't a Fuzzy. It was a bulbous-nosed metallic thing, floating slowly toward him.

"It's a snooper! Look, Herk; somebody's wise to us. They have a snooper in the duct . . ."

"Get the stones in the box! Right away!" Herckerd ordered.

"Ah, so there was something went wrong!"

He snapped the suitcase shut, shoved it into the box on the contragravity lifter, and fastened the lid, then snapped the hook of his safety-belt onto one of the rings on the lifter. There was a crash behind him, and when he turned, Herckerd was holstering his pistol. Then he, too, snapped his safety-strap to the lifter, and pulled loose the two poles with hooked and spiked tips, passing one over and slipping the thong of the other over his wrist.

"Full lift," he said. "Let's go."

He fumbled for a second or so at the switch, then turned it on. The whole thing, lifter, box and he and Herckerd, were pulled up from the ledge and swung out into the shaft.

"What did you have to shoot for?" he demanded, pushing with his boathook-like pole. "Everybody in the place heard you."

"You want that thing following us?" Herckerd asked. "Watch out; water-main right above!"

Maybe the snooper was just making a routine inspection; maybe Herckerd had finally panicked, after all his pretense of calmness. No. Something had gone wrong. Those damned Fuzzies had gone out the wrong way, somebody'd found them... There were more pipes and conduits and things in the way; he remembered the trouble they'd had getting past them on the way down. He and Herckerd had to push and pull with their poles and for a moment he thought they were inextricably stuck, they'd never get loose, they were wedged in here...Then the lifter was rising again, and he could see the network of obstructions receding below, and the white XV's on the sides of the shaft had become XIV's, so they were off the fifteenth level. Only five more levels and a couple of floors to go.

But he could hear voices, from loudspeakers, all around:

"Cars P-18, P-19, P-20; fourteenth level, fourth floor, location DA-231."

"Riot-car 12, up to thirteen, sixth floor..."

He swore at Herckerd. "Sure, it'll be a month before they find out what's happened!"

"Shut up. We get out of the shaft two floors up, to the left. They have the shaft plugged at the top."

"Yes, and walk right into them," he argued.

"We'll lift into them if we keep on here; we'll have a chance if we get out of this."

They worked the lifter around the central clump of water and sewer and ventilation mains, pushing away from it and then hooking onto handholds and drawing the lifter into a lateral passage, floating along it for a hundred feet before Herckerd could get at the lifter controls and set it down. Then he unsnapped his safety-strap and staggered for a moment before he found his footing.

It was a service-passage, wide enough for one of the little hall-cars, or for a jeep; maintenance workers used it to get at air-fans and water-pumps. They started along it, towing the lifter after them, looking to right and left for some means of egress. There should be other vertical shafts, but they would be covered, too.

"How are we going to get out of this?"

"How the hell do I know?" Herckerd retorted. "How do I know we're going to get out at all?" He stopped for a moment and then pointed to an open doorway on the left. "Stairway; we'll go up there."

They crossed to it. From somewhere down the bare, dimly-lighted passage, an amplified voice was shouting indistinguishable words. The passage connected with another, or a hallway. They could't go ahead; that was sure.

"We can't get the lifter through." He knew it, and still tried; the lifter wouldn't go through the narrow door. "We'll have to carry the suitcase."

"Get the box off the lifter," Herckerd said "We can't carry that suitcase ourselves; they'd catch us in no time. Get the suitcase out of it."

The box, four feet by four by three, with airholes at the top, had been necessary when they had the Fuzzies to carry; they didn't have to bother with them now. He opened it and lifted out the suitcase. No; they couldn't carry that, not and do any running. It was fastened with screws to the contragravity-lifter. Herckerd had his pocket-knife out, with the screwdriver blade open, and was working to remove the brackets.

"Well, where'll we go . . .?"

"Don't argue, goddamit; get to work. Is there any extra rope ladder in that box? If there is, we'll use it to tie the suitcase on . . ."

Over Herckerd's shoulder, he saw the jeep enter the passage from the intersecting hall a hundred feet away. For an instant, he was frozen with fright. Then he screamed, "Behind you!" and threw himself through the open doorway, stumbling to the foot of a flight of narrow steel steps and then running up them. A pistol roared twice just outside the door, and then a submachine gun let go, a ripping two-second burst, a second of silence, and then another. Then voices shouted.

They got Herckerd. They got the sunstones, too. Then he forgot about both. Just get away, get far away, get away fast.

There was a steel door at the head of the stairs. Oh, God, please don't let it be locked! He flung himself at it, gripping the latch-handle.

It wasn't. The door swung open, and he stumbled through and closed it behind him, hearing, as he did, voices coming up from below. Then he turned, in the lighted hallway beyond.

There was a policeman standing not fifteen feet away, holding a short carbine with a thick, flaring muzzle, a stunner. He crouched, grabbing for his pistol. Then the blunderbuss muzzle of the stunner swung toward him at the policeman's hip. He had the pistol half drawn when the lights all went out and a crushing shock hit him, shaking and jarring him into oblivion.

The operation-command room was silent. When the voice from the screen-speaker ceased, there was not a sound for an instant. Then there was a soft susurration; everybody in the place was exhaling at once. Grego found that he had been holding his own breath. So had Harry Steefer; he was exhaling noisily.

"Well, that't it," the Chief said. "I'm glad they took Novaes alive, anyhow. It'll be a couple of hours before he's able to talk." He picked up his cigarette pack, shook one out for himself and offered it.

Moses Herckerd wouldn't do any talking; he'd taken a dozen submachine gun bullets.

"What'll we do with the sunstones?" the voice from the screen asked.

"Take them to the gem-vault; we'll sort them over tomorrow or when we have time." He turned to the open screens to city police and Colonial Constabulary. The non-coms who had been on them were replaced by Ralph Earlie and Ian Ferguson, respectively. "You hear what was going on?" he asked.

"We got most of it," Ferguson said, and Earlie said, "You got them, and you got the stones back, but just what did happen?"

"They had a contragravity lifter; they used it to get up one of the main conduit shafts, and then they got into a maintenance passage on the fourteenth level down. One of our jeeps caught them; Herckerd tried to put up a fight and got shot to hamburger; Novaes ran up a flight of stairs and came out in a hall right in front of a cop with a sono-stunner. When he comes to, we'll question him and check his story with the Fuzzies'," he said. "How are you doing at Mortgageville?"

"We have the place surrounded," Ferguson said. "They might get out on foot; they won't in a vehicle. We have three Navy landing-craft loaded with detection equipment circling overhead, and Casagra has a hundred Marines along with my men."

"I can't help on that, at all," the Mallorysport police chief said. "I have all my men out making raids, and if you don't need that blockade around Company House any more, I want the men who are there. We have Ivan Bowlby, Spike Heenan, and Raul Laporte, and we're pulling in everybody that's ever had anything to do with any of them, or Leo Thaxter. We don't have Thaxter, yet. I suppose he's at Mortgageville, along with the Evinses, waiting for Herckerd and Novaes to bring in the loot. And we have Hugo Ingermann, and this time he can't talk himself out. We got Judge Pendarvis out of bed, and he signed warrants for all of them; reasonable grounds for suspicion and authority to veridicate. We're saving him for last; we've just started on the small-fry."

There wasn't any question in his mind that Leo Thaxter was involved in the attempt on the gem-vault. Whether Bowlby or Heenan or Laporte had anything to do with it was more or less immaterial. They could be questioned, not only about that but about anything else, and anything they admitted under veridication was admissible as evidence against them, self-incriminatory or not.

"Well, I'm going over and see what they've been getting from the Fuzzies," he said. "There ought to be quite a little, by now." He glanced up at the screen from Steefer's office; half a dozen people were there now, and he was surprised to see Jack Holloway among them. He couldn't have flown in from Beta Continent since this had started. "I'll call back, or have somebody call, later."

Crossing the hall, he joined the group who were interviewing the five Herckerd-Novaes-Evins-Thaxter Fuzzies. Juan Jimenez was there, so were a couple of doctors who had been working with Fuzzies at the reception center. So was Claudette Pendarvis. Jack Holloway met him as he entered, and they shook hands.

"I thought there might be something I could do to help," he said. "Listen, Mr. Grego, you're not going to bring any charges against these Fuzzies, are you?"

"Good Lord, no!"

"Well, they're sapient beings, and they broke the law," Holloway said.

"They are legally ten-year-old children," Judge Pendarvis' wife said. "They are not morally responsible; they were taught to do this by humans."

"Yes, faginy, along with enslavement," Ahmed Khadra said. "Mandatory death by shooting for that, too."

"And I hope they shoot that Evins woman first of all; she's the worst of the lot," Sandra Glenn said. "She's the one who used the electric shock-rod on them when they made mistakes."

"Mr. Grego," Ernst Mallin interrupted. "I don't understand this. These Fuzzyphones are simple enough for any Fuzzy to operate; all they need to do is hold the little pistol-grip and the switch works automatically. Diamond can talk audibly, but he simply cannot teach any of these other Fuzzies to use it. You don't have your hearing-aid on, do you? Well, listen to this."

Diamond used his Fuzzyphone; he spoke quite audibly. When he gave it to any of the others, all they produced was, "Yeek."

"Let me see that thing." He took it from Diamond and carried it over to the desk; rummaging in the top middle drawer, he found a little screwdriver and took it apart. The mechanism seemed to be all right. He removed the tiny power-unit and exchanged it for a similar one from a flashlight he found in the Chief's desk. The flashlight wouldn't light. He handed the Fuzzyphone to Mallin.

"Give this to one of the others, not Diamond. Have him say something."

Mallin handed the Fuzzyphone to one of the pair whom Lansky and Eggers had captured in the vault, and asked him a question. Holding the Fuzzyphone to his mouth, the Fuzzy answered quite audibly. Three or four of the humans said, "What the hell?" or words to that effect.

"Diamond, you not need talk-thing to make talk like Big One," he said. "You make talk like Big One any time. You make talk like Big One now."

"Like this?" Diamond asked.

"How does he do it?" Mrs. Pendarvis demanded. "Their voices aren't audible, at all."

"You think the power-unit gave out, and he just went on copying the sounds he was accustomed to make with the Fuzzyphone?" Mallin asked.

"That's right. He heard himself speak in the audible range, and he just learned to pitch his voice to imitate his own transformed voice. I'll bet he's been talking audibly for weeks, and we never knew it."

"Bet he didn't know it, either," Jack Holloway said. "Mr. Grego, do you think he could teach other Fuzzies to do that."

"That would be kind of hard, wouldn't it?" Mallin asked. "Does he really know, himself, how he does it?"

"Mr. Grego!" the police sergeant, who was still keeping half an eye on the communication screen, broke in. "The Chief wants to know if you want to go to the gem-vault and check the contents of that suitcase."

"Has anybody else checked it?"

"Well, Captain Lansky has, but . . ."

"Then lock it up in the vault; I don't have to do that. The Nifflheim with it. I'll check it tomorrow. I'm busy, now."

XXII

"You think four-fifty a carat would be all right?" Victor Grego was asking.

Bennett Rainsford picked up the lighter from the table in front of him and carefully relit a pipe that didn't need relighting. Now that he'd come to know him, he found that he liked Victor Grego. But he still had to watch him. Grego was the Charterless Zarathustra Company, and the company was definitely not a philanthropic institution.

"Sounds all right to me," Jack Holloway agreed. "You didn't pay me any more than that when I was prospecting, and I had to dig them myself."

"But four-fifty, Jack. The Terra market price is over a thousand sols a carat."

"This isn't Terra, Ben. Terra's five hundred light-years, six months ship-time, away. I think Mr. Grego's making us a good offer. All we need to do is bank the money; the company'll do the rest."

"Well, how much do you think the Fuzzies will get out of it, a month?"

Grego shrugged. "I haven't seen it, myself. I'll take Jack's word for it. What do you think?"

"Well, it depends on how much equipment you use, and what kind. If it's anything like the diggings I used to work, you'll get about a sunstone to the ton."

"We can move and process an awful lot of tons of flint in a month, and from Jack's description I'd say we'll be working that deposit for longer than any of us'll be around. You know, Governor, instead of the Fuzzies getting handouts from the Government, they'll be paying the Government's bills before long."

And that would have to be watched, too; it mustn't be allowed to become a source of political graft. Inside a month, now, the elections for delegates to the Constitutional Convention would be held. Make sure the right men were elected, men who would write a Constitution which would safeguard the Fuzzies' rights for all time.

Victor Grego, he was beginning to think, could be counted on to help in that.

Leslie Coombes held his glass while Gus Brannhard poured from the bottle, and said, quickly, "That's enough, please," when about fifty or sixty cc of whisky had been added to the ice. He filled the glass the rest of the way with soda, himself.

"And Hugo Ingermann," he said, disgustedly, "is completely innocent."

"Well, innocent of the Fuzzy business and the attempt on the company gem-vault," Brannhard conceded, pouring into his own glass. When Gus mixed a highball, he always left out both the ice and the soda. "It's probably the only thing he ever was innocent of, in his whole life. But he isn't getting away scotfree." Brannhard took a drink from his glass, and Coombes shuddered inwardly; the man must have a collapsium-plated digestive tract. "While we were interrogating this one and that one about the Fuzzy-sunstone business, we got a lot of evidence, all veridicated, to connect him with Thaxter's shylocking and Bowlby's call-girl agency and Heenan's prize-fight fixing and Laporte's strong-arm mob. I'm after him with a shotgun; I'm just filling the air all around him with indictments, and some of them are sure to hit. And even if I can't get him convicted of anything, he'll be disbarred, that's for sure. And this Planetary Prosperity Party of his is catching fire, leaking radiation, blowing up and falling apart all around. Everybody's calling it the Fuzzy-Fagin Party, and everybody who had anything to do with it is getting out as fast as he can."

"If we work together, we'll get a good Constitution adopted and a good Legislature elected. Or can we expect Governor Rainsford to agree with Victor Grego on what a 'good' Constitution and a 'good' Legislature are?"

"We can," Brannhard said. "We only have a few months before the off-planet land-grabbers begin coming in, and Ben Rainsford's as much worried about that as Victor Grego. Leslie, if you go into court and make claim to all the unseated land the company has mapped and surveyed, I am instructed by the Governor not to oppose you. What does that sound like?"

"That sounds like getting back about everything we lost, with the sunstone lease on top of it. I am going to propose the election of Little Fuzzy as an honorary member of the board of directors, with the title of Company Benefactor Number One."

Little Fuzzy climbed up on Pappy Jack's lap, squirmed a little, and cuddled himself comfortably. He was happy to be back. He had had so much fun in the Big House Place, he and Mamma Fuzzy and Ko-Ko and Cinderella and Syndrome and Id and Ned Kelly and Dr. Crippen and Calamity Jane. They had met so many Fuzzies who had been here and gone away to live with Big Ones of their own, and they had a place where they all met and played together. And he had met the two lovers, now they had names of their own, Pierrot and Columbine, and he had met Diamond, about whom Unka Panko had told him, and Diamond's Pappy Vic.

It had been to meet Diamond that Unka Panko and Auntie Lynne had taken them all in the sky-thing to the Big House Place, because Diamond had found out how to talk like a Big One without using one of the talk-things, and Diamond had taught all of them how to do it. It had been hard, very hard; Diamond was very smart to have found it out for himself, but after a while they had all found that they could do it, too. And now Mike and Mitzi and Complex and Superego and Dillinger and Lizzie Borden had gone to the Big House Place with Pappy Gerd and Mummy Woof, and they would learn to talk so that the Big Ones could hear them. And Baby Fuzzy was learning from Mamma Fuzzy, and tomorrow they would all start teaching the others here at Hoksu-Mitto.

"Pretty soon, all Fuzzy learn to talk like Big Ones," he said. "Not need talk-thing, Big One not need earthing; just talk, like I do now."

"That's right," Pappy Jack said. "Big Ones, Fuzzies, all make talk together. All be good friends."

"And Fuzzy learn how to help Big Ones? Many things Fuzzy can do to help, if Big Ones tell what."

"Best thing Fuzzy do to help Big Ones is just be Fuzzies," Pappy Jack told him.

But what else could they be? Fuzzies were what they were, just as Big Ones were Big Ones.

"And beside," Pappy Jack went on talking, "the Fuzzies are all rich, now."

"Rich? What is? Something good?"

"Well, most people think it is. When you're rich, you have money."

"Is something good to eat?" he asked. "Like *esteefee*?"

He wondered why Pappy Jack laughed. Maybe he was just laughing because he was happy. Or maybe Pappy Jack thought it was funny that he didn't know what money was.

There were still so many things Fuzzies had to learn.

Winner of virtually every award Science Fiction has to offer

THE SPIRIT OF DORSAI

By Gordon R. Dickson

The Childe Cycle is the lifework of Gordon R. Dickson. The centerpiece of that lifework is the planet Dorsai and its people. Here, in a special edition brilliantly illustrated by Fernando Fernandez, is, in the author's words, "an illumination," of the heart and soul of that people.

$2.50

Ace Science Fiction

Available wherever paperbacks are sold, or order by mail from Ace Science Fiction, P.O. Box 400, Kirkwood, New York 13795. Please add 75¢ for postage and handling.